WHILE
THEY
WERE
DYING

WHILE THEY WERE DYING

The Road to Iraq

A Novel

By

SAMUEL PETER SHAW

iUniverse, Inc.
Bloomington

While They Were Dying
The Road to Iraq

iUniverse books may be ordered through booksellers or by contacting:

iUniverse
1663 Liberty Drive
Bloomington, IN 47403
www.iuniverse.com
1-800-Authors (1-800-288-4677)

ISBN: 978-1-4759-5186-8 (sc)
ISBN: 978-1-4759-5187-5 (ebk)

Library of Congress Control Number: 2012917689

Printed in the United States of America

iUniverse rev. date: 10/05/2012

This book is for the fellow scribblers I toiled and swore and laughed with in newsrooms that stretched from Yorkshire to Africa to London—the free-wheeling, frustrating, enlightening, stimulating forty years that I spent and misspent in the company of committed warriors and lovable rogues. For better or worse, they helped make me and I would choose no other fellowship.

The statements and actions of the historical characters in this book, and the global and personalised reactions to them, are drawn from the public record and are integral to the overall story. Every effort has been made to ensure the authenticity, artistic interpretation and factual correctness of the historical characters and events, and in reflecting and balancing the opinions of the time.
All non-historical characters in the book, their lives and their actions, are entirely fictional and bear no intentional resemblance to anyone living or dead, or to any actions, present or past.

WHILE THEY WERE DYING

"The great showdown has begun. The mother of all battles is under way"—President Saddam Hussein, speaking as the United States and its allies launched Operation Desert Storm, January 17, 1991, to throw the Iraqi Army from Kuwait.

Prologue

Like a lonely toy on a piece of string, the boy Rolo was following the three girls, the older two in white tops and hugging jeans, the little one in a faded yellow smock, he trailing behind in the year's early heat, kicking that day's special pebble along the narrow, dusty path that bobbed up and down through the hummocks of the wasteland. It was where people took their dogs, dumped rubbish, made fires, smoked pot, drank booze, had sex, watched the sky, escaped the world. What you did depended on who you were and how old you were. That spring day in the second year of the 1990's, Rolo was eight years and 13 days, Katie Drummond and her friend, Mary Duff were eleven, nearly twelve, and Katie's little sister, Dodie, was three, nearly four.

At the top of the next hill, Dodie was waiting for him, watching as he threw cluster bombs at an Iraqi patrol, the stones falling short of the chirruping sparrows; trying, instead, a Tomahawk missile, the stick exploding among the Iraqis, the sparrows whirring away; the boy shrugging, running up the hill towards her, swishing nettles with a cane, puffing himself trying to catch a speckled butterfly; flopping down at her feet beneath a bushy tangle as if shot, the boredom of being pushed in each day with the Drummonds still a million times better than Big Mick.

Beneath the calm, hidden away among my hopes, I was scared shitless that it might all disappear, that this new life might fall apart like tea biscuits in warm custard; that I might start peeing the bed again and get sent back to the Home like the other times; that Mr and Mrs Rowlandson might not love me; that they might be lying when they said that this time, it was different. "You have our name and soon you'll make new pals—you'll see."

But I hadn't. Not close ones that would stick up for me. At my new school, it was all, "Orphan kid! Orphan kid!" and "You don't have a Mum and Dad, not a real Mum and Dad—you don't even have your own name."

I don't know which was worse: telling them I had a name, or telling them that nobody used it; telling them that I had real parents or telling them they'd dumped me on the front steps of the Home with a dummy, a dirty arse and half a Christmas card saying WARREN DUNCAN NICHOLS, March 20, 1983; *telling them that until I was nearly eight, I was Nico after my real parents, or telling them I was now Rolo after people I hardly knew.*

Before the Rowlandson's took me on, I had foster mothers, and one of them, fat old Mrs Groom, I liked a lot. But she died. She used to bawl at me for blocking the lav and for leaving a dirty line round the bath, and she'd laugh at me standing shivering in front of her, waiting for clean clothes. 'Look at you!' she'd say, 'You're as thin as a pencil! No bum and as thin as a pencil! As thin as that little widdler of yours!'

But she never hit me and she always gave me one of her sweets, the big boiled ones that looked like pink and white goldfish. If you sucked them too hard they made your tongue sore, and they got sharper and sharper. When they got small enough, she'd tell me to crunch them. But she couldn't do that herself because she had false teeth. And one day, when she caught me kicking the cat, she shouted at me so hard the fish caught in her throat and she threw a purple fit and died. Choked to death in front of me, lying on her back, kicking and gurgling, trying to roll over, the cat half way up the curtains, her dress up round her middle, her knickers pink and stretched, black hairs like Big Mick's crawling out over grey-white skin.

I liked Mrs Groom. She didn't send me back. She didn't pick me up and put me down like the others. Like they did things at the shops; looking at the sell-by dates, trying to get a cut-price bargain. Doing it for the money, not for me. For the neighbours, the teachers, the Care people, not for me. Not slapping but not cuddling. Not kissing and rubbing cheeks like real mothers did.

Then came Mr and Mrs Rowlandson.

That first time, when I was brought out to meet them, they didn't know what to do, didn't know what to say.

The second time, they gave me a Kit Kat—which I gobbled down in the lav when they'd gone so that nobody could steal it, smoothing out the silver paper and putting it inside an old comic to pretend it was treasure.

The third time, they took me home and let me sit in a posh chair and watch television and gave me chicken nuggets and asked if I'd like to stay there, if I'd like them to be my new Mum and Dad.

I said yes I would and they mussed my hair and tickled me and gave me another Kit Kat.

But then I heard her telling Mr Rowlandson that come Easter, she wasn't having any more of what happened at Christmas, having to take time off work to look after me, being stuck in the house with nobody to talk to and nothing on the telly but Bush and the fucking war in Iraq.

So when I broke up for Easter, I was packed off to the Drummonds in the next street, trailing round there every day with a bag of jam sandwiches and a bottle of pop—Janice, the eldest girl roaring in and out on the back of her boyfriend's motorbike; Katie bossing me; Dodie tagging on.

Watching him pretending to be dead, spread-eagled on the leaves, made Dodie giggle and she threw herself down beside him, lying on her back like him, nudging into him as he gazed up through the branches.

"I could've caught it, you know," he said. "I could've pinned it to a board and looked at it. But I let it go."

He drank some lemonade and gave her some, watching her glug it down, snatching it back before it was all gone; watching again as she suddenly gasped and squirmed, squatting down on her heels, little rubbery fingers rushing to pull her knickers out of the way; his cheek pressed to the dead leaves, his hand lifting her dress to watch the stream hissing from her, remembering Mrs Groom, looking for the black hairs.

She regarded his invasion gravely and without comment and when she was done, he jumped to his feet.

"Right! I'm a big monster and I'm chasin' you!"

She squealed and ran out onto the path, fleeing round the corner, the two of them bumping into the older girls as they made their way back to look for them.

"Dodie, where you been? What you been doin'?"

"Nothin'," said Dodie. "Rolo wanted a rest and he gave me a drink."

"Is that all?"

"Yes. We're playin' monsters."

The interrogation over, Katie switched her attack. "What *you* doin' here, anyhow, Rolo? We don't want you here. We're chattin'."

"I don't mind," he said. "I can just walk behind. Like I was."

"We don't want you," she repeated. "Go and find the others."

They left him, the little girl dragged off by one hand, waving goodbye with the other. After a minute kicking the dust and pebbles, making a canyon for the British tanks, he decided to climb a tree to see if he could spot the rest of the gang. To his right, three hundred yards away, a commuter train was rattling towards Waterloo, slotting in between the distant factories and the gas works like one of the maggots they'd watched gobbling up a dead cat. To his left, were the marshy bits and the Tube line. But behind him, squirming round, he could see the roof timbers of the half-built houses. It was only a guess, but he decided to try there.

Moggy's gang had been playing secretly among the new buildings ever since the workmen first arrived; what had once been nothing but a leafy resting place for used condoms, fag packets, squashed cans, and soggy tissues had become an Iraqi missile site blasted by U.S. gunships. And when they were fed up with the war games, it was exciting enough just to trespass, to swagger about like the workmen.

Jinking his way down to the site through a bank of high weeds, Rolo was suddenly pulled to the ground by a dozen hands, his mouth covered by a grimy palm, his legs held still.

"Be quiet! D'you want 'em to fuckin' see us?"

It was Moggy Moorhouse. He was already twelve and always had at least two fags stashed away in a little tin box for them to smoke in their den. He and his pal, Thumper Dyson, ran the gang and decided who got a drag and who didn't. A can of Coke stolen from home got you two drags, but a can of lager stolen from a corner shop while they all watched, got you three drags and three swigs. People who turned up with nothing had to pay a forfeit—like kicking dried dog shit, or wazzing as high as you could against a wall.

Thumper raised his fist. "Where you been, Rolo? Why you so late?"

"I've been no-where," he said, chest heaving. "I was with the girls."

"What girls?"

"Katie and Mary and Dodie. We weren't doin' nothin'!"

"Nothin'? I bet you were!"

"We weren't! Honest!"

Seeing a way out: "I was lookin' up their dresses."

"You *weren't*! They wouldn't let you!"

"I was! They did!"

"Whose?"

"Dodie's! She was havin' a wazz and I watched! It looked like a peach!"

They exploded into laughter, rolling about in the grass, the Iraqi soldiers forgotten, he also laughing, thinking he'd won them round.

"But you must've seen one before!" said Moggy.

"I hadn't."

"What about your sisters?"

"I don't have sisters," he said. "I don't have nobody."

Nobody but the boys in the Home, them and their fists. Them and Big Mick.

They stared at him, uncomprehending. Then Trazzer Wilcox said he was lying. Everybody had somebody.

"Forfeit!" shouted Mickey Dooley. "We should pull his fuckin' pants down and let them look at *him*!"

Hands dragged him back down into the grass and they started scrabbling at his belt, laughing at his little-boy wazzer.

But Moggy shoved them away. He was looking down on the missile site. The Iraqis were having a tea break, sitting on the other side of their rocket launcher, the new houses out of their sight.

"Rolo," he said, "you want to be a full member of this gang?"

"Yes,"

"The *youngest* full member?"

"Yes."

"Right! This is your forfeit." He picked up a large pebble, chalked a Union Jack on it and pushed it into Rolo's pocket. "That's a bomb. You wriggle through our secret hole, climb that ladder, walk across that plank like the men do, leave the bomb at the end of the plank, and come back down the ladder on the other side. If you don't do that, we tie you to a fuckin' tree, pull your pants down and tell the girls you've been touchin' Dodie's peach!"

The gang leader rolled his eyes at the innocent word and made lewd movements with a finger, the gang sniggering, pulling Rolo to his feet, ignoring his denials, strong hands pushing his shirt back in, yanking his belt, making him wince as they pulled it too tight, their actions a blur; his face working, trying not to cry, crushed by the realisation that he should have kept quiet. There was no escape.

He crawled through the weeds to the concealed hole in the fence, the watchers sneaking looks at each other, grinning nervously, shaking their heads, amazed that he had taken up the challenge. On the other side, they saw him stoop low and run to the foot of the ladder, glance around and begin to climb. At the top, he transferred to the scaffolding, disappeared for a moment, and then re-emerged, stepping on to the bendy plank that the men used as a short cut, they bouncing across in three strides, their hods and buckets held by one hand, the other ready to steady them on a high, makeshift rail.

Afterwards, when the police came, they said they hadn't meant for anything bad to happen, hadn't realised Rolo wasn't big enough, hadn't thought he wouldn't be able to reach the rail.

And when the questions got harder and they were scared stiff, biting back the tears, pushing them away with their knuckles, they said he should never have wobbled around like that, trying to get the bomb out of his pocket, fumbling about with it. He should have run across. But he just stood there waving his arms like one of those stupid clowns at the circus, the one you know can do the high wire but pretends he can't, and pretends he can't hear you screaming at him.

A mobile phone ringing.

"Mr Wolfson?"

"Yes, Bill."

"Mr Wolfson, can you get round here straight away?"

"What's wrong?"

"There's been an accident. A boy."

"What do you mean a boy? What kind of accident?"

"A little lad. Seven . . . eight. He must have climbed up."

"For God's sake! What was he doing on the site? Where were *you* lot?"

"He's hurt bad, Mr Wolfson."

"How bad?"

"Bad!"

"Bill, get a grip. Tell me what happened. What did he do?"

"He must have fallen off a plank. The men . . . ."

"And?"

"He went straight down."

"On to the ground?"

"Into the mixer."

"The mixer? The *cement* mixer?"

"Yes."

"Was it going?"

"Yes."

Wolfson closed his eyes, his mobile still clamped to his ear. A prayer, five words, rose from deep down and swam behind his eyelids. Please, God . . . Please, dear God . . . He looked back at the site meeting he was holding at a block of flats his company was building in Greenwich, some of the group peering at him, looking worried. "You all right, Mr Wolfson?" one shouted.

"Yes. You still there, Bill?"

"Yes, I'm here. The ambulance has just arrived. And the police. They want to see me. I'm the site boss. I've got to go."

"For the moment, say nothing, Bill. Tell them I'm leaving now. I'll be there in half an hour. Perhaps less."

He rang off, shouted, "Get on with it," and left without explanation, hurrying to his car, calling the firm's lawyers on the way.

By the time he had spoken to the police, inspected the hole in the fence, and the lawyers had rung the hospital that day, and for many days after that, and after the charges of negligence had been admitted and the fines paid and the compensation hurriedly, willingly, arranged, there remained within him a lasting horror, a laceration that wrought new channels in his mind, that shouted at him in the night, that mingled with the screams that he had not heard but would hear forever, that decreed that however much money he spent, however much he tried to turn sand into water, the boy in the mixer would never walk again.

And so when the Rowlandsons came to see me and just stood and looked at my legs and said nothing and gave me back to the carers and social workers, and I was sent to another Home, I got to be called Nico again, nobody there knowing about the Rolo bit, or about Big Mick and what he used to do to me, and not about how I used to float away from him in a dream about a magic cupboard; about how it sailed around in the clouds, a piece of paper inside it, stamped and signed, telling me who they were, my real Mum and Dad, and how many brothers and sisters I had, and what our dog was called.

But never getting a chance to read the paper.
Lying in bed, staring at the ceiling.
The cupboard forever sailing by.

"This is a victory for all mankind, for the rule of law and for what is right"—President George Bush, senior, February 27, 1991, after a six-week military campaign that drove Iraq from Kuwait. Eighty-eight-thousand tons of bombs and missiles were employed against targets throughout Iraq; tens of thousands of Iraqi soldiers and civilians were killed. But Saddam was left in power for a further 12 fateful years . . .

Chapter 1

Inferno 2003

Without planning it, his mind unfocussed, Colly Wolfson found himself in a small, unknown, unsought church, it's once white pillars and porticos dwarfed on all sides by the towering banks and office blocks of London's financial district, the City's fabled Square Mile. At the top of one of them was the venue for that day's conference—a friendly, cut-throat money meeting: on the one side, the investors, in the centre, the brokers, and on the other side, his advisors and himself, a quietly proud, prize-winning architect and builder.

If asked for a shorthand description of him, his friends might have first bridled at any inferred sycophancy, but, with a little smile, might then have added, "Oh I don't know . . . How do the glossies put it . . . ? 'Rich, youngish and of the day'—isn't that it?" But they would have drawn the line at spelling out the Knightsbridge haircut, the Jermyn Street shirts and ties, the Bond Street suits and shoes. Such details, in their circle, were taken as read—though the women among them might well have alluded, among themselves, to the lean, six-foot figure, the square shoulders, the small, tight buttocks, the Mediterranean skin tones . . .

Thus equipped, on the day of his money meetings, he would aim to arrive in the City early, and before he joined his team, would buy himself a coffee, rehearse his strategy, and then wander the gleaming, ever-changing streets.

But not *this* day. *This* day, because it was the twentieth of March; because it was already written into both their minds, his and Lizzie's; because, for years, it had been secretly, *doubly* special to *him*; because it had now been hi-jacked by a further horror—because of all that, this time, his steps had taken him to an ancient pew, an ancient haven of peace.

He saw that the new war—that day's war—was merely a catalyst, that the reality, *for him*, was the thoughts that were racing among the private, intimate parts of his life, the different years, the different places, the files that had been carefully hidden away—a computer mouse running amok, urging him to acknowledge what had shaped him and had shaped those who sought to love him.

But he wasn't ready for that. Not yet. All he could see were the images of that day's indescribable pre-dawn attack on another world, on the sun-baked buildings of another culture, the precursor of a second one-sided, hi-tech war there—the Starred and Striped father pressing the button the first time, racking up his multi-billion dollar war chest, his half-million invasion force, his hundred-thousand air sorties; but not allowed to finish the job, the driven son dutifully now arriving, that day, to nail Saddam forever.

So his eyes resting dully on the worn carpet between the choir stalls, his feelings suspended, refusing, for the moment, to allow any examination of his own connected inferno—seeing, instead, the televised Baghdad skyline, the gouts of smoke and flame, the jagged wreckage, the quivering flesh.

Resigned to the insistent banging of the drum, the unsaid, "Roll up! Roll up! Pull up your chairs! Watch the President's new reality show! Better than ever! No expense spared!" the accompanying blurb insisting that the single trigger was Iraq's refusal to destroy its weapons of mass destruction; making half-fiction out of half-fact, throwing in Saddam's alleged support of international terrorism, implying the attack on the Twin Towers, slating his violence against his own people.

So the audience confused, thinking that the talking and the threats of retribution would go on for ever. Pleased if they did, pleased if they didn't. Some, a few, cheering George the son and Tony the poodle; others, a huge mass of others, awed like *him* into silence by that day's bombardment, rejecting the temptation to slam the whole of Islam, acknowledging that behind it all lay the dictators, the bigots and the extremists, the intertwined, merciless tentacles of the hate-mongers; the lot of them forever ranting at the Great Satan and the old Empire Builders, screaming, rightly or wrongly, for the West to get out of the Middle East, for an end to blind support of Israel, for a just deal for the Palestinians—he suspecting that on that one, the Western millions would say, "Yes, but . . ." Would shrug it all away like the first time, would hide behind the smooth, trite, pronouncements of their leaders, would allow themselves to be convinced, and would get on with their lives as if the exaggerations and the faulty intelligence and the half-truths and the carnage was not happening, was not in their remit.

He sighed and bowed his head. For that day at least, he had gone as far as he could, ready now to admit that the inferno, that day's inferno, was not the only cause for his need for sanctuary.

—Lizzie, loving and kind, imagining that the reason for his wretchedness was the same as that filling her own mind that day, not the new war, something infinitely more personal, more compelling; trusting that what was in her mind was in his, but saying that, yes, of course he must go up to the City for his meeting, of course he must.

"It's only a short drive away and I'll be fine on my own," she had said, "of course I will," stinging him by adding, "I always have been," stating the opposite of her existence with, "You can't live in the past, Colly. None of us can," wounding again, not meaning to, not knowing, with, "You have to let go. You have to forgive. Even when there's nothing to forgive."

But what did *she* know? Thinking only of Robert, their baby son, of the way he, Colly, had blamed her, knowing she wasn't guilty, that it wasn't her fault, hating himself for thinking it ever might be, yet never able to cast from his mind the torture that she could have done more, that it might have been different had he been there with her instead of spending the night away on business.

So, yes, she was right. The inferno, his own, personal inferno, *was* to do with Robert. Both of them knowing that, both of them grieving, but only he thinking of Nico, she grieving Robert's birth that day eighteen years ago, but *she* without a thought of Nico, not aware that it was also *his* birthday, two years to the day before

3

Robert's; not realising that in his mind the two had become one, that Nico had replaced Robert, that Nico was his new son, that for the past three years he had been helping Angie to take care of him, calling in every other day or so, absorbing the boy's anger and frustration, helping him to dress and bathe, being there;

Lizzie not knowing this, knowing about the money, the compensation, the damages, but not being told about this later caring so as not to disturb the old wounds, cause new hurt; so that she would not realise he had replaced the one with the other, that the surrogate had taken over, that the few weeks of Robert's life had gradually merged with Nico's, that the only way he could deal with the guilt was to abase himself in the suffering.

So there it was—the grotesque fluke. On the day of the re-born war, the shared birthday, intertwining what was and what might have been with what was full stop; the bitter coincidence not allowing either the one or the other to be forgotten, to be put aside.

And this year, the day worse than ever, more involved, more guilt-ridden. For while Nico was not now, had not been for a long time, merely the second tragedy of his life, was instead the engrossing, intimate sun of it, the one around which he increasingly revolved, was drawn to, what Lizzie also did not know, had not yet guessed, been told about, was that there was now in his life another twinned pair, Chloe and Charlie; that he was craving for the one and already joined with the other, doing it for the sake of it, again and again, the slippery, gasping indulgences ever more hopeless, ever less likely to erase his terrible, unsought, unplanned deceits, Lizzie not knowing about them and none of them knowing about his new life with Nico.

"What I believe the assessed intelligence has established beyond doubt is that Saddam has continued to produce chemical and biological weapons . . . and that he has been able to extend the range of his ballistic missile programme . . . the document discloses that his military planning allows for some of the WMD to be ready within 45 minutes of an order to use them"—The British Prime Minister, Tony Blair, in the foreword to the government's dossier on its case against Saddam Hussein, published September 24, 2002.

Chapter 2

New Year's Day, 2003

He was standing in the shadows beneath the marble staircase, obscured by the dusty fronds of a potted palm, the size and sort, he supposed, that people casually situated in their vestibules to show how arty they were; standing silently, suffering his depression, drink in hand, thinking, for no good reason, of Blair and Bush and Lizzie's absence, watching Charlie and Howard Sinclair welcoming the various members of the Set.

It was like a mannered period play, a cavalcade of ridiculously exaggerated greetings, preposterous had the greeters merely been near-neighbours who saw each other socially once a year and would have been no less bored had it been once a lifetime, less so, he conceded, if, as in this instance, they were members of a group who had found a jangled rhythm. The Syncopations, said one wit. The Sink Set, said another, his joke within a joke more appealing, more lasting.

The Callows were the latest to make an appearance, shedding their furs and Barbours, stamping their feet, blowing on cold hands, signifying the raw, first day of the year, yet hot and bothered as always, pleading their unpunctuality, treating it as something important, when all their hosts clearly wished was to get a glass of mulled wine into their hands and let them tell it to someone else.

Before the Callows, in quick succession, had come the neatly attired Platt-Smiths, he joky but careful, she primping, wordless and tightly bound like an imperial Chinese foot, the sweaty pleasures of the bed, he pondered, still as far from her at forty as they had been in youth; in sharp contrast were the curiously carnal Leveringtons, duo-schoolteachers, duo-spectacled, he with a receding bush of hair, scruffy collar, and strangely withdrawn pelvis as if concealing an overcharged fantasy, she freckled, floppy and, as always, intriguingly bare-legged. Before the Leveringtons, if he remembered correctly, had come the excessively courteous, dry as sticks De Mangers, well-heeled landowners providentially begat from long lines of so-called gentleman farmers.

Then something different . . . new . . . interesting . . . Paul and Anna Brownlove ushering in two people he had not seen before: he tallish, thin-haired and thin-cheeked, with a prominent left eye and hands that gesticulated expressively, she also tall, but with red hair that fell to her shoulders, quiet hands that quickly caressed her glass, and a face both demure and worldly, fashioned, it seemed to Colly, from the skin of a pale, exotic fruit; lustrous, unblemished.

"These are our friends, Simon and Chloe," Anna was saying, "the ones we told you about."

"The ones you met last year in Vienna," Charlie recounted.

"Yes, just so. I'm sorry it's such short notice, but . . ."

"Don't worry for a moment," said Charlie. "We're only too pleased to have them—to have *you*," she added, apologetically, including the two strangers in the conversation.

They nodded dutifully, and as the Brownloves allowed themselves to be beckoned away, the man, Simon, made some remark about the holly and the ivy, the dangling paper balls and bells, his partner glancing upwards for a moment, but then choosing to look around, her green eyes taking in the various doorways before coming to rest on the man behind the palm, a smile touching her lips, an eyebrow arching sufficiently to draw Charlie's attention.

"Colly Wolfson!" she admonished, mildly. "What're you doing there, frightening my guests? Come along out and meet these people! Where's your long-suffering Lizzy? Simon, Chloe—this is Colly Wolfson. He's an absolute scoundrel! Don't say you weren't warned!"

6

To excuse her playful rudeness, she kissed him, not, Chloe noticed, on the cheek, but on the lips, uttering a loud, comic, "Mwa!" before teetering off to the kitchen, her red high heels clacking over the crazed black and white tiles of the hallway.

"Hi," said Colly, smiling but diffident, wiping his mouth on a paper tissue as if knowing that one would be necessary for just that purpose. Until their arrival, his place behind the palm had seemed perfect. Like most hidey-holes, it revealed more than might have been supposed—little tics and gestures, warning glances, winks, straying hands . . . Now he was out in the light, Simon seemed older, less generous, sardonic. But his partner still seemed without blemish, without a way in.

"Why Vienna?" he asked her. "Why not Baghdad?"

"Why Colly?" she countered, playfully. "Why not Columbus?" She smiled the same level, quizzical smile, quietly adding. "And why the palm? And why no Lizzy?"

He could see now that she was not quite so young as he had imagined. Thirty. Perhaps more. And from the way she wore her low cut, angora top, she was proud of what a jealous Lizzie, if asked, would call her page-boy chest, missing the point, sniffing at what *he,* if asked, would call her silk-shrouded lure. The silk, slippery, caressing, was his own invention, though he doubted that it would be any more inaccurate than Lizzie's.

During their exchanges, Simon had stood silent, his unequal eyes moving from one to the other, noting the undercurrents. Not wanting to play the game himself and anxious to replace the punch, he took hold of Chloe's arm, his grip unsettling her smooth perfection, and began shepherding her along the hall. "Sorry, old boy," he said over his shoulder, "quiz-time can wait for the drinks table. Why not lead the way?"

"No thanks," said Colly. "I'm sticking with the mulled stuff." He turned towards the dresser, then swung back and with a little wave of his hand, called, "Down there. Second left."

The woman Chloe, reading his wish not to appear impolite, smiled to herself and watched as he joined their host, Howard Sinclair, in his vigil by the door, reaching into the bowl, filling his glass, his conscience displayed to strangers, his thin, nonchalant frame concealed beneath an elegant, olive suit. She shrugged away a familiar stirring and followed Simon into the drinks room, aware that nobody else had yet progressed beyond the punch stage, perturbed, for once, that the trailblazers were themselves, the newcomers.

Simon's act of appearing racy had always been one of his basic attractions, as essential to her as the unspoken pretence that manners and mores were not qualities they much cared about. Recently, however, there were times when she thought she could see the first cracks in his façade. It disturbed her feeling of oneness with him, so that here, among this clan of like-minded, like-sounding people, she suddenly felt a strange, momentary need for obscurity. A gauze curtain . . . a potted palm . . .

"Ah! A woman after my own heart!" said a voice at her side. "I'll take the whisky when you've finished."

She looked up from mixing herself a whisky and ginger to find a short, broad-shouldered man raising his eyes from her cleavage. "Have you seen Hugo?" he asked.

"Hugo?"

"Hugo de Manger. I want to speak to him."

"But does he want to speak to you?" she replied, unsmiling. "If so, I can't help. I don't know a Hugo and I believe I don't know you, either."

"Ah!" he said, exaggeratedly, "brought together by a whisky bottle! You're no Sink, are you! Do allow me the pleasure—Herbie Kirby. As in Herbie's Van Hire. School—Borstal. University—Life. And you?"

She looked down into his wide-eyed challenge, wondering if his name was ever pronounced singly. Mata Hari, Walt Disney, Roy Rogers . . . Herbie Kirby.

"Chloe Jones," she said, chanting: "School—London suburbs. University—first year drop-out. Friend of the Brownloves."

"Venice!" he exclaimed, pointing his finger at her, pleased to display his knowledge, to prove his intimacy. "Did you do the Harry Lime thing—you know, the Ferris wheel? James Cagney?"

"Vienna, Orson Wells," she corrected. "Not this time. We . . ." But he was already turning away, his attention caught by the sight of a tall, thin man in red trousers, a faded velvet jacket and a creased orange tie.

"Sorry," he said. "There's Hugo now. We'll have another whisky later."

Herbie Kirby or Presumptuous Pete?

She turned from the table and was gathered in by the Brownloves, Paul saying, "C'mon, let's go and find Simon. He's wandered off," Anna apologising, saying they'd been waylaid by Keith and Jessica.

"Keith and . . . ?"

"Jessica. The Callows. The people we told you wanted to visit Vienna with us. You know, the perfect couple—good schools, good families, two point four children. Very nice people, but a weeny bit *too* perfect, *too* clever, *too* . . ."

She caught her husband's glance and stopped. "Sorry. Shouldn't go on. Yes, let's go and find Simon."

To Chloe, this bitchy, censorious side of Anna was, if anything, preferable to her usual style, which she found sugary and effusive. On the face of it, the Brownloves, or at least Anna, seemed to feel the Callows on their backs. But since she felt the same, or something similar, about *them*, her sympathies were only passing. They had met, of all places, in the queue for tickets outside the Vienna State Opera and had discovered that, back home, they lived in the same neck of the leafy Surrey suburbs: Simon, having divorced, in an old, rambling apartment, she in a nearby modern flat, the Brownloves up the hill among trees and lawns.

As it happened, the tickets for the Opera had run out before they reached the kiosk, so what more natural than that they all walk along Karntner Strasse for a meal? When they returned home, more meals followed—and Simon, it seemed, could not have been more pleased.

"Well, what's wrong with them?" he'd cried one day, sensing her mood. "It's not as if we live in their pockets—we only see them once a month. Less than that when I'm away."

"But it's more than that, isn't it? It's the regular golf thing for you and Paul, and the regular City chat thing ditto."

"We enjoy golf and we work in the City. I thought you and Anna got on fine?"

"We do, as far as it goes. But *you* don't have to put up with her African charities and her endless gossiping."

What was irritating her, what she left unsaid because it would hurt him, was the way he had changed; the way he was starting to conform. She realised it was inevitable—time passed and people changed. What was disappointing was that she would have liked to have changed with him, or at least been invited to do so.

So instead of agreeing to join in the search for him, she pleaded need of the loo and from there wandered back into the vestibule. With all the guests apparently welcomed in, Howard Sinclair was no longer attending the door, and the intriguing Mr Wolfson was nowhere to be seen. But the bowl of mulled wine remained on the dresser like a huge ruby and as it was still warm, she filled her empty whisky glass and slid behind the palm. The move astonished her—a thousand wild pissups, two broken engagements and a dozen years in advertising, and she preferred to hide! Not hide. Be still. Empty. Safe.

Before her mind had properly come to rest, a door opened across the way and two men emerged—Herbie Kirby's Heinz 57 terrier and the unmet Hugo de Manger's colourful Afghan hound. Seeing no one in the vestibule, Herbie continued what had obviously been a very private conversation.

"That's it then, Hugo. *I* get the six acres and the barns and *you* get a nice little something to help you out. O.K?"

To Chloe, shrinking behind the stairs, Hugo sounded crisp but hardly O.K. "That's exactly what we agreed in there, Herbie old boy. No need to repeat it. For obvious reasons, I'd prefer to keep the lid on."

They moved off down the corridor, with Herbie fussing happily at the other's heels. "Right you are, squire. No problem—anything to get a friend out of a hole."

Chloe winced on Hugo's behalf and silently congratulated Colly on his hidey-hole. Had she the chance, she would like to eavesdrop on *him*, on who and what he was. But since she was unlikely to be granted that particular wish, she moved off in search of further adventures.

The main hum of the party, she found, was no longer in the drinks room but in the lounge, a large room dominated by a huge, glowing inglenook, a grand piano bearing an elaborate arrangement of silk flowers but no music, and a truly hideous, four-seater settee.

It was bright yellow with red spots, a rash which had spread to two matching chairs, their sprawling arms forever scrolling outwards as if reaching for their next victim. Scattered around were a number of lesser chairs, the most popular being those furthest away from the fire, their occupants eating from laps or coffee tables.

Simon and the Brownloves were sitting in a deep bay, sipping gin and tonics, clearly awaiting her. "Ah! There you are!" cried Anna, snappily. "We couldn't find you. Where've you been?"

Without waiting for a reply, she added, "We've saved you a chair. Come and finish your drink and then, if there's any left, we'll go and find some food."

Leaning forward, she said confidentially, "That's the Callows across there on the settee. Keith and Jessica. Doesn't suit her dress, does it! Yellow, red and purple, were never good bedfellows. A bit like the Mayburys—the people with them," she added quickly, her husband beginning to glower.

Chloe looked across the room at Anna's current targets. They all appeared pleasant enough, the women slim and well enough dressed, the men in blazers and striped ties. She shrugged without comment. But Simon, in his new involved mode, asked what they all did.

"Well, the women have a bit of a tie-up. And they both have a sort of tie-up with Keith. Jessica Callows is an interior designer—not sure how good she is, but at least she knows where to go and get things—and Jill Maybury is an estate agent and puts work her way. She runs one of those up-market outfits that make a fortune for not much effort. She and Barns always seem to be getting something new. You know, new car, new house extension, expensive holidays. Obscure volcanoes, isolated high valleys—that sort of thing. All right if your name's Livingstone!"

She sniggered and Simon snorted with her. "Mind you," she added, "the Callows aren't far behind—as I said, she's an interior designer and he's a company director. One of the big building firms. That's the link with him."

"And the other guy? Barns?"

"Barns? Barnaby to his adoring mother. He's the odd man out—he's a weatherman on local television and rather . . ." hesitating for effect, " . . . nice. Surprised you haven't seen him on the box."

11

"He travels down to the television lot on the south coast," said Paul, severely. "You don't see him on the box up here unless you tune in specially."

"Whatever," said his wife. "Anyway, point is, Jill does her best to keep in with both the Callows. Well, you would, wouldn't you?"

"And why aren't they happy together?" asked Chloe, tired of the barbs about people she didn't know, irritated by Simon's interest in them.

"Who?" Anna asked.

"I thought you said the Mayburys weren't happy?"

"Did I?" said Anna. "I don't remember."

"C'mon," said Paul, hurriedly. "Drink up and let's go and see what's left to eat."

By this time, it was well past one o'clock and the wintry murk seeping into the dining room was met by six fat candles set in glass funnels among the food. Perversely, if anything, the tiny flames accentuated the gloom, their guttering glinting and gleaming on a host of well-visited dishes.

Despite the obvious feasting, Simon exclaimed, "De-de-de-dah!" his hands held wide, pointing to the table as if introducing the next act in a stage show. "Fear not, ye poor of Calcutta, the God's are generous!"—eager to raise Chloe's spirits, to laugh and fool around with her, to continue their careful, mutually approved intimacy. After the split in his marriage and the dark days with his conscience, she had carried him away, but had remained independent, separate, uncommitted.

"Cornu*copia*!" he said, a hand gripping each of her shoulders from behind, pointing her to the table, as if directing a child, as if the sight was worth nothing unless they saw it together. "It's like that place we go to, the Italian place in Brewer Street."

"Not Calcutta, then?" She looked up at him and knew she loved him, knew it or thought she knew it, knew, anyway, that this time it was different, that *he* was different; knowing that what had drawn her to him was his archness, his determination to have a good time come what may; knowing, too, that she would have liked this feature to have been deeper, to have gone on for longer; to be mixed with everything in him that was thoughtful and generous, but to have flowed everywhere; so that their early giddiness might still be bubbling into and over this New Year party; into and over and around their lives, their waking lives, their sleeping lives; might still be wrapping itself around them like the warm clamminess of musky bed sheets; she trying, but failing, to banish his disappointing formality there, his self-satisfying quickness; coaxing him, all the while, to let go, to join with her in those immodest, unmentionable intimacies that seemed beyond him, that seemed must live in her mind.

Checking her thoughts, shuddering silently, she cast aside the nagging, frustrating images of the bedroom and settled instead for the mundane, persuading herself that her mood was merely because she saw him settling, that she wished to settle with him, but had not yet decided when.

"No, *not* Calcutta," she added, too loudly, too brightly, "and not Brewer Street either. The Villa Francesca, perhaps! Or The Ritz!"

She laughed and clapped her hands, as much as at his sudden, uncertain frown as at her own silliness, and became aware that the group of people they had succeeded at the table had been brought to a standstill on their way out by a man telling a story about something that had happened at the airport at San Francisco. Everything about the man was either nondescript or plain shabby. He was neither tall nor short, and if he appeared thin, she saw it was probably because his shirt collar was two sizes too large. A brown tie more or less matched a brown, rumpled suit, but even this was spoiled by black brogues and lank brown hair badly in need of a barber and a bottle of thickener.

"And what happened then, Harold?" asked a wide-eyed Amelia Platt-Smith.

"Well, after the big Englishman had kicked off a bit more about being kept waiting at the boarding gate, he crossed swords with a tired looking Yank hanging over a barrier, a sort of laconic John Gregson fresh out from another 'B' movie. 'Settle down,' the Yank drawled, 'they'll not forget us.' 'I doubt it,' said the Englishman. 'They lost our luggage on the way in, now they've lost the bloody aeroplane.'

"And had they, Harold?" asked Amelia.

"No! Another ten minutes, they opened up the gate and we all got on."

"So?"

"So when we arrived in Chicago, the big Englishman pushed his way down the aisle and who do you think he found standing in the cockpit doorway?—the John Gregson stand-in! He was the bloody pilot! Laughing all over his face!"

The group shook their heads and raised polite smiles before moving off to the lounge, the storyteller exchanging glances with Anna. before following, exclaiming, "Yes, and then there was the time, when . . ."

As if on cue, a door opened from the kitchen and into the dining room swept Charlie, their hostess, followed by a tray of trifles borne by a black woman wearing an orange turban and a dusky yellow apron.

"Hello Angie!" said Anna, brightly. "How nice to see you. Don't tell me we're too late!"

"Of course, you're not," said Charlie, rather too sharply. "It's not the school canteen!"

Nevertheless, embarrassed by getting in Angie's way, they scooted around the table like naughty children, selecting their meal, making muted, unnecessary exclamations about how delicious everything looked, sliding out into the hallway with their plates, Chloe raising her eyes, Anna saying, "Oh don't worry! Silly cow should have checked."

In the lounge, the merry-go-round for seats was still underway. The Callows, spotting their difficulty, made room on the settee for Simon and, in the mix up, for a clearly reluctant Anna, leaving Paul and Chloe to wander through to the sparsely populated drinks room where they rested their plates on a table to cut up their food, then stood, plates in hand, eating with forks.

They were joined by Ozzie Leverington. But as soon as he had made the introductions, Paul asked to be excused. "If you don't mind, I'll just pop into the lounge for a moment—check if Anna's O.K."

"Check whether she's causing mayhem," said Ozzie as the other disappeared.

Chloe gave him a hard look, but was diverted. "Don't look now," she said, "but who's that going out? He was sitting in the corner."

"That's one of Anna's mayhems," said Ozzie. "Harold Wensum. She brought him along to one of our do's some time back. Turns up every now and again like a bad penny."

"What's wrong with him?"

"He's a shit. He bores everybody stupid with his travel stories."

"And for no reason than that, he resembles a pile of manure?"

"No, of course not. He's a shit because . . ." He hesitated and gave a weary smile. "You don't need to know. It should be enough just to look at him."

"Well, hardly," she said, tartly, adding, "So, when he's not getting under your delicate skin, what does he do?"

"Travels the world—hence his stories. From what he says, he's a paint salesman."

"A paint salesman?"

"Yes. If you ask him, he'll say he paints happiness."

"Fancy that," she said, affectedly, trying to smile as Paul Brownlove rejoined them, Ozzie sliding off with a casual, "See you."

"Where's *he* off to?" asked Paul. "Something I said?"

"Rather more something he trod in," said Chloe. "What he calls one of Anna's mayhems. Harold Wensum?"

"Oh not that again!" said Paul with a groan. "It really *is* time Ozzie stopped complaining." The sharpness of his tone advised an end to the subject and she waited. He seemed to have other things on his mind.

"What do you think?" he asked, looking around.

"To the party? Lovely house, lovely party," said Chloe. "Enjoying it."

"Yes, nice people, Charlie and Howard."

"They seem to be. I haven't seen much of them."

"No, I suppose they're busy. Doesn't help turning up so late for the food, though, does it? Or making cracks about your hostess."

She glanced at him quickly, wondering at first what he might mean, but then remembered. "Mmm. She . . . Anna . . . . she, er . . . she seems a little tense. But it was nothing! We're both having a lovely time."

"Good." He hesitated, then pressed on. "It's just that . . . nothing to do with this Wensum business. No, Anna . . . all that carping in the lounge. I just wanted to say, so that you might understand . . . Well, you've not seen Anna with this crowd before. She's fine normally, as you know, but when she gets with these people, the women, or most of them, they all have what she can never have. They have children. Mostly grown up now. But homes that are, or were, full of laughing, crying, worrisome, wonderful children. And she just can't quite handle it."

He raised his eyes and waited while she read the hurt and resignation.

"So when . . ." she said.

"So when we met you and Simon, there was no baggage, no children for her to fret over."

"To resent," she said.

"If you will."

"Sorry, Paul. I didn't mean that unkindly. I had no idea. She's never said. We did wonder, of course. You know—no children, all this charity work for kids out in God knows where. But we didn't know it upset her. I'm sorry," she repeated.

"No need for you to feel sorry. I just wanted you to know. Look," he said, suddenly uncomfortable, "if you'll excuse me, I'll go and see if they want more wine. Catch you back here."

But he was a little while. So, on a whim, she filled her glass with over-scented Australian chardonnay and moved back up the long hallway, hoping, cursing herself for a fool, but hoping, nevertheless—and failing to hide the tiny jump of excitement when she saw him beneath the palm.

"Hi," she said, smiling.

"Hi," said Colly. "Do you want to come under, or shall I brave the slingshots and arrows?"

She looked around her. Paul Brownlove and Simon were making their way into the drinks room, unknown voices could be heard in the cloakroom and the colourful Angie was disappearing into the kitchen with a tray of used plates. "The enemy has been repulsed," she said. "Why don't I *wallow* in the *wel*coming chair while you *appraise* from the *punch* table."

An eyebrow raised to acknowledge her droll eloquence, he moved to their new vantage point, looking down on her from his seat on the antique oak, his legs crossed, one hand planted by the punch bowl to support him, the other holding a glass of red. With his style repeated in her own pose, it occurred to her that they resembled one of those carefully staged Victorian photographs: the beautiful couple, the marble staircase, even a potted palm, formal yet charged, sensual, intimate.

Troubled again by her thoughts, she rose to her feet and resorted to inspecting her make-up in a scalloped wall mirror. Regarding him through the reflection, she broke an awkward silence by referring back to his earlier question, introducing the subject out of context as he had done. "Are you that depressed about Iraq?"

"Am I . . . ?"

"'Baghdad?' You said, 'Baghdad.' Strange choice."

"Sorry."

The silence resumed and was broken a second time by the de Mangers issuing from the cloakroom, throwing on their coats and hats as they moved to the front door, oblivious of them at first, she saying, "If you'd look after your things in the first place, you wouldn't lose them," he saying, "But Elizabeth, this is ridiculous! We've not even said goodbye to the others," she responding, "No, Hugo, it's *you* and your stupid deal that's ridiculous! You and that Herbie man! Stay if you must, but I'm off," seeing the two of them at the last moment, stopping short, fashioning taut, nodded smiles, he raising his hat, following her outside, still protesting, the door left ajar.

Glad of something to do, they both moved forward, their hands touching as they reached for the dull, brass knob, remaining there close together, smiling.

"Poor old Hugo," Colly said, softly. "Dog box time. What deal, I wonder?"

"Selling the family silver, I imagine."

"I don't think so, not Hugo."

"His birthright, then."

"His land? The silver is his land."

"So?" she asked.

Until this point, the little interchange had been light and joky, a mild flirtation, an exploration of their mutual attraction. Suddenly, by becoming serious, by showing herself to be in front of him among his own friends, Colly saw that she had somehow changed the rules,

17

made him, aware of her as a person rather than merely a perfumed fantasy, a New Year wish.

To reassert himself, he said, "It must be something to do with the vans. Herbie rents space from Hugo to garage his vans. Runs a fleet of them. Van hire. That's how Howard knows him. He sometimes uses the vans for his furniture business." He shrugged and smiled stiffly, holding her gaze.

"Ah!" she exclaimed, undeterred. "Methinks your palm tree did not reveal as much for you as it did for me. And now you're miffed."

"And why should I feel miffed?" he asked, the smile taking on an amused curiosity.

"Because . . ."

We're at it again, she thought, the wheels bouncing over the unknown track, the stones flying, the dust billowing. To keep the conversation centred, not wishing it to veer off into the doings of Hugo and the awful van man, she changed tack.

"So why no Lizzie?" she asked, softly.

The smile returned, recognising her ploy. "So why Vienna?"

"Oh that's easy. Simon's forever into broadening our horizons. You know, new sights, new sounds. We'd both been to Vienna before, but this time we were going on to Prague."

"Yes, Anna has said how much she enjoyed your company. And also since then. We—the Sink Set—we get together every now and then for a drink and a chat. We've been keeping tabs on you."

She noticed that there was still no mention of Lizzie, nor for that matter, of himself, of "Why Colly?" She knew already, if she remembered Anna's gossip correctly, that he was some sort of developer who won prizes, well off, fingers in pies. She also knew that he and Lizzie had a teenage daughter and that there had been two tragedies—a child's death and something about a boy, something complicated.

"Tabs on me? Hardly worth it," she said. "But you—how does one keep tabs on you? *Pour example, qu'est ce que c'est votre raison d'etre?*"

"German, too!" he mocked. "*Formidable!* I'm not sure about the *raison* bit, but *je suis un architecte*." He smiled at her, shaking his head, as if to a child. "But you knew that already, didn't you? As I'm sure you know all Anna's theories about my *raison*, about what she thinks makes me tick."

Alarmed at the slight edge that had crept into his voice, she offered conciliation. "Not at all. Forgive me, I'm sorry. We don't spend *all* our time talking about you. But you must have noticed how it's always the way-out people who attract the gossip."

"And does that include you?"

The face that had been poking around the lounge door every now and again, looking up the hallway—for all the world, she thought, like a cartoon woodpecker—now came into focus. It was Simon.

"It *might* include me," she said, moving away back down the hall. "Not for me to say, but I imagine that if you want to find out, you know where to find me."

"Who's miffed now?" he called playfully, her angora top as deep at the back as at the front, calling it out as if he had known her for years, not a micro-second; confounding himself, watching her walk away, a vision of swinging shoulders, wiggling bottom, brushing calves; her grey, sparkly shoes tripping along like a child's, her matching handbag twirling twice, low down by her side.

The party had now reached the comfortable stage. According to the state of their heads and stomachs after the previous night's New Year celebrations, everybody had eaten and quaffed their fill and old acquaintanceships had been renewed, some sincerely, others less so. Permissible, polite inquiries had been made about people present and not present, and a few guarded worries had been expressed about the looming crisis: whither the U.N? Could Blair keep Bush on track? Was it diplomacy or sycophancy—or was the Labour turncoat just being strung along? And what of the Tories? What Tories?

But in the main, the conversation had trilled along with its usual, required lightness, the *mores* of their social class decreeing that politics and religion should be largely set aside, that any such references were not for serious debate but made merely to set the scene, to show, however unconvincingly, that they had the partying in context.

If anything, the men observed these unwritten rules rather more strictly than the women, whose age-old contempt for male reliance on the use of force was matched by the confounding mystery to them of male camaraderie. Thus it was customary, at this stage of

Sink Set proceedings, for the women, and one or two renegade males, to withdraw to the fireside, leaving the bar to the men and their followers.

Resisting the urge to follow Chloe into the lounge—suspecting that Simon was already there—Colly found that among the bar crowd were Charlie Sinclair and her friend, Honey Leverington, each shaking her head, Charlie with no hint of a smile, Honey in mock disapproval, the rest of them hee-hawing at a joke apparently told by Charlie's husband, Howard, and just as apparently, extremely crude.

The two of them, he and Howard, had always been regarded as the closest of friends. It was how people saw them, decreed that they should be. And on the grounds that to demur might have demanded too many explanations, hurt too many feelings, he had allowed the issue to drift. It was far too late to jib publicly and far too complicated to provide an easy answer.

The man he had known for twenty years, was six foot six, clever, energetic, popular and from all accounts, a good boss. He threw great parties, invited his cronies along to his corporate boxes at Twickenham and Ascot, flew them around the country in his four-seater plane, and sniffed at the taxman, the lawyers and the Holy Trinity.

Blessings, like fivers, fell easily on Howard's plate—just as they did on his own. So the antipathy didn't stem from the man's personal fortune, his inherited furniture business, or his flair. And while he might long to have three offspring like Howard instead of his one, he couldn't blame him for what had happened to the dead Robert, and neither was he resentful of the young Sinclairs now sailing their privileged way through life.

So perhaps the problem was the relentless, sweaty maleness of the man, the jock image, the superficial attitudes, the boring, growing tendency to overdo the booze . . . .

"Ladies and gentlemen," Howard roared, banging the table with the flat of his hand, gulping his wine. "after such vulgarity, allow me to redeem myself—raise high your glasses and your skirts to Mr Colly Wolfson, head of Wolfson Associates bracket Architects unbracket and partner in that dubious money machine, Wolfson-McWhirter Construction. No better man has ever pulled his breeches up!"

"Nor pulled them down," said Colly.

"Oooh! Listen to him! We want none of that do we, boys? Come you to the table, Colly, for a glass of my finest wine. And whilst I pour it, you shall regale us with Tales from the Vienna Woods."

"Wrong man," said Colly, winking at a dozen widespread grins, hoping to deflect Howard's attentions. "Methinks thou confuses me with Brother Brownlove. T'was he who recently communed with the great Johan."

"Verily," said Howard, winking back, "but 'twas you, was it not, doing your own spot of wifeless communing—up the hall with a certain tasty red-head, who, I am led to believe, has also recently dallied on the Danube. So come clean: honour us with racy tales from Vienna."

Of the men, only Herbie Kirby responded gleefully, impervious or uncaring of the changed mood, the need not to encourage their suddenly truculent host.

"Steady on, old boy," said a voice from the back. "He's hardly been snaffling her into the bushes!" It was Roger Platt-Smith, moving forward, trying to ease Colly's discomfort. "C'mon! Let's get the chap a drink! And I'll fill you up, too, Howard."

But their host was not to be deflected. "Nah, nah, nah! I wanna hear about Colly and the redhead. C'mon Colly, you can tell an old mate! She a bit of all right then, your red-head?"

It was clearly intended to be light-hearted, conspiratorial. But the drink had got there first. And before Colly could think of a suitable reply, wondering instead why Charlie had left the room quite so abruptly, he was saved by Honey Leverington.

"Hang on!" she cried. "You pipe down for a moment, Howard. Colly, I'm no redhead and I can get by without The Blue Danube. But I haven't seen you all day. So I'm going to appropriate this nice bottle of whisky and then I'm going to have my unprintable way with you?"—sweeping him out of the room and into the hall, followed by false ooohs and aaahs.

Once in the hall, she kissed him on the cheek and presented him with the whisky. "I think you'll find Charlie in the kitchen," she whispered. "Be kind to her, Colly." She smiled at him encouragingly, willing him to do as she bade, her Good Fairy wand shedding treason.

Nonplussed, ruffled by Howard's heavy humour, Colly watched her drift off into the lounge, and stood undecided, unable, for a moment, to focus his thoughts. He knew—didn't he?—that the joshing had been friendly, drunken but friendly. And he knew—didn't he?—that nobody would take any notice. So why was he so irritated? And why the message from Honey about Charlie Sinclair?

As it happened, Charlie wasn't in the kitchen; he could see her at the front door, seeing off a jostling crowd of friends, Harold Wensum, saying that, yes, he'd be off again in the next few days; the Brownloves trying not to encourage him; Simon Mount looking down the hallway, pinpointing him with his protruding eye and its ridiculously raised brow, but without any sign of his earlier bonhomie; Chloe Jones glancing his way, taking in the whisky bottle, but declining to hold his gaze.

A moment later, wrapped up against the chill, they all moved outside, and with Charlie now engaged with the departing Mayburys, he slipped into the brilliantly lit kitchen, partly because it was what Honey had suggested and partly because he didn't want to be found dithering around.

Across the room, twenty feet away, was Angie Maketi, the maid, her apron replaced by a dark maroon anorak, her flamboyant headgear by a grey woollen hat.

"You having your own party, Colly?" she asked.

"No! No! No, it was just . . ." He placed the bottle on the worktop. "It's a long story, not worth it . . . . You off then?"

"Yes, I've got to get back. Time I went. He'll be expecting me. I'll be round back here in the morning to tidy up properly."

She began to open the back door, and they looked at each other for a long moment, suddenly serious, their eyes switching to the sight of Charlie Sinclair entering from the hall. She glanced at Colly, then quickly, brightly, too brightly: "You're off, then, Angie? Thanks again. See you tomorrow."

"Right you are, Mrs Sinclair. Bye, Mr Wolfson."

"Bye, Angie."

For the first time that day, for as long as he could remember, they were alone, enclosed in a bright, functional world of purring gadgets, glass-fronted cupboards, shiny, patterned surfaces, none of it touching them, arranged neatly all around but not part of them. It was like a giant, glaring cell, an open prison from which they could escape at any time, but chose not to, he confused, alarmed, aware of Charlie's anger but able only to hazard a guess at its source, its direction, guessing one part of it, the part Lizzie had told him, about how things had gone wrong in the Sinclair bedroom, he suspecting more, hoping he was wrong, not knowing if he wanted it broached.

Perhaps he *was* wrong, he thought. Perhaps it was just his new feelings about Howard. Perhaps it *wasn't* treason. Perhaps Honey had sent him along to the kitchen to listen and sympathise—a sort of stand-in for Lizzy, Charlie's confidante. But if it was that, why didn't Honey do it? She was just as close . . .

Jesus . . .

She was stacking the plates that Angie had been washing, sorting them out, crashing them together, head down, working fiercely.

"Charlie . . ." hesitant. Then louder, firmer. "Charlie!"

"What?" Looking up, face strained.

"Charlie, you don't need to do that. Angie's coming tomorrow. You know she is."

"I need to get on."

He crossed the room, took a plate from her hands, then held them. "You need to take it easy. You're jiggered and upset about . . ."

He was interrupted by loud voices and raucous laughter outside the door. "C'mon, you silly fart," Roger Platt-Smith was saying, "let's get you into that bed of yours."

"Nah, nah . . ."

"Yeah, yeah," said Roger, humouring his reluctant host, emphasising his resolve with a final, "Oh yes! Oh yes!"

Charlie was already half way across the kitchen. "I've got to see to him. Be a dear, say my goodbyes to the rest of them, will you?"

For something to do, to give his mind time to sort out a blurry thought that he couldn't quite place, he finished the stacking, then followed her out. The remaining guests were getting their coats on, hanging around, undecided, watching Roger and Herbie Kirby come back down the marble stairs, smiling, shaking their heads, Herbie announcing, needlessly, with too much relish, "That's going to be one helluva hangover!"

Colly moved among the leavers, shaking hands, kissing the women, passing on Charlie's goodbyes, saying he would stay on for a while, see that everything was O.K.

They all Happy New Year'd him, Roger punching him on the shoulder, Honey Leverington giving him an extra kiss, holding his face between her gloved hands, her eyes shiny bright.

With tears! Bright, sad, happy tears! Jolting him. Her face smiling, he saw, but her eyes weeping.

Then they were gone and he was wandering about collecting the last cups and glasses, piling them on a tray; sitting on the dreadful settee, watching the fire eating into the last of the logs, envying its mindless existence, wondering what the hell Honey was crying about. Then not thinking at all, not for an hour, not until she joined him.

Looking at her, seeing her through the mists of the preceding years, shrouded from him always by Lizzie's friendship. Not for him—not, until this particular party, this moment—a shuddering, exuding woman. Merely his wife's friend, his friend's wife, someone Lizzie had met while visiting a photographic exhibition, Charlie the model; not emerging from the mists, not for him, until now. Even now, still indistinct, wreathed by the final wisps of her shroud, her course unknown.

From what Lizzie said, Charlotte Anne Ford had started life in the meaner streets of 1960's Wimbledon, the daughter of an accounts clerk who, when she was sixteen, had proudly landed his little film star a job in his office. At five foot ten, with the approximate face and hair of an Elizabeth Taylor and the legs of a Betty Grable, it was no surprise to anyone but her father when she quickly got out from behind the adding machine and, with mother's help, fled to a modelling school and thence to an agency. While the rest of her gender ranted and railed for Women's Lib, Charlie Ford reinforced her cuticles, brushed her sheening hair and dieted herself onto the catwalk and into the glossies. When Howard Sinclair found her at the Paris Motor Show, she was twenty and draped semi-nude over a phallic bonnet. From there to the altar of a somewhat higher order took her only a few whirlwind months, their first child following less than a year later.

"I do love him, you know." She had settled herself into the middle of the settee, near to but not touching his sprawling legs, sharing his view of the fire, dressed now in a high-collared, ankles to ears soft blue dressing gown, the red shoes and the black and red dress discarded upstairs, speaking as though she were continuing an earlier conversation.

"I suppose so," he said.

"I do! I really do."

"Would you like me to make us some coffee?" he asked.

"Coffee? You want coffee?"

"No, I don't. Not really. I thought you might."

"Well, I don't. I want . . ." She threw her hands up and allowed them to fall. "I want to sit and talk. If you want a drink, have a brandy or something."

He rose to his feet, as much to end the perplexing banality as for any urge for further alcohol. He left the room and returned a minute later with the bottle of whisky from the kitchen, two glasses and a box of chocolates.

"I couldn't find the brandy," he said. "This'll do."

He poured the drinks and slid one along the glass-topped table in front of them, took a chocolate and slid the box along.

She watched him munching and sipping . . . the black wavy hair . . . the sallow skin . . . not watching her, watching the fire, splaying his legs, digging his heels into the carpet. Unnerved, she jumped up, catching the table, spilling the drink.

"Fuck it!" she said, stamping her foot, rubbing her leg.

"Never mind! It'll clean. Angie'll do it."

"She won't! It'll be too late!" She hurried out and returned with a cloth, kneeling down, rubbing furiously, a sob mixing with her quick breaths.

"Charlie, for Christ's sake," he said, walking round, pulling her up, allowing her to cling to him. "C'mon, now. There's no need to get upset! It's only a drop or two. And if it's about Howard, he'll sleep it off and be fine tomorrow. You know he will."

He was offering her a way out, a straw to clutch at, suspecting, knowing, that it wasn't Howard, not entirely.

A second sob ended with a deep intake of air. "It's not about Howard. You know it's not. You know I can cope with

Howard—you've watched me do it ever since I met him. Picking him up, patting him on the back, setting him off again on the right course, the right direction. It's not about Howard—it's about you!"

"Me?"

"Yes, you!" Pouting, reproving, a red-tipped finger drawing a line down his cheek, her body beginning to move, seeking him. "You know it is."

"Do I?"

The words drawing her away. "Stop teasing! You know it's not about Howard and not about Lizzie. It's about *you—you* and a red-haired tart called Chloe!"

To interrupt her, to give him more time, he sat her down on the settee, settling beside her, allowing her to grasp his hands, knowing that to call a halt, he needed only to kiss her gently on the forehead, free his hands from her lap, and walk out. Say nothing but, "I'll ring you in the morning," and walk out.

"Chloe?" he said, chidingly. "For goodness sake!" He paused, watching a vein beat in her throat, sighing, knowing there was still time to go, but not wanting to hurt her. "What is it you want?" he asked.

"How do you mean?"

"Well, you say all this—about Howard and Lizzie. About how it's not to do with them. But others *are* involved . . ." ending lamely, not wishing to say which others, not certain whether he wanted another complication . . . whether he wanted to listen to a sudden new recklessness within him, to throw his life in the air and cry, "Why not?"

She released his hands and when the caresses failed to follow, she read the signs and he watched as she stood up and began to walk slowly from him, turning as she reached the door, her voice low.

"Colly, I'm not proposing the end of the sodding world! I want *you,* not the rest of mankind. When you leave, put the catch down. And when your balls catch up with your scruples, let me know . . ."

Drifting from the firelight, her vulgarity dissolved by welling tears.

"Un Chief Kofi Annan: No Case for Iraq War"—Independent, Jan 1, 2003.

"Hold Your Fire, Tony"—Cabinet rebel, Clare Short, The Mirror, Jan 13, 2003.

"This War is Wrong"—Simon Weston, Falklands War hero, The Mirror, Jan 23, 2003.

"Mandela Denounces Blair over Iraq War"—The Times, Jan 31, 2003.

"Non! Chirac Rebuffs Blair on Iraq"—The Mirror, Feb 5, 2003.

Chapter 3

Hen Party

Every few weeks, the Sink women shrugged off their men and went out on a jaunt, or merely gathered in one of their homes to nibble and sip and dish the dirt. There was nothing formal about these occasions and there were only three don'ts: no talk of offspring, supermarkets or personal illnesses unless they involved sex or scandal; a fourth condition, that members of the Set should bring a friend of their own gender, was easier met.

That spring evening, the women had arranged to meet at the Callows' brand new home, a five-bedroom mansion on a new estate off the road to Guildford, its rooms, they assumed, as tidy and gleaming as Keith and Jessica were publicly perfect. Nothing, it seemed, ever went wrong in their lives, or, as the Set guessed, no blemish was ever admitted to—a characteristic that set people's teeth on edge.

For some of them, the hen parties themselves were one blemish too much. Amelia Platt-Smith welcomed personal friends to her tea table but was highly nervous of dipping her tiny toes into the larger pool of female introspection, its scones-and-butter blandness offset by the usual half-teaspoon of sugary spite. Others, like Honey Leverington, Charlie Sinclair and Jill Maybury, got by with the handbag set, but favoured the wider, simpler stimulus of the male.

So not everyone attended all the time.

On this occasion, however, with the chance to scrutinize Jessica's interior design skills, the attendance was higher than normal—a fact noted with pleasure by the hen party originator, Anna Brownlove.

"Another coup for you, Anna," remarked Jessica, reviewing the number of bobbing, chatting heads, tweaking the faultless cuffs of her crisp, striped shirt.

"Well, I think so, don't you?" Anna replied, aware that Jessica was more likely to be attempting to boost their friendship than proclaiming support for her innovation. "Don't want the chaps on top of you all the time, do you?"

"Who doesn't? Don't tell me you've been saying no to your sex god, Anna?" It was Honey Leverington, pushing by, winking at Jessica, her bare legs still brown from last year's sun.

"I was just saying . . ." Anna began. But Honey was already on her way to join Charlie, and the explanation, unnecessary, boring, died in the air.

When the Set coalesced some years ago, the Brownloves had been welcomed partly because of Paul's friendship with Howard Sinclair, and partly because of their tennis court, a beautifully maintained all-weather affair blessed by a generously stocked bar—a haven for anyone who could, or could not, hit a ball. Of the two of them, Anna was far the better player and mixed easily among her tennis cronies—but not, she was aware, among the Sink women, most of whom were not only blessed with productive wombs, but managed to combine their motherhood with that other keenly felt omission of hers, a career. Illogically, despite her family money and her charity work, she felt inferior and regarded them as a challenge to be overcome—thus her idea for the all-female gatherings.

With this on her mind, she turned to her guest, Chloe Jones, and tut-tutted her disapproval of Honey's gibe. "They're all so damned smart, so certain—kids, careers, whiz-bang husbands, glossy homes, Honey among them—though a pair of tights and a super-lift bra wouldn't go amiss there, would they?"

Chloe smiled, used by now to the older woman's underlying lack of self-esteem. "More like a fork-lift truck," she contributed. "She didn't mean anything, you know. It was just a remark, a joke."

"Very generous of you."

"Maybe, but true. You might not have their kids and their jobs, but from what I hear, they have a great regard for you and Paul."

"You don't say," said Anna, dryly.

"Oh yes. Your work for your kids in Africa, particularly."

"I suppose so," said Anna, the damning thought still with her that it took no sort of skill to inherit money, nor to offer help to the beleaguered charities.

With some of the other women gathering around to greet Chloe, Anna drifted away and it was some time later that her friend found her in deep discussion with Elizabeth de Manger.

"I do sympathise," Anna was saying, "you just can't trust some people," looking up, seeing Chloe, adding without a second thought: "Elizabeth was telling me how Hugo has sold off a few old barns and a bit of land to Herbie Kirby. He thought he was doing him a favour, and now it looks as if he shouldn't have bothered."

"Shouldn't or needn't?" asked Chloe, nodding to Elizabeth, noticing her quick, uncomfortable withdrawal.

"Both, I imagine" said the impervious Anna. "Point is, it looks as though Herbie is planning to sell the land on. Some helping hand . . ." the sarcasm dripping freely.

"Perhaps nothing will come of it. Best not to concern ourselves," said Elizabeth, rising, smiling tightly.

They watched her walk away, her unfashionable dress fluttering over unfashionable shoes. "Oh dear!" said Anna. "Makes you wonder who was doing the favour—Hugo or Herbie. Very touchy! Must have just happened."

"No," said Chloe. "It was at the Sinclair's New Year party. I caught them at it. The more interesting question is why?"

"Oh that's easy. Hugo can't keep off the horses. Or, come to that, the roulette wheel. It must be that—and the fact that it's her money, not his. You might have told me, though."

"I didn't think it was important," said Chloe, knowing the opposite, glancing around the room. From the odd word or two she was able to pick out between the laughter, four of the women were dissecting Cherie Blair's style guru, and another four were giddily comparing Jude Law with Hugh Grant. Among the faces were several she had met at the Sinclairs. But once again, it seemed that Lizzie Wolfson was not among them, which was a pity because—*cherchez la femme*—she now needed more than ever to understand Colly.

During the past couple of weeks, after an initial silence, she and Colly had exchanged six tingling phone calls: two to invite each other out to lunch, two to say how much they had enjoyed themselves, and two subsequent ones—both from Colly, but not now concerned merely with lunch. From his trail of self-deprecating, subtle markers and signals, she could see that he was offering her the chance to make the decision—either to get out or to get in deep. And she could feel the same slow burning.

But after the sex, the initial excitement, would there be a point? Would there be something further? Would she wish him to be a permanent replacement for the sexually repressed Simon? Would he be capable of leaving Lizzie? Or was he merely offering her a passing affair within her present affair, an inconsequential romp like her others? The answer, she sensed, would depend, not so much on her, but on him, on what sort of man lay behind the secretive, diffident mask that she had so far barely lifted. For her safety, it was time to know more—if not through Lizzie, then through her friends.

"So is everyone here?" she asked, artfully, leading Anna on, her masquerade exciting her.

"Just about," said the other, still rankled at her friend's earlier obtuseness, unaware of her tumbling thoughts. "Jill Maybury's not here and I haven't seen Lizzie Wolfson."

"Mmm," said Chloe, congratulating herself, "she wasn't at the New Year do, either, was she?"

"No, I don't believe so. One of those convenient headaches." A scoffing laugh.

"Convenient? Why? Doesn't she get on with the Sinclairs?"

"On the contrary! They're very good friends. Well, Lizzie and Charlie are. And everybody else thinks the men are. No, it's Lizzie and Colly."

"Oh dear." He had said nothing, but she had presumed as much.

"Yes," said Anna, "they're very nice people. Lovely. But I'm afraid they're finding their mountain hard to climb. Let's go and get some more of that red wine, shall we—we'll be eating soon. If Angie's prepared it, you remember Angie, don't you, from the Sinclair's place, if she's prepared it, it'll be worth having."

Chloe silently cursed Angie and the Burgundy, but half an hour later, armed with fresh wine and a beautifully decorated plate of poached salmon, she managed to manoeuvre her source into a secluded corner, filling a lull in their small talk with: "You're right, you know—we all have our mountains to climb."

"Surely not you and Simon," Anna demurred. "He's such a dear. Paul finds him the perfect golf partner."

"Maybe, but he's only now getting over his divorce—and he wasn't married anywhere near as long as some people, Lizzie and Colly, for example."

She held her breath, but need not have bothered—the bait was taken.

"I didn't say the Wolfsons were about to get divorced," Anna corrected, reprovingly, "merely that they're finding it hard going. They should have got over it all long ago, but, well, you know how some people are . . ."

"All I know is the little you've told me, something about . . ." Hesitating, artful. "If you'd rather not go into it, Anna . . ."

"No, no. So long as we don't shout it from the rooftops. It's just that, years ago, Lizzie and Colly lost a baby. A boy. Cot death. He was away on business somewhere and when she got up in the morning, she found the baby dead. It was their first and as you can imagine, they were devastated. Apparently they ended up blaming each other."

"How awful for them," said Chloe, hushed. "Terrible. But what did the boy have to do with it?"

"What boy?"

"The accident. The one in the accident?"

"How do you mean? The boy had nothing to do with it! Not at all! That was years later. The baby died some time in the Eighties, '85, I think, Sally was born two years later, and the accident was some time after that. 'Ninety, 'Ninety-one."

She looked around her, making sure no one was within earshot, hearing instead, the reproachful voice of her husband. "But Paul," she had protested on several occasions, "I was only repeating the truth or giving my opinion. Am I not allowed a mind of my own?"—a mind that within this group of career mothers, refused to believe that social intercourse must be bound by the exorbitant cost of child minders, the relative absorbency of tampons, or the trustworthy elasticity of condoms—or the Pill, for that matter. All these, she granted, had their moments. But, for pity's sake, what happened to all the rest of it . . . the rest of life?

With most of the guests now upstairs oohing about the two-person, state-of-the-art whirlpool bath and the accompanying full-length, rose-tinted mirrors, the coast seemed clear.

"In all conscience," she went on, "the cot death was bad enough, it would be for anyone—the social affairs people, the inquest, the hurtful questions. Lizzie told me she thought she would go mad, Colly withdrawing into himself, the two of them losing faith. But they gathered themselves, and had Sally as a sort of replacement. Lizzie thinking they'd got through, that they'd made it. But then the boy. The accident. The boy—I hope you're ready for this—falling into a cement mixer—"

"No!"

"Oh yes! Like a rag doll! His legs . . . his arms . . . The men, the workers, hearing his screams . . . hearing the other boys . . . but too late."

"Was Colly there?"

"No. He did everything possible. To make it easier, he said from the start that he was willing for his company to admit complete liability. Of course, his insurance people said it would never have happened had the boys not trespassed in the first place. But he blamed the security firm for that.

"It was a nightmare, a total nightmare for both of them. And it got worse. It turned out that the boy had only just been adopted—been in homes or been fostered all his life. When he came out of hospital, the new parents couldn't cope. You can't blame them, really, there'd been no time for proper bonding, and they'd not exactly signed up for a . . ."

"Cripple?"

"A boy in a wheelchair. I never met them, of course, but Lizzie says they were scumbags—the money, a huge amount, a lot of it from Colly's own pocket, was in a trust and she said they resented not being able to get their hands on it."

"Appalling."

"Mmm. I think it was more that they weren't fitted. The man took off after a lot of fighting and bickering and the woman stuck it out for a while. But then a new boyfriend came along—and he said it was either him or the boy. The long and the short of it was that, p.d.q, they gave up their adoption and the boy ended up back in a home."

She paused to allow Angie to clear their plates, complimenting her on her cooking, re-introducing her to Chloe, Chloe adding her own compliments, wondering how the woman fitted in.

The two of them alone once more, Chloe sought her informant's eyes, encouraging her to continue, aware of Anna's grim enjoyment in purveying other people's misfortunes, Anna seeing the show of languid, disaffected interest, but knowing she had her fish firmly on the hook. "Look," she said, "there's not much more, but let's flit around a bit first, otherwise the others will think we're ignoring them."

They moved from group to group, sometimes together, sometimes apart, ending up at the bathroom and going from there to the small upstairs room that Jessica had claimed for her snug. Curled up in an armchair with the door closed, Anna relaunched her biography.

"After the shock of it all, Colly was in pieces. And Lizzie says she had a terrible time persuading him to step back. 'He's got his new parents,' she said. 'He'll be OK. You've got to move on. Your family is here, we need you.' He saw what it was doing to her and Sally, and picked up the threads again.

"Two years or so later, when he heard from somewhere or another that the boy was back in a home, it all started up again. And this time, Lizzie had to fight even harder. The boy, it appeared, was profoundly disturbed. 'So am I,' she told Colly. 'So is Sally. I don't want to know the details,' she said. 'Just sort things out once and for all. And keep it to yourself—I don't want to know.'

"And that's it. He threw himself into his work and made them richer than ever. As you've perhaps gathered, he's still remote and secretive, and with a company as big as his, she never quite knows when he's coming or going. But as regards the boy, he's in the past . . ."

She gave a little smile and shrugged away her loose-tongued indiscretions.

"Garbage—U.N. Inspectors trash Bush's 'evidence'"—The Mirror, Feb 22, 2003.

"Divided Security Council awaits Blix's assessment"—The Independent, March 7, 2003, on the Chief Weapons Inspector, Hans Blix.

"U.S. sets deadline without second U.N. Vote."—The Mirror, March 18, 2003

Chapter 4

Flotsam

He had said he must be off, must abandon her in the reeking bed, imagining after what had gone before, after she had sunk back, that he was in control, could withstand her pouting lips, could tear his eyes from her unblinking challenge, could ignore the slowly trailing finger tips, the slow, breathless patterns of her crimson nails. So that when it came to it, his departure was an uncontrollable span later, a magnificent, possessing, indeterminate parcel of existence that clawed and strained and teetered along the exquisite, jagged edge, that had him praying for the agony to last for ever, yet craving an end, seeking the trigger that would release her, that would allow him to escape.

"And now, Charlotte Anne Ford," breathing the words, calling her by the name she was known by when he first met her, that he had heard chanted at the wedding altar, "I really *must* go, go I really *must*," sliding out of and from her, slapping her once famous model's bottom, pretending that she would ensnare him again, knowing that after this last time, he was safe for the moment.

He showered quickly, washing her from him, trying not to think how easily, how casually, he had succumbed to his depression; how he had thrown his scruples to one side: a few days and that had been

35

it!—and was almost dressed, believing her to be asleep, when he found her looking at him, her eyes clouded, questioning.

"What is it?" he asked. He was sitting on the bed, tying a shoelace, craning his head, looking at her sideways. "What's . . ."

"Am I important?" she asked. "Am I important to you?"

"Like water in the desert! Like wine at dinner! Of course you're important," he said lightly, reaching out, taking her hand. "You've always been important."

"Colly, I'm not talking about before—about all the years gone by—I'm talking about now."

"And what makes you think I'm not? *I'm* talking about now. You're important to me *now*."

"Now that you're fucking me?"

He released her hand slowly and withdrew a little, staring at her, his young-old face puckered. "Why say that? Why spoil things?"

He stood up, and began putting on his jacket, moving to the door, upset that she was allowing him to go with her crudity still in the air.

But she was suddenly with him, a gleaming silk dressing gown drawn tightly around her; coral pink collar, white throat, black hair, the crimson nails digging into his shoulders, the gorgeous gentian eyes searching, troubled. As always these days, her loveliness made him light-headed, made him wonder why him.

"Colly, dear Colly," she was saying, softly, urgently, breathing the words as if they might be her last. "I don't want to spoil things. I love you making love to me. I love your nearness. Your smell. The way you laugh and tease me . . ."

"So?"

"So I have all this and I love it. But then you leave me. You go out of that door back to Lizzie and I don't know what's going on in your mind. I know your body, but I don't know your mind. I don't know where we're going."

"Perhaps I'm *not* going back to Lizzie," he said, smoothing a strand of hair away from her face, playing as with a child. "Perhaps I'm going to a world that you don't know about. That nobody knows about. A never-never world on another planet, a different time-scale, a different dimension. A plum pie, icing sugar world that only I know about—me and the funny little people who live there."

36

"Stop it! I'm serious."

"So am I," he said. "I am so, I so am!" nuzzling her, trying to make her smile, troubled by this new mood. "We don't need to know where we're going at the moment, Charlie. We're going where life takes us. It's a fun fair! It's magic! Bury your face in the candy floss, come with me, see where it leads!"

He kissed her lightly but tenderly, then strode to the door. "It was wonderful just now," he said. "I'll ring you."

She moved to the window and watched him climb into his car, turning right at the end of the drive, not left as she had supposed.

Once clear of the leafy suburbs and the clogging high streets, Colly allowed the Jag to pick up speed, swooping along the Kingston By-Pass, flashing slower vehicles out of the way, not wishing to waste a moment, his mind nibbling at that day's candy floss, but excited, as always, at stepping from one existence into another.

As he neared central London, he turned off the main road and after a series of shortcuts, came to rest under a laburnum. He was in a road of worn out, gentrified Victoriana. Like scores of others all around, the house before him was a gabled two-storey; what made it different was a large ground-floor extension built out onto what had been a corner plot garden.

He turned his key in the latch, swinging open the heavy, glazed door, calling out, "It's only me," a woman coming through from the kitchen, her skin dusky, her apron shiny yellow.

"Hi! Angie."

"Hi! Colly."

They touched hands in a brief greeting that passed for a handshake, the contact seemingly inadequate but confirming their closeness, saying more perhaps, he thought guiltily, than Charlie's other world tumescence.

"You O.K., Colly?"

"Yeah, I think so. You?"

She nodded. "It's just you look . . . . Oh! Listen to me!" she cried, throwing up her hands, laughing, moving off back to the kitchen. "Why don't you go through and talk to his lordship. He's been in a rare good mood today. Don't know why. Probably because you're coming. Go through and I'll bring some tea."

Colly entered a small, interior hallway and rapped twice on a wide door, wincing at the sound of heavy rock from within, knowing that he would not be heard. He pushed the door open and saw that the boy was on his computer, gazing at the screen, grinning at his latest e-mail message. Beside the computer, on a large cream-coloured desk, were two small loudspeakers and a printer; on a matching desk, ninety degrees to the first, were two much larger speakers either side of a television and its accompanying video and DVD players. A radio, an elaborate, wall-mounted tape recorder and several cassette holders completed the scene.

Elsewhere, there were two low bookcases packed with computer and rock magazines, each shelf arranged so that the latest editions displaced earlier ones; four modernistic tubular chairs for guests, a table and a fridge. On the walls, were garish rock posters and blown-up photographs of wide-eyed children caught in the world's wars and famines.

"Hi, Nico!" To make his presence known, Colly had walked round one side of the big desk and had spoken leaning sideways. He received a cold wink by reply and a chiding wave from a pencil. A few bars later, the latest craze in the heavy rock world crashed their way to a climax and the boy reached forward to switch off the tape machine, using a remote control to do the same to the CD player.

"I don't suppose they'll mind that too much down at the centre, will they?" he said, sarcastically, screwing his face up, signing off from the net. 'Bi 4 now,' he wrote, 'mus have T wi piss artist.'

From where he stood, Colly could see the last two words. He shrugged and went to sit at the table, where he waited while the boy wheeled himself across to join him.

"Won't mind what too much?"

"You! Saying, 'Hi Nico' on the tape. Still, better than, 'Kiss my arse.'"

Colly rode the coarseness and apologised. "Sorry, didn't realise. Thought you were supposed to be in a good mood today?"

"Who says?"

"Angie."

"What would *she* know? She doesn't even think I should be taping stuff."

"Perhaps she's right."

"Well, I'm not selling it, am I? I'm not making a fortune. I'm just doing a favour for a few poor sods who can't get a ticket on T. Blair's gravy train."

"And why's that?"

"Because all the good teachers've pissed off to where *you* live. Places like that. No good teachers—no exam passes. No passes—no jobs. Not good ones."

"But you don't want a job."

"I'm not talking about me. Anyhow, who says?"

"Well, do you?"

"I might, I might not."

Angie entered the room with tea and cakes, breaking into their conversation. "You might not what?"

"I might not want this bossy, over-paid git telling me what to think."

"Nico! Colly's not come all this way to hear stuff like that."

Flaring up. "So what's he come for? To see *me*? Or to see *you*? To talk to *me* or just to bath me in between seeing *you*? It's no different, you know, him bathing me! No different to when *you* did it!"—leaving the thought in the air, suddenly off on another tangent. "I'll show you something!"

He spun the wheelchair around, knocking the table, spilling the tea onto the tray, and made off to his adjoining bedroom, where they could hear him rooting in a drawer, cursing. They awaited his return, resigned, used to his mood swings.

"Look at these," he said, back by the table, four snapshots on his lap, still addressing Angie. "This one was when I was nine, still in hospital, him and Mrs Rowlandson standing beside my bed."

She took the photograph forbearingly, looked at it briefly and placed it beside her, accepting the second one.

"And this one is when I was eleven, you and him pushing me over the lawn at the home," flicking it over to her, continuing, "and here's one of just you and me at this house when we didn't see him for years. And finally, happy families again! All three of us drinking my eighteenth birthday champagne!"

"I've seen them," said Angie.

"I know you've seen them! We've all seen them! The point," he said, his voice rising, still addressing her, "is all these years—all these years of him being around, in and out of my life, and I still don't know the first fucking thing about him! He never tells me!"

Swinging now to face Colly: "D'you think I don't know what you must have gone through? I'm not always just thinking about me and my bloody legs, you know! D'you think I don't know about guilt, that I can't imagine it?

"What I *don't* know is *you*. I know what you do, I know about your contracts and your building workers and your cars and supporting Chelsea but preferring Arsenal—stuff like that—because you tell me and I read the business stuff in the papers. That's the easy bit. But what do you do at home? As a person? With your wife? Your daughter? Your friends? You never tell me about that . . . about them . . . about what you think, who you are."

He paused, swinging his gaze from one to the other. They sat patiently, knowing from past occasions that he was not yet spent.

"Shall I tell you what *I'm* thinking? I'm thinking that if it's only guilt that brings you here, it's not enough. It's no longer enough. Not for me, anyhow. I don't want your guilt. I don't want your pity. I don't want the crumbs off your table."

Angie jumped to her feet. "That's enough, Nico! Don't be so damned rude! If it weren't for Colly, you'd be nowhere. You'd be sitting in a home, going mad, like you were when . . ." She broke off as Colly rose and strolled over to the window, motioning her to be quiet. For the second time that day, he was being told his fortune. It seemed that life was catching up, that the icing on the cake was melting.

He was aware of the wheelchair passing behind him, going off to the bedroom. When he heard the door close, he returned and sat by Angie. "Don't be upset," he said. And when she continued to say nothing about the outburst, saddened, he knew, on his behalf, feeling that it was her fault, he switched to the other, lesser reason for his visit—paying the bills, signing a couple of cheques for her, discussing some repair work that she said was needed to the roof. That done, she said she was off to cook the evening meal.

"You're more than welcome to stay, Colly," she said, despondently. "He'll come round."

"I know. Thank you, but perhaps next time."

"Colly . . ." Tentative, nervous.

"Yes?"

"You will be careful, won't you?"

"About the boy?"

"Not just the boy. Yourself. All of us."

"How d'you mean?"

"Perhaps I'm speaking out of turn. It's just that, the other day, I overheard a certain conversation, a certain young lady, already spoken for, asking a lot of personal questions. Or at least, receiving a lot of very personal information from someone who should have known better."

She watched as he grimaced. "There are already a lot of people depending on you, Colly. It's like having two families."

She left, not waiting for a reply, not needing one.

He sat for a moment digesting her words, sorry that she should have been put in an embarrassing position but intrigued by her news. The fact that Angie was worried about an affair in the making rather than an unknown one in full swing, he found ironic. But there were plusses and minuses: adding Angie to the list of people he was deceiving saddened him, but the thought of Chloe Jones asking questions about him elated him—so much so that his celebratory rap on Nico's bedroom door was misinterpreted.

"No need to break the bloody door down," the boy shouted. "If you can't take what I had to say, bugger off!"

"Don't be a silly arse! C'mon, Nico, open up." He heard the lock snap back, waited a moment or two for the chair to reverse, and then entered.

Like the living area, the bedroom's walls were covered in dull black paper, this time with a few repeated swirls of purple and red. Along one wall was a white wardrobe and cupboards, along another a bookcase revealing a preference for science fiction and the occult. A barred bed with a hoist above it, a wide door leading to the specially designed bathroom, and a wall-mounted television completed the main features.

Colly moved some clothes from a chair and sat down.

"You know you're talking crap, don't you?"—his voice quiet and reasonable, having learned long ago that with Nico, loud demands often brought loud, violent responses.

"Am I?"

"You know you are—all that stuff about Angie, about me coming to see Angie. Can't you see that's insulting, hurtful, especially to her?"

"I know. I didn't mean it. I just say it. It just comes out."

"You'll need to say sorry."

"I will. But it doesn't change the other stuff, does it?

"About me?"

"About you being a bloody stranger. About coming here, two, three times a week—and I know more about the milkman!"

"You don't have a milkman!"

"Exactly!"

Colly acknowledged his defeat and they exchanged tight smiles.

⸻

"Look," said Colly a few days later, feeling for his words. "I don't have to tell you, things are complicated. They were complicated then and they're complicated now. I thought you understood. You say you do, but . . ."

He went to the fridge, opened two cans of lager and gave one to the boy. "After the financial settlement, the money business, the lawyers and executors, the inquiry—after you'd come out of hospital and gone back to the Rowlandsons—I thought it was all sorted. So I bowed out—"

"And left me."

"Well, yes. I—"

"Why?"

"Well, I didn't *have* to, not exactly," not wanting to involve Lizzie, to admit that he had put her and Sally first. "It seemed for the best—it seemed best to let everyone get on with things."

He ignored Nico's soft, derisory snort and went on:

"Then one day, Angie rings me at the office. All I knew of her then was that she was one of the carers set up by the hospital. Anyhow, she rings and says you're back in the home and you aren't doing very well. You aren't co-operating. Disruptive. The psycho's phrase was 'profoundly disturbed'. You remember it, don't you—shouting your head off, chucking stuff about? And that's why I got involved again."

"What, 'cos you felt responsible?"

"I put you in a wheelchair—it was up to me to follow up."

"Why? 'Cos you had the money?"

"It wasn't just a question of money. There was the fund, after all."

"Which *you* set up."

"Not just me."

"So you fixed things with the social workers, bought this house, adapted it, lured Angie round here with your wallet, gave me to her to look after—and then fucked off again!"

"I didn't just fuck off. I told you—it was complicated."

"Complicated? You want complications, think about me, think about all the other kids in the home."

"I can't help everybody, Nico."

"Face it, Colly. You did it 'cos you felt guilty. Nothing more."

Plenty more. Like you are the ghost of my dead son. Like the two of you are sometimes the one person. Standing side by side, merging into one, then back into two. Merging in and merging out. Like one of those trick photographs. Now you see it, now you don't. Loving him through you. But never able to tell you. Never able to say, "The real reason I'm here is because you have taken the place of my dead son." Because that would be too hurtful, too cruel. And in any case . . .

It was early evening, the daylight was fading and the oldest of his many guilts was again creeping up on him, gnawing at him . . . Lizzie . . . not being with Lizzie . . .

The boy's voice continuing, " . . . and that's why we didn't see you again for years. You come in and fix things like a fucking plumber. And then you float away. 'Bye bye! I've done my bit. You just get on with it.'"

"I came back, didn't I?"

"Oh yeah! 'Cos Angie asked you to! For *her*, not for me. 'Hello, Mr Wolfson? Nico's started getting a hard on when I wash him and I don't think it's right and he won't have anybody else in to do it. Can you come and wash his arse for him, Mr Wolfson?'"

"It's not like that, Nico, and you know it! Never was. I come here because I want to. I want to help. I want to make things easier. For you and for Angie. If you don't like it . . ."

The boy swung the chair and went to close the curtains. At the time, for a long time, the idea of his tormentor washing his arse had seemed the supreme irony. It had not soothed his humiliation, but had developed into something deeper, more decent.

"I'm sorry, Colly. I really like you coming round. It's just that . . ."

"You want more."

The other shrugged and changed tack. "Am I going to get a bath tonight, or not?"

Colly smiled, forbearingly, and helped Nico undress. The mental wounds that had gone deeper even than the metal blades, that had combined with the agony and the frustration, that had produced the anger and the resentment, were still there plain to see. Miraculously, there were signs that they were healing, that although adolescence and beyond had brought more than the usual crop of problems, it seemed that the boy might yet win through. Physically, his spine and his legs would never mend and there were still question marks about his arms and hands. But the constant physiotherapy was beginning to show, and looking at him lying full length in the bath, Colly felt a secret pride and realised with a jolt that it was more than time to stop thinking of him as a boy.

He waited while Nico washed the parts he could reach, then completed the job himself, sloshing fresh water over his head, helping him up into the special chair, his hands sliding around the soapy body, ignoring the waving erection.

Exasperated, humiliated, Nico tossed his head.

"It's just the same it was with Angie," he said.

"No matter."

"But it *does* matter. It worries me."

"After all you've been through? C'mon!"

"What? My accident? What's that got to do with it?"

"I wasn't thinking of the accident."

"What then?"

"You know . . . the others."

"What others?"

"Sorry," said Colly.

"What others?"

"You know . . ."

"No, I don't know. Give us a clue!"

"Let's leave it."

"Oh, yeah, sure. Just walk away." For a minute, he busied himself drying his hair, his head under the towel, his hands rubbing as furiously as his arms would allow. Then:

"Big Mick? Fat Alf? The men in the homes. Is that what you're talking about? How did *you* know?"

"I know. I was told. That's why you . . . . how we, Angie and me, how we understand, try to understand. That and the accident. What amazes me is how well you handle it."

"Just a fucking hero, that's what I am," said Nico, the sarcasm smacking into the other's face.

"I'm sorry," said Colly. "I didn't mean to . . . It's just that I've been waiting for you to tell me. All these years, wondering what to do, what to say, how to help."

"Well, thanks for the thought," said Nico, seeing the hurt, regretting it. "Look," he said, gently, "it's something I try not to think about. If you think about it, it stays with you. You've got to make yourself believe that it never really happened, that it was only a sick dream, sick, unhappy bastards taking advantage. So you think yourself away. Doing it then while it was happening, doing it now. Float yourself up and out of it. Sometimes into a really special place that smells of newly baked bread and has a Dad mending your bike. And later, like now, you tell yourself it wasn't too bad, it was better than being blown to bits in Iraq—"

"—or falling . . ."

" . . . into a cement mixer. That, too. So stop worrying about it. It could have been worse." He hesitated, then shook his head. "You don't need to know how much worse; what other boys went through. Like I said, I don't think about it."

He looked up, held Colly's eyes and allowed the towel to slip slowly from his lap, the momentary gentleness overtaken by a sly, lascivious challenge.

"C'mon, Nico," said Colly, the words quick, chiding, but not heated, "one minute you're a hero, the next you're playing games. You don't think I'm that way, do you?"

"I wouldn't know," said Nico. "You never talk about yourself."

"Not much to tell. I come here for Angie's food—that and the sparkling conversation."

"Bollocks!" A pause. "You know I'm not gay, don't you? Not really."

"Yes, I know," said Colly.

"And you're not gay, either, are you?"

"No, not really."

They laughed, Nico content, playful, Colly concerned.

As if he had turned a new page, he saw that he was caught in a net of his own making. His wife, his lovers, their men, the boy, his dead son, his daughter—all of them entwined in the mesh, gaping in the murky currents, fighting for life, waiting for him to lift his spell.

———

"U.K.'s Biggest Peace Rally—The Guardian, February 15, 2003, on the million-plus anti-war demonstration in London, part of a day of organised protest by millions of people in sixty countries, three-million in Rome alone.

"We have only just begun to tell the truth about this unjust, immoral and unnecessary war"—Methodist Bishop Sprague at the rally in Daley Plaza, Chicago (Chicago Tribune).

"I ask the marchers to understand this: I do not seek unpopularity as a badge of honour. But sometimes it is the price of leadership and the cost of conviction"—Tony Blair speaking at a Labour Party conference elsewhere in Glasgow, as fifty-thousand protestors marched into the city centre. (Speech text).

"Evidently some (people) don't view Saddam Hussein as a risk to peace. I respectfully disagree"—President Bush, Boston Globe, February 19, 2003.

Chapter 5

Mr and Mrs Wolfson

As a boy—and later, as a man—he would sit at family gatherings—other people's family gatherings—and watch how they behaved, all the people there. How they coughed and sniffed and whispered and talked and shouted and laughed and cried. Sometimes doing all of these together, like at weddings and big anniversaries, and sometimes in pairs, whispering and crying when the coffin was brought in; talking and laughing at the wake.

Apart from two ancient cousins on his father's side whom he'd never met and was never likely to, and his mother's cousin twice removed who lived somewhere in Australia, there were no Wolfson relatives. It didn't seem to matter, not to begin with. But then he started to notice and ask questions, and all he could remember, all the way back to him being a child, was them, his parents, telling him they were "the end of the line," saying it as though it was a weight to be borne, as though it automatically ruled out wide friendships, rumbustious parties; the lonely, sad phrase filling their existence, filling his.

Depending how you judged these things, he supposed they weren't what might be called, bad parents, his mother and father, not that bad, anyhow. Introspective, private, careful were three of the words he knew people used about them. Ultra was another. Ultra-private, ultra-careful . . .

And he supposed it was true. Even with trivia, they seemingly forever examined their motives, assessed their attitudes, each with the other, making sure they were on the same track, the *right* track; closing up when people asked their opinion, his father glancing at his mother; keeping to themselves, being unobtrusive, speaking when spoken to.

Typically, or so it seemed to him, they never took him on holidays abroad. That was for other people. For them, it was quite enough to go to a caravan for a week, or to a B&B, usually Norfolk, but sometimes a more interesting coast with rocks . . . Devon . . . Cornwall . . . The first thing his mother would do was to inspect the toilet, looking down her nose, leaving the landlady in no doubt that they wouldn't be staying unless it passed muster. But she was quite happy to sit for hours on a blanket on a windy beach or a splashy promontory, looking very English in a long raincoat and a navy blue sunhat with a stiff straw brim . . . buttering sliced bread for their cheese and tomato sandwiches . . . reading a book while he and his father played French cricket or fished in the rock pools.

Careful, then, about everything, his parents, especially him. Never a moment not making sure he had the best, the best they could afford; the best clothes, the best books, the best education, scraping together the fees for a private school, doffing their hats to the teachers, his mother trying not to look too pleased when he won a place at Oxford.

Of course, on the way, things happened. People thought they knew his parents. But they didn't. They didn't know how generous and pure and shy his father was. Or how enigmatic.

And they didn't know that when he was twelve, his mother came into the bathroom one day while he was towelling himself down and started talking about sex, about how to do it, what he might expect, parting her bathrobe, showing him the exact place, saying it was what men did, what they were there for.

And they also didn't know that a year later, she slid into his bed while he was sleeping and he woke to find her showing him again. Except that this time, she wasn't talking.

So they had no idea of that, either. But, apparently, demeaningly, crushingly, his father had. He never knew how. Perhaps he'd heard them, heard his fading protests. Perhaps *she'd* told him. She was indifferent enough, cold enough, obsessive enough. Perhaps he'd watched the grooming and had guessed. So he never knew how, because the act was never referred to, never spoken of; suffering the guilt alone until he went off to university, waving to the two of them standing at the gate as he jumped on the bus, receiving his father's letter three days later.

It came in an envelope postmarked Manchester, two-hundred miles from where they lived, a place that meant nothing to him, a place they'd never been to; a single sheet of A4, no return address, no clues, just a brief, sad, wounded message that his father had known of the bedroom visit all along; that because he loved him, to give him stability, he had decided to stay on— "while it was necessary."

The letter had a second paragraph, wishing him well, urging him to be "his own man", to make the best of his talents, and not to be afraid.

"When I've had more time to think things through and when you are rich and famous," the letter added, "then perhaps we can get together again. And who knows, perhaps (if your mother will allow it!) we might even be friends."

From the seething, silence-filled conversation he had with his mother on the phone that evening—pretending to her that it was a casual courtesy call, not yet knowing whether the letter was merely a crisis for him, or for them all—and from his subsequent, flying visit home, it appeared that after waving him goodbye, his father had gone upstairs, packed a bag and had left. Not a word; just left.

A year later, he received a second unforeseen message, this time from Newcastle, from a woman who said she was his father's wife. Mr Wolfson, she said, had died of a heart attack after a short illness. He had not wanted her to trouble anyone and she had had him cremated. Could he please settle the enclosed bill.

A month later, his mother died from an overdose.

———————

"In this conflict, America faces an enemy who has no regard for conventions of war or rules of morality . . . the people of the United States and our allies will not live at the mercy of an outlaw regime that threatens the peace with weapons of mass murder . . ."—President Bush, 0418 GMT, March 20, 2003, announcing the start of the war against Iraq—the so-called, 'Operation Decapitation.'

"It is in the spirit of friendship and goodwill that we now offer our help"—Tony Blair addressing the Iraqi people on Toward Freedom TV, March 21, 2003.

Chapter 6

Easter

Before his breakdown set in, before the four years of disintegration and recovery, had he been asked to define the parameters of his marriage, the Sink Set would not have been at all surprised had Colly Wolfson cited Ozzie Leverington's parties, the ones he threw every decade or so, on or about the tenth of April, to celebrate his move up the timescale. And had the Set been asked to be specific, they would have said the second such party and the final one.

Ozzie's decade idea arose from several factors: 1, while a student, he couldn't afford to hold a bean feast every year; 2, to do so might have been seen to be ostentatious, even egotistic; 3, it would have underlined the unfortunate fact that each of his birthdays seemed to be surrounded by death and suffering.

If it wasn't always bullets and bombs, it seemed to him you could take your pick from mendacity, paranoia, hatred or just plain failure. And if that wasn't enough, since each birthday fell on or around Easter, you could go to Church and suffer with Christ on the Cross.

At the beginning, the omens looked good—while he was slipping into the world in 1953, Khrushchev was slipping into Stalin's bloodied seat and a newly elected, much loved Swede called Dag Hammarskjold was slipping into the Secretary-General's seat at the U.N. Naturally enough, much of Britain had its eyes elsewhere, licking horrified lips over the Notting Hill serial murderer, John Christie. But whether they were or weren't, tough luck, things got sticky for Ozzie's two charmers—Khrushchev lost out over Cuba and poor old Dag bought it while trying to sort out the mess in the Congo.

By the time his first adult party hit the scene, Ozzie was twenty-one, Israel's gritty grandmother, Golda Meir, was resigning as prime minister, the French, or some of them, were mourning Georges Pompidou, Nixon was still trying to wriggle out of Watergate, Vietnam and Cambodia were moving towards their American catastrophe, and just by way of something different, U.S. heiress, Patti Hearst, was making world headlines as a screwed-up kidnap victim.

Much of this failed to register significantly, at least on the day, because what Ozzie remembered about that first adult birthday was that it was held in the spacious apartment of generous friends, and that it was the first time he met Cressida Grammaticus. She was twelve and he was in his final year at Edinburgh, the party being intended as a consummation of his student friendships and of the view they shared with a particular ancient Greek that change was the only reality; that permanence was an illusion. Their drinking toast was thus "Hail Heraclitus!"—and to beef him up, they decreed that all things had their origin, not in fire, but in each separate mind, and that try as they might, each and every individual would always fail to describe fully his or her own personal truth, would never wish or be able to delve deeply enough.

To expose a twelve-year-old to this uneasy mixture of ancient concept and modern appendix would have been risky enough—but definitely not the sexual freedoms that flowed around it, a point Ozzie made despairingly when Hector, his flatmate, rang to say there had been an awful cock-up, that he would have to bring his kid sister to the party.

"The parents have gone off to worship with the Greeks again," he said. "They've sent Cressida up by train for me to look after during the hols. She's only just arrived and I cannot, really cannot leave her alone all night with Wensum."

Harold Wensum was the uninvited arsehole they sub-let a room to. They had him down for a sexual deviant with hygiene problems and despised him.

"You're right—she'll have to come," Ozzie said. "She can stay in the kitchen with the door closed. I'll get her some comics and Coke and ice cream, and if she washes the glasses, I'll give her a fiver."

Nine years later, the Gandhi film was busy winning its eight Oscars, the campaigners for nuclear disarmament were busy trying to emulate his passive resistance, Thatcher, with no such ambition, was busy planning her landslide re-election with the sickening promise of more Philistinism, and Ozzie was busy welcoming guests to his "Thirtieth to end all Thirtieths."

To help pack out his flat in Hampstead and to justify the title, invitees were urged to "bring someone—anyone!—interesting."

Howard Sinclair, a rugby pal, had brought three people: a sultry goer with dead fish eyes dubbed "Your Plaice or Mine" and a young couple called Colly and Lizzie, blissfully hi-jinking towards marriage, an event to which they had immediately invited him. Much more importantly, among the others, Hector, lovely, loving Hector, had brought his sister, Cressida, plus a few of her girl friends.

"You remember, Cressie, don't you, Ozzie? The one in the kitchen?"

"Amazing!" he said, gazing, enraptured.

In the short space of nine years, the unremarkable child had turned into a wide-hipped, thick-waisted earth mother with large breasts, wonderful muscular calves and a fascinating mop of unruly, frizzy hair. Her eyes were alive and dancing and as dark as glossy Greek olives, and there was a wonderful, light spontaneity about her that drew him like a moth.

"Of course I remember her," he said, jumping to sit theatrically on the end of a dresser. "Cressida—the gift from the Greeks! The faithless lover! I shall marry you! And to keep Troilus at bay, I shall call you Honey."

"Honey?" she laughed, jostled by her friends, enchanted by his foolishness, astonished that he was no longer the intimidating giant of the past.

"Why Honey?"

"Because you shall be my pure gift from the earth—together, we shall sow the Trojan furrow."

As the clock ticked around his fortieth—a quasi-sombre event celebrated in a disused church to "venerate the passing of my youth"—AIDS was claiming Rudolph Nureyev, cancer was doing for football hero Bobby Moore, the French were routing their Socialists, IRA bombs were going off in mainland Britain, and the world was watching Texas as the Waco siege ended in mass immolation.

Ozzie tipped his cap to the first two and carefully edited out the rest. Of his own world, Hector had long been a closet gay, the creepy Harold Wensum was still, thankfully, God knows where after netting, of all things, a double first, and Colly and Lizzie were immersed in their two tragedies. The only genuine bright spots were Howard Sinclair's happiness with the stunning Charlie, and the sowing of Cressie's furrow with five eager offspring.

By the third year of Christ's second millennium, Ozzie imagined, wrongly, that of all the parties so far, his fiftieth, would be quiet, reflective, sentimental, an opportunity for him to wander around his garden with tried and trusted friends. "Come and share my memories," he wrote, "you are the precious stones in my crown of joy."

"You can't put that on the card!" Honey had shrieked. "It's schmaltzy! You'll embarrass people!"

"Perhaps I feel schmaltzy. Perhaps it's time to let them know, to say I love you. Look at us—the two of us. Cast your eyes around. The first-born's preparing for Oxford, I'm Head of History and you're on the way back to full-time teaching. But we're still here. Still the same. And it's the same with them. I know I'm older than the rest of you, and probably soft in the head, but I think it's time to celebrate our lovely, eternal friends."

She regarded him—his shock of tortured, springy hair, his large square head, his sympathetic, forgiving eyes, his meaty, competent hands with the fingernails cut too closely. Physically, she was happy how he was. They were a matching pair. But his open-heartedness, his unquestioning faith in others and how they saw him, his generosity of spirit, his refusal to recognise that change bit deeply into people's characters not merely into their creations, this side of him both inspired and dismayed her. It wore her out and he knew it. Yet here he was, even with something as innocuous as a birthday invitation, stretching the boundaries, making the big play, when it really should be as obvious to him as it was to others that the friends he venerated from as long as thirty years before, were not now quite the same people.

Perhaps he really didn't realise. Perhaps there was something in him, some tiny flaw, which, despite his credo, prevented him from seeing that the process of decay was universal. Perhaps it was she who was wrong . . . her own family, her own marriage, were her rocks, her unchanging foundations. But Lizzie's? Charlie's? Couldn't he see that Heraclitus was at work there as much as anywhere, as much as the Brits and the Yanks busy knocking Iraq to pieces?

Heraclitus! The soothsayer of change. Ozzie didn't know it, but she hated the man, hated his melancholic assertions, hated how his followers gaily tore down everything that had gone before, throwing it over, kicking it into touch, like a cur whipped into line, shown no respect, no acknowledgement. Doing so for the past decade or more, up and down Britain, the new Puritans throwing their stones of instant change at the wise windows of evolution—the uncomprehending Church, the universities, the great institutions and corporations—clamouring for change, but giving no compelling reason. Because it was new and therefore somehow good? Or was it merely to tear down the sacred walls which they, the changers, had been themselves unable to scale? Or scaling, had found themselves to be insufferably puny against the fused legions of those who had gone before?

She shivered. If the rule of Heraclitus really *was* universal, then should he not also be dancing over their own lives, hers and Ozzie's? Disrupting their happiness? So far, their dugout, their old rambling home in the Surrey woods, seemed curiously unaffected. It still had no television. There was still a piano and a harp in the lounge and violins and tennis racquets in the dining room and piles of books and art reviews on top of the fridge. The door to the bathroom still hung crazily. And in the kitchen, a long line of cereal packets were still flanked by miniatures of David and The Age of Bronze, their proud, masculine displays confounding Ozzie's own, curiously bent posture.

In the same way, she could feel little change in herself, in her body and attitudes; could still feel little regret at pointing Colly Wolfson at Charlie; could not deny the flickering tingle that Ozzie still found her generous belly and naked calves as provocative as the look-a-like Moores and Hepworths out in the garden.

The guests had now arrived and were strolling around as Ozzie had hoped.

"A case, perhaps, of reproduction all round," she heard Anna Brownlove say, acidly, sniffing at the statues, smirking at her pun.

"Yes, dear," said Paul sadly, glancing at Honey, hoping fervently that this was not to be another of those days when he and the others celebrated the fruits of life while his wife celebrated her emptiness.

The de Mangers walked by, aware that his gambling debts and the sale of the barns to Herbie Kirby was common knowledge discussed in detail by all and sundry, she still fuming about it, he humiliated. As a pair, they were typical of that middle class phenomenon—people either just above or just below the required station, never quite in tune; included and apparently well liked, but rarely talked to, lost amongst others' friendships, worn like a badge by the thrusting, of-the-day Sink Set, its members acknowledging the de Manger pedigree, tolerating the boredom.

"Poor Elizabeth," said Anna, quietly. "Soldiering on in the pocket of that dreadful Herbie."

"Hardly," said Paul.

"Perhaps not," she conceded. "But having to watch while Herbie cleans up Hugo's mess. And from what Ozzie tells me, making a mint out of it, doing what Hugo could have done in the first place."

"And what's that?"

"Getting planning permission on the barns, turning them into houses and flats. Into money! Easy enough—so long as your name's not Hugo. And in any case," she continued, transferring her irritation, "where have all these people come from? I thought Ozzie had given up these open invitation events."

She gazed from face to face, spotted the Platt-Smiths, waved, and walked over to them, leaving Paul to grab a couple of Pimms from a tray borne from group to group by their beaming host.

"See Anna's found Roger and Amelia," Ozzie exclaimed, by way of excusing the throng.

"Who?"

"The Platt-Smiths."

"Oh yes," replied Paul, masking his bitterness with a grin, trying to sound casual and disinterested. "A touch of local muck-raking first—so much easier when it's people one knows, don't you find? She'll be getting round to your other guests later."

"Keep your pecker up, old boy," said Ozzie uneasily, moving off. "And tell Anna that if she discovers any of the guests' names, to let me know."

He skirted the base of a huge holly bush—"You'll have to chop it down, it'll scratch the children," Honey had said, and he'd said he would, but the scratches had healed faster than his resolve—and found Lizzie Wolfson perched on the edge of a bench, alone.

"Happy Easter!" he said brightly, sensing depression.

"Easter?"

"Yes. Not 'til next week, actually. Tomorrow's Palm Sunday."

"If you say so," she said. She accepted his offer of a Pimms and sat with the drink in her left hand, the ice chinking, the cigarette trembling in her right, looking, with over-bright, unblinking eyes, up a glade of vivid, uncut grass.

"I didn't know you smoked," he said, searching for a topic, unnerved by her agitation. First Paul Brownlove, now Lizzie . . . .

"Neither did I until a few months ago. A year. Perhaps longer. But you have to have something in your life, don't you? Everybody does! So they say! Even if it's only the dreaded weed."

He joined her on the bench, placing the tray between them, doing so slowly and carefully as though she were a timid bird or a sleeping child. Honey would be waiting in the kitchen, ready to give him more Pimms. But he couldn't leave now. Not immediately.

He took one of the two remaining glasses from the tray and sipped carefully, aware of a dear friend in distress, one he had imagined unchanged from the person he had first met twenty years before, sitting now, as then, in a pretty dress with a summer jacket, the lovely lines of her face and throat still resisting time. He realised, with a start, that it had been almost a year since they had last met, she missing the New Year's Day do and he missing a couple of get-togethers the previous summer.

"This doesn't sound like you, Lizzie."

"And how should I sound? How would you know?" The words soft but cracked, turning to him, shrugging, excusing her challenge. "You wouldn't know, would you, Ozzie? None of you would. Not because you don't care, because . . ."

He waited for her to finish, but she was drawing on the cigarette again, inhaling deeply, keeping the smoke within her, feeding on it.

"Because it's tough at the top?" he said, joking inanely, trying to ease her out of the blackness. She smiled in response, but remained silent.

"Haven't had a chance to see Colly, yet," he said, still trying to find his way. "Where is he?"

"I wish I knew," she murmured, rising, bending to place her empty glass on the tray, saying again in the same tone, "I really wish I knew," moving away, up the glade, leaving a dark track through the wet grass, he knowing he should go with her, but nervous of intruding, returning instead to the house, meeting Herbie on the way, having to listen to his plans for the barns.

"God, does that man prattle," he said, puffing into the kitchen, nodding to a busy Angie Maketi.

"Who?" Honey asked.

"Never mind," he said. "Have you seen Lizzie?"

"No, not yet."

"Well, have you seen Colly? It's Colly I want."

"He'll be ranting about Bush and Blair, or he'll be with Lizzie."

"No."

"Then try the playroom. Being there pleases him. And if you see Charlie, point her this way."

Unlike most other rooms in the house, the playroom, up under the tiles, had been the scene of regular change, each beloved plaything left as a memorial or for some subsequent sibling—piles of gently rotting board games with pieces missing; broken, faded wooden lorries and railway engines; worn out, much kissed, much abused dolls, their blue eyes staring into the spidery depths; one-potato, two-potato skipping ropes, frayed in the middle; make-believe costumes for pirates and fairies and Joseph and Mary; over-flowing toy boxes . . . .

They had noted, long ago, that Colly liked to spend quiet moments there, knowing why but not commenting on it, either to him or to Lizzie. Especially not to Lizzie. But he wasn't there. So he began peering down from the playroom's dormers, a picture of Lizzie in his mind, of her walking up the glade, thinking, for a few ridiculous moments, of an earlier blue sky, of doing it with Honey under the apple tree, spotting Colly at last across the way, standing by the stable, under the outside stairs that led to the loft above.

And Lizzie was with him.

They were framed in the sealed loft window like an old silent film, he standing woodenly, unspeaking; she agitated, her hands flailing, tearing her hair, pointing at the little crowd that had gathered, pointing always in the same direction, at, it seemed, Charlie Sinclair; her fists pounding on his chest before turning, struggling past Howard and the rest of them, the Callows and the Mayburys; the Brownloves detaching themselves, going after her, Chloe Jones standing white-faced, staring at Charlie.

And the old Greek, looking down from a far greater height than Ozzie, relishing the thought that for that moment at least, to the Sink Set, what had gone before no longer mattered.

Could no longer matter again in quite the same way.

The musky apple tree, the precious toys, the fond friendships.

The friendships Honey had known, had always known, could be as fragile as an eggshell.

That Ozzie had been convinced, determined, would last forever.

That Honey knew would now break all their hearts.

Chapter 7

Jetsam

If pushed, Warren Duncan Nichols, orphan, would concur that he had a combination of three constants in his life that were peculiar to him, that elevated him above the norm, that nobody in their right mind would crave, but, having acquired the first, might need the other two, or at least their equivalent. Like many foisted things, he hated the first, grudgingly loved the second and both hated and loved the third.

In a guessing game, the first of his peculiar constants was easy—he had no legs, not ones that worked, anyway. These days, there was the odd time when he could pretend it really didn't matter one way or the other; that he'd got used to it. Even so, whether ignoring it, or cursing it, you didn't have to be Einstein to guess the first. Everybody got that one.

But not the other two. Challenging his pals, egging them on, knowing they were likely to take the piss and say things like, One—Not Scoring for England and Two—Not Shagging. So only a few guessed Angie Maketi for the second, and nobody at all guessed Colly Wolfson.

They guessed Angie because she was always there doing for him in the background; unlike the nurses when he was a kid, interfering, ordering him about, over-friendly, pushing into his life. And not like Mrs Rowlandson and most of the foster mothers.

He was twelve when he first told Angie that he wished she were his mother.

"Your step-mother?"

"No. My mother."

"But I'm . . ."

"You're black and I'm white. So what?"

Two years later, when he'd said it again and she'd smiled and ruffled his hair, he'd said, "Well, all right then, my step-mother." But she'd sat and taken his hands and said, "We don't need to do that, Nico. We don't need to change things. You've had enough change, enough different faces. I'm here for you. You're not just my patient. You're my special boy, my special person."

"Yeah—delivered and paid for by Mr Columbus Wolfson!"

"That's unfair."

"OK, it's unfair. I have a black servant who doesn't want to be my mother and I have a white bill-payer who doesn't want to be anything."

"I'm already you're mother, Nico. It's just that you can't see it."

"And Colly?"

"You'll have to ask him."

But he didn't dare.

He'd stopped talking about it, the mother bit, when he was watching her one day hanging out the washing, reaching up to the line, slim, healthy, her tits outlined against the sky, her frilly dress blown high by the wind. It seemed to him that if you fancied the woman you wanted to be your mother, if you started getting a hard on in front of her, lying there in the bathwater, you had no right. You forced your disappointment back down into your belly and pretended to tell her to naff off. Not meaning it—meaning, "Stay and be there for me, but stop tormenting me!"

Which was how Mr Pay-the-Bills came back into his life, sliding in to do the bath duty, easing his conscience, but never admitting it. Wiping him down, drying him, his hands everywhere, but never saying, "How about me being your step-dad?" Steering clear of it so obviously that he got the message."

All three of them keeping Colly's part in his life secret. Angie saying they needed to because he didn't want to give people the chance to say he was paying conscience money. Him saying bollocks, he's already spent a fortune in the courts doing that, it can't just be that, and she saying he could believe what he liked. But if he cared for Colly, if he was grateful, he'd keep the secret and he'd stop pestering him. So he did—and they got the wrong message about how he felt about it all.

Which was why he blew up. If they'd listened, if Colly had listened, they'd have realised that the father bit was still important; have realised that although he was now a man, not a boy like they still thought him, there had to be something more than just living in Colly's house, taking his money, being cared for by his nurse.

So he said what was true. That after all this time, all these years, he still knew fuck-all about him, that if Colly couldn't hack it, if he couldn't stop treating him like an arms-length gaga charity case, then he couldn't hack it, either.

And it worked! The Great Provider sat down one day and told him about his life, his work, not just his present contracts and stuff like that, but going all the way back to when he was starting out, how he'd made his mark designing houses and offices and warehouses, and had taken risks with his building business, pushing and manoeuvring, bidding and counter-bidding until it won him prizes and made him rich. Rich as Croesus!

And he told him about taking Lizzie to Ozzie's party before they were married, how they'd been so happy, how they'd honeymooned up in the mountains and that it was still like that; the two of them still happy up there in the peaks, rolling around in the high meadows.

And for the first time, he also spoke about Sally, not just in passing like he usually did, as if she didn't count, but how she made him laugh, how proud he was of her, how she was sailing through school, how she always seemed to pick the right boy friends.

Repeating how happy they were, the three of them . . .

"So there's just the one girl?"

"Yes."

"Nobody else?"

"Nobody."

"Nobody at all?

"Like who?"

"Like . . . like parents?"

"No parents."

"They dead?"

"Yes."

"Were they old?"

"No."

"But you don't want to talk about them?"

"No."

"So nobody else?"

"No, there's nobody else. You know there isn't. Don't tell me you and Angie don't chat about it."

"Of course we do. She tells me all about the wild parties, the police raids, the marijuana cakes, drawing keys from the hat, that sort of thing. And she tells me all about your friends. What they look like, what they sound like. What they get up to."

"Wow! Not *all* of it, I hope!"

"No, I don't suppose so! I knew you had the one daughter, though—I was just testing."

"There you are then."

"Yep. There I am."

———————

During the long years between being rescued from the care home and being seventeen, Angie or one of her stand-ins would chat to him and drive him backwards and forwards to his swimming and the physio and the hospital and the barbershop and the youth club—places like that. It was only now and again that Colly would turn up and take him somewhere different, usually a Chelsea home match at Stamford Bridge.

But the football was never enough to stop the shutters coming down, to stop him deciding that if he couldn't have all of it, *all of him*, he didn't want any of it. So he lost himself in his CD's and his computer and the crap on TV.

He still met people—but only on the phone and the chat lines and in Angie's stories about the people she met while catering and skivvying at one of her parties, pushing back the walls for him, illuminating his life, even though the characters were phantoms, their lives wafting in and out of his fears and frustrations like wispy, see-through pictures on billowing silk.

And he could tell that from the way she spoke—laughing and wistful at the same time—that Angie's on-off life with Anna and

Herbie and Hugo and the rest of them filled a need in her as much as for him, fed their yearnings, made them forget themselves.

And it was like that for ages, party after party.

But by the time he was twenty, after the New Year do at Charlie's and Howard's, things changed; a buzzer went off, worrying him, warning that perhaps the stories might not go on forever, that Angie seemed no longer able to stand back.

"Where've you been this time," I sang out, hearing her in the hallway. "I can't remember."

"I told you," she shouted, bustling through to the kitchen, dumping bags there, poking her head round my door on the way back for more. "It was Ozzie's fiftieth," snapping at me, taking in the empty Coke cans on the floor.

"I know, I know—I'll move them. It's just that you're back so early. What happened? Did Ozzie finally flip? Is there a mass grave with missing arms and legs?"

No answer.

And it was the same the next day, she and Colly spending ages in the kitchen with the door closed, and then him leaving without bothering to call in, and she as ratty as Hell.

"What's up?" I asked her.

"Nothing. It's all right."

"What, *you* all upset, *he* not bothering to say hello, and it's all right? You two haven't finally, you know . . . ?"

"Don't be stupid," she said, snatching up one of my jerseys, folding it, stuffing it into a cupboard, banging some books into a pile. "Get that idea out of your head—it isn't going to happen!"

"Yeah—but you'd like it to happen, wouldn't you?"

"But it hasn't and it won't!"

"Well, *something's* happened! Or am I just a cripple in a wheelchair that everybody looks clean through and doesn't see?"

"It's not like that! So stop talking rubbish! Colly and me—it isn't going to happen. It's not what either of us *wants* to happen."

"If you say so."

"I *do* say so. It's just that you'll have to shower in your chair the next few nights. It won't kill you. Colly's got something on his mind; things to do. He won't be able to spend much time here."

"Why not?"

"He'll tell you himself."

—————

"Angie, I know! I got it wrong! Like you say, I should never have made him think my life was so bloody perfect. But I didn't know Lizzie had seen through me, did I? I didn't know she was going to shout her head off about Charlie in front of everybody, did I? God knows what Ozzie thinks. And Honey and the rest of them."

"Never mind them. It's the boy you need to think about. In the end, lies will always find you out."

"Is that so! Just listen to Miss Moral. Well, I'm not going to start telling him about Charlie. That's nothing to do with him. Or with you for that matter. I'll have to think up another story."

"Not a story, Colly—the truth! The truth about you and Lizzie and Robert. And about that worrying daughter of yours. Everything! No cotton wool clouds and no eternal laughter."

She was helping him to thrash out the mess, waiting for him to take the way she was pointing. She could see him looking at her, her eyes, the contours of her face, thinking he was gathering his thoughts, trying to decide what to say, what the new account of himself should be, *not knowing that I was overwhelmed by her beauty, by the way, in certain lights, at certain times, the hollows of her cheeks seem filled with a curious glow, a wispy haze of green fire that flickered across the oily blackness* . . .

"You do understand why you have to tell him, don't you?" she demanded. "I know you weren't trying to fob him off, telling him a fairytale. I know you were trying to protect him, keep things lovely for him. But now this Charlie business has happened, especially now, he needs to know *all* of it."

"C'mon," he said, casting around. "He's got *you*, your influence. I thought that if I could give him sight of another person like you, another life like yours, it would settle him, make him happy."

"But it was a lie! It was a lie then and it's even more of a lie now! And, anyhow, what's so special about me? You can't keep talking to him about you and me. We're two people, we're not . . . together. He dreams the fairytale bit, the happily ever after bit. But it's not going to happen, is it? It's slipped by. If you'd wanted that to happen, Colly, you wouldn't have chosen Charlie."

But I didn't choose her. She was given to me by one of her friends like a birthday present that you rip open without caring too much what's inside. Howard failing her and me failing everybody. Lizzie, Robert, Sally, Nico, my father, my mother—and you. Knowing, as I had always known, that I was hurting you, plagued by it as much as by the others. But setting you aside, not seeing you clearly until it was too late, too complicated . . . the green fire still shimmering, filling the hollows of your body as it might have done . . . dancing between us as it might have done . . . drawing me into you as it might have done . . .

"What he needs," she was saying, "is the truth. If you and Nico are ever going to have the relationship you want, one that's going to keep the two of you sane, then you've got to give him something to put his faith in. You've got to tell him what's happened. Right from the start. The whole of it."

Not the whole of it. Not about you, the way it could have been you. Not Chloe. Not my mother. Not my father. And not my son. My dead, resurrected son.

———

When you have time, like I have, sitting in a wheelchair, like as not on the outside, you learn to second-guess people—their movements, their voices, their eyes, even the way they breathe.

When Colly visited that next time, coming straight in to see me without calling on Angie first, his stride quick and certain, his face neither friendly nor unfriendly, I knew that he must have come to some sort of a decision, thinking it had to be something to do with Angie or me, thinking that perhaps he'd run out of money for us or didn't care any more; not considering for a minute that he was going to tell me it was another woman, that he'd been shagging Charlie Sinclair!

"So who cares," I said, relieved that it was nothing directly to do with us, but wanting to be cruel, to pay him back for Angie, and for me—for it not being about us. "I thought for a minute it was going to be something important."

I saw his jaw tighten. But before he had time to bollock me, I remembered the guff he'd told me about the mountains and the flowers.

"So your loving wife's a lie then? Why tell me if it's a lie?"

And he said all he'd done was not tell me that things had changed, that he and Lizzie had lost each other, but that he'd not wanted to worry me. That he'd not thought.

"Well, I know somebody you could have thought about, somebody very unhappy, even if she is only your paid help."

But he just tightened his jaw again and said he was moving out, that he was going to live in a cottage belonging to the de Mangers. As soon as he was settled in, he said it'd all be the same as ever. Angie and I wouldn't know the difference.

"Really?" I said. "And will it be like that for Lizzie and Sally? And for Charlie and Howard?"

Mind your own damned business, he'd snapped, the cold control breaking at last. What the fuck did I know about Charlie and Howard?

"Enough," I said. "No surprise that's she's beautiful and that he gets on your tits, irritates the shits out of you."

So who's a clever bastard then, he'd said, snarling it out, frightening me. Just keep your nose out. You wanted to know! Now you know!

Roaring off in his Jag, showing me that he wasn't all piss and wind. Not just a holy do-gooder, a rich geezer, all dough and no heart . . .

Just ordinary. Somebody who got angry. Who cared.

It was good he got angry. Really good.

"In the first wave alone . . . American warships fired 320 cruise missiles at Baghdad and its suburbs—more than were fired in the first Gulf War . . ." The Times, March 22, 2003.

Chapter 8

Scam

It had always seemed to Howard Sinclair that the creaking, bleached veranda was the perfect place, the ends glassed in against the weather, the front flaky, white-railed, a sanctum, everyone knowing that when at the beach house, he was always likely to be snoozing there, or listening to the radio or reading his maps, yelling up to him, "Coming for a swim, Dad?" . . . "Coming for a sail, Capt'n?" . . . she whispering, "Yes, my darling, but let's go inside, not here, let's go inside."

Sitting there that Easter Sunday, his trust in the sun betrayed by the occasional surge of cold air, one deceiving him, the other chilling him, darting into his flesh like a sword—Charlie's new dagger, his *friend's* new dagger; huddling his large frame within the canvas of the chair, trying to keep separate what the doctor had to say about the ache in his head and what Lizzie Wolfson had to say in her tirade about the state of his marriage; putting both to the back of his mind, aware of early bees, a poignant robin, bickering, faraway gulls, the veranda a hideaway within the larger hideaway of the dormered house, the place they kept on the south coast, its whitewashed walls looking down on the clinking moorings and the windswept links.

And yet thinking only of her.

Loving her, hating her, drawn by the mystery of her; the switched on perpetual model, the cool, statuesque clotheshorse, getting off, or seeming to, at the click-click of the camera, the prance down the catwalk; snapping into and out of her work, a strange mixture of haughty style and girly exuberance; dividing her favours, some for the glossies, some for him; excited by his business coups but not in the day-to-day; pretending an interest in his golf, but preferring, if pushed, a gentle game of tennis, enough to flush her cheeks, to lead the way to an icy sun-downer; visiting the cottage only when he and the family were there, never sharing his love for it, yet crewing for him, sticking it for days at a time, looking forward, as he knew, to the next port of call, showering and powdering for the bar, her smooth, shaded make-up, her marvellous eyes, her tanned limbs—the very *essence* of her transforming faded denim into a million dollars, turning heads . . .

After the numbed, silent drive home from Ozzie's, the row hadn't started until the phone rang, interrupting their thoughts, goading him to snatch it up and smash it back down, the caller unanswered.

"Gathering like vultures," he had said. "Alerted by carrion."

"Don't be absurd," she scoffed, regretting it, kicking herself for not ignoring him.

"Oh it's *me* being absurd, is it?" he said, glaring. "And I thought it was *you*. *You* be*having* absurdly, and me just *feeling* absurd, standing there listening to that poor woman telling the world that you've been shagging her husband!"

"And when half the world is doing that, is that so absurd?"

"It is when *she's* your closest friend and when *he's* supposed to be a chum, a mate!"—crossing the room, grabbing three framed photographs from the bookshelf.

"Look!" he said, tossing them one after the other on to the settee next to her. "*There* are the four of us in Rome! *And* Paris! *And* New York! Four of us, but apparently only two happy and trusting!"

"Don't give me the trusting bit," she said, twisting a handkerchief in her fingers, throwing it from her. "Don't tell me that you've never broken my trust in you, that you've never been with some floozy."

"If I have, she was just that—a floozy. Not a friend! Not one of the gang! What in God's name were you thinking about? If I wasn't enough for you, you could have had anyone! Why foul your own doorstep? Why choose Colly Wolfson? Why break Lizzie's heart?"

"And what about *your* heart? Have I broken *your* heart?" Scoffing again.

He stared at her, frowning, his face working. "You have no idea, have you? You're so brainless, so bloody wrapped up in yourself, you have no idea."

He could see that the insults had jolted her, set her face, dried her words. He crossed the room again, this time to the drinks cabinet, and slugged whisky.

"Do, by all means, turn to the booze," she said, "—to your work, your chums, your yacht, your plane and your bloody golf. But never me! Not when I'm down here on the ground with you. Only when you've got me up on your pedestal. Up on view with my legs in the air. Letting the blokes know that when you fuck, you fuck the best!"

"Who's being absurd now?" he asked. "*And* obscene!"

His glare beat against her obduracy and found no way in. If it was going to be like this, if she was going to respond like this, it was over. *He could never tell her about the ache, about his head.*

"So why Colly?" he had repeated, this time quietly—*sitting in the canvas chair, looking out to sea, still trying to make sense of her reply.*

"Whatever I say," she had said, "it'll look as if I'm criticising you, comparing you. Which would be wrong because you're two totally different people. You're like a barn door, he's thin and neat. You dash into things head on; he's deeper, more thoughtful. You have your heart on your sleeve; he hides his feelings a mile down."

But not, he failed to hear, not telling him what had led her to gasp and groan against the hair and flesh of another body—his friend, the husband of her friend—not telling him what it was that she craved, that sparked her into "Come and take me, come and be where my husband has been for twenty years, come and fuck my cunt." Able now to say that word, even though he'd never thought it of her, never referred to her that way in his mind, as ashamed by the crudity, even now, as if he'd spoken it out loud, as if her adultery had not demeaned him.

"So he's different," he had said. "So what? You just wanted to wipe me away."

Horrified. "No, I didn't! You're not a fly on a windscreen! I care about you, our lives, us and the kids, our home. You were never supposed to know. I didn't want to hurt you, would never have planned it that way. It's just that I love him. I suppose I always have."

"'Love?' 'Always?' 'Suppose?'" Questioning, deriding, making her purse her lips, raise her chin, fight to control the tears.

"C'mon Charlie! You know better than that! Colly Wolfson's in love with everything and nothing. He takes because it's there, but he never knows what he wants and he hardly knows what he's taking! He's that sort—the spoiled brat, the quirky outsider, the great agoniser. Look at him over Iraq! What's that all about? What makes you think that even if you do love him, even if you're prepared to give everything up for him, that he feels the same about you?"

"He does! I can see him clearly. I trust him. And you can't say he sits on his hands. He didn't make a fortune by doing nothing."

"Neither did I—but it seems my money is no longer good enough!"

Desperate now, heading off her protests. "OK! OK! Business-wise, he's smart. But what about the cot death? What about how he treats Lizzie? And what about that accident—the smashed-up boy? The lack of care . . . the hand wringing . . . no follow through. Doesn't that tell you something?"

He found her looking at him, shaking her head, slowly, sadly. "And you ask, 'Why Colly . . . ?'"

———

To start with, he thought it was stress. Disagreements with his directors, cash flow, staff problems, the usual ebb and flow of running a big company, nothing exceptional; the kids, his son and daughters, doing great but never quite doing what he wanted; a few worrying rows with Charlie—trying to understand her, to match what she seemed to need; feeling that it wasn't enough, that he was in one of his dreams, trying to get to the office but on the wrong bus, the wrong train, the wrong station.

When his eyesight started playing up, he switched the blame to that and felt silly and relieved. But while the new spectacles helped, the headaches persisted—the fuzziness of not being quite in touch, of not being able to work things out quite so easily, of somehow drifting out of character, puzzling people, boozing, offending Charlie, making her think he no longer cared.

Trying to get through on his own, knowing it wasn't just his eyes, that it couldn't be. Holding out for as long as possible, pulling strings to by-pass their family doctor to make sure it remained his secret; going to a friend of a friend, a Harley Street specialist, and from him to a private hospital he and Charlie had never used before, pretending he was away on business trips, knowing there was something wrong, something bad. But not wanting to tell her, if at all, until he was certain.

The examinations, the tests, the X-rays, the scans, the futile extravaganza, had all come and gone, the medical people accepting him as Monty Sinclair of the house by the sea, sending their letters and bills there, phoning him only on his mobile; pretending to her all the while that he was in a different city, doing different things.

But still not being able to tell her. Not because there was something there in his head, killing him. And not because there was nothing they could do about it. But because of her affair—standing there at Ozzie's, listening to Lizzie ranting and raving, revealing a totally new crisis, a nightmare he'd never suspected, a ghastly smear in an otherwise flawless window; his own *private* nightmare still fresh, the full meaning of the tumour unveiled to him only a week before Ollie's party. Heeding the doctor's advice to tell her immediately, but then deciding to gift her one final, carefree party with the Set. So delaying his news for a week, deciding to tell her the day after the party. To hold and caress her; to turn her lovely face to him, to say to her, "You're the love of my life. Despite all that I may be, you are the one I have lived my life through, the one who has brought me joy, the one who now has to be strong for both of us."

Except he couldn't say that now. Couldn't say, "I need you to help me die," because her hopes wouldn't be with him. She would tend him, she would nurse him through the hopeless therapy, but she would have Colly; she would have the comfort of knowing that her widowhood would release her into happiness.

He had never thought beyond his death, had never imagined her with a new, immediate life, had thought that she would grieve like other women grieve; that eventually, after a decent period, she would emerge and cast around for a new existence.

So what now? Be a sacrificial, uncomplaining hero? Or grab his humiliation like a club and smash his friend down? Crush the dark, wispy curls into his forehead, into his finely drawn, playboy looks, demanding, "Is there anything else of mine that you would like to smear yourself on?"

But he didn't fancy the hero bit. And with the clawed hand scratching at his door, the idea of violence seemed pathetic.

So he sat on the veranda and fashioned something out beyond himself, beyond either of *them* . . . a subtle game . . . a game of love and vengeance . . . a cosy roulette in which *he* would throw the dice and *they,* the adulterers, would both win *and* lose. Arranging his death in such a way that for those first few terrible hours—days?—*they,* the two of them, would think themselves the single, direct cause of his obliteration; arranging it so that they would learn about the tumour only after their initial torment; so that they would have the chance to relieve their guilt—*but would never know what, precisely, had lain in his mind.*

Sitting there looking out to sea, *he and his beautiful clotheshorse whisking through the waves, the flume stinging their faces, hauling in the flapping sail, laughing at their daring, delighting in their togetherness,* silent tears slowly coursed while he pondered the wider reaction to his coming death—the shocked, white faces of the Sinks.

Was it an accident or deliberate?
Was it the adultery?
The cancer?
Or both?

———

Lizzie Wolfson's view of the domestic wreckage was from her own hideaway, the little upstairs room at the front of the house that was known as her study, but which was nothing more than that, a hideaway, the place she went to think and be still, more comforting, she realised, sadly, than the previous day's Easter service at the cathedral, seeking anonymity and peace there, but her prayers unanswered amid its cold, impersonal vastness.

It astonished her that although a week had passed since Ozzie's party, the secret little glance she had seen there was still printed in her mind like the image left when you close your eyes after looking at a light bulb or a bright window. A glance, no more than that. But a revelation, a confirmation of all the hitherto unconnected, unrecognised signs and signals, a give-away that had readied the two of them for stoning, dressed them in adulterers' sandwich boards: "Look at us," the glance had said, hot, engorged, spilling guilt and smugness, "we're shagging."

Back within the privacy of his own house, resenting the humiliation of her public flare-up, he had denied that it had been going on for more than a few weeks.

"Have the decency to admit it!" she had shouted, throwing the oven cloth at him, beating him with her hands. "Stop thinking about Bush and Blair and all the poor people in Iraq! Have the decency to tell me the truth! For three years now, you've been disappearing out of this house. You've been seeing her all that time!"

"No, I've not," he said, quietly, his face drained, the easy charm stripped away. "I really haven't."

"I don't believe you. If you were truthful, if you showed me some respect, some love, we could talk it through. But you're lying."

"No! I'm not lying. I only started up with Charlie at the New Year. The rest has nothing to do with her."

"'The rest?' What rest? What does *that* mean?"

But she was asking the impossible. He could find the words that would bring transparency, that would fashion a frank, honest response. But not without destroying her. Not without revealing his parallel, unmentionable, unforgivable deceit over the boy. Not able to say, "It's not been Charlie all that time, it's been Nico, the boy whose life I ruined, whom I now love, whom you refuse to recognise, who has become the son you let die."

She returned his wordless stare, saw that she could push him no further, and shrugged.

"Without the truth," she said, quietly, "there's nothing."

The next day, while she was kneeling in her forlorn cathedral, wondering why God was so hard to find, he went to live in the de Mangers' empty gatehouse, closing his own front door quietly as if not to interrupt the sound of their daughter's weeping.

The weeping, she knew, was still going on inside, even when, as now, Sally was somewhere or other with her friends. And she was surprised that she could know this and do nothing about it, shutting herself away in her little room and doing nothing but turn things over in her mind, again and again, seeking the place where she had gone wrong.

Gradually, her mind recoiled from the turmoil, and she began registering the minutiae—the fading wallpaper, the carpet stain where the Callows boy had upset his cocoa, the mark where Colly had allowed a heavy suitcase to catch the wall . . .

Enjoying the respite, the soothing irrelevances, when, suddenly, there was a sudden crunch of tyres on the gravel and through the gates beneath her swept a familiar Mercedes convertible, its roof down, its driver Howard Sinclair.

She hurried into the bedroom to frizz up her hair, put on some lipstick. Normally, she wouldn't have bothered, Howard not being the sort of man she really warmed to despite them all being long-term friends. But since her explosion at Ozzie's, it seemed important to keep her end up, if not for herself, then for him.

She opened the door and turned without greeting him, not knowing what to say, leading the way into the kitchen, offering him a cup of tea.

"No thank you, Lizzie," he said. "It's very kind, but . . ."

"It's only tea," she said, impatiently. "Perhaps you'd like coffee—or something stronger?"

"No thank you," he repeated, their presence in the kitchen thus unnecessary, its rejected utensils heightening their awkwardness, moving from it to the less demanding contours of the lounge.

"I thought it might help if we met," he said. "I wanted to come before this, but I've been busy . . . things to do . . ."

She noticed that he was speaking slowly, less decisively than usual. He seemed to be taking the split badly.

"Have you been keeping all right?" she asked. "You don't seem yourself."

"No," he said without inflection, leaving the word unexplained, nevertheless coming to life.

"I wanted to ask you whether you had any inkling of this, whether Colly had said anything. I don't want to upset you, but I need to know. It would be nice to know."

Surely he must have suspected, seen some sign? "Haven't you asked Charlie?"

"No. I didn't get the chance. We had a row . . . we're not talking. I don't suppose it really matters—they've been together . . . enjoying themselves . . . She says they love each other . . ."

He seemed defeated, strangely empty of rancour. If it didn't matter to him, why was he asking if she had realised? It annoyed her, exasperated her. "For what it's worth, Colly says it started at your New Year party. But I wouldn't take that as read. Not for a minute. And of course it *matters*! We shouldn't just give in! Don't you love Charlie any more?"

"Yes," he said. "More than life. But I'll have to leave the fighting to you."

He lowered his eyes and she watched him clasping and unclasping his hands, trying to gather himself.

"But if you love her, why leave it to me?"

The eyes rising again. "Because I don't have the time."

The flat, unexplained words stirred her irritation into astonishment.

"The time? Of course you have the time! What's more important than fighting for your marriage?"

"Lizzie, I mean it. I don't have the time. Accept it!" A deep breath, then: "There's no easy way to say this. I don't have the time because I have cancer. I'm dying of cancer. So there's no point me making a fuss. I just wanted to . . ."

She froze, her mind closing down, trying to take in his news, not listening to the rest of his words.

"Cancer? Where? What . . . ?"

She screwed her eyes, swallowing, one hand fluttering to her face as he told her, briefly, of the hospital visits and the prognosis.

"Does Charlie know?"

"Yes. I asked her to say nothing." The lies escaping her!

"And Colly?"

"I believe she's told him."

"The point is," he continued, "the reason I'm telling you, is that Charlie won't accept the cancer, won't talk about it. And she also won't talk to me about this business with Colly. So that means I can't tell her how I feel about the one and about the other. About how I've loved her, and how sorry I am."

He held his hand up as if to quieten her, but her words were already in the air.

"It's not your fault, Howard! You didn't ask for this, any of it! Neither of us did! But you *can* tell her—you can write her a letter!"

"No, I can't write a letter—not even one for later. Not now I know about what's been going on. If I ignored that, it would sound false; if I included it, it would be too bitter, too complicated."

She watched him slowly shake his head as if to clear it of what had gone before.

"What I came to ask, the reason I came, was to ask you if you would do it for me, if you would make sure, if anything happens, that Charlie knows I came to see you."

"But what am I supposed to say?"

"Just tell her I came to see you and that I love her and forgive her."

"But you're broken in two—I can see!"

"Perhaps. Perhaps not. I'm sorry she's stolen Colly, that it's got to be him. I wouldn't have wished that on you, Lizzie, and I've told her. But if it's going to make her happy . . ." the words trailing away, then picking up again. "The affair, I could have coped with. But not now, not with this thing in my head."

She took a little embroidered handkerchief from her sleeve and bit on its folds. This huge, hulking, infuriating, poor man . . . A bitch for a wife, a Judas for a friend . . .

Tears came to her eyes and she wiped them away with her fingers, forgetting the hanky. "I'm so sorry, Howard! I launched off at Ozzie's without thinking. It was so unkind to you . . ."

"No, no."

"Yes, it was."

She sought the hanky again and smoothed it out, looking up suddenly, alarming him.

"You said, 'If anything happens . . .' If what happens? What are you trying to tell me, Howard?"

"I'm asking you—"

"Yes I know. But—"

"If it does, just tell Charlie I came to see you."

He rose to his feet and she followed him to the outside door, where he turned and enclosed her raised, clasped hands in his own.

For a long moment, she tried to see deep into him, deep down beyond his words, trying to fathom the reason for his visit. But he turned abruptly and left her on the doorstep, his light kiss flickering on her forehead, its imprint a question mark.

"Air raid sirens blared, and yellow-and-white tracers from Iraqi anti-aircraft fire streaked across the city. Several large explosions rocked the capital, and a ball of fire flared in the southern sky. As the sun rose higher, street lights flickered out and the city fell into a ghostly silence"—Los Angeles Times staff writers on the opening attack on Baghdad, March 20, 2003.

"We set off a load of missiles and they headed the right way"—British pilot. The Times, London, March 22, 2003.

Chapter 9

Pay Off

Despite her initial, curiously deep feeling that she had been let down, Chloe Jones nevertheless managed to persuade herself that her shock over Colly's fling with Charlie was more to do with the nature of Lizzie's denunciation than with her own involvement. She and Colly, she reasoned, had merely made eyes at each other and had got no further than a couple of lunches, exciting, suggestive, but vinaigrette and tomato, hardly musk and mattress. Charlie's presence in the equation still rankled but had been agonised away on the grounds that the affair must have flowered well before she had a claim, and was thus excusable. Indeed, if she were to give in to Colly, pursue her madness with him, his fling with Charlie could, in fact, prove a Godsend, absolving her from any blame in his break with Lizzie.

About Simon, she had no answer, nor, at this stage, her nagging worries about Colly.

So when her phone rang and it was his soft, urgent voice telling her the day was too gorgeous to waste in an office, she was ready to say yes, she would meet him, she would play truant, she would come and sit on a park bench in the middle of London, the plane trees towering over them like a green basilica, the sunlight filtering on to the altar of his face, his arms spread like a cross along the backrest.

Apart from his initial polite greeting, he was unsmiling. "I'm sorry you had to find out like that," he said. "It must have been pretty awful."

"Oh, I don't know," she said, belying her mood. "An admirer with a wife *and* a full-time lover . . . so much the in thing! Does wonders for a girl's pride! Awful, yes. But then, who am I?"

Alarmed, thinking perhaps that she was trying to tell him it was all over, that the scene at Ozzie's was too hurtful, he said, uncertainly, "But you're here . . . you care enough to see me."

"Enough to see if there's anything left."

"For us?"

"For me. For me to make sense of. To discover what sort of person you are. I thought I was getting there. After what Lizzie had to say, I'm not sure."

He closed the space between them to a few inches, but instead of pressing against her, he swivelled his shoulders, his face still near enough for her to catch the tang of perfume and mint.

"Pretend there are just the two of us in the world. Just one man, one woman." He was breathing the words, bantering, coaxing.

"But there aren't," she said, fighting the seeping entrancement, the sensation that they were already naked, that his fingers were not merely entwined in hers, down there on her lap, but were beginning to . . .

"But there could be."

"And Lizzie?"

He released her hand and sat leaning forward, wrists on knees, fingertips gently drumming against each other.

"We're living separately. I can't see it changing."

They paused while a child of three or four left the path by the lake and skipped towards them, her blond curls catching the sunlight, regarding them impassively for a moment before flitting away beyond the bushes.

"And Charlie?"

He continued to look before him, as if still seeing the child. "I only started with Charlie, that way, the day I met you. Lizzie doesn't believe that, but it's true. We were unhappy, we lost the map."

"And have you found it again?"

"Enough to know the way to a good coffee shop!" he exclaimed, impishly, pulling her to her feet, acknowledging without words his failure to convince her. "Come with me! Come and explore the mysterious alleyways of old Constantinople!"

"Mmm! *Turkish* coffee . . ."

"Well, bog English, anyway," he said, laughing, leading her to a nearby bistro, steering the conversation towards her, what she had been up to, avoiding further mention of the recent upheaval until they were crossing the pavement to her cab.

"Don't think I don't care about Charlie and Lizzie and Howard," he said, the light-heartedness gone; his voice deep and level, his face drawn. "I do and I'll do what I can to smooth the pain away. God knows how, but I'll try. But when I've done that, when I've proved you can trust me, I'll be in touch. Watch out for me, won't you?"

—standing on the pavement, waving goodbye to Chloe Jones, convinced, at that moment, that of all the elements in his world, she might be the one to absolve and save him, wash him clean, allow him to start again, not knowing that only the previous afternoon, a vengeful Howard Sinclair had been sowing certain lies in Lizzie's ear;

—standing there waving, the taxi disappearing into the traffic, thinking of its passenger, unaware of the coming nightmare, of a little plane that even then was circling the Sinclair homestead, buzzing and dancing round and round, blipping its wings; a pretty little blue and white plane coughing its way towards the clouds, slowly looping over, hurtling down and down into the green, welcoming woods, spinning like a corkscrew;

—so no time for him to settle things and no easy way of him ringing Chloe, of continuing the delicious build-up to their affair. Because what he now had to tell himself, had to deal with, was that it wasn't merely the end of a marriage, of two marriages, but the sudden, violent, fiery death of the friend he had turned from.

"The Battle of Iraq is one victory in a war on terror that began on 11 September, 2001, and still goes on . . . any outlaw regime that has ties to terrorist groups and seeks to possess Weapons of Mass Destruction is a grave danger . . . and will be confronted"—President Bush declaring the end of major hostilities in Iraq, May 2, 2003.

Chapter 10

Inquest

As she had planned, Jill Maybury arrived early, choosing to sit at the back in the corner, a dozen seats along from the heavy swing doors of the public entrance. The room was small, low ceilinged and soulless, a bleak example of public money spent to bad effect: cheap wood panelling, badly hung velvet curtains, ugly cast iron radiators, frosted windows and fluorescents that would have graced the 'Fifties. Not quite the Old Bailey, but well enough suited, she imagined, to the dismal purposes of a coroner's court.

She was on her own, Barns pulling his old woman act, deciding at the last minute not to ask for a day off.

"C'mon," she'd pleaded, trying to make a joke of it, "there'll be plenty of weather for you to get wrong when you get back—I'm told there always is."

"Maybe," he'd said, not in the mood. "Thing is, I don't know why you want to go. The Callows aren't going—Keith says it's only the formal details. We know who he is and we know what happened—his plane crashed."

"I know."

"So what's the point in going?"

"I just thought we'd . . . I just thought it might be nice for Charlie to know that someone was there for her."

"What about your friend, Lizzie? Who's flying the flag for *her*?"

"Lizzie won't be there," she said, patiently. "You wouldn't expect it. I'll see Lizzie some other time. Are you coming with me, or not?"

"Perhaps I'll make it to the second hearing," he said.

Selfish prick . . .

The thing was, and she knew Barns thought this but didn't want to say anything in case it caused a row, she had her own reasons for going. From the start, the time when the Callows had introduced them to the Sinks, she had felt an outsider, in awe of the Sinclairs' flamboyance, afraid of Colly's intensity, uncomprehending of the Leveringtons' intellectual mateyness, and so on. It was silly, really, because being in the estate business—and more to the point, the proud owner of a small string of lucrative agencies—she knew her views were highly respected, the Sinks all being of the breed that stood in reverential awe of property, not necessarily buying into the boom but forever giving the impression of being about to do so. Nevertheless, she couldn't escape feeling that she and Barns were only tolerated because it amused them to rub shoulders with a television weather man, albeit a provincial one, and because she was a friend and associate of Keith Callows, the builder, and of Jessica Callows, the ostentatious interior designer.

Lately, Jessica herself had also become a problem, gradually detaching from their friendship and cultivating the acidic Anna Brownlove. This was upsetting but at least made room for her own preferences—the sad, kindly Lizzie Wolfson, the beauty and style of Charlie Sinclair. Their sudden bust-up, before she'd had a chance to develop a threesome, was a deep disappointment, but also, perhaps, a moment of opportunity.

After a while, people began drifting into the room, among them the dreadful, on-the-make Herbie Kirby. She smiled at Roger Platt-Smith's exaggerated take-off of the man they secretly dubbed 'Orrible 'Erbie and, misunderstanding, he smiled back and came to sit next to her.

"Hello, Jill," he said, breezily. "What you doing here?"

"The same as you, I imagine," she responded tartly, her dislike not preventing her from silently admiring his surprisingly sleek charcoal grey suit, white shirt and quiet blue tie. Until now, she had seen him only in what he called his "party gear"—a mixture of Caribbean shirts and shorts for patio parties, loud checks for indoors.

"What's that then?"

"You know—showing the flag, keeping an eye on things . . ." annoyed at her lack of verve, his sartorial transformation quite off putting.

He glanced round the room. "None of the others here then?"

"No."

"Rum do," he said, presumably, she thought, meaning Howard's death.

"Terrible," she agreed.

"Yes. You'd have thought they'd have been here."

Before she could rescue herself, they were called to order and the inquest opened and closed within the space of a few terse, dispassionate sentences. Yes, witnesses would confirm the aircraft had been registered in the name of Howard Montefiore Sinclair. Yes, they would say he had been seen taking off in it. Yes, thick woods had prevented the emergency services from reaching the crash scene. Yes, the pilot had been incinerated. Yes, DNA showed it was the said Howard Montefiore Sinclair.

Were inquiries continuing? Yes.

Could the funeral take place? Yes.

Adjourned.

After being called to their feet for the coroner's departure, they remained standing, Herbie stretching, though still not quite reaching her height.

"Idiot," he said.

"The coroner?"

"Howard."

"Howard! What gives you the right to say that?"

"No right. But I knew him and I liked him. A few years back, he put business my way when things were bad. He was a good bloke, really good."

"Yes, but—"

"No buts, Jill. He was an idiot. Threw it all away. Crashed his plane because that wife of his . . ."

"You don't know that."

"I know he worshipped her. And I know I could have helped him."

"The way you're helping the de Mangers?"

The switch in subject was made levelly and without heat, but he quickly recognised its catty, loaded content.

"You people," he said, smiling, shaking his head sadly. "Hugo gets in trouble and you think I'm fleecing him. Yes, I've bought some of his land—but he got the going rate. Small corner down by the railway, the place I've been renting his old sheds for my vans. Sheds, not barns, mark you. And yes, I'm going to knock 'em down. I have a deal with the local council. I get to build a new centre for my van hire, and on the rest of the land, a housing association gets to build loads of very necessary, absolutely essential, low-cost housing for folk who need a leg-up."

He stopped as suddenly as he had started.

"The de Mangers—" she began, defensively.

"The de Mangers," he interrupted, "would only have wanted big houses and would never have got planning permission. This way everybody wins. You're an estate agent—right?"

"Right," she said, weakly.

"Then *you* should know," he said, not unkindly.

He suddenly became aware that they were the only ones left in the room and began edging along the row, smiling back at her, uneasily. "Thanks for coming today," he called. "Good to know I'm not the only one who cares. But do yourself a favour—stop listening to Anna Brownlove."

On the day of the funeral, there was a howling wind and cold, stinging rain, the petals of the wreaths dancing briefly before sticking together, the ink on the tributes smudging, one of the pall bearers losing his bowler, two hundred mourners packing the crematorium, overflowing into the aisles, trying to arrange their sodden clothing but glad to be inside, the elements, for the moment, taking the edge off their varying degrees of sorrow.

At the rear of the chapel were Howard's business associates, general friends and neighbours. In front of these, were his flying and sailing cronies and the golfers, followed by several pews of employees. Between these and the two families, in a thin line all the way across, were the Sink Set, for once quiet, respectful and dressed soberly, grieving their friend but jolted by the sight of Lizzie and Colly arriving together, followed by Sally, their eyes looking only for a seat; turning, pushing into a pew further back, Sally sitting between them like a barrier, Lizzie staring straight ahead, never once looking at the grieving wife, but accepting Colly's argument that on this one occasion, they should face it out side by side.

So there were two nuclei for the Sinks to ponder on—the three Wolfsons and the larger gathering of Sinclairs, the lot of them guessing at Charlie's feelings, trying to penetrate the famous catwalk stare.

—he not looking at me as I passed by behind the coffin, so not seeing my yearning for him, for it to have been him sitting beside me, holding me, consoling me—knowing that there, in the middle of the throng, in the middle of anywhere, that this was impossible, but wanting it with a tautness that dragged at my groin, stopped my breathing, praying that it was the same for him, that one day, he would allow me to smooth away the horror . . .

After the coffin had disappeared beyond the curtains and the final tears had spilled, the mourners drove to Charlie's house for the wake, sharing cars, dithering on the pavement, no-one wanting to be the first to arrive.

"I take it they're not coming back? Colly and Lizzie?"

"Herbie, for goodness sake! Of course they're not coming back! The funeral was one thing, coming back here . . ." Honey Leverington allowed her voice to fall away in disbelief.

Jill Maybury, alarmed by her sudden, unexplained urge to intervene, could see that the Set was beginning the long job of learning to face the consequences of the tragedy, getting themselves used to the new situation, not merely Howard's death but the break-up of the two marriages. Perversely, she reasoned that the death removed one quarter of their embarrassment. But whether it would be enough to allow them to continue as before, to accept the new liaison, to re-write history, was a problem not yet resolved. For the moment, it was clear to her that there must be no wild talk, no cross words, that in the circumstances, the affair and its consequence must be left in the undergrowth, not exactly hidden, but not advertised, either.

Like the rest of the Set, her nerve ends had been exposed; unlike them, she had already been thrown up against the only one of its members rash enough, at this time, to call a spade a spade. Curiously, it had not so much been Herbie Kirby's comments about Howard that had stayed with her, but the way he had manipulated the land deal with the de Mangers and the insight it had provided.

Circulating at the wake, she resisted talking to him, his nod and raised eyebrows acknowledgement enough of the note she had sent to his office.

"Those who hide their light under a bush," she had written, *"often find themselves misunderstood. Should your housing association need help with the marketing, it shouldn't cost you more than a working lunch."*

At the time, the note, though irksome, had seemed the least she could do—an apology without actually saying sorry. Now, with him only feet away, breathing and scenting the same air, it seemed nothing but an obvious, unsophisticated come-on! Dismayed by her gaffe, but, if she were truthful, knowing that she was half-ready for some coarse excitement should he take her up, she sighed frustratedly and clicked her tongue.

"Not to worry, dear," murmured the boring, dependable Barns, jumping to the wrong conclusion. "The whole business will be over before we know it."

It was such a silly remark that she couldn't be bothered to reply, walking off in search of another sherry, irritated as much by his failure to understand her as by his casual, uncaring forecast—his failure to appreciate that with the inquest yet to take place, the matter was not likely to merely blow itself out like one of his storms.

———

With the courtroom's dreariness now made tolerable by the alternating hum and hush of an expectant gallery, a neighbour of the Sinclair's took the oath and spoke of seeing Howard's plane circling the house—"as it had on previous occasions."

"And what was different about this time?"

"This time, instead of flying away, wiggling its wings, it climbed up and up and then came down like a dive-bomber—straight into the woods above the house. It was if they were a target, as if he was aiming there."

A fireman confirmed there was nothing they could do. "We couldn't get the appliances anywhere near. There were broken branches and thick undergrowth everywhere. The tail plane and the wing tips had been ripped off, and the nose was embedded in a crater. The earth was soft," he explained, "it had been raining."

"And the fuselage?"

"Surprisingly, the fuselage and the cockpit had stayed more or less intact."

"And this had caught fire?"

"Yes. A very fierce fire. By the time we fought our way through, all that was left was the airframe."

"And the pilot?"

"The pilot was . . . there was nothing left."

Airfield witnesses said Howard had taken a flight plan to Newcastle and had asked for the plane's tanks to be brimming. One of them said that at the last moment, he had produced a pink envelope and had asked for it to be posted as soon as possible.

"Was he calm about this?"

"No, he was very insistent that I shouldn't forget."

"Is this the envelope?"

"It looks like it. It's got the same name and address on it."

"And whose name is that?"

"His wife's."

A police sergeant said Mrs Sinclair had not been at home on the day of the crash; they had traced her children and obtained her mobile telephone number, but the device had been turned off. In the event, it was six hours before he had been able to inform her of her husband's death.

"I said that due to certain information in our possession, I had to ask whether she had any reason to believe that Mr Sinclair might wish to take his own life. She said, no, she hadn't. The next day, her lawyer rang to say that a letter had been received."

"In a pink envelope?"

"Yes. It had been opened."

"And is this the envelope and the note it contained?"

"Yes."

"Will you read out the note?"

"'*Darling, I cannot bear it. Love you always, Howard.*'"

Mrs Charlotte Sinclair, in a dark grey suit with a black silk scarf, gloves and shoes, received the coroner's sympathy impassively. It was necessary, he said, for him to understand clearly what the note might mean. Could she help?

Looking out over the heads of the Mayburys and the Callows and the rest of them, centring on the face at the back, the lovely, beautiful, sculpted face of her lover, wanting always to have it there before her to kiss and stroke, their love-making nothing without his eyes on her, without her making them close and flutter . . .

"I cannot say what frame of mind my husband was in that day, nor for a little time before that. We had been living as . . ."

" . . . as strangers?"

"Yes."

"Your marriage had broken down?"

"No!" The face still there before her, his eyes unblinking, the line between them, eye-to-eye, for him, for her, as straight and as bright as a white laser, the rest of the room in shadow, her forceful, hurt denial of the coroner's question shrivelling.

"I'm sorry," she whispered, gathering herself, the court waiting patiently, understanding her misery, not wanting to intrude; she now looking down, afraid, for once, of what she might see on his face.

"Yes, our marriage had broken down."

"And where were you on the day of the crash?"

"I was in London. Knightsbridge . . . Mayfair . . . I was on a shopping spree. I was depressed."

"And the phone?"

"I wanted to be alone."

Thinking, remembering forever, that that day, she had wanted him, her beautiful lover, to visit her, to go to the house and drink and talk and lie with her, so that she could comfort him, smooth away Lizzie's wounds . . . but he had said he was too busy, that there was someone, it didn't matter who, that he needed to see. So she had taken herself off up to London, anywhere to get out of the house, away from the lonely booze and the sight of the empty bed.

The inquest over, members of the Sink Set gathered on the pavement outside, acknowledging each other with brief nods and handclasps, their usual effusive greetings shunned.

"Ozzie and Honey have taken Charlie home," Anna Brownlove told them. "They're trying to help her through it."

"Her children didn't come, did they?" asked Jessica Callows.

"No. She didn't want them here. They're at the house. Lizzie's not here, either."

"I thought I saw Colly," said Barns Maybury.

"Colly? Are you sure?" Jessica was incredulous.

"Jessica . . . ." said her husband, shaking his head, warning her away.

"Oh yes," said Barns. "He was on his own, near the door. That's who she was looking at. Thought you realised."

"Don't know about that," said Roger Platt-Smith. "But, yes, he was there. He's gone to tell Lizzie."

"Lizzie?" exclaimed Jessica, ignoring Keith's headshake.

"Yes. He feels he should be the one to break the news, the verdict."

"Very noble," said Jessica, the sarcasm jarring the air.

"Right!" said Keith, alarmed at the turn in the conversation, furious his wife was the cause. "I think we all need a brandy or something. There's a pub down the road."

But he had no sooner got them moving than they were joined by a seething Herbie Kirby.

"Bloody coroners!" he said, grinding out the words, stopping suddenly, blocking their way, choosing for some reason to address Jill Maybury.

"Them and their la-di-dah verdicts. Death by this, death by that . . . labelling sane people insane . . ."

"But it wasn't that, was it," said Anna Brownlove. "He got it right—Howard took his own life *while the balance of his mind was disturbed*. It's axiomatic, a catch-all."

"All right, Anna, we don't need a lecture," said Jill. "Herbie's upset, that's all."

He was still staring at her, tears clouding his eyes, looking lost, his voice choking. "He was such a good bloke," he said.

"Of course he was," Jill said, striding up to him, slipping her arm through his, grasping his hand, forcing him along with her. "Of course he was," she repeated, peering at him, smiling wanly. "Let's go and get that drink."

*During the 43-day Iraq war, commanders of the U.S-led coalition
made 30,542 requests for targets to be hit; 25,240 were approved;
19,898 were hit. Total Coalition military personnel deployed against
Iraq, 467,000. Total number of aircraft used, 1,801, 113 of them
British*—The Independent's 'A Year of War,' March 17, 2004.

Chapter 11

Fall-Out

At the age of twenty, after all that had happened in his life,
Warren Duncan Nichols had turned out to be one of those rarities,
a pragmatist with cynical judgement but some hope. The old man
in him, the shell that had grown up around his suffering, decreed,
snidely, that it was merely the hope of youth, a fire that would die
with the quickly passing years. So even on his good days, he wasn't
such a prat to think that it could last forever, that anything worthwhile
could come of it, that in the long run, he could never be more than a
sad, bitter cop-out with no legs.

Sometimes, when Angie was watching one of her soaps and
Colly had pissed off back home, always saying sorry this and sorry
that, sorry he had to go and sorry he couldn't have come sooner,
he would sit and think of the steps in his life, the childish ones like
in his book on the Great Wall of China, or one of those forts in
the Robin Hood films. Or come to that the Foreign Legion—Beau
Geste, the fort in the old black and white Beau Geste.

He could remember the ladder—climbing the builder's
ladder—and if he tried hard enough he could just about remember
running up and down stone steps—Errol Flynn dashing about like
a fucking mountain goat with the Sheriff of Nottingham trying to
stick a sword up his arse. Racing up and down with their swords, but
never falling. Never dropping like a stone.

It wasn't that kind of step he was thinking about, anyway. He
was thinking about people, the people in his life, the ones that had
been his steps. Frank was always at the top of his list because he

was the first person who'd been kind to him. He didn't know his other name. Never had. Funny little caretaker bloke at one of the homes, one when he had legs. The big kids took the piss out of Frank because he was so small. But he always had a smile and a sweet for the little kids.

One day, when Frank was locking up before going home, he found Big Smithy forcing him to do it, pushing his face into his flies, twisting his ears to make him open his mouth. Frank told Big Smithy to bugger off. And he did. But the next day, Frank was limping about the corridors with a bad leg and two broken teeth. And a week later, after a black eye, he left and Big Smithy just carried on like before.

So Frank got on the list going up, and Big Smithy and another man like him at another place, but worse, much worse, they were always on the list going down.

When he'd first met them, Thumper Dyson, Moggy Moorhouse and Mickey Dooley had all been on the list in a big way. They were his new life, Rolo's new life. But after they made him climb the ladder, they went down so far, they came off the end of the page. He didn't give them a second chance and he didn't want to think about them. Not then, anyway.

Some of the hospital lot also got on the list. But the doctors and nurses only seemed to care about him when he was a patient, and the social lot were *paid* to care. So they didn't really figure. For a time, Mr and Mrs Rowlandson figured—stepping onto the list high up with their Kit Kats but then slipping away. These days, he hardly thought about them at all.

Angie was always there, usually stepping up, but sometimes down like after catching him watching porn on the internet with his hand down his trousers, or worse than that, like when he finally realised she wasn't going to marry Colly.

When Colly started shagging the Sinclair woman, he took a step down and another one down when he snapped at me for laughing at her husband topping himself. A life of bloody Riley and the first time something goes wrong he climbs into his plane and tops himself! Just because she'd fancied a bit on the side with Colly! No big, ugly, fat bastards twisting your ears, bending you over. No sitting around in a fucking wheelchair waiting for people to do things for you! Just, oh well, what the fuck, let's end it!

"For Christ's sake, stop sniggering!" Colly had shouted. "Don't you understand? I've killed him! I might just as well have shot him, strangled him."

"Bollocks!"

"No, it's *not* bollocks! When you've been around a bit more, when you have friends, you'll understand. Do us all a favour—get a life!"

He had no fucking right to say that! And it wasn't the first time, either. He might have been a kid the first time he said it, but he wasn't one now. And he wasn't a no-hoper! He knew loads of people down at the disabled swimming and they were always asking him to the club at the Community. And Colly Shithouse knew he knew loads of people there because he met them at the clinic.

Trouble was that even now, even after Colly had opened up and started telling him stories and stuff, he still didn't know him. But he knew enough to see that he was all over the place. Turning Angie down for Charlie Sinclair, beating himself up about No-Hope Howard, leaving Little Lizzie in the lurch—what did all that say about him?

And where did it leave Angie and him?

One step up or one step down?

Still, if that's what the sad bastard wanted him to do, that's what he'd do! He'd get a life all right! He'd stick two fingers up to Mr Colly fucking Wolfson and he'd get a life!

A real life.

———————

It was with much the same blend of sympathy and poison and unexplained anger—such was their closeness, their cloying familiarity, their differing loyalties—that also now rippled through the Sink Set.

In the Callows' case, Jessica's tactless comments after the inquest led to a row that ended with Keith questioning her growing friendship with Anna Brownlove. Instead of 'friendship', he had used the word, 'intimacy,' a clumsy choice she would normally have ignored or laughed at. This time, being pulled up in front of the others still rankled.

"And what intimacy is that? Mother and child's? Husband and wife's? Or something rather different? What is it they call it between two women?"

"You've lost me."

"Then make yourself clear next time. You sound like Precious Roger in one of his amateur theatricals."

"Who? Roger Platt-Smith?"

"Who else!" she cried, happy to win the point, knowing it wasn't over.

The Platt-Smiths themselves appeared so deeply affected by the twin events that Anna Brownlove said she could have sworn that they, at last, felt the earth move—a sort of climax by proxy!

Apart from her jibes, Anna was saying nothing. Unfulfilled herself, she observed the disintegration of four of her closest cronies with a mixture of outward concern and inward gloating; Paul grateful for her silence, but knowing it stemmed from the old problem: their failure to produce children—Charlie and Colly, despite their faults, both managing the miracle but not deserving it; not if you were Anna.

At the heart of the tragedy, the Leveringtons spent their days grieving—Ozzie for two credulous men who should have known better; Honey for interfering, for pushing a footloose Colly into bed with an unhappy woman, intending it to be a game that would clear the air, lift their depression.

So the Sink Set mourned, preoccupied, anchorless, drifting through space like lost planets, failing to notice the possible birth of a new star—Jill Maybury and Herbie Kirby, the two of them gyrating far out in the universe; the one bored, the other lonely, mixing their grieving with excited dreaming, their eyes suddenly opened.

———

Colly Wolfson, standing in his rented cottage surveying the lighted windows of nearby houses, wondering if the occupants quarrelled as bitterly as he and Nico, was surprised to see a familiar Mercedes convertible sweep through the gateway. The surprise, he noted, was mixed with more than a streak of guilt and dismay.

Charlie Sinclair stepped into the little room, removing her headscarf, fluffing her hair. "Don't I get a kiss?" she asked, pouting, pretending light-heartedness.

"Of course you do."

He leaned over and kissed her on the cheek.

"Coffee?" he asked.

"If you want," clearly miffed at the peck.

She sat at the table while he busied himself, sensing her tears, his back to her like a barrier.

"Been up to much?"

"Not a lot," he answered without turning. "Busy at work. New contract. You know the sort of thing."

When he brought the coffee over, she rose and like an echo of her past, sashayed over to the empty, untidy fireplace.

"Can't you understand how I feel?" she asked, the words spilling out, bouncing off the bare white walls. "I've just had my life snatched away! I didn't hate Howard, you know, I just loved you more. And now I've lost him and I'm losing you!"

"You not losing me! What are you talking about?"—still sitting at the table, upset but controlled.

"It feels like it! It's three weeks since the funeral and I've hardly seen you."

"We've spoken. We're in touch."

"On the phone! Always on the phone!"

He sat clasping his mug, sipping the coffee, frowning at her anger, watching without comment as she crossed to the sink and dashed her drink onto the unwashed dishes, cursing himself for not realising when he started the affair, *before* he started it, that he wasn't the only manipulator; knowing now that when it came to manipulation, he'd lost hands down, Howard beating him to the tape, pinning his death on him like a loser's medal.

"Charlie, I've told you—we can't carry on as if nothing has happened. As if Howard . . . There are too many people hurt. You need to give me time. I'm not a machine."

Their eyes met and he saw the anger that he had heard down the phone these past three weeks:

—at Howard for not being angry, for not showing more fight, for not kicking her out, for not trying to win her back, for branding her;

—at herself for not seeing ahead;

—at Lizzie for blurting it all out in public;

—and at him. The anger and the pain reflecting on to him, ricocheting like unexplained bullets.

For trusting him?

For misjudging his love?

For having to face the hostile stares alone?

Or was it the fear that although they were still together, still talking, he had already retreated?

Aware of her misery, but detecting now a new tone, soft, urgent.

"I know how you hurt," she said, coming to sit with him, pushing on to his chair, her softness, her scent, alarming him; what had once so many times inflamed him and, afterwards, had smoothed and calmed him, now took on a different shade, once glowing with colour, now sombre greys and blacks, "because I hurt, too. But we can't hurt forever," declaring it like an ancient truth, "and we shouldn't take all the blame."

She took his hands and searched into him with wide, unblinking eyes, seeing his tenseness, he seeing Howard, she trying, he knew, to transfuse her passion, to mend the invisible cord.

"Who says we shouldn't? Who says *they* shouldn't?"

"Who?"

"Blair and Bush. They started something and now it's turned into something else. Like us."

"I don't want to talk about Blair and Bush! What are we talking about them for?"

"But it's true! They told us one thing, the Weapons of Mass Destruction thing. And now they're saying something different; they're turning it on its head. Like us!"

"Colly! With them it's about politics, arrogance, power and fear. With us, it's about us. You and me. Nobody else."

She leaned forward and slid her hand up his back, into his hair, running her fingers through the loose curls, her other hand pressing against his cheek, trying to turn his head.

"Silly Billy," she whispered, as if he were a child. "Look at me. Please look at me."

When he didn't respond, she moved closer, pressing her cheek against his, her tears melting into his. "Please don't send me away," she whispered. "Don't lock me out. I couldn't bear it. I need to be with you. I need to know that I'm not a monster," starting back at his sudden show of irritation, his rejection of her exaggeration.

"It's true," she said. "That's what they think!"

Sorry for her now, shaking his head, replacing her hands on his face, allowing them to move downwards, the palms flat, pressing hard, searching for the spark that had held them together.

"Let me stay . . ." whispering the words, breathing them . . . "Please let me stay."

He found himself holding her, lightly, carefully, his hands, his lips, unmoved, his mind producing a vision of Blair and Bush exchanging high fives in the shadows, but overlaid now by a second vision—Howard's charred body; the embers turning to dust, falling to the bottom of the upturned cockpit, wondering if his mind would ever let them stop falling.

"Of course you can stay," he murmured gently, sadly. "If you want, of course you can. But we can't . . . I can't . . . I'll sleep down here. I won't mind."

———

Sally Wolfson, searching for the happiness she couldn't find with her parents, was eight when she started sleep-overs at friends' houses, ten when she went on holiday for the first time with her cousins to her uncle's Spanish villa, and twelve when she fell in love with her gym mistress. She was a languid thirteen when she discovered that prolonged French kissing gave her something more to think about than sad parents; a dissolute fourteen when heavy petting proved to be even more effective; and an angry sixteen when she ended up on her back, two fingers stuck in the air at the father who had failed her.

The boy she had chosen for the honour was no one special—merely the first to answer his phone the evening her father walked out on them. Point was, he wasn't really a boy and she wasn't even sure she liked him. He was black, twenty-one, had a tattoo of the Devil on his thingy and came from some God awful council estate. But he had a Suzuki 650, took her to pubs with his mates and their bimbos and knew all about condoms and joints and poppers; doing it to her, that first time, as if he couldn't wait to get back to his bike, the stars spinning over the park bench, holding on to his leather jacket, clutching, yelling, the stretched Devil reaching her heart, driving up and up, it not minding the heart being broken, he not perceiving until later the unexplained agony.

"Yeah!" she had said, her school pals drawn by the hot, loaded whisper, "I'm with this big black guy. So what! He's cool, real cool. And I tell you—he'll do anything for a laugh. Anything!"

So she wore Leroy like a badge. He was better than smashing windows or bunking off school or stealing stuff from shops, like some of her poxy friends, the stupid cows. Or getting slaughtered on coke and pills.

Even so, with things the way they were at home, one of her parents not there and the other like as not pissed, and neither of them caring a stuff about her, she realised that her act of defiance was useless—as a way of grabbing their attention, of bringing them together, even if they were only united against *her*, the sex bit, even with somebody like Leroy, was futile. On its own, it was futile.

"I see you've reverted to the Neanderthals, darling." The speaker, her mother, was leaning against the kitchen door, her dressing gown hanging open, her hair in urgent need of the best coiffeur on the High Street, an empty glass in her hand.

"Mother, cover yourself up! What's that there, then," nodding at the glass—"your breakfast bottle, your lunchtime bottle, or an advance on your five o'clock bottle?"

"Don't be so bloody rude"—moving to the dresser, pouring another gin out of spite, demonstrating her sobriety.

"Then don't be so bloody disgusting about my friends."

As usual these days, her mother's words were uttered without heat, a sign that the real crisis lay elsewhere, that they were already well schooled in the charade that allowed them to cope as a twosome, not a threesome.

"Am I to meet this black person?"

"I shouldn't think so."

"So all I'm to see of him is his back as he carries you away from the gate on that death trap."

"Or his face as he brings me back."

"Are you in love with him?"

"I might be."

"Then your not."

"Then don't be ridiculous!"

A pause.

"He's a big boy, then?"

Their eyes locked on like missiles, Lizzie haughty, challenging, disgusted with herself for resorting to the implied crudity, yet needing to know the state of the relationship; her daughter's defiance waning, turning her away.

"I thought so," she said, tartly, her self-disgust diverted to the ring in Sally's nose, irritated again by the long-running row over her refusal to remove it. "You're behaving like a tart! Going off at all hours on the back of a motorbike with a boy you hardly know! If your father was here, he wouldn't allow it!"

"Well he's not here, is he? Haven't you noticed?"

More respectfully, she asked, "Have you told him?"

"About your sudden predilection? Not yet, no. It's a delight I have yet to inflict on him."

She laughed briefly, trying to make the sound light, uncaring, cursing Colly beneath her breath, but not yet ready to talk about him. She sipped her drink, trying to make it last, diffusing the sudden tension by asking, "Are you seeing him tonight, the boy?"

"Leroy? No, not tonight. Perhaps tomorrow."

"I thought perhaps he might be taking you to the theatre. I'd love to go to the theatre again. The lights . . . the atmosphere . . ."

"The theatre! Where've you been, mother! People like Leroy don't go to the theatre! It'd be like going to church! 'I say, Leroy, old boy, have you seen what's on at the Old Vic? Or the National? Or perhaps you fancy a touch of opera?'"—choking on her thick Afro mimicry, forcing cracked laughter into the livid air, her mother amused despite herself, glad of the chance to enjoy the moment.

"So where's he going tonight?"

"Mother! How do I know where he's going tonight? I don't have a clue! I don't give a shit!"

Lizzie sighed, wondered what she had done to deserve such a life, and moved to the breakfast bar, where she hutched herself up onto a high stool, pulling the robe around her, ready now to make an effort.

"It would be nice if we could get by without words like that," she said, mildly, gazing down the garden. "Your father used to enjoy doing his roses," she said. "It was about the only time I knew where he was."

"Oh c'mon! 'Cept when he was working, drumming up contacts, that sort of thing, he was never, rarely, out late. He always seemed to be around."

"Yes, but where did he go? He'd swan in here at five, stay for an hour, go out for three hours and come back without a word. Never a word. Sometimes, when he was late, I'd ring the office and they'd say he left an hour ago. But he still didn't turn up here until eight or nine. You know he didn't!"

"Well perhaps he went for a drink. Or to a club or the dogs!"

"The *dogs*?"

"Well, somewhere! We've been through this a million times. Why didn't you ever ask him?"

"Don't be cruel! I did ask him! You know I did! He wouldn't tell me."

"So it might have been anything. It might have been Charlie! It might have been another woman, not Charlie! Who knows! I'm sick of it! He's gone and I'm fucking sick of it!"

She ran to her room and stayed there.

Leroy got stoned that Saturday night and didn't turn up until Monday, meeting her out of school, smirking at her friends, roaring off through the traffic, the two of them transformed into Action Man and Action Woman, black helmets, shaded visors, the bike's throbbing, dangerous power like a monstrous vibrator, coursing up into them, expelling their troubles, yammering at them. They were going nowhere and everywhere, zooming around aiming for nothing, the howling, beautiful machine carrying them away.

But not, it seemed, always away from their childhood, Mr Whippy's Ninety-niners clutched by thin, young fingers as they perched on a nearby bench, their bottoms on the backrest, their feet on the seat, licking their icecreams, nibbling the chocolate. "What d'you wanna do? Go to my place?"

"No," she said.

"C'mon," he said, nuzzling her. "I've got something for you."

"Oh yeah?"

"Yeah."

"Another Ninety-niner?" sniggering, trailing her tongue into his mouth.

"Yeah, another Ninety-niner! C'mon, let's go!"

"Not yet."

"What then?" asking it as if fornication was the only possible item.

"I wanna stalk somebody."

"Stalk somebody?"

"Yeah, you know, like these nutters do."

"What for?"

"For a laugh. We'll cruise around, pick up some sad prat and stalk him, see where he goes, what he does. If he's not interesting, we'll pick somebody else . . ."

He laughed and punched her on the shoulder, making her nose dip into her cornet.

"Ain't you just the queer rich bitch!"

"Less of the rich," she said.

He went to the machine, threw her a cloth for her nose, opened the bike's panniers and pulled out a leather riding suit and a pair of boots.

"Put them on," he said.

She sat stroking the soft, black leather, looking up at him, feeling herself being drawn in.

"Where'd you get these from?"

"You don't wanna know."

Drawling it, exciting her.

"Coalition" casualties to November, 2007: U.S. 3,866, British 171, Other allies 133. Iraqi civilians killed during the 2003 invasion and the ensuing coalition operations: 76,000 minimum—*The Daily Telegraph, November 4, 2007, on the then latest official estimates by the Iraq Body Count group.*

Chapter 12

Fall-Out II

The woman in the red BMW pulled down her sun visor, reviewed the state of her make-up in the vanity mirror and waited for the lights to change. Behind her were two London double-deckers, a cab, two cars and a motorbike. Instead of sidling up to the front, the bike's two riders were acting out of character, waiting patiently in line, clearly uninterested in a quick getaway, the man's feet planted either side of the machine, the girl sitting balanced, seemingly weightless.

They had latched on to the Beamer as it emerged from the side entrance to Buckingham Palace, thinking its driver must be somebody special. They were now on the Chelsea Embankment, travelling west, Leroy Pinkerton bored out of his mind, wondering why he was bothering. It wasn't as if he and Sal were daft on each other, they were just enjoying what was on offer and, like as not, would eventually drift away, she back to her prissy middle class Englishness, he back to some girl his mother would like and say yes to. Black. Wide hips. Big arse.

As the lights turned green, he followed the woman down the King's Road, across Wandsworth Bridge, and a million boring hours later, into Richmond. Once there, he and Sal watched as she dived the BMW into the narrow driveway of a nondescript house under a plane tree. Within seconds, she was inserting her key into the front door and letting herself in, rubbing her foot against her calf as she did so.

"Home to hubby," said Leroy, lighting a fag. "Hubby, two kids, one manqué dog and athlete's foot."

"Athlete's foot! Where'd you get *that* from?"

"Because she's got an itch and she's too old to get it where you get it."

"Don't you think of *anything* but that?" She punched him in the back, once, twice, playfully.

"Yes I do! My feet up in front of the telly, you on my knee and no more of this fucking ridiculous game of yours. Three times! We've followed a no-life from Islington, once to the fish and chip shop, once to the bookies and once to the local knocking shop . . ."

"You don't know that!"

" . . . . and a queer from South Kensington to the toilet at Oxford Street Circus. Very exciting—hope he met the man of his dreams. Now where are we?—we're stuck in snooty Richmond."

He turned to receive recognition of his drollness, but without much hope. So far, she hadn't bothered to ask where he lived, assuming the worst, probably guessing right. She knew nothing about him and apparently didn't want to. He wasn't complaining; she made him laugh, she was a good fuck, and she looked good hanging round his neck when they went clubbing, his pals winking at him, eyeing her tits, watching his hands . . .

"Well, so long as we're in snooty Richmond, you can drive a few miles further and drop me off at my snooty home. But before that, I'll make a deal with you. One more stalk and if nothing comes of it, that's the end of it."

"No!"

"C'mon, Leroy! Get cool! One more stalk! We go to Kingston. I get to choose and afterwards, you get whatever you want for as long as you want."

"I get that, anyway."

But he gave in and having set him up to believe that this last choice was going to be as random as the others, she was careful not to direct him along the road where Wolfson Associates had its offices, choosing instead to park at the nearby corner, at the place where she knew her father would emerge in his Jag.

It now being May, Colly Wolfson grudgingly thanked President George Doubleyer for announcing the end of hostilities in Iraq, joined the hollow laughter that this could be so, and listened with his customary resentment as the White House and No 10 continued to chatter out their belief that Saddam's alleged Weapons of Mass Destruction would still be found.

Sickened by the unproductive violence, numbed by the propagandist repetition, he was now trying not to absorb, not to read every word on the subject . . . at least not until he felt strong enough, felt able to withstand the blaring headlines; tearing out each offending page, folding them carefully, stacking them away to be read later . . .

Lizzie and Sally—what in God's name must they think of him? Normally, he'd be able to picture it. But not when he was so numbed by Howard's death, by the thought that he'd been directly responsible . . . and not when he was so sodding confused and mortified by his impotence with Charlie . . . not that that, not being able to do it or even want to do it, should matter a jot. What mattered was the way he'd spoken to Nico. All right, the boy had been out of order, mocking him and scorning Howard. But telling Nico, of all people, to get a life was pathetic.

So he jabbed the button to silence the Iraqi war reports and concentrated on the tedious drive that he was making through south London to try to put things right.

A couple of times, cruising along the A3 and then later, after he'd turned off, he was aware of a motorbike in his mirror. Strange thing was, it was still behind him as he wiggled his way into Sydenham, but then purred by, unconcerned, as he slowed to look for a parking place. The riders had matching black helmets and leathers and they were travelling slowly enough for him to notice that the hands on the controls were not the expected white.

Any other time, he might have given more thought to it—the fluke of him and the bikers sharing more or less the same destination. But with his mind now preoccupied, rehearsing his words of peace for Nico, he failed to notice that the bike had stopped behind a furniture van a little way round the bend and that the pillion rider was crouched behind a nearby S.U.V. and was watching as he walked up a short, tiled path, let himself into the house on the corner, and closed the door behind him.

———————

"Angie! It's only me," he called.

"Hi," she called back from the kitchen. "I wasn't expecting you so early."

"No," he said, walking through, drawing himself a glass of water. "I came straight from the office. I wanted to settle things with Nico. It's been on my mind."

"Good move, bad timing. He's down at the Community Centre. Take a seat, I'll make some tea."

"Is he going to be long?"

"No telling. He'll ring if he can't get a lift back. He goes down there a lot these days. Likes the company. Says you told him to get a life, so he's got one."

She smiled sadly, not wanting to hurt his feelings. "Still, at least he listened to what you had to say."

"Perhaps," he said, resigned. "But I said it badly. I messed it up. These days, I'm pretty good at that."

"You hurt him. But you've not messed it up. He'll come round. He thinks the world of you."

He watched as she busied herself making the tea, reaching up into a cupboard for biscuits. Her movements were still lithe, still as graceful as a girl's. He'd never thought it through completely, but it came to him that he'd outlived fancying her long ago; that these days he no longer thought of her as a possible lover. She was his friend. His closest. Or, at least, the one he would always be able to trust.

For some moments, they sat munching their biscuits. She could see that he had lost weight. He looked tired and lonely and despite her disappointment at the way he had recently managed his life, she would have gladly hugged and comforted him. But he might have got the wrong idea, so she allowed him his stillness.

Reading her thoughts, knowing her that well, he said, "I'm sorry it's all turned out like this. One minute I'm the guy in charge, the next I'm nowhere."

"Sometimes, these things happen," she said, excusing him, giving him an easy way out.

"It's not as if I spent years fancying her—Charlie. I didn't. And it wasn't a whirlwind, either. It just crept up. And I let it."

"Yes, but once it was going, once you realised what was happening . . ." She was still letting him off all lightly.

"Oh once it was going, yes, we tried not to hurt anyone . . . to keep it quiet. But we didn't fool Lizzie. And poor old Howard couldn't take it. I let them down. We both did."

"Well, *we're* still here," she said, forcing the brightness. "I am and Nico is, even though it's changed him."

"I don't deserve you. Either of you. Anyhow," gathering himself, finishing off his tea, "who're these new friends of his?"

"I don't know," she said. "I drop him off down there and sometimes I fetch him back or they do it. There's quite a gang of them, boys, girls, you know the sort of thing. Some are from the swimming club and I know some of *them*. But not the new ones."

On an impulse, he asked, "I don't suppose one of 'em's a tall black bloke with a motorbike? One of those big powerful jobs?"

"Not that I know," she said. "But I shouldn't worry. Nico's hardly likely to get a ride on that, is he?"

"No, I suppose not," he said, allowing her wrong assumption. He pretended a rueful smile. "It doesn't matter. Just a thought."

They chatted on other subjects for a while, and when Nico still didn't turn up, Colly arranged to visit the next afternoon. He let himself out and walked to his car.

The motorbike was nowhere to be seen.

———

When it came to social graces, Leroy Pinkerton was one of those people who liked to run with the flow, merge with the background. It was no good being cool if you looked and sounded shit—like a naff Yank mouthing off on the Centre Court; or a Geordie rivet man at the opera; or an Afro-Caribbean mumbo-jumbo plumber at Henley. Or for that matter, anybody making sure that their regional accent gave them away at five hundred yards. Like the naff celebrities on TV, the ones that pissed him off.

Leroy's idea of an acceptable accent for himself was to be able to speak without people realising he was black. Whether he sounded south London, north London or pure East End didn't matter. Not that he was ashamed of his colour. Far from it. But it impressed the stupid Whiteys and kept them guessing.

What really *was* stupid was him wasting Saturday afternoon sitting in a lousy pub waiting around for Sally-bloody-Shaghead while she stalked the bloke with the Jag. What was so fucking wonderful about him, he had no idea. But it was the second time they'd tailed him, this time from the same business park in Kingston down to a cottage near Esher. Half-an-hour wait there and the Jag was on its way again—this time all the way to bloody Sydenham along exactly the same bloody route as before. Big deal! It wasn't even as interesting as the Oxford Circus bloke—the gay. But there he was—sitting with a tattooed moron of a porky barman, watching crap on Sky, while she fannied around outside . . . nervy, hurting like mad. But she bought their pot and she was a good screw, so it wasn't all bad. Strange kid, though.

Suddenly, she was trailing into the pub, plumping herself down beside him, announcing: "I'm like a whacked out gay with a pork pie—fagged out and fed up! I also need the loo. Be a good Afro-Caribbean," squeezing his arm, "get me half a cider and go and do the last stint. It's important to know how long he stays. You can take the bike."

She smiled tiredly while he protested, but compromised by promising to join him as soon as she had sunk her drink and agreeing to leave if their quarry had still not emerged.

Five minutes later, wearing her helmet, she walked back down the road, expecting to find Leroy concealed behind the apparently permanently parked furniture van. But for some reason, he was out in the open, sitting on the bike with the engine running. And as she walked up behind him, who should go by but her father in his Jag. She saw him turn and stare at the idiot Leroy before accelerating up the road, forced on by tooting cars.

"You fucking prat!" she shouted. "He's spotted us. Get moving!"

The bike roared off in the opposite direction, twisting away down the side streets, stopping at some lights.

"I don't know why you're so pissed off," said Leroy. "So he spotted us! So what? Mission accomplished."

"You and your crap. Mission aborted, more like."

"Not so," said Leroy, triumphantly. "I saw him come out. And I saw the black mamma with him. And I saw the ever so lovey-dovey kiss she gave him. He's like the rest of the rich geezers—he's visiting his side show."

———————

After spotting the bike, Colly's despondency deepened, in the space of a few seconds, to a point he had never imagined. It seemed there was always another layer. This one took him from a patchy mist to an impenetrable fog and he caught himself wondering which layer death was on. At the moment, he knew he still had some way to go, if for no other reason that the fog was lit by his anger, the flashes diffused as in heavy rain.

The day had begun badly. After a night spent with the bottle trying to forget Howard, trying not to think of Charlie and Lizzie and Chloe, trying to decide what to say to Nico, he'd arrived in the office late and had spent an hour trying to conceal his hangover from his staff, especially since they were giving up their week-end to hit a target date. Pathetically, they always seemed able to guess his state. So as soon as he could, he'd left for Angie's—and had found Nico quite chirpy. Too chirpy as it turned out.

"Hi, Nico. I popped in yesterday to see you, but—"

"But I was out. Angie told me."

"Yes. Right. I wanted to say—"

"You wanted to say sorry for being a heartless bastard."

"Nico! If you'll just let me—"

"Colly! I know what you're going through. But you can stick your apology. You don't need to explain."

"I'd like to."

"You don't need to. You were right! You said it wrongly, but you were right. I needed a life. And as if by magic, I've got one. All the mates I ever needed."

"Do I know them?"

"How about, 'Well done!' How about, 'I'm pleased for you.'"

"Of course I am. I just wondered—"

"They're *my* mates. You don't need to wonder. Just chill out. Relax. And stay off the booze. If your head'll let you, why not fetch a towel—I take it bath-times are still in order?"

Letting him out of the house half-an-hour later, Angie smiled at him. "I told you it'd be all right, didn't I? He doesn't bear grudges, not even against you. He's just growing up, that's all. It's taken a time, but he's growing up. He wants his independence."

"Some independence," he said, bitterly.

"As much as he can manage," she said. "It's early days."

"But where does that leave *me*?"

"It's not about *you*, Colly. It's about *him*. It's always been about him. Or should have been."

He stood on the doorstep, his arms hanging listlessly, his head bowed, reflecting on her gentle admonishment, looking up as she cupped his face in her hands and, in a rare gesture, kissed him tenderly on the lips.

"You're a good man, Colly Wolfson. Despite everything, you're a good man."

"I doubt that," he said, ungraciously, turning without another word, walking to his car, the attempted, unsuccessful balm of her farewell washed away as he saw the man on the motorbike, sitting there by the kerb, looking at him; the same bike, the same man, the same smaller figure in the background.

By the time he had managed to turn the car and go back, they had gone, and although he raced around the streets for a while, he couldn't find them. Back at his cottage, the whisky bottle out again, he sat and pondered. He had no doubt now that he was being stalked. And he had no doubt that the stalker, and possibly his accomplice, had seen Angie's kiss and would get the wrong end of the stick.

At the very least, they knew where Angie lived.

And if they knew about Angie, what about Nico?

He put the whisky down and had a long drink of water. He was going to have to go out.

Journalists from around the world killed in Iraq during the 2003 War: 30 plus; 13 of them in the early days of the fighting—official figures.

In the fighting since then, the number of journalists and media contributors killed has risen to 230, more than in the entire Vietnam War or the Algerian Civil War—Reporters Without Borders, 2012.

Chapter 13

Fall-Out III

On arrival, not having been to the Wolfson house before, Jill Maybury was looking forward to seeing the lounge or the drawing room, or whatever Lizzie called it. Instead of that, she'd had a gin and ginger pushed into her hand and had been ushered into a well-used snug cum television room. Magazines were slipping from a footstool, a box of chocolates lay open, surrounded by tinfoil wrappers, a pair of slippers had been kicked under a chair, one upside down, and the carpet needed vacuuming. But with Lizzie huffy and half sozzled, she realised that the intimate, book-lined little room was better suited to her task: the building of a closer friendship. Now, after two hours of difficult, apparently aimless chat, and with Lizzie in the kitchen making tea, she concluded that, if nothing else, her visit had at least broken the ice.

As the other reappeared, tray in hand, to excuse her long stay, she glanced at the wall clock and again begged forgiveness for inviting herself around. "I just wanted to show that there was at least one of us thinking of you," she said, innocent of her presumption.

Lizzie smiled wanly. It had been kind of Jill to come. But in truth, apart from a few opening words of sympathy, the steady intake of gin had somehow diverted her into a boring, estate agency monologue, and they had scarcely touched on her new, man-free status. Why she was bothering to serve tea she couldn't imagine.

However, a sudden mention of the Maybury offspring brought another change of tack. "All this talk about me and my boring business!" Jill exclaimed. "I've not even asked you how poor Sally is. Must be hard not seeing her father."

"Not really," said Lizzie, lying. "What with his work and so on, she didn't see a lot of him when he was here." It was a second lie, but the woman opposite had done little to make her want to share her daughter's suffering; or her own, come to that. "Not much difference really to *you* and *your* kids—you don't see them all week because they're away at school, and,"—she indicated their meeting with a wave of her hands—"you don't see them all the time at the week-end, either."

Jill flushed at the obvious put-down, but stopped short of pointing out that at least she and Barns were still together. Instead, her mind clicking on togetherness, she found herself mentioning Herbie Kirby. "Yes," she said, "Herbie wonders why we do it—send them to boarding school. He says if he had kids, he'd want them around him all the time."

To show that Herbie was of no great consequence, she laughed and veered away, probing again. "Just like Ozzie—his kids all around him, but always going on about Anna's friend, Harold what's-his-name, the one who tells the airport stories—"

"Wensum."

"Yes, Harold Wensum! Being very rude about him! Not really wanting him around at all."

"Really?"

"Yes. Seems a perfectly ordinary type to me. Makes you wonder why Ozzie's so worked up about him. Won't say much and Anna's pretty tight-lipped, too, so it *can't* be serious!"

She laughed again, this time at her own drollness, trying to draw the other into her amusement that Anna Brownlove could be tight-lipped about anything. "All she'll say is that it goes all the way back."

Lizzie nodded wistfully. In the times when she and Colly had been at peace, they would sit around after a party or a dinner recalling the high spots, dissecting the conversations. She remembered him once telling her how Harold Wensum had been taken in by Ozzie and his friend, Hector Grammaticus, to help with the rent when they were students in Edinburgh, and how, according to Ozzie, there had been a rapid falling out, a real shouting match, Hector telling Harold he was disgusting, sneering at some rumour or other, something to do with Harold's apparent inability to make it with girls of his own age. Not that that should have worried Hector, she thought. But Ozzie had apparently muttered something about how, soon afterwards, they or someone else, had seen Harold in a children's playground. So, since they didn't get on anyhow, they'd asked him to leave.

She remembered Colly being quite intrigued by the story. "There's surely more to it," he'd said, "otherwise Ozzie wouldn't allow the bloke to hang around, even if he is only on the edge of us." But the inquisitive Jill Maybury didn't need to know any of that, at least not from her.

"Yes, I suppose Anna's right," she said. "Best not to ask. You know what these men are like."

Outmanoeuvred, Jill reverted to an earlier theme, suddenly realising that despite the passing time, there had been no sign of the Wolfson girl.

Is Sally *in*?" she asked.

"I'm not sure," said Lizzie, managing a tired smile, suppressing her screams of boredom, praying for an intervention—anything to end the other's tedious, empty presence.

As if on cue, the doorbell sang its cheerful chimes, interfering with her own mood.

"Perhaps that's Sally now," said Jill.

But it wasn't. It was Colly, standing in the porch, looking at the garden, swinging round as he heard Lizzie open the door. He appeared angry and tired, the lines on his face accentuated since she'd last seen him.

"I'm sorry I didn't ring you," he said, moving forward as he might have done when they were together, but stopping suddenly. "There's something we really need to get straight." Looking around, agitated, asking, "Whose car is that?"

"Not that it needs to concern you," she said, the gin mellowing her voice. "It's Jill. Here to cheer me up. She's been leaving for the last hour."

He caught her eye and they smiled, briefly, warily. "Come in.," she said. He waited in the hall while she went through to the snug to announce his arrival, remaining standing, clearly not intending to retake her seat. Jill took the hint and gathered her things without a word.

"Hello, Colly," she said, guardedly, kissing him on the cheek, accepting one back. He was looking dreadful. "You're looking well."

"You, too, Jill. How's Barns?"

"O.K."

"And Herbie?"

"Herbie?"

"Yes. Round at Charlie's the other day, she said you'd been round there chatting about Herbie. Saying what a different sort of person he is once you get to know him."

The two women glanced at each other, Lizzie sharply. There had been no mention of such a visit during two hours of conversation.

"I was just trying to keep in touch, Lizzie," Jill explained, hurriedly. "Trying to . . ." She'd been about to say, "rescue things," but bit the words off. "Nobody seems to go there any more. To Charlie's." With no reply from either of them, she added, "I'll leave you two together. I'm sure you have a lot to talk about. Perhaps we can do this again, Lizzie . . ."

"Yes, perhaps . . ." Non-committal, empty.

Lizzie waited by the door until the other's car disappeared, then turned to remonstrate with Colly. He was standing at the back, under the stairs. "Do you have to be so bloody tactless? Mentioning your tart in this house is bad enough! But embarrassing that poor woman like that is pathetic! She's stumbling around like the rest of us. She didn't deserve that."

"Sorry."

"No, you're not," she said. "You wouldn't know what the word means. Never have."

"If you wish. But Charlie's no tart."

"Some would say so."

"Some might. But, if you please, not you to me."

She shrugged and he followed her into the lounge and sat on one of the settees, hands behind his head, his tiredness and the booze invading him, not knowing that she had the power to lessen his suffering, that there was another reason for Howard's death, one at least as persuasive as the break-up of his marriage.

Not knowing this, so also not knowing that Lizzie wished she had told them, Colly and Charlie, straight away; that every passing day made it harder for her to say, "For God's sake lighten up! Stop the boring castigation, the ritual chastisement! You're off the hook! He had cancer!" when she knew that, now, weeks on, doing that would make her look heartless and vindictive, and that just as Howard had obviously planned, it wouldn't let them off the hook in any case. Not totally.

"Anyhow, never mind all that," she said. "Do pray tell why the sudden visit?"

He hated it when she acted all cocky and stagy, a manner she resorted to when she was hurt but wished to appear hard. He brought his hands forward and slowly massaged his face, watching her through his fingers, her offhand pretence bruising his conscience.

"I want to know something," he said, equably. "Are you having me followed?"

"I don't understand. How d'you mean?"

"It's quite simple! I mean, 'Are you having me followed?' You don't need to, you know. I'll admit the lot. It's just that I thought you might have told me you'd gone to the lawyers already, that's all."

"Colly! As far as I'm concerned, nobody is following anybody! And I haven't gone to the lawyers! Not to gather evidence, anyhow. You're getting paranoid."

"Rubbish!" he said. "Somebody *is* following me around. And I can't think of anybody with a better reason than you."

"Well, rest assured, it's not me. Not yet, anyhow. Perhaps it's your office making sure you've not lost your marbles . . . or perhaps it's your lady friend checking on whether you've got anybody else in tow."

The arrow, intended as nothing more than a random insult, hit its mark without her realising. He stared at her, wondering how much she knew. Surely nobody knew about Chloe? He jumped to his feet.

"Stop sodding about, Lizzie," he said roughly, covering his alarm. "I'm serious. Somebody is following me and it's got me nervy."

"So I see," she said, dryly. "But you don't know who it is, and now you've got my denial, you don't know why they're doing it."

"It's a bloke on a motorbike. Him and a sidekick. Smaller. I don't know whether the smaller one's a man or a woman. They're always covered up with helmets and leathers."

"So you don't know the first thing about them?"

"No, I don't! I'd tell you if I knew! All I know is that they ride around on a bloody great powerful motorbike! One of them's small and the other's tall and black."

"Black?"

"Yes. I saw his hands."

"Well, I can't help you, Colly," rising to mask the concern on her face, suspecting that she might *very well* be able to help him, wanting now to get rid of him before Sally got back, before he saw her saying goodbye to a tall black man on a powerful motorbike . . .

"Have you tried ringing the police?"

"Of course not! Not yet, anyhow! After Howard, we don't want another story in the papers, do we?"

"We certainly don't," she mimicked, parodying him, though thankful that the. police weren't involved. "I don't know what to say. You'll have to sort it out yourself. But it's nothing to do with me."

She held the door open for him and he stood on the step for a moment.

"I'm sorry, Lizzie. I should have rung. I didn't mean for any of this, the break-up, to happen. You know that, don't you?"

"But it has," she said, looking anxiously at the gate, more worried for the moment about this possible new complication involving their daughter than with her own predicament.

"Yes, it has. Please tell Sally I miss her and that I'd love her to come and see me or meet me somewhere. Will you do that?"

"Sally will see you when she's ready and I'll not stop her. Goodbye, Colly."

She closed the door before he had time to reply, her palms flattening against the oak, her nails seeking to dig in as if she were on a rock-face, steadying herself, holding on, checking from the hall window to make sure Sally was nowhere in sight, watching her husband's car nose out into the road.

———

Despite the official end of hostilities, large-scale bomb attacks continued unabated against the nationals and allies of the United States: among them, in May, 2003, in Riyadh, 34 people were killed; 41 in Casablanca the same month; 13 in Jakarta in the month of August. In November, 2003, gun and bomb attacks claimed a further 17 victims in Riyadh; 23 in Istanbul; and 27 at the British Consulate and HSBC bank offices, also in Istanbul—Press reports.

Chapter 14

Revelations I

Sunday morning.

Out early.

Damp. Fresh.

Muddy river roads, chunky tyre tracks, white trainers, limbs taut, lungs laboured, breasts trickling sweat, patching her top.

Turning away, swinging to where she lived, dwarfed by odorous oaks, their veined trunks thick and stiff, saying hello to the man who lived opposite, the man in her dream castle, entering her world, taking her, not asking, just sliding in, fired by her submission, taking her, knowing she was waiting, the heat billowing through her, the furnace floating her away, her body with the man, her mind hovering above, wondering where Colly was, what he was doing, what he was thinking. Missing him. The man drifting in, drifting out, walking off now with his dog, unknowing as he always would be.

The hiss of the shower, the steaming scents of the suds, the bubbling rivulets, the tingling potent crevices; the man with her again, as blatant, as reeking as the oaks, crowding her, coaxing her, dizzying her—but the image elusive, fading, banished into the mists by the cold requirements of the day ahead.

Annoyed with herself at such nonsense, she towelled down briskly, sprayed herself with the perfume that she knew Sally liked, and dressed and made up carefully but casually. On this morning, there must be no sign of the boozy, errant mother.

By the time she went downstairs again, it was nine o'clock, which meant she would have plenty of time to assemble her thoughts before her daughter's usual late Sunday emergence.

Of the previous day's two visitors, the most revealing and the one carrying the most important messages, was Colly. But Jill Maybury, silly woman, had also been enlightening. From what she had to say, it appeared that the Set was shunning Charlie. Which was gratifying, but not necessarily accurate. She couldn't believe that everyone had cut her off—Honey Leverington, for one, was still bound to be close to her. What was clear was that Jill herself was lonely; that she and Barns weren't exactly on fire. Otherwise, why the guilty mention of Herbie Kirby? Why try to cover it up?

She smiled at the thought of jerky, corny little Herbie trying to make love to the tall, stylish Jill, clambering in among the beautiful, gym-honed limbs, fastening to her like a love-sick beach crab. It occurred to her that Barns wasn't all that tall, himself. Still, whatever her preferences, it seemed that Jill wanted to be friendly. Perhaps it had just been a bad day for her.

Colly, on the other hand, had been totally typical—his usual mix of urbane charm, amused spite and immature temper. Whether his regret over their break-up was sincere, whether it made any difference, was something she'd have to think about. It seemed to show a wish for appeasement, if not reunion. At this stage, she wasn't sure she wanted either.

Rather than that, the crucial question at the moment was the new, urgent one: the man on the motorbike, the black man in black leathers, and the smaller person with him. She might be wrong, she hoped she was, but the coincidence was too great. It *had* to be Sally and her idiot boyfriend. What he thought he was doing, God only knew! But it had to be Sally acting out her grief. And she had to get her talking about it without it all turning into yet another dreadful row.

Hearing movements upstairs, she waited a few moments then went up and stood outside the bathroom door. "Sally," she called, "I don't know whether you've anything on today, but if you're going out, I'd like a few minutes with you first, dear. That O.K.?"

There was a mumbled groan from the other side of the door. Satisfied, she went downstairs and started preparing toast and coffee, emptying the dishwasher, tidying things away, fluffing her hair in the hall mirror, smoothing her lips, still nervous about her opening tack.

The girl appeared in the kitchen like a wraith, fluffy grey slippers gliding across the tiles, a robe of heavy grey silk down to her ankles, its hood pulled up around her head, framing her face.

"Won't you be rather warm in that, dear?" The words, innocuous at any other time, slipped from her, involuntarily, dismaying her.

"What was it?"

"Sorry, I didn't meant to . . ."

"Never mind that. What did you want to see me about?"

"Have some toast and coffee."

"Yes, I'll have some. What do you want to see me about?"

"I just want to see you, talk to you."

"What about? It's not like you to be up and dressed. Not these days. Are you taking me out or something?"

"We could go out to lunch, if you want. Just the two of us. That would be nice."

The girl poured herself some coffee, no sugar, no milk. It was a taste she'd learned from Leroy.

"But that's not what you want to talk to me about, is it?"

"It could be," her mother said.

"But it isn't."

"No."

They fell silent, Sally for once waiting patiently, sensing that whatever it was, it was serious.

"Your father, he was around here yesterday." Saying it as quietly and gently as possible.

"Dad? Round here?" Appraising her mother's smartness, her hair, her lipstick. But getting it wrong. "Did he stay? Have you two made up?"

"No, no. Nothing like that. Sorry! I didn't mean to . . . He stayed for just a short time, a few minutes. He came to ask me something."

"What?"

"Two things, really. First," she lied, "he came to ask if you'd see him, if you'd let him take you out."

"What for?"

"He misses you. He's concerned. We both are."

"You're concerned about yourselves. Always have been. I don't exist."

Lizzie stared into her coffee, trying to make out her reflection. Failing. The girl was right. It was shameful, but in some twisted way, from the night she was conceived, she had not existed. They both loved her, always had. But, somehow, they'd never got past thinking of her as anything more than a replacement, a visitor, a being who had materialised and would soon drift away with hardly a wave. It was a terrible vision and she could find no words to reply.

But the girl was not about to withdraw the dagger.

"My dear unknown, pathetic brother," she murmured, bitterly. "If only you'd lived . . ." the thought one that Lizzie recognised, that had persisted through the years. A rarely spoken, but ever-present family incantation.

"Well, he didn't. And he wasn't pathetic. He was a perfectly normal, beautiful baby boy who died in his cot. It happens! But your father could never accept it."

Why did it always come down to this? Why couldn't her baby lie in peace? She rose, binned her toast and threw what remained of her coffee down the sink. There were times when she could gladly strike her daughter. Not once. Again and again. Like she would an intruder—

"For God's sake, don't let's go into all that," Sally cried, regretting her earlier words but not prepared to show it. "So what's the second thing? What's so important? Don't I get to know?"

"Yes, you do! But can you stop being cruel? Can you stop believing you're the only one who hurts?" With the girl silent, she plunged on. There seemed little point now in gentle kindness, even if she felt it.

"You can tell me why you and your boyfriend are following your father around."

"Who says we are?"

"I do."

"What do *you* know? You haven't seen us."

"No, but your father has. He hasn't twigged it's you because he doesn't know about your black boyfriend. He thinks—"

"Leroy."

"He thinks Leroy is my private eye gathering divorce evidence. But it's not. It's the two of you stalking your father. If you're not careful, he'll go to the police."

"You haven't told him, then?"

"No. Of course not. Though I wonder why I bother."

The crisis over for the moment, she poured herself more coffee.

"When I was your age," she went on, sitting down, trying to smile, "I ran away for two whole days. With a girlfriend, true, but ran away. We didn't get up to much. Bought some cigarettes and some cider and shared them with some boys in a park. Spent the night necking. They were nice boys and I'd like to think Leroy is a nice young man—"

"You'd be wrong—he's an evil prat!"

"Then why are you giving yourself to him? Why are you defiling your body with rings and for all I know doing drugs and God knows what? To get back at me? To get back at your father?"

"Top marks! Ten out of ten!" The heavy sarcasm disfiguring the girl, lacerating her mother.

"But why follow him?"

Sally's head remained bowed, her eyes peering up from beneath the hood. Before her, across the table, was a woman in her forties. She was decent and gentle and kind and caring. And she'd been there all her life, mostly in the shadows, giving herself, but never, it seemed, giving all of herself, sitting there with her hands on the table, her flaky red nails, her lovely face, her life crumbling around her, knowing, surely, that it was happening because of herself, because of her weakness; that had she been stronger, she could have stopped it, withstood her father, helped him wipe out the picture of their poor, pathetic child lying dead in his cot.

She was so sick and tired of the deadness that she felt dead herself. Weary and dead. Weary of never coming first, of knowing always that if they were to be a happy family, it was she who had to be happy, who had to laugh and urge them on, desperate to see them smiling, not at her, at each other, to see them together, happy, not with her, with each other, to see the two of them sharing the joy of the moment, recognising her love for them, putting her first, forgetting the baby.

It must have happened sometimes. Surely it must. But she couldn't remember.

So she sat there peering at her mother, seeing the sadness, realising she was already close to defeat, deciding that the part of her that wanted to pay her mother back, destroy her, was the part that had to overcome, that as always, she would try again—she would try to get her mother to make her No. 1.

She would always do this and she would never tell her the truth; she would never tell her what Leroy had discovered about her father.

"I wasn't trying to get back at you," she said, "I was trying to help you. For years . . . two . . . three, all I've heard is, 'Where's your father? I never know where he goes, what he does.'" I used to think, 'What is she banging on about? So he goes out. So what?' But when you, when the two of you split, I thought you might be right, that he had a secret. And that it wasn't just Charlie, couldn't be."

"And that's why you followed him?"

"Yes."

"And did you find his secret?"

"I don't know," she lied. "Sometimes," the lies coming easier now, "he'd just drive around. Sometimes he'd go to a pub or go for a walk on the Common. There didn't seem to be a pattern. Perhaps that was his secret."

"What was?"

"Perhaps he was just lonely and he didn't know how to tell us."

"I don't think so!"

"Perhaps we weren't listening."

"Perhaps one day, he'll tell us."

"No," said her daughter firmly. "It was his deep-down secret. He'll never tell us."

"Like Leroy is yours?"

"Maybe."

"And is he evil?" Knowing the answer, praying that she was right.

"No. He's sweet. He's a prat, but he's sweet."

They looked at each other and smiled. There was a new understanding.

But only one of them knew the truth.

"So whenna we gonna trail da geezer wiv da Jagwar again?" It was Leroy messing about, pretending to be something he wasn't, happy to have the run of the flat while his family was away.

They'd already done it in front of the telly and were now lying in his bed, coupled again but blasé, the passion not yet ruling him.

"What fink you are?" she countered. "A fuckin' rapper?"

"No, baby, no. But no need to swear."

She pouted. Leroy in his holy mood was worse than R.I. To get her own back, she began to move rhythmically. He smiled and pressed her down, stopping her.

"Well, are we?"

"Are we what?"

"Going to trail the Jaguar geezer?"

"No. He's just one of life's casualties. Sad, ordinary."

"Bollocks!"

"Who's swearing now?" she asked, and again began moving her pelvis, this time provoking a response, but jolting to a halt when her mobile rang.

"It's yours," he said. "Aren't you going to answer it?"

"What! Now?"

He reached across to the bedside table and plucked the phone from her bag.

"Here you are."

"Get off me then!"

"No need. Billy and Gayle do the mobile thing all the time. Say it's real cool."

She lay unsmiling, trying to sum him up, watching his eyes motioning her to become another Gayle.

"It's my mother."

The eyes widened in mocking delight. Not to be outdone, she pressed the button.

"Hello, mother," closing her eyes as the tensed black buttocks slowly began their dance.

"Hello dear. Look, I'm only thinking of the food, you know, what to cook. I couldn't remember whether you said you'd be home tonight."

"No. I'm at Sandra's. I'll probably stay over. That O.K.?"

"Yes, dear. Are you all right, dear? You sound strained."

"No, I'm fine. Must go. Somebody's coming!"

Joining in the final convulsion, collapsing in a heap, laughing their heads off.

Her mother! Her poor, bloody innocent mother!

Thinking about it, she was staggered that she'd not gone through with the humiliation bit, telling her mother about her father's black honey bun; waiting for years to humiliate her, but when the chance came, bottling it, going soft. What amazed her, excited her, was that the silly cow had not thrown a fit when her father called round, had obviously not started screaming and chucking things. And the fact that he'd been able to call at the house suggested that he wasn't exactly consumed by hatred, either.

She knew she was on dangerous ground; that all the ifs and buts didn't necessarily add up. But two bickering parents under one roof were better than one sad one, especially if they could learn to get on. The first thing was to get rid of Charlie Sinclair and the black lover—who knows, she thought, perhaps both in one go!

Relying on Leroy's faulty conclusion about Colly and Angie, bypassing the unknown, intricate twists and turns of adult emotions, she began work on the second part of her plan, spinning it into shape, this time not involving her boy-friend.

For what she had in mind, like her mother, he was altogether too decent.

"When you make an enemy of the United States, you'd better watch out. Sooner or later, we will get you"—Paul Bremner, U.S. Administrator of Iraq, July 2003.

Chapter 15

Revelations II

"Strange, isn't it? How people change?"

The muse was Honey Leverington. They were sitting in Charlie's summerhouse by the rose garden, drinking Pimms, Honey's bare legs propped up on a cane table.

"Well, not you," said Charlie. She had rung Honey and Ozzie a couple of days before, imploring them to come round, desperate to start picking up the pieces. Not realising that the pieces were about to shatter into even smaller pieces, that in the post before they arrived was a bombshell, an allegation that Colly had a second lover. No warning and no proof. But humiliating enough not to be able to tell even such close friends as the Leveringtons.

All she wanted now was to be alone to decide what to do. Consequently, she rebuffed Honey's obvious effort to draw her out, attempting, instead, to keep the conversation light—and hopefully short.

"Certainly not you," she emphasised. "For instance—your legs! I've never seen you in stockings in all the years I've known you. Woolly socks, perhaps. Stockings, no."

"Like knickers, it saves having to take them off—such a fag!" quipped Ozzie, sitting opposite, sniggering at Charlie, sensing her mood.

"If you've quite finished, Ozzie," Honey said, archly. "As you very well know, I don't wear stockings because I find them irrelevant. I do wear knickers—sometimes," she added, laughing in memory of rutty bygones, trading playful blows with her husband.

Any other time, she would have included Charlie in her mock ticking off, but stopped short, fearing that to do so might not be

125

entirely proper with a woman who had recently lost her husband and was now in difficulty with her lover. For the same reason, she broke off the spontaneous horseplay with Ozzie. The way forward, she decided, was to be philosophical, not emotional.

Ozzie took the hint. "All right, all right!" he exclaimed. "How strange, she says, that people change," working himself in, entering the discussion against his better judgement. "What people? And why strange?"

When Howard had died and Honey had broken down and confessed her involvement, he had been horrified, directing his feelings not so much at Charlie as at his wife. Swapping partners was one thing, a custom that Heraclitus would surely have approved. But in this case, helping Charlie with her love life had meant being disloyal to Howard, a deed to which he had objected strenuously. Now, here was Honey muddying the waters again . . .

"Well," she responded, dismayed that she was centre stage, not Charlie as she had intended, "here's poor Charlie being blamed, wouldn't you say, for a tragic consequence out of her control?"

"It's happened down the ages," said Ozzie, tritely.

"True. But that doesn't make it right. It doesn't justify it. It merely means that people still refuse to see beyond the end of their noses."

"I ask again: what people?" Ozzie understood his wife's tactics, but was growing increasingly uncomfortable. Like her, he wished it were Charlie doing the talking. But to stop now might be worse than continuing.

"Noses have a habit of growing," he added. "The more difficult the situation, the longer the nose."

The contrived bantering suddenly had the effect they sought.

"Will you two, for God's sake, stop tip-toeing around? It's bad enough half the gang ignoring me without being wrapped in cotton wool by you two!"

"I'm sorry," said Honey. "It's just I think it so unfair."

"Honey, I didn't expect to be exposed as the scarlet woman, not at least quite so soon, and I didn't expect my husband to up and kill himself. But you can't conjoin with the male half of everybody's favourite couple without realising that if things go wrong, you're going to be tarred and feathered."

Ozzie, hearing the ice breaking and sensing that his presence would be a hindrance, murmured a few disconnected words, placatory, apologetic, asked to be excused and slipped into the garden without waiting for an answer.

"And how *is* the male half?" Honey asked, quietly, watching Ozzie disappear behind a pergola. "Is he being more supportive?"

"Supportive? I don't think he knows the word!"

"You know what I mean . . ."

"I know what you mean! But I doubt that an impotent lover could be supportive, even if he wished it."

She swung round and gazed into her friend's troubled face.

"He says it's the shock of it. After Howard's death . . . the guilt of it . . . . He can't . . . . Whether it's just me, I don't know."

"What do you mean, 'Just you?' I thought you were an item?"

"So did I. And for all I know, we may still be. I shall know tomorrow. But not a word. Not to anyone."

Charlie's eyes were suddenly glassy with tears, but before Honey could respond, she had jumped to her feet and was holding out her hand.

"C'mon," she said, "Let's go and find Ozzie. We'll have one very large, very stiff drink, and then I shall have to ask you to leave—things to do."

Through the post had come a plain brown A4 envelope. In hand-written, scraggly block capitals, some sloping backwards, some forwards, it was addressed to 'Mrs C. Sinclair,' and marked 'Personal.' It had seemed one of those tiresome advertising con jobs. But inside, instead of the usual, eminently forgettable printed offer, was a sheet of paper containing a jumble of variously sized letters. They had clearly been cut from the headlines of several different newspapers and had been glued down to make a message. It was unsigned, but was both flowery and succinct:

"CoLumbUs sAils tHe SeAs with a TaRt like you in EveRy port. HaS dOne foR yEArs. IF yOu Don't BelieVe, heave-Ho to . . ."

127

She had screwed the sheet into a ball, squeezing it hard, as if to kill it, to wring the poison from it, her anger giving way to dismay and panic, her feet slipping into the chasm, seeing beneath her the broken plane, Colly straddling her husband's smoking embers, looking up at her, winking slyly.

She remembered staring at the morning chat show, the bleeding hearts betrayed, as usual, by enduring shallowness; the studied, irrelevant clothes of the morning bimbos; hearing but not listening to their clucking concern over the latest twist in the Iraq scandal: a cooked Government dossier on WMD, a BBC reporter, a troubled Government scientist, a furious No 10 spin merchant . . .

Caught amid her own tragedy, she had chanced on the story only here and there and although she scarcely knew what they were talking about, the tightly clasped ball of paper suddenly seemed her passport to a secret, shadowy world of her own.

As with Iraq, her life seemed out of control: she'd taken her husband's friend as a lover, her husband had killed himself in despair, if not retaliation, and her friends, or some of them, were shunning her. Now, she was being told that she had made a poor choice: her lover was busy elsewhere.

Inevitable questions plunged through her like stabs of ice. Where? With whom? Surely, Colly would not do this to her? Surely, he was too decent? Too needful?

But then the drips: his recent claim of impotence, his lack of tenderness, his obsession with guilt, a picture, emerging from nowhere of his car frequently turning in the wrong direction when he slipped from her bed. Going right instead of left. Left to his home. Right to where? Another lover?

As for who had sent the note, Lizzie, the wronged wife, was clearly top of the list. But would she stoop so low? Would she throw away all memory of their lovely, former friendship? Surely not. Surely it had to be a jealous crank?

After the Leverington's departure, trying to rationalise, trying to calm her nerves, to stop the questions drilling their way into her, she concluded that there were only two real alternatives. She could place her faith in Colly and throw the message away. Or she could do what it suggested.

Her doubting fingers carefully unscrewed the ball of poison and read the address of Colly's alleged dawdling. It was somewhere in south London and meant nothing to her.

Over breakfast, she studied her A to Z road map, her hair gathered up into an anonymous bun, her clothes likewise: a navy blue shirt that had seen better days, and a pair of faded jeans and tatty trainers that she used in the garden. For transport, she chose the Range Rover that Howard had used to pull his boats. It was a little big, but she'd feel secure in it, and if she were sitting around for a long time, she'd be able to stretch out.

Perhaps because it was a rainy Sunday, her journey traffic-wise was not as tedious as she had expected. She went the long way—all the way up the A3, anti-clockwise round the South Circular, turning right down into Sydenham. The side roads had proved a problem, but only because she was a stranger to the area. If Colly used a more direct route, he would do it much faster.

The only distinguishing feature of the house now diagonally opposite her was a large, single-storey addition built within the V formed by the road she was parked in and another, lesser road running in from the rear. If Colly chose the back door, she would miss him; there was nothing she could do but hope.

In an effort to make herself less conspicuous, she had scrambled into the back of the Range Rover and had pulled the rear blinds down. She was now sitting in the corner by the pavement, keeping watch on the house through the driver's window.

Nothing but the banal happened: three dog owners, one of them dragged along by an Alsatian; two black women with large white shopping bags; four down-at-heel youths, scurrying quickly, heads down, talking excitedly about football; a little girl on a pink bicycle, a man calling, "Stay on the pavement, Emily. Stay on the pavement," the child pedalling to the point of the V, waiting for the man to catch up, then turning, going down the other side, ten minutes later, reappearing, chanting, "C'mon Granddad! C'mon Granddad!"

This and similar—but no-one going to the house, not even junk mail zombies; and after two, perhaps three hours, nothing to take her mind off a throbbing headache, a legacy, she presumed, of too much vodka, too much stress. She had aspirins but nothing to wash them down. Getting out of the car was to risk being seen, but she also needed to stretch her legs and go to the loo, so she hurried the few yards to a pub on the same side of the road beyond the V. It was dark inside but not so dark as to hide her wrinkled nose from a podgy barman polishing glasses.

"Yes, darling?" Stuck up bitch.

"Could I have some water or some Coca Cola, please?" she asked, stiffly. "I have a headache coming on." Fascinated, revolted, she saw that beneath a green string vest, his flesh was covered in blue and red tattoos: two dragons, their tails linked around his neck, their bodies travelling down his chest and belly, their snouts disappearing beneath his jeans into God knows what.

"Which do you want first?" Dressing down, but posh and stuck up.

"I don't want both!"

He watched her trying to read the slogan on his right shoulder.

"Water," she said.

"What kind?"

"I don't mind—Evian, whatever . . ." She saw now that there was another slogan on his left shoulder.

"Not the *brand*. Still or fizzy?" Stupid cow!

"Oh I see! Sorry! Fizzy. No, still!" Watching him pour it, remembering that she'd left the aspirins in the car. Ye Gods! What was wrong with her? What was she *doing* in this stinking pub, anyhow? If only Howard . . . If only she'd not . . .

She managed to get some money out of her purse and while the man was counting out her change—staring at his hands, trying not to imagine what the dragons were getting up to below his belt—she asked, blurting it like a nervous child, "Do you know who lives in that house down there at the V, the one with the extension?"

"Don't know nothin,' lady. Don't live round here."

"I see," she said, trying to keep the distaste from her face. If he wanted to make himself look hideous, it was none of her business. Lots of people did.

"You a friend of the black bloke, then?" Back polishing his glasses.

"What black bloke?"

"The black bloke wot was in 'ere. 'E was drinkin' lemonade, pretendin' it was gin. I know all the tricks. '*E* was lookin' at that 'ouse. I saw 'im. They were bikers." Why was he telling the silly cow all this crap?

"Who were?"

"The black bloke. 'Im an' 'is girlfriend. They were bikers."

"Perhaps they were thinking of buying it," she said primly.

He guffawed at her silliness, his black and red hands convulsing, snapping the stem of a wine glass, cutting a finger.

"Fuck it!" Yelling the curse at the glass, as if it was it, not he, that was at fault, throwing it violently into a bin, bending forward over the bar, clasping his bleeding finger, squeezing it, the slogans on his shoulders now plain to see: "For God and Country."

"Dearie me!" she said, swivelling on her heel, walking quickly from the pub, laughing unbelievably at herself as she hurried back to the Range Rover. Dearie me? Where did she get that one? And who was she to dearie anybody?—the proud possessor of a dead husband and a wilting lover. She couldn't even order a drink! Couldn't even remember to take the aspirins into the pub! And now she'd walked out without touching her glass or going to the loo! Priceless!

All she wanted was to get back home. She wriggled away the message from her bladder, switched on the engine and was busy gunning herself out of the parking place, still cursing herself, when she saw a familiar figure walking up the garden path to the house. Colly! Carrying a bunch of flowers!

She watched as he inserted a key into the latch and opened the door, stepping back as it was suddenly pulled wide by someone within. She could see quite clearly that, of all people, it was Angie Maketi! She was looking at Colly, shaking her head fondly, admonishing him with a smile as people do when making up after a row, allowing him to kiss her on the cheek, accepting the flowers, standing up close to him, drawing him into her home . . .

"In Iraq, a dark and painful period is over."—President Bush, December 2003, on the arrest of President Saddam Hussein.

Chapter 16

Revelations III

Another dream.

This time, a blue and white dot in the sky, Howard's voice travelling through the ether, terse, detached, calling ground control, apologising, retracting.

"Charlie Alpha, Charlie Alpha. So, so sorry—no I'm not, no I'm not.

"Charlie Alpha, Charlie Alpha. So, so sorry—no I'm not, no I'm not."

The same silly words again and again and again, scrambling her mind, bobbing her about in one of his boats, water slopping over the side, wetting her belly, trickling across the guilty, exciting, impervious stains, rubbing at them with long-nailed fingers, her burning, betraying innards churning like before, like when she was with him, *him*, not Howard, her face raised to the heavens, sea-sick vomit dribbling from smudged lips, searching for him, screaming, "Sorry or not? Sorry or not? Which *are* you? Which *are* you?"

But her voice strangled by the waves and by the Sink Set, each of them wearing Colly's face, trudging round and round her, their feet sloshing through the spray, the women pretending to be dumb, pointing their fingers at Howard, the men naked, a squawking parrot perched crazily on each tortured penis.

"Pretty boy Colly! Pretty boy Colly! Pretty boy Colly!"

And suddenly everybody looking at the shore, at a black Lizzie racing over the rocks, keeping pace with the boat, her body covered in dragons, their snouts gobbling lewdly, her arms waving frantically, her yells bouncing from the surf. "Some friend *you* were! Some friend *you* were!"

All of it jumbled, simultaneous, so that the words scrambled into an insane black and white alphabet, the letters higgledy-piggledy, refusing to stick down, all of them swarming after her, chasing her to the cottage, to the veranda, snickering at her still moist knickers hanging from a chair; their cottage on the outside, a salt-stained corrugated iron shithouse on the inside, the letters pinging from the reeking, wavy walls; her hands—*his* hands?—scrabbling to get her skirts up, gasping, pissing her life away, the whole of Sydenham laughing at her.

It was the putrid, sickening, numbing nightmare, as much as anything, that made up her mind. Until then, she'd been ready to tough it out, to wait for Colly to recover himself and carry her off. But here he was, deceiving her with Angie just as he had deceived Lizzie. With Angie and with her. She loved him. But now that Angie was on the scene, the agony was unbearable. She couldn't eat, she couldn't sleep. She needed help to stop the dreams, to smooth her guilt.

Upset, incoherent, it seemed to her that the only person able to do this was Lizzie. It was obvious that she was the author of the note—who else? And if she *were,* then quite clearly she was aware of Colly and Angie and must be suffering herself—doubly so. If she and Lizzie could get together, they might be able to pool their misery, might find some way forward.

At the very least, she might discover what Lizzie intended to do about Colly.

Lizzie Wolfson's first reaction on receiving Charlie's note was even more violent than the sender's had been a week or so before over the hate mail—she tore it to shreds, screwed them into a ball and threw it from her, angered further at the sight of it coming apart, the bits scattering across the carpet like dying petals.

For several minutes, she stood leaning against the patio doors, arms crossed, chest heaving, gazing unseeing down the garden, moving to the lounge, pouring a drink. Not gin, it was too early, sherry, slugging the first, sipping the second, mulling things over, ready now to consider Charlie's plea for forgiveness, her recognition that they could never again be friends, her suggestion that they meet to smooth things out. The first she labelled pathetic, the second banal and the third insolent.

But a fourth point intrigued her, something about not being able to bear it alone any more, '*not now I know about Colly.*'

So what more was there to know? He was charming on the outside and self-lacerating on the inside; he was a brilliant architect and businessman whose wealth and prizes were for nothing; he was a loner, a withdrawn father, a never-there husband, an adulterer. Everybody close to him knew all that. And still loved him. So what more could there be? How worse could it get?

She dialled a number and heard a familiar voice.

"Come today at three," she said, replacing the phone, not waiting for an answer, knocking back the last of her sherry.

The early afternoon slipped by with a couple of gins and a sandwich. Sally rang—suddenly, pleasingly, considerate—to say that after school she'd be seeing Leroy. Half-an-hour later, Jill Maybury called to suggest lunch at Cobham and a look round the boutiques.

"You come into money, Jill?" she asked, tartly, rudely.

"No, but I shall enjoy watching you spend some of yours. I thought you might like a trip out."

She hesitated, wondering whether she wished to spend several hours in the company of this lonely woman. Two sad cows together. What the heck . . .

"Why not. Give me a day or two and I'll ring you."

"Oh good! Seen any of the gang?" The crucial question, the reason for the call.

"Been too busy," she lied. Then suddenly, shockingly: "How's your friend Charlie?"

Silence.

"Seen much of her?"

"Er, no," said Jill, stumbling. "I wouldn't say that."

"She's due round here in ten minutes. Tell you all about it when I see you. Bye, Jill."

She hung up with a wry smile, satisfied that she had set the hare running.

When Charlie arrived in the big Merc, sweeping around in front of the house, spraying pebbles into the flowerbeds as she always used to, she opened the door without a word and led the way into the lounge, gesturing her to one of the settees, sitting opposite her on the other. She saw no reason why she should make it easy for the woman, nor did she want to be too near her.

The contrast between them was marked. She, the cuckold, had made every effort with her appearance to show that she was none too affected; Charlie, on the other hand, had quite obviously dressed down, but had been unable to remove the tautness from her face, nor the anxiety from her eyes.

They sat and regarded each other for long moments before Lizzie asked, a little too brusquely, too pointedly, "Still going to the beauty club?"

The other extracted the barb and sent it back. "Still cycling and dreaming about the man across the road?"

In a light-hearted, unguarded moment an age ago, Lizzie had confessed her fantasy and was not now able to stop her resentment showing.

"Lizzie, I've really not come here to cross swords and score points. I just . . ."

"You just wanted to come and crow."

"No! What I said in my note I meant. I feel so sorry. I think we should look to the future. To what's going to happen."

"So that you can settle down with lover-boy? I don't want to play ball and I don't see why I should look to the future. What future?"

"We've all got a future, Lizzie. It depends how we play it, how we arrange things."

Lizzie rose to her feet, walked round to the back of the settee and stood with her hands resting on the top of it. She wanted to be as far away from this patronising, sanctimonious cow as possible.

"I don't need you to do any arranging for me, Charlie," she said, grinding the words out, not recognising herself. "I don't need you or want you in my life. You've got my husband; I don't need your pity!"

"And what makes you think I've got your husband when you know I haven't, when you know you've been trying to humiliate me."

"If I have, who could blame me! Humiliate you? I could *kill* you! If things have gone wrong for you, that's your fault, not mine. This is not about me and it's not about you bleating about some hiccup! It's about you wheedling me into giving him up, about not getting in your way."

Charlie hung on to her calm, determined not to allow the row to break into a blaze.

"It's not about that," she said, quietly. "It really is not. It's about you closing your mind, refusing to . . . Lizzie, I *know*! I *know* about the other woman . . . !"

Transfixed, her grip on the settee tightening, Lizzie sought to harness this latest turn in the conversation. Until now, she'd felt in control . . .

"What other woman? *You're* the other woman! What are you talking about?"—mistaking the other's hesitation, not ready to accept that Charlie, like Sally, did not want to destroy her, had never actively, deliberately wanted to hurt her.

"Lizzie, you *know* what other woman. The one you told me about in your pathetic little note!" She rose quickly, snatched a sheet of paper from her bag and threw it onto the settee, returning to her seat, leaving the grotesque letters staring upwards, shouting their message.

"Not very nice, is it, Lizzie? A poison pen letter! Mental blackmail! Why couldn't you have told me yourself? Why do it like this?"

Lizzie crossed to the drinks cabinet, forcing herself to walk sedately, scorning the gin, not prepared to fiddle about mixing one, selecting what remained of the sherry, pouring just the one, walking to the window, saying "If you want one, help yourself," taking a handkerchief from her sleeve, dabbing her face, pictures of the past floating through her mind: of Colly's persistent absences; of him saying he was being stalked; of Sally admitting it, but saying she had discovered nothing.

"I never sent you that," she said, softly, the passion stripped from her, realising that her daughter must have been lying; that she *had* found something but had decided not to tell her. Why not? Why go to all that trouble only to bottle it up? Because she was frightened? Because she didn't have the courage to tell her?

"Well somebody did," said Charlie, relentlessly. "Somebody who hates me. Who else but you? Whoever it is, knows what I know, what you know. Face it, Lizzie, admit it! Colly's been at it for years—not just a few months with me!"

"Charlie! I know nothing of the kind! I've never seen that address before and I don't know of any woman. If you're so certain about it, why not tell me? Why not get it off your chest?"

The other looked at her pensively. There was no other way.

"Lizzie, I . . ."

"Just tell me!"

"Angie."

"Angie!" Erupting into scornful laughter. "Don't be stupid!"

"It's true, I've seen them."

"Where?"

"At that house, the house there in the note. A few days ago. I'm so sorry."

"No, you're not! You're sorry for yourself! You thought you had him and now you've lost him! If it's true, you never had him in the first place!" Bursting into more laughter.

Charlie spotted the rising hysteria and tried to console her.

"Lizzie—"

"Don't you 'Lizzie' me! You thought you were so smart coming here, didn't you? So smug. So why don't *you* do some owning up? Why don't you tell me about the cancer? About why you never mentioned it at the inquest?"

"What cancer? What are you talking about?"

"You *know* what I'm talking about. He *told* you!"

"I haven't the foggiest. *Who* told me?" Framing her words, asking them gently, as she might have done when they were close, seeing the anger disappear from Lizzie's face.

"My God!" she breathed. "You don't know, do you?" Incredulous, horrified.

"*What* don't I know? *What* cancer?"

But instead of her pressing home her attack, Lizzie had retreated, both hands raised to her mouth as if in prayer, her mind suddenly grasping the reason for Howard's visit to her.

"So that's it," she said, speaking aloud, but to herself. "It has to be. I thought I'd never understand . . ."

137

She re-emerged from her thoughts and turned to Charlie. "Howard—your so dear husband—he told me he'd told you. But he didn't, did he? He was lying! He tricked me! Just like he tricked you!"

She laughed, disbelievingly. "Charlie! You thought you knew Howard, didn't you? Thought he was all loving and generous and open, didn't you? But you didn't know he was dying of cancer, did you? He told *me*, not you!"

"Rubbish! Why would he tell *you*? He would have said! I would have known!"

"No! He kept it to himself. He asked me to tell you he loved you. He said: If anything happens, tell her that every moment of my life with her was wonderful. The cancer bit was obviously meant to come out at the same time. He must have wanted me to tell you after the crash, after you'd got his note!"

Charlie shouting: "So why didn't you? Why in God's name leave it so long?"

And she answering: "Because it would have been too soon! He wanted you to suffer—and so did I! *I wanted the two of you to walk through Hell!*"

She was gulping, ringing her hands, twisting the handkerchief between her fingers, trying not to let go, horrified by her malice, triumphant at the other's shocked silence. When she spoke again, the decibels had given way to the old, quiet bitterness.

"So, this future of yours, Charlie—do you still want to share it with me?"

———

Within the inner London tangle, a few short miles from the wealthy south-west suburbs, Warren Duncan Nichols was sitting in his wheelchair, his eyes closed, nodding to the blaring genius of *Bohemian Rhapsody*, mouthing the verse in sync with Freddie, lost, it seemed, in the world of Beelzebub.

Immersed in the screaming guitars, but hearing another kind of music, one he'd only recently come across—the infinitely variable, heart-stopping music of having a girlfriend.

One that counted. Really counted. Not some low-life hanging round the rich boy, doing it because wanking a grateful cripple was a good laugh, because it fed some sick power craze; and not one of the fawning, sentimental softies going all mushy on him, sighing their sorrow, nothing but charity—tears, tits and charity.

This one was utterly, totally genuine! And right at the top of all the special things about her—drinking and laughing and eating with her, smelling and touching and kissing her—were two that were absolutely astonishing: one, she said she felt the same way about him, and two, her name was . . .

"Is this the real life? . . . Is this just fantasy? . . . . Escape from reality . . . Open your eyes . . . look up to the skies . . . And see . . ."

"Can you reach me a fresh shirt?" he had said to Angie.

"Dressing for dinner, are we?" she'd joked.

"No, afterwards I'm going out."

"Oh yes?" Interested. Guarded. Nervous that the dreadful row with Colly, though now fading, had unbalanced him, made him impulsive.

"Yeah. Ivan's Dad is coming round. He's dropping us down at Drake's Hall."

Drake's Hall was a community centre that in the evening was nothing more than a big pub frequented mostly by young people; Ivan she knew from the disabled swimming, a spoiled brat ruined by parents trying to make up for the leg he'd lost when his father had turned the car over.

"You didn't say . . ."

"No, well . . ."

"And what do you think you're going to get up to?" It was the wrong approach, the wrong question. But she was worried—from being a near recluse, he was suddenly branching out with a kid like Ivan Snell.

"Oh you know—a bit of pill popping, shagging the odd bird on the snooker table . . ."

"No need to be crude! I've told you about that before! Crude means rude. Crude people never get anywhere. Never!"

"Especially cripples with black nannies!"

"Pathetic!"

"I know. I'm sorry. It's just—"

"It's just that I'd like to know! I'm not just the maid who fetches a clean shirt for you! I *care* for you."

"I know you do. You don't have to remind me. And you don't have to worry. I'll be back in one piece. And I'll be the same person."

But half-a-dozen visits to Drake's later, he wasn't the same person. Because by then, he'd discovered old faces and laid to rest old devils.

"Mama, just killed a man . . . put a gun against his head . . . pulled my trigger . . . now he's dead . . ."

In reality, he felt that it was *he* who had been killed, that his life had been taken away then given back, handed another chance, but squandering it, getting snotty with Angie and Colly, refusing to go out, refusing to accept that although he'd never walk, never be like other people in that way, there were many other roads, and until now, he hadn't realised they were there for the taking . . .

"Mama, life had just begun, but now I've gone and thrown it all away . . .

"Mama, didn't mean to make you cry . . . Sometimes wish I'd not been born at all . . ."

That first time, Ivan Snell had stumped up to the door of the Community Centre on his tin leg and had waited while his Dad got Nico into his chair. "O.K. Dad," he called, "see you later. C'mon then," he said to Nico, "let's go and get a fucking beer. I don't know whether you're going to like this lot," he said, bumping the wheelchair off both walls of the corridor, "they're a load of tossers. But the birds aren't bad."

They sat quaffing pints at a table beside a small dance floor, he summing Ivan up as a sad wanker who thought vulgarity made him sound tough; Ivan sniggering about a girl at work who gave blow jobs in the storeroom.

"I suppose you wouldn't manage that," said Ivan, glancing at Nico's legs, irritated by his lack of response.

"How would *you* know?" said Nico.

Memories of his days in the homes were seeping in through cracks opened up by the other's ignorance. He was trying not to listen. Instead, he was looking at three girls sitting at a table across the floor, hardly able to believe his eyes. If the blond was who he thought she was . . .

Ivan, aware that he'd lost his audience, followed his gaze. "Doesn't take *you* long, does it?" he said.

"Do you know her?"

"Which one?"

"The one doing the talking."

"'Course." To prove it, he added, "Bit of a misery. Her sister died a year ago, perhaps more."

"Which one?"

"What?"

"Which sister?"

"Fuckin' 'ell! What's it to you! Her *older* sister. Came off the back of a Triumph. She looked after her for years. Never left her. But it didn't help. Anything else you want to know?"

"Not at the moment." Of course it had helped! It must have! What a prat!

He spun the chair and wheeled himself across the dance floor.

"Hello, Katie."

She broke off her conversation with the other two and turned to look at him. "My name's Kate," she said, evenly. "I don't think I know you."

"Yes you do," he said. "You're Kate Drummond and that," he suddenly realised, "is your little sister, Dodie."

"Dorothy," corrected the girl.

"Dorothy," he repeated, allowing the change to sink in, turning back to her sister. "You *do* know me," he said, "I'm Warren—" following their example, dropping the childhood nickname, feeling awkward and foolish at the strange sound of it.

Kate peered at him, ran her eyes over his chair and abruptly jumped to her feet, spilling their drinks. "Jesus Christ!" she said, "If you've come to haunt us, you can piss off now!" Pushing past his chair, striding across the floor followed by the other girl at the table, leaving Dorothy alone with him.

"That other one's Mary Duff," she said. "I don't think she knows who you are. But Kate does and I do. You're Rolo—the boy who looks up little girls' dresses"—extracting her vengeance twelve years late.

"Yes, that was Rolo, Dodie's little pal," he agreed, pretending not to notice her blush, "and he's very sorry. But I'm not Rolo, now.

Before I was Rolo, I was Nico and after I was Rolo, I was Nico again. But if you're now Dorothy, and Katie's Kate, I'm Warren."

"Cool," she said.

And that was how it had started . . .

He settled himself in his chair, ready to enjoy further happy recollections, closing his eyes as the Queen masterpiece reached its crescendo—

"So you think you can love me and leave me to die

"Oh baby, just gotta get out, just gotta get right outa me"—when the doorbell rang.

He sat inert. It'd be Angie. The silly cow had gone out shopping and now she'd be standing outside the front door not wanting to put the bags down to get her key out, the song now hanging on the thread of Freddie's exquisite pathos:

"Nothing really matters, anyone can see,

"Nothing really matters"—the doorbell ringing again, insistently—*"to meeeeee."*

"For Christ's sake, Angie!" he growled, bundling through into the hall, annoyed at being disturbed, but guilty, too, at not going to the shops with her, of never going with her. He reached up and snapped the Yale open, backing away, calling, "Well, push it then! Push it!"

Lizzie Wolfson did as she was told and stood like a vacuous waxwork, staring downwards, totally uncomprehending of the vision before her.

She'd stuffed Sally's note to Charlie in her pocket and had driven to the address in south London. Arriving there, she'd summoned up all that remained of her courage and had walked quickly to the front door and rung the bell, ready to pretend she had lost her way if it wasn't Angie, convinced that if it was, she'd find a houseful of light brown children.

But it was no such thing! It was a young white man in a wheelchair; fair to light brown hair, medium build, a pleasant enough face, but closed and guarded. When no other picture emerged, when he failed to say anything, she departed from her prepared script, blurting: "I'm sorry, I seem to have got the wrong house. I'm looking for Mrs Maketi."

She stood waiting for a reply, becoming uncomfortable, irritated by the young man's glowering silence. She began to back away, thinking that perhaps his mind was also affected, saying things like, "Never mind . . . sorry to trouble you . . ." when he suddenly wheeled his chair backwards, making room for her.

"You'd better come in," he said. "She's out shopping."

She stepped inside and stood by the open door. The hall was wider than she had imagined and the internal doors were also wider than normal, presumably for his wheelchair. The carpets were newish and expensive, and good quality prints of the Impressionists hung on well-decorated walls. What looked like a state of the art kitchen lay behind him, and from somewhere, some other room, she could hear a rock song, not one of Sally's, one that she thought she remembered herself.

"We can be heroes—just for one day."

"David Bowie," he said—not really, she saw, much more than a boy, but now suddenly chatty, awakened by her interest in his music. "When you rang the bell, it was Freddie Mercury. I like the oldies. I like the guitar playing. The electric guitar. The further back you go, the better it gets. Angie doesn't mind it, but it sends Colly bananas!"

He laughed without taking his eyes off her, seeing her start, returning her stare, realising that she must be from Colly's other life, the one he wasn't allowed to share. No one from it had ever called on them before, had ever tried to get in touch. They were Colly's secret. Outside this house, outside their own lives, he and Angie didn't exist . . .

The thought angered him, fanned the old bitterness. But it also intoxicated him. To show her that he wasn't just a cardboard idiot, he sat trying to fit her to one of Angie's over-the-top characters in her charades of the Sink Set. The woman in front of him could only be one of two people . . .

"You're Charlie, aren't you? You're Colly's . . . ."

"I'm not Colly's anything," she said, bristling, alarmed. Her mind seemed to be unravelling. What was happening?

"Yes you are," he said, smiling, enjoying himself. "You're Charlie, you're Colly's woman. And I'm his other plaything, his son. Sick, isn't it?"

"I'm *not* Charlie and *you're* not his son," she cried, horrified, stepping backwards, one hand clinging to the doorknob. "I'm *Lizzie*! Mrs *Wolfson*! His *wife*! His son, my son, died!"

"Bollocks!" he shouted back, enjoying the charade, *his* charade, his five minutes of fame, knowing he should be keeping his mouth shut, that Angie and Colly would go ape-shit. But so what? So fucking what? He was sick to death of the two-faced pretence . . .

"His son didn't die! He didn't let him!"

"He did!"

"No, he didn't! He didn't die—he just fell and broke his fucking back!"

She staggered as if struck, the young man laughing maniacally, delivering gross exaggerations of the Sink Set, their names and sillinesses, chattering them out like a runaway machine, spinning her head, faster and faster.

"Stop it!" she shouted. "Stop it!"

He broke off as quickly as he'd begun and sat stooped as though the hilarity had been a fit that had worn him out. "I'm sorry," he said, suddenly contrite. "You didn't deserve that. Forget it. Forget all of it."

The easy way, she knew, would be to turn on her heel. But that would settle nothing. She wouldn't get the chance to confront Angie—and it wouldn't quieten the dreadful voice in her brain telling her that the foul-mouthed boy in the wheelchair was dragging her to something unspeakable, something she had never been prepared to accept . . .

She began to speak, but he interrupted her, his apology not yet complete. "Charlie might deserve it. And probably Colly. But not you. I'm sorry, but if you really are Mrs Wolfson, you'll know who *I* am. We don't need a guessing game. I'm Warren Nichols, the boy in the cement mixer. Believe it."

She squeezed her eyes shut, then opened them. The picture was still refusing to come. "But you can't be," she muttered. "He sorted all that out. I told him to. It was all over years ago."

Then suddenly angry, realising that if the boy was telling the truth, then Colly was not merely duping her with Angie, he was duping her with the boy—he had built a family for himself! He had a substitute son!

She began praying, hitting out. "Is it him filling your head with this junk?" she yelled. "Well, is it? Or is it the tart who lives here?"

"It *might* be me, Mrs Wolfson," said a voice behind her, "but I'm no tart and if you choose not to remember Nico, that's up to you."

She whirled round to find Angie standing behind her, shopping bags in each hand. *Nico,* she was saying to herself. It really *was* the same boy! It had never been sorted out and left behind—it had been going on forever! Nico and Angie!

She staggered again and would have fallen but for the other woman dropping her bags, vegetables scattering across the porch, ignoring them, catching her, lowering her gently to the doorstep, sitting there among the tomatoes and mushrooms and sweet potatoes, hair flopped over her face, leaning against the frame, trying to think, listening to them talk, their voices low, knowing she could hear them, but not wishing to disturb her, provoke her.

"I'm sorry! I didn't mean to! I just flipped. He'll go ape-shit," said the first voice, panicking. "Send her away! You can't tell her any more of it, he'll be—"

"It's too late to keep us secret, now," said a second voice, a woman, kind, gentle, picking things up, putting them back in paper bags. "She's got to know. She's got to face up to it."

"But I sent him off to settle it," said Lizzie.

They turned and saw that she was talking to herself, like a child. "And he did. For years, we were free of it."

"Yeah! And we never saw him," said Nico. Bitter, brooding, his mood changing again.

"Nico," said Angie, her tone sharpening, "don't you have to go and get ready to go out?" Going over to him, bending to place both hands on his shoulders, looking into his face, cajoling him. "Trust me," she whispered. "We've got to be gentle with her, but now this has happened, we have to tell her. It should have been done years ago. Best if you leave it to me, eh?"

"It's my life, too."

"Trust me. I've not let you down yet, have I? Well, have I?"

He looked from one to the other before slowly spinning his chair.

Angie watched him go and then helped Lizzie into the kitchen, mortified by the embarrassment, cursing Colly beneath her breath, but trying to keep things light. She sat her down at the table and Lizzie watched the familiar black hands put the kettle on, clatter out the cups and saucers, pour sugar into a bowl, understand the tut-tut as Angie remembered that she sweetened her coffee, but not her tea.

"There," she said, sitting down herself, "that's better."

She sipped at the tea and encouraged her unsought guest to do the same, edging her cup nearer to her. It was time to start talking. But instead of taking the cup, the woman opposite threw a sheet of paper onto the table.

"You'll be wondering how I found you," she said. "That's how! It wasn't sent to *me*. It was sent to Charlie Sinclair *by my daughter*—I've just found out. She's like Nico—she's looking for a father."

"But . . ."—scanning the note—"but how did she know?"

"Simple! When you've got a father like Colly, you stalk him! She and her boyfriend. It was the only way—should have tried it myself years ago. Pathetic, isn't it?"

She sipped her tea, knowing that it was only the anger that was keeping her going, her eyes visiting Angie's face before flicking slowly around the kitchen, talking while they did so.

"Nico's got a broken back, my daughter's got a broken heart and I've got a broken marriage," her words now gluing her gaze fully on the other. "And we know what good old faithful Angie's got, don't we?—she's got my husband!"

Angie shook her head. "One step at a time," she said, quietly. "I've sent Nico away because he tends to get upset. He thinks he can cope. But he's too near it. He sees Colly as his father. That's what he would like. But Colly won't allow it—not openly. That's mainly because of you—and your past. But the fact is that whatever he will or won't allow, Colly has treated Nico as his son for years."

"I wouldn't know that," said Lizzie, the bitterness eating another piece of her, "unlike you, I've never seen them together. But if I'm honest, yes, I know he felt that way, years ago. Truth is, I didn't want Nico in our lives. I resented him, who wouldn't? Not because Colly saw him as our son—because he was *replacing* our son, our *real* son, with Nico, wiping our real son out as if he never existed;

blaming me. Openly, then secretly. And not only that—letting me down with you and Charlie at the same time!"

She tried to laugh, but cut the sound short, jumping up, looking out of the window. Tired grass, crumbling red bricks, cracked grey slates.

"Yes and no," said Angie. "You've got the Charlie bit right, but not me. He and I, we've never done that, been that way. He fancied me, on and off, I knew that. But he chose Charlie. He set Nico and me up in this house years ago when I told him the boy was stuck in a home, losing his mind. He was such a brave little boy—he and his broken little body and his broken mind. And when he got bigger, and I couldn't cope, Colly started helping me, coming here to this house, nursing his sadness over his son and you and Sally, trying to deal with his guilt over Nico, keeping him at arms length, not telling him anything for years, not until recently. But Nico wanting so much to have him as his father, and me dreaming for a while that perhaps we could be a threesome, realising long ago that it would never happen, that the two of us would never really be more than Nico's carers."

She waited for Lizzie to turn and look at her. "I'm not Colly's lover, Mrs Wolfson, I'm Nico's pretend mother, his carer. I love them both. But soon, it'll all be over and I'll lose them."

Lizzie saw the lovely brown eyes blinking away the tears and could stand it no longer. She snatched up her bag and ran from the house.

" . . . what I have been told is that the government knew that the 45-minute claim was questionable . . . before they wrote it in their dossier. I have spoken to a British official who was involved in the preparation of the dossier, and he . . . said: 'It was transformed in the week before it was published, to make it sexier. The classic example was the statement that weapons of mass destruction were ready for use within 45 minutes. That information was not in the original draft. It was included in the dossier against our wishes, because it wasn't reliable . . .'"—Andrew Gilligan, the BBC Radio 4 defence correspondent, speaking on May 29, 2003, an hour after broadcasting his sensational scoop calling into question the British Government's September 2002 dossier on Iraq.

Chapter 17

New Life

Publicly, true to their kind, the close-knit, socially sensitive members of the Sink Set affected to deal with Howard Sinclair's death as one, coalescing on accident rather than suicide, muttering their private opinions about him, his wife and her lover, to their partners, or in some cases only to themselves, unaware, so far, that two of their number had an altogether fuller insight into his death.

For Lizzie Wolfson, Howard's confidences had been unsought and unwanted, an encumbrance that had obstructed her own grief over Colly's infidelity with Charlie. It had fed her bitterness and had given her a power over them that she couldn't help thinking she had not wielded wisely. Keeping quiet had undoubtedly made them suffer. But while. Sally's intervention had missed the mark regarding Angie, hitting instead the equally unwanted truth about Nico, the knowledge was worthless unless it also removed the girl's pain and confusion.

It was time she refocused.

Returning from Angie's, she showered away her humiliation, tied her hair in a simple ponytail, creamed her face and sat within a soft pink robe in the silent lounge, waiting for her daughter, praying that she would come home before her courage failed.

An hour, perhaps two hours later, she heard the soft purr of the motorbike and composed herself.

"I'm so glad you're back," she said, smiling, the girl framed in the lounge doorway in her black leathers. "I fancy a cocoa. Why don't you jump into bed and I'll bring some up?"—the girl frowning, about to refuse, but catching herself, saying O.K.

So she sat on her daughter's bed, gently threading her way through the girl's torment, begging her forgiveness, admitting her wrongs, blaming Colly for some of it but trying to be fair, telling her of how two people had lost their way.

"So Dad's not tied up with Angie?"

"No. Not from what she says."

"He only goes there to look after this boy, Nico?"

"Yes."

"And you believe her?"

"Yes."

"But that's all it is, he's not adopted him or anything?"

"No. That's all it is," wishing it was, knowing it wasn't, lying to save the girl's feelings.

"And Howard died in the crash and had cancer. He didn't—"

"That's right." Hurrying on, not wanting the girl to start dissecting another half-lie. "What I think we've got to do, the two of us, is to see things as they are and to be happy with what we've got. Which means no more stalking and no more letters like the one to Charlie;" telling her that her father need never know, praying that Charlie and Angie would keep their mouths shut.

"As for why Howard really died, would have died in any case, I think we'll let Charlie tell your father about that. It's their business now. But at least we know where he disappears to—and why. And we also know there's only Charlie."

As if by way of an afterthought, taking advantage of the moment, she added, "And by the way, that boy friend of yours—I don't care if he's black, brown or blue, rich or poor, or too old. Just tell him to take care of you."

All of which, thought Lizzie with a grim smile, left Charlie on the scene but up the creek. The poor little model girl still had her paddle, but she knew nothing about Colly's relationship with Nico and she still believed that Angie was her rival.

The smile widened.

Charlie Sinclair, bored, beautiful and biddable, was well aware, over the years, that the constant glamour and riches of her life had wrought their changes, persuading her, as they invariably do, that with a snap of an indolent finger, all things were possible; that while money could well nigh buy everything, and often did, enough of it also brought a feeling that nothing could touch her, that she, like others, could get away with anything—thus her eventual disillusion with the persistently unsophisticated Howard and the whim of her adultery with the amoral Colly.

Her mistake, she realised, was that she had fallen in love with her lover. Since his moneymaking was almost as good as his lovemaking, this wasn't necessarily a problem. The problem was that he came with a scheming wife, a teen-age tearaway, and now, of all things, a kitchen maid with her skirts up. Throw in his pathetic principles and his emasculating guilt, and there was much need for creative thinking.

In the case of Angie, she decided that it was best to tread lightly. Accusing Collie of betraying her when she herself had betrayed her husband *and* her best friend would sound ridiculously hollow and might rebound—he might choose Angie! Best leave him in the dark and get him to shed her along the way.

As for Howard's cancer, she only had Lizzie's word for it. But if Lizzie were speaking the truth, it seemed to her that most people would find her silence horrifying but understandable—Colly and Sally among them. Lizzie, the devious bitch, would realise this—and say nothing.

So she would do the same! It was simple! She would merely tell Colly that she had found out about the cancer by accident—that way would not set him raging at Lizzie . . . would not reveal Lizzie's suffering . . . would not risk the two of them wiping the slate clean. What she needed was proof. With cast iron proof, she could liberate Colly from his depression and gently ease him back into her bed.

But it would have to be done quietly. If Howard was dying of cancer, if that could be shown to be the major reason for his suicide—perhaps the *only* reason?—the last thing she wanted was a hullabaloo, people milling around trying to be helpful, scaring Colly off. She would need time to plan, to spread the news quietly and gently to Colly and her friends. Done properly, the trollop might yet win a few sympathy votes . . .

A search of Howard's study revealed piles of glossy sales manuals—mostly from his factory but also of cars, cabin cruisers, yachts and light aeroplanes, what to equip them with, what to wear on and in them. There were also drawers packed with old correspondence and jottings, and, surprisingly, two folders of holiday memorabilia and a large collection of family snapshots. But nothing more.

A day later, she scoured the entire house and looked again through the cases of personal belongings sent from the factory after his death, among them several files and a number of computer floppies. Nothing. A quick phone call to the general manager brought a respectful assurance: yes, everything had been returned; no, there was nothing of a personal nature on the hard disk. "Just tidying up, making sure," she replied.

Widening her search, she affected a pain in her shoulder and went to the doctor, making sure it was a day when her usual G.P. was on his day off, and that she would be seeing the one used by Howard. It had seemed a natural port of call from the start, but one she had been avoiding. Doctors and their probing questions made her nervous.

But the visit was a dead loss. "Apart from this pain of yours," the doctor said, forbearingly, "how are you keeping? Are you sleeping?"

"Mostly," she lied. "My main problem, I suppose it always will be, is wondering why he did it. Alright, our marriage wasn't what it was, but he had so much going for him . . . I can't help wondering if there was something else."

"Like what?"

"Well, it wasn't money or anything to do with work. So perhaps it was his health."

"How do you mean?"

"Well, he couldn't stand being ill. Never could. Even a cold would send him into a black hole! If it was something more serious . . ."

"Mrs Sinclair, I don't think so. I went through his records with Dr Jenkins. He was as fit as a fiddle. Death is often difficult to accept, especially when . . . I think we'd better give you something to settle you."

She walked from the surgery, frustrated, throwing the unsought prescription for sedatives into a waste bin by the church wall, regretting her action, stooping to retrieve it, her sudden movements startling a pair of white doves into abandoning their gravestone for the safety of the church tower. They reminded her fleetingly of the seagulls wheeling above their beach house, strident and greedy, somehow emphasising her lack of feeling for the place, the effort she had to make to share Howard's love of it, the gulls zooming around, hovering in the wind, settling on the roof as lightly as floating fluff . . .

Drip by drip, a new realisation percolated through her misery. After he left her, after he went away, between that time and the plane crash, what better hideaway . . . !

"There was political spin put on the intelligence information to create a sense of urgency. It was a political decision that came from the Prime Minister. We were misled: I think we were deceived in the way it was done"—Clare Short, three weeks after resigning from Blair's Cabinet in protest at the war; The Daily Telegraph, June 2003.

Chapter 18

Tennis

This time, instead of under the stairs, he was standing within the dense cascade of an enormous, much admired tree in the Brownlove's garden. They thought it was some kind of walnut and on very hot days would sometimes take tea there, sitting inside the cool curtain of leaves that kissed the lawn in an unbroken ring. For the Brownloves, it was a conversation piece, a beautiful curiosity. That day, for him, it was a sun-flecked dome of peace, a deleter of dead babies, broken bodies, broken hearts, a filter of the sights and sounds without.

It was the June solstice, the day, or thereabouts, that the Sink Set gathered each year for iced tea, mint juleps, margaritas and languid tennis. Nobody could quite remember the connection, if any, between the day and the American South and nobody much cared. But if the weather was dry and warm, it was pleasant enough to loll about between matches, tittling and tattling, the conversations as indolent as the white-clad figures on the red shale. He had decided not to go, convinced his presence would be too embarrassing, too divisive. But Anna had overcome his better judgement. It'll be bad enough without the other three there, she'd said—show your face, build for the future. But his nerve had failed—he had slid in the back way and had sought the refuge of the giant tree without being seen, content to listen to the voices filtering through the leaves.

"Well, I don't know what *you* think, but I'm not sure we should be here *at all* this year."

It was Amelia Platt-Smith doing her hand on heart conscience stuff, working herself up towards her customary theatrical climax. It was hard to believe it was only once a year that she and Roger were pressing them all to buy tickets for their latest production in some church hall or other—suffering the acting, aching for the nearest bar.

"You mean because of Iraq?" Honey Leverington's incredulity rasped through the leafy canopy.

"No, no! Not Iraq! Who said anything about Bush and Blair?"

"Who would want to?" said Ozzie, whooping.

"Quite," said Amelia. "No, not all that spin and deceit, Honey. And not all the slaughter, although . . . No, not because of that!—*Howard*! Because of *Howard*!"

"Ah," said Ozzie.

Within his dome, he edged silently behind the walnut's huge trunk, wondering how he was going to escape.

"I'm sorry," said Amelia, "but don't you think it strange, a load of fops playing tennis—and Howard so lately dead?"

"I rather like being a fop," said Ozzie. "C'mon, Amelia! Stop treading the boards. Join the mewling throng!"

"You know what I mean," she replied, miffed.

A new voice, the rather hard tones of Jessica Callows: "So you will also know that dear Howard was thinking cancer rather than adultery. Plenty of deceit there, Amelia."

"A desperate man in a desperate fix," responded Amelia grandly, adding, "I suppose you heard about the cancer like we did—from Jill Maybury? Rather convenient for the lovers, don't you think?"

"What—hearing it from Jill?" asked Ozzie, spitefully.

"Don't be obtuse—hearing it at all!"

"It's not just from Jill, you know," said Ozzie, bypassing the more loaded question. "I've seen the correspondence—from the consultants and the hospital. There's really no doubt that . . ."

They were moving away, reluctantly answering Anna's call for partners for the next set. He hadn't realised Charlie had been in touch with Jill, or that she had shown Ozzie the hospital stuff. Clever of her! Before his irony turned from comment to query, and before he had the chance to leave, new voices settled into the unseen deck chairs.

"If you would pass me the Pimms, Jill. Thank you." To the sound of clinking ice, the matching cut glass tones of Elizabeth de Manger. "Do you remember how he used to lace into this stuff after slogging the ball about, pretending he wasn't trying, but the sweat still flying?"

"Who could forget it—anything to beat Colly!" said Herbie Kirby.

They all laughed in agreement—and laughed again at his next quip. "Howard the Slogger! Anywhere would do! Didn't you once collect one in a certain unmentionable place, Hugo?"

"Looked worse than it was, old chap."

"Not if you believe Elizabeth! She said it kept you out of action for a week or more!"

"Oh *really*, Herbie!" said Elizabeth, severely. "But he could certainly hit the ball. Lovely, big, fine man," she said, wistfully.

They were silent for a moment or two before Herbie added: "Lizzie also collected one, didn't she? On the head! Pity she's not here, I like her."

"We all like her, Herbie dear," said another voice: Jill Maybury. "But it's not possible at the moment, is it?"

"Suppose not," he said. "Pity the innocent have to suffer, though."

"Best not get into that—dangerous ground," said Hugo. "At least they know they weren't to blame."

"Only possibly, "said Herbie.

"The pity, if there is to be pity," said Jill, "is that poor Lizzie has taken it very hard. Never goes out. Of all people, Charlie went to see her not long ago. But she won't talk about it, just sits and broods about Colly."

"Hmm," said Elizabeth, "I wonder what he's up to *now*?"

If only you knew, he breathed, tip-toeing away, keeping the trunk of the tree between himself and the little drinks party, emerging into the sunshine on the other side. On his way down the garden to the rear gate, from behind a shrubbery, he spied Chloe Jones on the tennis court. She was partnering Simon Mount—who else?—against the Brownloves. All four of them were good players, stroking the ball around without putting too much energy into it. But it was the tanned, lithe Chloe who filled his eyes, that and the memory of their latest session.

Strange thing was that in bed, she and Charlie were pretty much the same: Charlie was taller and tended to lose herself more easily, but their limbs and their bellies and their breasts came from the same mould, and they were equally bold and forward, coolly leading him into their reeking pleasures, unaffected by Lizzie's limiting modesty. It occurred to him that the only real difference lay not with them, the two of them, but with him, his reactions to them—robotic lust with the obsessive, driven Charlie; tingling ardour with the carefree, promiscuous Chloe.

Humiliating though it had been, if he were to tell the truth, his temporary impotence after Howard's death had been something of a relief. It had allowed him to examine his feelings for Chloe and had forced him to cool his affair with Charlie. Somewhere in the back of his mind had stirred a betraying thought that had the coolness carried on long enough, it might have produced a welcome ending, a tame, sad letdown. But before this could happen, she'd rung him at the office, her voice tearful, but excited.

"It's Charlie! Don't go to the bar or wherever tonight, Colly! Please, please come to the beach house. I've got something to tell you, to show you."

"Tell me now." Cold, not wanting to play games.

"I can't. I need to see you. If you love me, you'll come. Please, please come!"

Unable to refuse without causing a scene, not sure in any case that that was what he wanted, he had climbed the salt-bleached wooden steps and had found her clutching a wad of unbelievable letters, their message no longer merely the factual, dispassionate details of discovering and coping with cancer, nor even their accompanying sympathy for Howard, but the initial wonderful, warm wash of relief that the two of them had not been to blame for his death. Not solely. That he would have died, anyway!

And just as he had given in to his lover's blackmail—the implied, 'Drive all the way down here or I'll do something desperate'—so he gave in to her desperate need to share the moment, his body answering, able at last to join her in her mourning—and in her celebrations.

Later: "So you found them here? But how, why?"

Accepting her answer, unaware of the lie: "I came down to tidy up—I'm thinking of selling. And there they were—stuffed into an old pillowcase in the linen cupboard!"

"Poor sod."

"Howard? Poor sod nothing! He should have told me!"

"Perhaps he couldn't bring himself to."

"No! He wanted to make us suffer. Remember the note: *'Darling, I cannot bear it. Love you always.'* Two-faced bastard—saying one thing, meaning another."

"I want to believe it—but . . ."

"He was your friend, but it was me who lived with him. I *knew* him. And I'm *sure*," she had said, "sure enough for both of us. Trust me"—praying that he wouldn't see through her lies and omissions, her decision to say nothing of Howard's malicious conversation with Lizzie.

So he'd taken up with her again, a faltering congress of mind, a rampage of flesh, a togetherness based on her faith that Howard would never have killed himself merely because of her adultery. And to keep the crushing guilt at bay, he went along with it, still not entirely convinced, but not wanting to question her, feeling the growing entanglements, not knowing how to escape.

For a short while, there was an edgy happiness between them, a nervy awareness, their laughter frequent but brittle, their togetherness taut and quivering. More and more, her talk was of them setting up house together, of him divorcing Lizzie, of her selling her home. As time drifted by, he found he was neither embracing the currents of her life, nor fighting against them, allowing them, instead, to waft over him, to carry him where they would.

And then the drifting over! Chloe picking up the phone, inviting him to share her fragrances! Like one of those tiny sample snapshots that you pay to enlarge and sometimes enlarge again, revealing more and more of what's in them, she expanding into him, filling him, bestowing him with a new universe, an endless velvet land of ecstasy and wonder.

That first time, like a nervous schoolboy, arriving on her doorstep already unable to breathe, curbing himself, clutching her to him, her dizzying invitation, demanding, "But why now? What's made you . . . ?"

Accepting her tender replies, marvelling and swooning over her, slipping into her mind, encouraging her into his own dark alleyways, discovering that while his goatishness held no terrors, she shied like a foal from words like love and forever and devotion.

So he stowed them away, his true feelings, knowing she saw through him, allowing her the pretence that he was drawn only by what had first intrigued him: the mocking indifference, the whimsical search for passing pleasures; rejecting the insidious thought that with Lizzie forsaken, she was merely seducing him away from Charlie, doing so for a bet. With herself? With Simon? Rejecting this, but afraid, knowing that for her, it might be so; that what excited her was his entanglement, his desperation, his loathing, unspoken, of her continuing bolthole with her curious, cock-eyed lover, of her safe sanctuary with him, of his guardianship, of the thought of his cold, cock-eyed jism on her bored, unmoved belly.

"Makes you tired just watching, eh!" It was Ozzie Leverington, carrying two mint juleps through the secluded back gate, arriving at the car before he could drive away, handing one of the glasses in through the open window, opening the door, getting into the front passenger seat. "Have a drink with me, Colly," he said. "It's been a while."

"Yes." On guard, but accepting the drink.

"Still brooding about Blair and Bush?"

"Among others. I tend not to like sham, especially when it kills people."

"And Howard?"

"What about him?"

"Bit of sham there, I hear."

"Perhaps."

"But you're all right about it now? Y'know—the cancer bit . . . It must have been . . . ." In deep, searching for words.

"A relief?" Exasperated.

"Well . . . yes."

"Suppose so. Better that way than the other."

"But you and Charlie—you're . . . all right again?"

For the first time, he looked Ozzie full in the face, wondering how much he knew, how much Charlie had confided to Honey.

"It was all a bit of a shock, Ozzie, the death and everything. Knocked me sideways. But, you know, you pick yourself up. Have to."

To escape the sudden intimacy, the embarrassment, they both pretended interest in the restrained laughter of a group of people standing on the other side of the laurel hedge—by the sound of it, Paul Brownlove's office pals listening to a man telling a story. " . . . a New York air stewardess trying to quell my nerves, telling me not to worry, we were on a British airliner with Rolls Royce engines—a 'Back One One One', she said, not even knowing it was pronounced 'B-A-C One-Eleven!' And me with this dreadful hangover!"

"Is that who I think it is?" asked Colly.

"Got it in one," said Ozzie, bitterly. "Harold Wensum. The rotten apple at the bottom of the barrel"

"But . . ."

"No buts, Colly. Queen Anna must have her way. It's not enough for her to know what Hector and I think. All she says is that people change, that I more than anyone, should know that. When I said, some time ago, that a leopard doesn't change its spots, she said perhaps Harold didn't have any spots in the first place."

"Makes you wonder," said Colly, thinking about the spots, being misunderstood.

"Makes *me* wonder, too! She should tell him to stay away."

"And what's she say to that?"

"She says he just comes and goes. If Hector can't stand the sight of him and has to stay away, tough."

"Like Howard and me," said Colly, switching himself back into the conversation, losing interest in a student fall-out that had somehow remained unexplained through the decades and seemed too boring to pursue.

Ozzie drew breath, thought better of it, and said nothing, each suffering their respective ghosts in silence, unaware that only that morning, Anna, in response to Ozzie's grumbling, had cornered

Harold; he arrogant, flagrant, casually slipping his hand round her bottom, thinking she wanted to talk him into another assignation; she not demurring at the hand, seeking, instead, further scandal, attempting to tease out of him his shared history with Ozzie and his brother-in-law, Hector Grammaticus, about why Ozzie should be quite so antagonistic—being left to unravel the innuendo in his throwaway, "Oh, I don't know about antagonistic. It's all the way back. We were students. They had each other. They didn't need poor old me."

Into their silence came further voices. The latest match had apparently come to an end and Anna could be heard thanking her partners for the game, saying to her husband what a pity Simon and Chloe would never be able to play Howard, regretting that Colly and Charlie had not felt able to come, the lot of them strolling away.

Funny thing was, it wasn't Chloe's lovely, eager body he was thinking about now, nor, for that matter, the absent Charlie's. He was wondering why Charlie had gone to see Lizzie. And the picture in his mind was of Lizzie, sitting at home, alone.

"Eight month's ago . . . Andrew Gilligan . . . cast doubt on the Government's dossier on Iraq . . . a vital plank in its case for war. In the ensuing furore . . . government scientist, David Kelly, who was revealed to be Gilligan's source, was found dead in the woods. Lord Hutton, appointed by Tony Blair to hold an inquiry into the circumstances surrounding Dr Kelly's death . . . said Gilligan's assertions were unfounded . . . criticised the BBC . . . (and) said Dr Kelly had broken the rules governing civil servants in talking to journalists. He exonerated Tony Blair, cleared Alastair Campbell and attached no blame to the Government for the naming of Dr Kelly. So was this all an establishment whitewash?"—The Independent, January 22, 2004.

Chapter 19

Crash

Without planning it, almost as it were by accident, Colly Wolfson awoke to the fact that, in the parlance of the time, he was now running four women, four because he had not yet rid himself of Lizzie, legally or mentally, and because Angie was as much a part of his life as the rest of them.

Perversely, the thought of a pirouetting quartet caused his pulse to rise only slightly, if at all, and he wondered what the average chauvinist scored. In his case, rather than a sense of his *own* power, it seemed that for most of the time, the four were running *him*, chasing around his consciousness and his crotch, exciting him, dulling him, elating him, depressing him, gathering themselves together then falling apart like a child's building blocks.

Waiting for them to stand them up again, to answer his questions, solve his puzzle:

If Lizzie knew about Charlie and was right, and Charlie thought she knew about Angie and was wrong, did Chloe know about all three? Or just the two? And just as important, did anyone at all know about the *real* Angie? The one caring for Nico? And if they did know, what was to be done? Where, in God's name, did he go from there?

Sprawling in a chair at Angie's place, his eyes closed, his mind racing, the faces revolving, gathering pace, their assurances, their tears; dwelling on his puzzle, unable to wipe it away, the questions repeating and repeating, aware, somewhere at the back of his mind, of the long, gathering depression, knowing that he needed to answer his puzzle.

Among all this, he could feel her eyes on him, critical, admonishing, on the verge of uttering her female wisdom, trying to judge whether it was worth it.

To stop her, without opening his eyes, he muttered, "Angie, I've just had a bloody awful day at work with those effing prats up in *Birmingham*,"—singing the word out in a passable, insulting shot at the local dialect—"and I don't need more crap when I get home. I just need to be left alone."

She noted his reference to home—loose language or a Freudian slip?—but allowed it to pass.

"Colly, it's *you* doing the talking. I've said nothing." Forbearing, equable.

"Angie, you don't need to."

Rising to the irony, she said, "Sorry about your bad day, but it's not *me* that's been drinking."

"Oh c'mon! I stopped on the way back for a couple, that's all. You'd do the same if a ten-mill job disappeared down the plughole. One last week, one this week."

"And is it you without your mind on the job, or are you blaming someone else?"

Silence.

"So, like you do these days, you went for a drink and missed Nico—and that's what's bugging you!"

"It doesn't help. Out with his pals! These days, always out with his pals!"

"Hardly," she said, his eyes still closed to her smile. "At the moment, he's very pleased with himself. Been cramming calcium and vitamins down himself for months and doing exercises to strengthen his arms. Pumping iron, he calls it. Haven't you noticed? You saw him last week."

"Only in a rush."

"Yes, but he'd rather have you doing for him than me or Esme or Mary. They're great carers, but you know very well that if he knows you're coming, he always stops in or goes out later."

"So I have to make an appointment to see my own . . ."

"Your own what?" Leading him, encouraging him.

"Stop stirring it, Angie! You know what I mean."

"I know what you'd love to say, but daren't. You never dared because of Lizzie. I'd say that means she's still around . . . in this room . . . in your head."

"And I'd say that good friend as you are, like my work, that might not be any of your business. I don't want to quarrel, but—"

"Then don't—just think about your life, what you're doing to yourself, and about Nico."

She got to her feet. "You need food, not booze. Why not eat with me and wait for him? But better not tell Charlie."

"What the hell's it to do with Charlie?"

"Have you been telling her about this place, about me and Nico?"—aware that after Sally's poison pen letter and Lizzie's visit, her question had been cast into deep waters . . .

"Of course not!"

"So she knows nothing?"

"Not from me."

She sat twiddling her wedding ring. She could end the conversation there—or she could use the moment to insert a thought into his mind . . .

"You say that," she said, equably, "but at the tennis do, I had to swallow a certain pointed innuendo."

"Was she at the tennis do?" Disbelieving.

"Yes—briefly. She came into the kitchen, took one look at me, made a face and said she couldn't face it. She left without seeing Anna or anybody."

"And you took that as an innuendo?"

"Yes."

"About you and me?"

"I guess so. Seems she thinks she's not the only crumpet on your plate . . ."

"Rubbish!" Startled, praying that Angie had got it wrong—that there was no innuendo; that if there was, it was about *her* and not Chloe Jones!

She laughed, teasing him.

"Maybe. But what would a man know . . . ? All I can say is that she seems to have something on her mind. It might be kind to let her into our secret."

He opened his mouth to reply, but found she had moved into the kitchen.

He stayed in his chair, brooding about the multiplying, inter-linked questions until she called him to the table. By the time Nico came in an hour later, he had finished off the wine and the blackness was rising. He grunted his thanks to Angie for the meal, noted her early diplomatic departure upstairs, and joined Nico in his room. He was wearing a T-shirt that said, THE BEST. But, peevishly, he decided his arms looked no different.

"So," said Nico, reaching for the music centre controls, turning down the volume, "are you still in with Charlie?"

"As a matter of fact, yes I am. You could have asked me that last week or the week before."

"What—with you racing in, racing out? 'Wash this, wash that and stop getting a hard on!' I'm a cripple, not a plank of wood."

"You're disabled and old enough to show some control. And I've stopped saying that, anyhow."

"You used to, though. You still can't imagine that I have the same feelings, the same emotions as you or anybody. Just because I spend my life sitting down doesn't make me different. And for years before you yanked me out of the Home, I wasn't *in control*, I was in *care*—remember? After all this time, I thought you might have got the message."

"I have . . . I have!"

"Really? I don't think so. The way you go on, anybody'd think it was going to jump up and bite you. You know why it happens and you said you didn't want it. Ages ago. So why go on about it?"

"Because—"

Wanting to say because you're too hurt, because I'm too ashamed, because even without Lizzie, but now with Charlie and Chloe—and they unknowing—I still don't have the courage, the words to tell you how much I want to feel you in my veins, to love and honour you. But not that way. Not any more. Not ever. As a son. As my son.

"Because I'm a prat! Let's leave it—I have a lot on my mind. I'm not in the mood."

"You never were."

"Not for that. And you weren't, either."

Saying the necessary lie, setting the boy free, losing him. "I thought we were agreed on that? I know what happened to you, I know about the homes, and the men there, and I know it's difficult, but—"

"But you'd rather mope and make up stories in your mind about me. Once a queer, always a queer! But I never was! I was *used*. And yes, there was a time if you'd wanted that, if that was the only way to get you to love me . . . but I've moved on, and you still don't know, still can't see."

Colly lowered his head to cover his shame and blew softly into his hands.

Why couldn't he be honest? Why couldn't he match him? Tell it as it is? Accept his love? Lizzie's love? Sally's love?

"I do see. I try to," he said quietly, raising his face, forcing a sympathetic smile, trying to heal the boy's wounds. "I do try. I know how you feel"

"*Felt*," said Nico. "I doubt if you ever knew at all."

Colly opened the palms of his hands, gesturing his disagreement.

"Well you don't!" the boy went. "You think I don't pull birds like other blokes—but that's not true. There've always been nurses and carers ready and willing. It's what happens. You can't do what they do for me without caring and you can't let them do it without getting close to them. Not Angie for Christ's sake"—responding to Colly's sharp glance—"others. Some genuine, some . . . y'know . . ."

"But—"

"But Colly—you don't! You don't even know the first thing about my music! It's kept me sane for years, but because *you* don't like it, nobody can like it."

"I've bought you loads of it!"

"Yes, but you don't *know* it, you don't *share* it with me! For instance, who's this?"

He zoomed the sound up so that the beat crashed around the room making Colly wince.

The boy laughed, scoffing. "Well?"

Reluctantly. "It's not Queen . . ."

"Of course it's not bloody Queen! It's Radiohead. One of the best bands ever. But of course, you've never even heard of them."

"So what's the piece called?"

"*O.K. Computer.*" He pressed the controls, changing the CD. "And this? You should know this. They're an old band. American. Wonderful. Trailblazing. The new age of sex and drugs. Telling it like it was. Suffering it. This is when they were coming out of it"

Colly closed his eyes and listened. "Who is it?"

But Nico had gone to the loo, pissing into a bottle, emptying it down the pan, washing the bottle, singing along with '*Californication,*' wheeling himself back in, not using the electric motor, exercising his arms, proud of his new power, resentful that Colly hadn't said.

"So?" he asked.

A shake of the head.

"Red Hot Chilli Peppers."

"Nico, I know I should know stuff like this. Or some of it. And I do. It was always on at the parties and the gigs at the uni, that sort of stuff. But I was never really interested. For me, life was all about design and drawing, shapes and colours."

—that and fighting to keep his mind from dwelling on the actions and deaths of the two people he should have been able to trust, the two people who brought him into the world . . . and left him dangling . . .

"Sure. *I* know that. But you never told me. I had to work it out for myself."

"I'm sorry. I should have thought. I suppose some of it might be the age thing—you know, your generation, my generation."

"You mean father and son stuff?"

"Yes, I suppose."

"But you're *not* my father."

"No, but—" Caught out again, allowing his guard to slip.

But give me a second chance to say, 'No, but that's what I want, what I've always wanted. Will you be the son I lost? Will you join me, make me proud and complete?'

Knowing, pleading, that the answer would be *'Yes! Yes! Yes!'* But never able to ask the question, not even now. Never sure he could deliver, afraid always he would let him down, like he seemed to let everyone down. Aware always of Lizzie and now of Chloe, of his craving for a new beginning with her away from the ghastly complications, the inter-linked, overcooked nightmare . . . Realising that the question, as ever, was more about him than about the boy . . .

Saying instead, "No, but there's something of that in it."

"Bollocks," said Nico, matter of fact, unemotional. "There might be, could be, if you were my father, but you're not. You're a middle-class, conscience salving, rich as Croesus aid worker, and I'm your broken slum kid from Baghdad."

"Baghdad?"

"Yeah, Baghdad! That's what you're always banging on about, isn't it? Angie says you've got a thing about it."

"Never mind Angie. What about these friends of yours?" Refusing to be sidetracked, but smarting, accepting that the boy's pen-picture was at least half right.

"What friends are those?"

"The ones you're always out with."

"Oh! *Those* friends!" Toying with him. Smug. Careful . . . Brought up by Angie to respect this man, to believe in him, not only because of his kindness, but because she said he was trying to repay a debt that could never be settled, a sort of wound, she said, that could never be healed. And he'd bought that, as a kid, and was grateful for it. But he also knew Colly hadn't got where he was by sitting on his arse. He was quick and clever and basically selfish. Not so much selfish as self, concerned with self. So that when he wanted something, he went and got it. And then, like as not, left it. One of those gifted sods that switched on the charm and rolled people over with one glance, his eyes blue and wide and frank. Involved with people, but apart from people; both at the same time. So when it came to talking about his friends, it paid to be careful—especially when the friends included some of the kids from the building site gang. Because Colly would never understand. He would either play merry hell and piss off in a huff, or he'd be muscling in, trying to get to know them, trying to discover how a broken back counted for nothing, how it could bring them all together, how it was that *their* guilt could be forgotten and forgiven . . .

"So who are they, these friends?" Casual, persuasive.

"Well, you know most of the ones who're down at the swimming, 'cos you've been to watch me."

"Not for a while, though."

"No, Mary usually takes me." He laughed and told a funny story of how Mary had nearly fallen in one day, leaving blank what sometimes used to happen a long time ago in the cubicle afterwards. It was none of his business.

"And are the exercises helping with the swimming? Angie tells me you're pumping iron!"

"I'm not doing them for the swimming. Not particularly. I'm doing them so that I can get about, be more independent."

"So long as you don't end up a second Arnie Schwartzenegger." Joking. Failing.

"Why not? I don't notice it doing *him* any harm!"

Colly's blackness edged a little higher. They were talking, which was good. But he was off-key, off-balance, continually tripping in his efforts to keep up. He needed something to help him along.

Inside Nico's fridge, he found four large bitters and a four-pack of extra strong lager. Without asking, he opened two of the beers and they sat for a while discussing booze before suddenly returning to the original conversation.

"So what about the rest of your friends? Where do *they* hang out?"

"Here and there." The gates still shut, irritating him, depressing him, causing him to push too hard.

"But you don't *go* here and there, do you?"

"I don't zip around in a fucking Jag, no! Doesn't mean I don't get out."

"Nico! Will you stop fighting your bloody corner! What happened to sociable? To friendly? All you're doing is kicking my arse."

"Then stop acting the Gestapo."

Instead of the questions, he could have told about his awful day. If he'd thought, he could have told about all sorts of things. But the moment had passed. Instead, he muttered a soft, "For fuck's sake," walked dejectedly to the fridge, and opened another bottle, convinced that he'd blown it.

"One for me, too," Nico sang out, dryly.

They sat for a while quaffing the beer, Nico listening to the music, Colly trying *The News at Ten*, clenching his teeth when the lead story was once again Iraq, the latest violence, the row over Weapons of Mass Destruction, or rather the failure to find them, Blair and his spin men defending desperately, the Tories nowhere, the Lib-Dems, like him, too raucous, too over-keen.

"Have you ever had a snake bite, Colly?"

"A what?" Switching the TV off, the question pushing in through the angry denunciations.

"Not a what—a snake bite! Let's have a *real* drink!"

He watched as the boy poured two of the lagers and added several squirts of blackcurrant juice. It looked revolting, but seemed to go down O.K. If this was what it took, then so be it.

"O.K?

"Tasty."

"Fancy a smoke with it?"

"A smoke?"

Nico shook his head, amused. "Hang on," he said. "I'll be back."

He re-emerged from his bedroom ten minutes later with two homemade fags.

"Are those what I think they are?"

"Could be," said Nico. "If Angie finds out, they're yours. I don't normally use them in the house. But tonight," he added, theatrically, "we have something to celebrate—you in your cups!"

He lit one, inhaled deeply and passed it to Colly.

"Suck it in, keep it in and blow out slowly. Your troubles will melt away.!" More ironic theatrics.

They finished the spliff in silence, measuring its effect, each drag sliding Colly back to his days at the uni. What with the concoction sloshing around in his belly and the heavy, oily smoke in his nostrils, it was a moment or two before he realised that Nico was talking again, this time without the barbs.

"I meet some of my pals at the gym," he was saying, "and some at the Community Centre. Sometimes, there are jigs for the disabled there—it's like a bloody chariot race at the Forum!" He laughed and Colly's smile floated in the air, riding on the smoke.

"And do you enjoy it there, at the Centre?"

"Yes, I do. It's great. But I like it best when it's just an ordinary do, you know, for everybody."

"With people who are not disabled . . ."

"Yes. No chips. Not sitting about being second class. And not pissing about proving themselves, compensating for what they've not got."

"You still get that, Nico, even with legs. Anyhow, not all wheelies are like that—*you're* not."

"Suppose not. But I'm not a wheely, I'm a person. An unsociable, unfriendly tosser."

"Touché," said Colly, cursing himself, aware suddenly of the changes wrought by the passing years, seeing the vulnerability, but aware now of the boy's new, brave determination to forge himself into a complete person.

They sat in silence for a while, mulling over the stalemate, Colly with his eyes closed to stop the room spinning. "So," he said, "these people with legs—what do they get up to?"

"All sorts of things. Apart from killing themselves in ego-trip aeroplanes, what do *your* friends get up to?"

"No need to be so bloody cruel, Nico. You know what my friends do because I know Angie tells you. We're talking about *your* friends."

His friends, he could have told him, were even more wounded than he was. Hard as nails on the outside, locked into the building site on the inside—he tied to a wheelchair, and them tied to their guilt. And he trying to untie them. Because if *they* weren't free, *he* couldn't be free. Thinking a thousand times, that he hadn't had to walk that plank, that he hadn't had to fall. If he hadn't been such a prat, trying to show how brave he was, none of it would have happened. All of them would be free.

What Colly didn't know was him going to the Centre with Ivan Snell and meeting Kate Drummond. It was his first time there, and it was her first time since her sister died, ages before. And him and Kate clicking, And she going off to where they used to live miles away and bringing Thumper and Trazzer back with her. And them being on their guard, wondering if there was a catch, but getting to know him, loosening up, having a laugh, showing that no legs didn't equal idiot. And them saying that, no, they couldn't get Mozzy and Mickey to come because . . . well . . . because they were the ones that had sent him to walk the plank and they'd never got over it. And him saying 'Keep telling them it was my fault, that I can't be whole again until everybody's whole.'

So he couldn't tell Colly about Kate and Kate's dead sister and how she'd cared for her and how she was now working as a carer for one of the local councils and how he loved and loved and loved her. And he couldn't tell him about Dorothy and about Mary Duff and about his pals, Jim Dyson and Jerry Wilcox, and especially not about the other two who wouldn't come, David Moorhouse and Mickey Dooley.

—Because he wouldn't realise.

—Because he'd blunder in and louse it up.

—Because he cared too much.

—Because he was sliding off the rails.

"Colly," he declared, pouring two more snakebites, lighting the other spliff, dragging in deep, passing it on, "one day I'll be glad to tell you about my friends, who they are, what they do. But not until you're ready to hear it."

"And what's that supposed to mean?"

"It means what it says on the tin. At the moment, you're not ready. When you're ready, you'll not need to ask what it means; you'll know."

"Very deep," said Colly, his sarcasm provoking the other into more actorish faces.

"But not hogwash!." He waved an impudent finger, reached for the spliff, took a drag and handed it back.

Listening to the boy, watching him as if for the first time, it came to Colly that it wasn't he who had been strong, had been doing favours, but Nico. That it was Nico who had been the rock, Nico around whom they had circled, that without Nico he would have been that much less of a man. Even now, he wasn't sure he felt a *real* man because a *real* man would be loved and trusted. And although Angie was always assuring him that the boy cared for him, he clearly didn't trust him.

His mind elsewhere, he sucked too hard on the last of the spliff and burned his lips, ending up swearing and spitting, trying to dump the stub into an ashtray, missing the first time, telling himself that he didn't care a stuff, that he could handle them all—even this emerging, patronising boy-man sitting stoned in his chair, head lolling about, mumbling something to him about Lizzie, about meeting Lizzie.

Floating across to him, shaking him. "Wake up! You're talking crap! You've never met Lizzie! C'mon, wake up! Admit it!"

But he couldn't rouse him. Instead, he wheeled him through to the bedroom, fixed the hoist straps around him and swung him onto the bed. Once there, he removed his shoes and trousers and threw a cover over him.

"There you are, boyo. You can't say I don't try."

He stumbled back into the other room and regarded the bed settee, rejecting it on the grounds that he didn't want to risk more grudging toleration in the morning, convinced now that it was too late, that he really had blown it. He stepped out into the night, tested the cool air, decided he was O.K., and slid into the Jag's driving seat.

For some reason, he couldn't find the ignition, couldn't even remember where it was, finally getting the key in and reversing out onto the road. A black cab chugged round him, pipping self-importantly, as if they weren't the only two on the road.

Exhilarated, replying to the challenge, he put his foot down and passed the cab within a few yards, tore round the bend and saw green lights turning to amber, illuminated in them a car, a baby Fiat going the same way as himself. He pressed the pedal again to beat the red, grinning with anticipation, failing to realise that the car in front had not yet cleared the railings on the pedestrian island, that there was no room to pass.

All he remembered was the word 'Lizzie' floating on heavy wreathes of spliff smoke, and of Nico talking crap about seeing her.

—that and the contemptuous voice of the taxi driver, the cold, matter of fact traffic cops, and the flashing lights of the ambulance for the people in the Fiat.

". . . And what of the central issue that Lord Hutton felt he could not address? If the September 2002 dossier which helped persuade the nation of the urgent need for war . . . was indeed reliable, where, exactly, are Iraq's weapons of mass destruction?—The Independent, January 29, 2004.

Chapter 20

Games

An hour before Jill Maybury was due to arrive on her second visit—enigmatically inviting herself to afternoon tea on the grounds that a good chat was often better than a good you-know-what—Lizzie Wolfson received a telephone call from, of all people, Angie Maketi.

"Look," she said hurriedly, obviously afraid that Lizzie might hang up, "I know you must be wondering why I'm calling you—I'm just trying to do what's for the best. It's just that . . . what makes it awkward is that Colly, Mr Wolfson, doesn't know I'm ringing and—"

"What are you trying to tell me?"

"You won't say anything, will you? This is for you."

"I won't say a thing. What is it?"

"Two things, really. First—and he's alright, he wasn't hurt—he's been in a car crash."

"Wonderful," said Lizzie, wryly. "Where?"

"Just down the road from here. A week ago. He's been charged."

"What with?"

"Drunken driving. Driving without due care and attention whilst under the influence of drink and drugs." Reciting it, saying it as quickly as possible.

"Drugs?"

"Pot."

"What—at your house?"

"Lizzie, it doesn't matter where. I'm telling you because he might need you. He's not coping."

"What about dear Charlie?"

"He can tell Charlie himself. It's you that I thought should know."

Thanking her stiffly, the bitterness welling up, spurting like a fountain ten minutes after Jill Maybury's arrival on a visit that started on one track and ended on another; that made the weather man's lonely little wife the bearer of the sort of inside information eagerly sought by gossips such as Anna Brownlove . . . and by worried suitors such as Simon Mount.

———————

No one could put a date to when Simon's left eye became prominent. One day he was a normal enough, reasonably good looking young man, tall and skinny, a fine, almost pretty nose above sensuous lips, the next, so it seemed, he was a lop-sided Cyclops, his left eye the feature you were most likely to notice, its brow more or less permanently raised and the eye cruel and demanding. According to the wicked folklore among his circle, he had made so much use of the eyebrow whilst playing the fool that it had stuck—except, they sneered, when he was discussing money, or, as Jill Maybury was soon to discover, when persuading his women into bed.

Wicked or not, the folklore proved generally accurate—lounging on the couch listening to his lover, Chloe Jones, once again analysing the scandal involving the 'filthy rich architect,' the 'bimbo model,' and her 'pillock of a pilot husband', there were enough elements present of each strand of the theory to bring his two brows perfectly level.

Not that he was so interested in the scandal, or in Chloe's over-descriptive view of it; more that it had within it the seeds for him of a growing jealousy, a feeling that she seemed unhealthily drawn, a spellbound cat curled in his armchair, fascinated, not by him—but by the flutterings of yet another defective, eternal triangle.

"I know I've been over this before," she conceded, wary of his mood, conscious that although it was the danger of secretly baiting him this way that made it exciting, she had to remember he was no longer quite the freaked-out hedonist of old. If he tumbled her, God knows what would happen . . . .

"But don't you think it's intriguing? Why would a man, a man with money to burn, burn himself instead, even if he had cancer? Wouldn't he do something about it, or choose another way?"

"I can't imagine," he said, refusing to play her game, playing his own.

"But what about the bimbo? You've always had, shall we say . . . plenty to offer," teasing him, trying to interest him. "Would *you* fancy her after something like this?"

"I wouldn't know, depends how good she was in the first place," still not playing, still watching her closely, noting that whenever they had this conversation, she never used names, as if the three people in the triangle were merely bit parts—First Tosser, Second Tosser, Third Tosser—as if names might make them too real. Too revealing. Of *them*—or of *her*?

"That's typical of you," she said, mildly. "But seriously, if you were *him*, the other one, would you be able to continue? Not just the sex—"

"Is there anything else?"

"Bastard! Not just the sex, everything else?"

"No idea. You'd better ask him." Cold, affecting disinterest.

"Only playing!" she exclaimed. "Big Chief no need get green-eyed."

"Big Chief tired of pow-wow," he said, stretching languorously, reaching for her. "Says slave girl talk too much. Says wants make papoose."

And although she did eventually allow him to make love to her, though with conception strictly ruled out by both of them, he noticed again that she seemed to be listening for someone else, hearing another voice, awaiting a different touch. Without doubt, he could feel her cooling. And where once it would not have mattered, now it did. Because now he wanted an end to the wandering. He cared. And he wanted her to care with him.

At various times, Anna Brownlove's money-raising campaigns for the kids of Africa afflicted her in much the same way as many another voluntary worker—she had the distinct feeling that people who sat on their backsides regarded her either as an irritating saint or a toiling fool. The feeling spawned a resentment that joined with the deeper, chronic disappointment of her barren womb and led her to mix her virtues with a morbid, well-known curiosity in human duplicity.

So when Simon Mount rang, there was, immediately, a mutual, unspoken understanding. By him making the call himself rather than leaving it to Chloe, she suspected an underlying reason; for his part, because of her instant wariness, he knew that he would have to jump through hoops, but that in the end, like a she-wolf with cubs, she would cough up what he sought, good or bad.

After the usual opening pleasantries, he added, regretfully, "Yes, long time, no see," aware that her tennis party was not long back down the road, but not wanting to be the first to mention it.

"The tennis . . . ?"

"Well, yes!—I meant just the four of us."

"Ah! You're right, it has been quite a while."

"Mind you, the tennis was great. Lovely day. I don't think I properly thanked you."

"Not to worry, dear. Chloe did. Lovely girl."

"Isn't she just!"

"So busy, too! Diary always full. No time for a girlie lunch—not these days."

He registered the gratuitous, curdling information and changed tack.

"Suppose not. But she really enjoyed the tennis. We both did."

"So you said." Waiting patiently.

"Yes. She's such a good player—except for that game we had with you two, I could hardly get near her for the crush!"

"All the chaps?"

"Yes. This one . . . that one . . . even Colly Wolfson!" Here it was! Her pulse quickened.

"Colly? Didn't realise he'd turned up."

"Oh yes! Spotted him. Busy man . . ." His allusions as adroit as hers, a recognition not lost on Anna, whose mind was already smugly recalling the carefully stored memory of the last Sink hen party—of Chloe's persistent interest there in all things Wolfson. And that was months ago . . .

"Oh I don't *think* so, Simon," she said, showily, anticipating his next query, leapfrogging it not so much to save him the embarrassment, as to demonstrate her crystal ball insight.

"No, not for a *moment*, dear. Anyhow, he's got his hands full, what with Charlie and the other thing."

"What—Howard?"

"No, no, not Howard! Well, Howard, yes, of course. But haven't you heard? It's being kept quiet, but Jill Maybury tells me he's been in a bit of a shunt. His fault. Something to do with drugs. If only he'd have . . ."

Her voice trailing away, her mind performing somersaults. If only he'd what? Fancied *her*? Been shagging *her*? Astonished, angry with herself, aware that such thoughts would have lain fallow had he not started it up with Charlie and now, from Simon's abrupt, apparently confirmatory interest . . . with Chloe? The whole lot of them in some sort of sexual frenzy merely because a gorgeous man . . . because Lizzie . . . because he couldn't say no to Charlie's easy pickings? Instead of . . .

"Sorry, dear—lost in thought. Thinking about poor Lizzie. But don't worry about the other thing, dear. Colly Wolfson might be ever so dishy—not my cup of tea, mind you, never did trust the pretty ones—but I'm sure your Chloe can cope. Oh yes, I imagine so."

———

Thinking it over, analysing Anna's nuances, setting them against what he already suspected, Simon was left with few doubts: Chloe was enjoying the same treats as Charlie Sinclair. With similar diversions in the past, she had only involved herself for the amusement, for the challenge, knowing, when she eventually admitted her latest coup, that he would laugh and snigger with her and carry on as before. This time, however, it was different—even before she had met Wolfson, he could feel her drifting away, falling behind. Perhaps, without her realising it, she was now drowning . . .

He needed to know more. And from what Anna had said—another of her encrypted messages—he knew just the person.

"Hello! Jill!" saying the two words separately, breathing them down the phone. "How is my very *favourite* estate agent?"

"Is this . . . is this Simon?"

"Flatterer! Right first time! I was sorry to miss you at the tennis. You know, Anna's do."

"I was there."

"Oh I know you were there. I mean, missed playing with you."

"Playing with me? Are we still talking the 'love-all' stuff, Simon?"

"Sounds ace to me!"

"Ha! Ha!" she said, affecting sarcasm, but following with, "And why would little old you want to play ball with little old me?"

"Come out to lunch and I'll tell all—that is, if you think Barns won't mind. You don't think so?"

Having attracted, but so far failed to lead astray, the uncouth but morally correct Herbie Kirby, the impressionable, forlorn Mrs Maybury was still looking for adventure.

"Barns," she replied, "will be chasing his isobars."

The restaurant he took her to was one of those exclusive places away from the High Street. Exclusive and seductive.

With their starters eaten and with the second glass of wine poured, she leaned up close to him, her best perfume blending with the Muscadet on her breath. Half whispering, she told him that she really didn't mind his hand on her knee, but wasn't it time he started telling.

"Does there have to be a reason for this?" Whispering in return, his hand staying, the thin, caressing fingers the rhythmic wash of a gentle tide.

"You said there was."

Brazenly, the hand remained while the waiter served their main courses, his face impenetrable, the trained eyes of servitude unseeing, the hand withdrawn on his departure to begin the task of demolishing the exquisitely arranged *supreme de canard aux figues*.

"It's simple. I really did miss seeing a lot of you at the tennis and thought, well, that going out to lunch might be fun."

"And so it is. But . . ."

"Look! We've known the Brownloves for more than a year. Met them on holiday. And they brought us to meet you all at Charlie's New Year do. And it was great! Loved it! But since then, we haven't had much of a chance to get to *know* you all. So I thought—"

"You thought you'd quiz little old me in the back of a restaurant."

"Ah! My subtle is your obvious."

She laughed—and wished the hand were back on her knee. "What do you want to know?"

"Nothing specific—just what makes people tick. It's so much easier to make friends if you know their background."

They ate in silence for a while. Having thought about his request, she began with herself and Barns, passed on to the Callows, then the Platt-Smiths.

"And what about the big love affair business? It must have been a bit of a shock to you all."

"Not as big as Howard's death . . . ."

"No, suppose not. Charlie seems such a nice person. Very easy to know. Different again to the Wolfsons. Lizzie we've not met, but Colly is . . ."

"Mr Inscrutable?"

"Absolutely! What's all that about?"

She repeated the brief history, a la Anna Brownlove, of the Wolfson's blighted marriage, the cot death, the injured boy.

"Ah yes," he said. "Chloe told me of this boy. Became his patron, didn't he? Set him up years ago."

"Yes, very generous, I hear. What I also know, just between the two of us," preening herself, eking out her knowledge, her judgement diluted by the dizzying thoughts of the prize clearly on offer, "is that he never gave up. He's been seeing the boy secretly every week for years. And something else the Sinks don't know—the boy's carer, the person Colly pays to be in charge, is none other than the party bottle washer, Angie Maketi. Lizzie's only just found out."

He raised his famous eyebrow. "And . . ."

"And that's about it," she said, finishing her wine, accepting more from a second bottle.

"But you know more than that, don't you?" he said, raising the eyebrow again, playing her like a gulping trout.

"Do I?"

"Well, perhaps not. Don't you know that he's on a charge for pushing heroine?"

"No, he's not!" she exclaimed, bursting out laughing. "And you know he's not! He's been smoking pot with the boy. Problem is that he also had a lot to drink and crashed his car."

He wagged his finger at her to show that his challenge had been right.

"And is that all you wanted to know?"

"Is there more?"

"There could be." She now playing the line, reeling him in. "And it could be the most interesting of all. But not here."

"Where?"

"I'll leave that to you."

On her way home from his flat three hours later, the adventurous Mrs Maybury cosseted herself in the back of her taxi and reviewed her amazing afternoon.

Within minutes of their arrival at his flat high up in a tower block, he was pressing a brandy on her, and was sitting up close on a black leather studio couch. She noticed that his left eyebrow was now quite level and sensed that like her, he was savouring the moment, working hard to make her do his bidding, encouraging her to slot into place the final piece in their separate games.

"So just what is this tantalizing nugget of yours?"

"Which one is that?"

"The one you're sending me mad over." The words breathed against her open lips, the thin fingers retracing their steps.

But it wasn't until they were between the sheets and he was above her and she was straining to reach him, the hunted, salving tip poised but withheld, tormenting her, demanding her part of their bargain, that she finally said it was Charlie, that when she'd told Charlie about the car crash and where it was, she'd shouted, "And you know why it was there, don't you? Because that's where he fucks his black angel, Angie Maketi!"

Gasping her gratefulness as the smirking Tantalus was at last unleashed.

The next day, putting it all together, arranging it in his mind, Simon Mount made two phone calls. The first was to a friend on the local newspaper, seeking information without giving any himself; the second was to the man whose name he had been given by the first, and to whom he spoke for a long time and in some detail.

Having done so, he sat back to wait, unaware that his latest conquest, after wilfully breaking the vows of her boring marriage, was now riven with guilt.

Not for Barns.

For Herbie.

"It (the Hutton Report) is a whitewash, basically. The danger is that it is so one-sided a report that it is going to lose credibility. People just aren't going to believe it"—the Labour Party M.P., Austin Mitchell, The Daily Telegraph, January 29, 2004.

Chapter 21

Revenge - I

When he checked again, remembering Angie's words, yes, it was clear that Nico's bodybuilding was working. He was taking a shower, levering himself about under the spray in his special chair. And where before he had looked thin and wasted, that now applied only to his legs. Above his hips, along his shoulders and arms, even his stomach and back, muscles flexed and swelled healthily. He was pleased for the boy, proud even. But in the end, the fact that he had missed the change, had had no part in it, added to his depression, his sense of redundancy.

Back in Nico's room, he watched him gel his hair, sticking it up in tufts. He found the style faintly ridiculous, that and the gold ring that had suddenly appeared in one ear. But, well, what the hell—what did *he* know?

"Are you staying here tonight?" the boy asked, peering into the mirror, twiddling his brush, dropping it, cursing mildly as he manoeuvred his chair to pick it up, glancing across at Colly, grinning. "Can't even hold a brush," he said.

For the first time, Colly saw that Nico was happy. The vision was like putting on a new pair of spectacles, the surprise of the sudden sharpness and clarity, the regret of not doing so earlier. As with the muscle building, he had missed the boy shedding his bitterness, coming to terms with himself, still nervous, uncertain, untrusting, but looking outwards. Perversely, he wondered if the old problems were merely stored away.

"These friends of yours, the ones I'm not allowed to meet, they've certainly got you going," he said, their eyes converging for a long moment, Colly uncomfortable under the direct gaze, embarrassed by his ferreting. Into his mind jumped several similar, dead-end conversations with Sally.

The boy shrugged and reverted to his original question. "Well, *are* you staying?"

"Would you like me to?" Grovelling for the old dependency.

"It's not a question of like."

"Rather more you keeping an eye on me? Doing a proper job?" He watched as Nico gave his hair one last tweak before turning round, grinning.

"That's right! So that this time, we can get you *properly* motherless! So that you don't have to go out and mow down the other half of south London! Mind you, I think the rest of the baby Fiats must have fucked off by now! Scared shitless!" He laughed and shook his head disbelievingly. "Plonker!" he said, throwing the hairbrush at Colly, laughing again as the other ducked out of the way. Then, seriously: "—So that you can spend some time with us and not sit around clutching a bottle, moping about your women."

"—So that you can get me into court tomorrow morning in a fit and proper state."

"That, too," said Nico. "And for God's sake, stop worrying! What's done is done. If I hadn't passed out, it wouldn't have happened. But I did. Do what that hot-shot bloody lawyer of yours says, Sam what's-his-name. It's your first offence and the couple in the other car weren't badly hurt, they were just knocked about a bit. So look on the bright side! They're not going to send you down—and you don't have to mount another 'Save Warren Nichols' campaign."

So, sadly, the bitterness was still there . . .

But the boy was right about the court. He followed Sam Stirling's advice, pleaded guilty to everything, made no mention of Nico or Angie, said he had been given the spliffs at a party because he had been complaining of stress at work, and made a short speech of shame and contrition. In return, he was given three months suspended, fined £500 with costs, disqualified from driving for a year and handed one-hundred-and-twenty hours community service.

After completing the necessary formalities, he emerged from the courthouse, pumped Sam's hand, said they must get together for a drink, and with the lawyer disappearing round the corner, took a deep breath to rid himself of the day's humiliation. As he did so, he was confronted by two people: his wife looking up into his face, and seconds later, a photographer who danced around in front of them, his camera whirring, before jumping onto the pillion seat of a waiting motorbike and disappearing into the traffic.

"For God's sake!" Lizzie cried, startled. "What was all that about?"

"You tell me! Where did *you* spring from?"

"It had nothing to do with *me*," she said, flaring.

"Of course not."

She looked at him sharply, but failed to spot any sarcasm.

"You do believe me, don't you?"

"Yes."

"And you don't mind me being here?"

"No. Not now. Not if you don't mind having your picture in the paper, screwing things up."

"I'm sorry, Colly. I am, really. I've been waiting for you to come out. I came because I thought you might need some support—I heard on the grapevine that Charlie wouldn't be here."

"For obvious reasons," he said. "She and everyone else."

"Yes, foolish of me not to come inside."

He watched her wrestling with her emotions, her face thinner than he remembered, her make-up not quite so certain. But for the fracas with the photographer, he would have been happy to see her. Grateful even.

"Look," she said. "I still don't know what's happened to you. You can either take me for a drink and tell me there, or I can read it in the papers."

"I feel shattered," he said. "Let's go for a drink—there won't be much in the papers, anyhow."

Early the next morning, Tuesday, he had a meeting with his welfare officer and was briefed on his community service tasks . . . clearing up the rubbish at a couple of picnic sites . . . cleaning out the toilets . . . serving food to the homeless . . . signing up for courses at drug and alcohol dependency clinics. The latter was clearly a waste of time, but he said nothing. Afterwards, he bought a copy of every national newspaper and scoured them, heart in mouth. A couple of the so-called quality papers and one of the red-top tabloids had short, down page accounts of the court case, all of them with variants of the headline, "Top Architect Clobbered." But apart from that, there seemed little interest.

The middle of the week came and went. The community work was as it was supposed to be—irksome and humiliating, rewarding even, if done properly. Not enough to make him jump over the moon, but, if he swallowed hard . . . Ok—unlike the alcoholics class, a bunch of worried men and women, some old, some young, sitting in a circle stuttering out their demons. When it came to his turn, he said he didn't have any demons, he didn't have a drink problem and he didn't know why he was there—looking around for support, finding none. Angry about it, knowing that somehow, he had let them down . . .

The Wednesday night he spent with a pleasurably sympathetic Charlie and on the Thursday he had been hoping to see Chloe. But for some reason she wasn't answering her phone. Which was disappointing and a bit of a mystery. But at least there were no further reports in the nationals. And although, as he feared, his local paper splashed the story on the Friday, even there it was restricted to what had been said in court and was angled more on his "remorse and sorrow."

Saturday also started unremarkably, dawning with him still in one piece and with rising hopes that the worst of the bad publicity was over. He spent a couple of hours weeding the pathways in what one of the locals called Dog Shit Park, and then trailed back to the Tube to go to a men's hostel to work in the laundry. That done, he jumped on a bus to Nico's to help him with what he called his "week-end ablutions."

During the scrubbing, he heard that Nico was sleeping over that night at "some flat or other" after a night with his friends at the Community Centre. Angie, it appeared, was taking the opportunity to visit her sister. So there was no point staying there.

It was now early evening. And it was while he was standing at the front gate, waving goodbye to the two of them, feeling a sudden need for Charlie, for her to wipe away his day—coming to the conclusion, only an instant before, that there was no point in searching around for some way of breaking it off with her, of upsetting her, not until he and Chloe had got properly together—when his mobile rang.

It was a man with one of those cheery, brisk voices, the ones found in people experienced at dealing with strangers, at hurrying them along, not taking no for an answer; an authoritative voice, bidding him the time of day, asking him if this was Mr Colly Wolfson? Since the crash, he had become used to similar calls from the police, his lawyer, and various court officials and aid workers, and had come to recognise that authority ruled. When you were in the wrong, when you were paying your penance, the easy way was not to argue.

"It is," he said, repeating the phrase twice more as the voice rattled out his new home address and his office address, asking if they were correct.

"And," he said, not unpleasantly, "am I allowed to ask who *you* are? I've paid my fine, surrendered my driving licence, been to the drugs clinic and started my community service. Is there something else?"

"You tell me," said the voice. "I've got several more questions. Not questions exactly, because we know it all. More wanting your comments on certain points."

"What points? You know everything relevant. Are you the police, or what? I still don't know who you are."

"Perhaps we'll leave relevancy to our readers, Mr Wolfson. Oh sorry! Didn't I make it clear? No, not the police, Mr Wolfson—this is one of those nasty Sunday prints that the great unwashed read." He gave the newspaper's name and introduced himself. "Mike—"

But Colly was no longer listening. He was cursing himself for being conned.

"I don't care a flying fuck who you are! I've done the court bit and I've nothing further to say. Piss off!"

He rang off, but with him scarcely across the road, his phone played its silly, ersatz tune again. "Don't you understand good old Anglo-Saxon?" he snapped.

"I do. *Very* colourful! What *you* don't understand, Mr Wolfson, is that this is your chance to balance our story."

"I balanced the story in court. Read the transcript!"

"Hmm! But the court story is like an iceberg, Mr Wolfson—we only saw the part that you put on view. Bear with me. When I asked if you were the well-known architect, the Mr Colly Wolfson who lives here and works there, I could just as easily have asked if you were the same Mr Wolfson who was involved in the crippled boy case. Strange how the boy now goes to a Centre well known for drugs and that you crashed your car on his street . . . and correct me if I'm wrong, but the *same* Mr Wolfson who is the father of runaway, broken-hearted Sally, the sixteen-year-old clubber and biker. And the *same* Mr Wolfson who is now running not one, but *two* lovers: one of them Mrs Charlie Sinclair—what a pity it was, such a pity, about her husband—and the other one, the woman who cares for the boy—what's her name?—Oh yes, the black skivvy, Angie Maketi . . .

"So I'm doing you a favour, Mr Wolfson. I'm giving you the right of reply, the chance to balance our story."

"Bullshit!—the chance to dig my grave."

"Think about it."

"I don't need to think about it! Half of what you say is a pack of lies and innuendo and the other half is my private business and nothing to do with you or anyone else."

"All we're doing is putting your court case into context."

"Rubbish! All you're doing is what you do best—dredging for stuff that's not there. All my friends know that I'm involved with Charlie Sinclair. It's no secret. It began before her husband's plane crashed. And there are no question marks there—they've been cleared up. He was suffering from cancer,"—taking a chance—"he did it because of that, not because of Charlie and me. As for Angie Maketi, it's totally untrue that I've been sleeping with her. Who's feeding you this garbage? She's a wonderful, honourable friend and I'll sue anyone—"

"And the boy?"

"What about the boy?"

"There seems to be a feeling that you see rather a lot of him."

"What *is* this? He was disabled in an accident on one of my building sites. We admitted liability. What was I supposed to do—walk away?"

"He was lucky you were rich enough—"

"He can't walk! Never will! You call that lucky? Angie Maketi is his carer. Other people are also involved and I help as often as I can.

So, yes, I do see Angie regularly. But the last twelve years haven't been about her, they've been about Nico."

He paused, out of breath, searching for a way to explain himself, to vanquish his caller.

"Is that it?"

Anger flooded through him and he found himself shouting, the reporter's call one humiliation too many, the twin tragedies of his life whirling around in the black hole, the four cloying women woven into them; deciding, in an instant, that if his life was to be disgraced in this way, then why not tell it as it was, match Nico, let go of the dead baby, reveal what had lain hidden . . .

"No, it's not bloody *it!*" he said, babbling, desperate to break through the reporter's impervious shell. "We're not talking about some faceless charity case! We're talking about a beautiful, brave boy! He's my life! My reason! My son! Anybody who doubts that is a fool, and anybody who says I've been carrying on with Angie is a liar."

Sitting in the cold, quiet cottage, the whisky bottle open beside him. Glass in hand. Glass empty. Mind empty. Glass recharged. Mind still empty. His phone ringing again. Not the harrying, devious reporter. Angie. To say she was sorry they had not been able to stay with him.

Hearing his silence, asking if he was O.K.

Yes, he was fine. Just fine.

Wondering if it was her, Angie, who'd pulled the plug on him. Gone insane looking after Nico . . . cracked with jealousy over Charlie . . . But no, it couldn't be Angie. Surely not Angie.

So if it wasn't Angie, who was it?

Nico? Fed up waiting for a father? Seizing the moment to pay him back? Possibly, even a short while ago. But surely not now? Not now he was happy. Why *was* he so happy?

So was it some jealous bastard at the office? In some rival office? There were plenty with grudges, with reasons to resent his success. But where would they get the gen? How would they know?

Charlie? No not Charlie, never Charlie. She loved him, needed him. Like Lizzie once did.

Lizzie? The cot death . . . Nico . . . Charlie . . . Plenty of reasons for her. Was that why she'd turned up outside the court? To finger him? To play Judas? A woman scorned? Possible. Anything was possible. Even Sally! Perhaps the two of them—Lizzie overcome, losing her senses; Sally on the road, deciding if she couldn't have him, nobody would . . .

He drank more whisky, sitting for another hour, his mind again blank, cursing silently. Cursing them, him, them, him, mainly him. Cradling the bottle, he shambled off up the stairs, the curses following him—but stopping suddenly as a jubilant thought began to form, sustaining him, holding him together.

The man on the phone, the man cataloguing his failures, his deceits—there'd been no mention of Chloe! And there would have been, wouldn't there, had the man known? Because—three lovers instead of two, actual or not—wouldn't that have made his story even better . . . ?

Which meant he'd got away with it!

There was still something left!

There was still Chloe!

He raised the bottle and drank deeply to celebrate his victory.

"The (Hutton) report leaves big questions unanswered because, inevitably, they were not addressed. We are still no closer to determining whether this country went to war on a false prospectus. We need an independent inquiry to find out why that happened"—the former leader of the Liberal Democrat Party, Charles Kennedy.

Chapter 22

Revenge II

Late that Saturday, the grossly overweight Mike Lampeter was sitting in his paper's vast newsroom, a beached whale among a sea of grey computer terminals, the lateness of the tide washing away all but a distant couple of users. He was chewing on a mildly warm meat and potato pie, his feet up on the desk, catching up on the day's football after a busy shift. Except for his own stories, the sports pages were the only part of his paper that he deigned to read, although even they rarely matched his taste.

The night editor, chained to the newsroom in case a major story broke, walked down the aisle and flopped into an adjacent chair.

"Doesn't Mr Scoop have a home to go to, then?"

Lampeter raised his eyes from the Manchester United report. His marriage had broken down months before, a fact known to the entire office since he was now shacked up with the hard boiled, don't-give-a-toss deputy news editor.

"Give it a rest, Locksley. I'm knackered from keeping you lot on your Cloud Nine salaries—another wincing, red meat exclusive."

"Wincing?"

"Wincing. Another slice of dirty diversion for the mindless masses."

"C'mon! Let the masses be—they care like you and I care!"

"Oh yeah—let's do that. Let's pretend that while they're lapping up my story about the adorable Mr Wolfson, all they're *really* wanting is to care about the boys dying in Iraq. Let's pretend the dying won't go on and on. Let's pretend the masses care as much as Tony boy says *he* does."

"So what? When Iraq's over and the masses have forgotten all about Tony, the pricks and the losers will still be out there waiting for you to write about them."

"Yeah—and like Colly bloody Wolfson, they still won't care a stuff."

"How d'you know? Did you ask him?"

Like Mr Lampeter, Charlie Sinclair did most of her best thinking sitting down, the Sunday morning sunshine streaming in through the beautiful glass lantern in the ceiling, highlighting her hair, playing on the ruffles of her dressing gown. She was perched on the edge of her chair, leaning forward, reading that morning's newspaper, hugging herself as people do when they're cold or trying to comfort themselves.

They were in the kitchen, she at the table, Colly at the window looking down the garden, catching himself looking outward, wondering whether people had noticed, whether they judged that he, his mind, was trying to escape into the distant vista, into whatever he was looking at; whether seeking the seemingly simpler life of the distant vista was the same for them.

He was waiting for her to finish reading the story about him—about them all, flinching at the lurid, double-page spread reflected in the window, his life laid out before him, each element given its own, inflamed headline. If he moved his eyes to another pane, the reflection disappeared; in one pane that part of his life that weighed like a ton, in the other a clear view, a fresh start.

He remembered hearing the first half of the reporter's by-line and practised saying the whole name, breathing it on to the glass. Mike Lampeter. Mike Lampeter. A simple, straightforward name, crisp, to the point, like the voice. He wondered what the man was like, what he looked like, what he thought, whether he enjoyed lifting stones . . .

After the phone call, after he had got over his anger, he did some thinking of his own. Since Lampeter's newspaper wasn't the sort any of his set were likely to dirty their hands on—they were all ever so slightly too hypocritical to be caught enjoying its wares—he was going to have to let them into his life, one by one, before they heard it on the drip-drip. His life might be out of control, and explaining it all personally might be tedious and degrading, but at least he didn't need to look more of a shit than he was . . .

Fired by his rear-guard action, he locked his latest bottle away in the drinks cupboard, phoned for a mini-cab for the whole of the next day and was up at seven, ready to begin his task

His first port of call was the newsagents, where he verified that it was only Lampeter's *Screws of the World* that was running his story. He bought a coffee for his driver and ten copies of the newspaper for himself and the people he was about to call on.

The first on his list would have been Angie and Nico, but they were both out overnight. Which wasn't a good start. Neither, it turned out, was his second choice—his wife, Lizzie. Explaining away his faithfully recorded quotes on "his son, Nico," was never, in the circumstances, going to be easy. But any faint hope of parleying quickly disappeared when he found her waiting for him, dressed in shirt and slacks and looking remarkably calm. "So what took you so long?" she asked.

He frowned, irritated at being so easily second-guessed. "I need to talk to you."

"I don't think so," she said, blocking the doorway, keeping him out on the porch. "If that's a copy of your life story that you're holding, don't bother. I know all about it. Your daughter, Sally—remember Sally?—she phoned hours ago. Just the sort of thing you want to read, don't you think, on your way home with your friends from clubbing—what your father finds important?"

"What! They bought one?" Incredulous.

"Of course not! They found it on the train. You can buy them in London late at night. All the papers. It's what *we* used to do. Or have you forgotten that, too?"

"I'm sorry. I didn't plan it this way. That's why I'm round here now."

"The trouble with you, Colly, is that you don't plan anything. Me, I've got used to your obsessions, your work, our son—the totally innocent death of our son, not me, nothing to do with me, just a common or garden cot death—even Charlie, even Nico, even if you substituted him for our baby without asking me, even if you were screwing her while you were screwing me—"

"I wasn't."

"So she tells me . . . Colly, at a pinch, just at a pinch, I could take all that, all the lies, the deceits, the self, self, self, even when it all gets splattered over that disgusting newspaper. But couldn't you have said just one kind word about your daughter? In that diatribe of yours, couldn't you have defended her, mentioned her just once?"

So he was now with Charlie, banging on her door at eight o'clock in the morning, wandering into the kitchen, newspaper in hand, asking for a drink. A real drink to chase away Lizzie's words. Slugging it, gazing through the window, realising she was no longer reading, turning to her.

"I had to come round," he said. "I had to make sure you heard it from me, not someone else."

She was slowly sliding the open newspaper across the table with her fingertips like a naughty child, watching its hundred pages slither to the floor like a lurid, oozing sewer, rubbing her hands on her robe, the child absolving itself from the act, the adult removing contamination.

"Oh! So kind you are," she said. "So *very, very* kind."

The fury following.

"Why didn't you tell me about this boy, this Nico? That you were still seeing him, still involved with him after all these years? Why go around carrying secrets? And not only that! Coming to this house, rushing away from my bed, letting me think you were going off home or somewhere, when all the time you were going off for some more at Angie's! I don't need to read this rag to know that—I've known for ages!"

"How? How do you know? How would you think that?"

"Because I got an anonymous note. It was like something out of a horror comic. I went to where it said—to Angie's house. I saw the two of you."

"What, me and Nico?"

"No! You and Angie! Kissing! What was I supposed to think? What would *you* have thought?"

"I might have given you the benefit of the doubt."

"What doubt?—you weren't scared to death, you hadn't just received a poison pen letter! I didn't know Nico was there and I didn't know what to do. I took the note to Lizzie. I thought *she'd* written it. I thought we could come to some understanding."

The news that the two of them had been getting together behind his back jolted him, threw up other questions.

"Are you telling me that she *also* knows where Angie and Nico live? That if you gave her this note, *she* knows, too? Has she *also* been there?"—it occurring to him that apart from that one oblique reference, Lizzie hadn't told him about her meeting Charlie, that if she was keeping that a secret, what about Angie and Nico . . . ? And then suddenly remembering Nico babbling on about seeing Lizzie . . .

"Yes, perhaps she's been there," she answered, enraged again, this time by his interest in Lizzie. "I suppose so. I don't know. We're not talking about Lizzie—we're talking about Angie and this boy."

"But I've told Lizzie—like you've just read—that there's nothing in it! There's nothing between Angie and me! There never has been!"

His denials rejected, met with more anger.

"So why do you think Lizzie let me think the opposite? Why do you think she did that?—to get back at me or because she still cares for you?"

"I don't know."

"No, but I know *this*—what would you say if I told you it was Lizzie who told me about Howard's cancer? I didn't just find the letters and all that stuff from the hospital like I told you—I made that up! *She* told me about it—how Howard had cooked up a plan to make us suffer! But the sad cow didn't tell *you*, did she? And *I* didn't tell you because I was trying to save you from the hurt, from you stirring it all up. And what do I get for my trouble?—I get told in this rag about this ridiculous boy and that I'm *lying* about *Angie*! That anybody who thinks you're screwing Angie is a liar!"

She swept aside his attempts to interrupt her and sailed on. "And not only *that*—but that this precious boy, this precious Nico, is your whole life! Not *me*! *Nico*! And not just Nico, *Lizzie*!"

"Lizzie?"

"You saw her at the court! You told me not to go. But *she* did! Look at the photograph! Look how she's looking at you! Look at them *all*!"—gesturing violently at the faces looking up at them from the floor. "A snivelling wife who's kicked you out but can't keep away, a black lover who we're all supposed to believe is *not* your lover, and a crippled boy who's *not* your secret son! You can have them. But you can't have *me*! Not now, Colly!"

———

The phone ringing in the cottage. On and on. Again and again. Checking each time for a message, expecting it to be Charlie to say sorry, to say she didn't mean it, to say anything but what she had just said. No messages. Checking the caller's number, hoping, praying, it would be Chloe. It wasn't Chloe. It was Angie. Each time it was Angie. Either her or Nico.

He knew he should be ringing them, that he should have gone to see them, chancing that they would be in. But after Charlie, he needed time to think.

Perhaps the next time Angie rang, he'd be ready . . .

When she did, and he finally picked up the phone, it was to more agonised ranting. And despite his tactics, he was still caught out, unable to deal with the awfulness.

"Angie, I . . ."

"Colly! Thank you so much for the glowing character reference! And so public! I can't wait to put it in my C.V. It'll look so good there, don't you think, a cutting from nothing more than a porn rag! You weren't born yesterday, Colly—everybody knows that denying something to these people in that manner is as good as striking a match."

"If you say so."

"I *do* say so—you should have said *nothing*!"

"The stuff I said about you—you know I didn't mean it to sound like that. I meant it literally."

"And what you had to say about Nico—was *that* literal? Or do you expect him to take it with a pinch of salt? What he'd been waiting to hear all his life, Colly, and you tell him he's your son in the middle of a story about sex and drugs! *You* having sex with every woman in sight and *him* hanging out in a drugs den! What were you *thinking* about?"

She paused, waiting for him to respond. But he could find nothing to say that would sound decent.

"Are you still there?"

"Yes."

"Colly, you're the boss, you pay the bills, but we're *friends*. And a friend would tell you that Nico didn't need the great fanfare. A quiet word would have been more than enough. Having it dragged out of you by some hack on a tabloid humiliates him. What do you think his friends are going to say?"

"Can I speak to him?"

"That wouldn't be a good idea. Deep down in him, it's different. But at the moment, he's seething about the drugs and he's wondering if he wanted the son bit in the first place. He might come round, he usually does. But you're not the only person in his life any more. You'll have to give him time."

"So I stay away and you cope on your own?"

"Yes. I've done it before. He's stronger now and he's got his friends and his other carers. We'll cope.

"Bye, Colly."

———————

Looking down the apple tree garden from his cottage window, the sash cord poking out beyond the bobbin, frayed at the end, seeing it as a tiny, droll commentary on his life. Sitting there, reviewing the wreckage: Angie and Nico, Lizzie and Sally, all four of them blown like leaves across an uncut lawn by a fitful wind. Two of them the future: young, quivering, scurrying along; the other two caught by the tufts, waiting for a gust that might never come.

But none of them with time for him . . .

Which left his two lovers . . .

By the time the call finally came from Chloe, easing the despair gnawing away inside him, he had already decided not to tell Charlie that he forgave her outburst, and not to try to change her mind. It was clear that when it came to Charlie, Howard had won; his poison had dribbled between them, burning into them like the cancer that would have killed him.

So, while the decision was still fresh and before that day's whisky took hold, he wrote her a note, kind, affectionate, telling her how wonderful their love had been, regretting his lapses, agreeing with her that their time together should come to an end, that however much they might wish otherwise, there seemed no future for them.

It was half-an-hour after he had returned from the post-box, after he had poured himself another drink and was looking ahead, wondering how Charlie—how all of them—would take the news yet to come, the news about his secret affair with Chloe, about the life that lay ahead for the two of them, that the phone rang and her voice floated into his consciousness like the sweetest incense.

Greeting her, trying not to sound too grateful, too desperate, telling her how terrible his misery had been, how the newspaper was wrong, assuring her the nightmare was now all over. "It *is* all over, isn't it?"

"Yes," she said, kindly, softly, "it's all over. All of it."

"And you don't mind about the trial and the crap in the paper?"

"We must meet," she said. "Today. Now. Come to the flat."

Taking the stairs two at a time, checking his hair, rehearsing the words he would use to tell her about the other parts of his life, about how he had stored them away, put them on hold, about how his thoughts were now only of her, about how they could *do* and *go* and *be* whatever and however and wherever she wished, about how they could live their fairytale.

But when the door opened, he found it wasn't Chloe standing there, it was Simon; thinking at first that the poor bastard must have arrived by coincidence—what a toe-curler for him! But then noticing that the sneering, challenging eye was more pronounced than ever, deciding instead that the man's presence couldn't be chance, that she must have called him over to break it off with him . . . that somehow he had run up the stairs too fast . . . arrived too soon.

Once he was in the flat, whilst all three of them were still on their feet, he waited for their greetings. He wasn't sure how he should greet them, and they were saying nothing, not even something fatuous like, "Hello, what fun this all is!" staying silent, saying instead, Simon saying, abruptly, cruelly, "Perhaps you'd better know straight off that Chloe and I have set a date for our marriage."

"Marriage?" Staring at Chloe, seeing that where there might have been tears, there was a sort of defiant, self-sustaining coldness. He imagined that she had carefully manufactured it to meet an impossible circumstance, and clutched at the thought that it had nothing to do with him, with the two of them; that it was really intended for Simon, that Simon's words were for nothing.

So why this sense of dread? This spawning supplication?

"Yes," said Simon. "We're getting married! People do!"

Facing Chloe, his back to Simon, his prayers now rising in waves.

"You never . . ."

—told me? Whispered to me? Said:'Oh! By the way, my darling, this time, before you kiss and honour every inch of my body, before you bury yourself in me and tell me that no matter where you are, what you're doing, your cock will always be there, a million miles up into me, before you do all that, I think you should know that I'm planning to shrug you off, scrape you from me.'

"When . . . ?"

Simon answering. "Christmas. The Saturday before Christmas."

"No, not *that*! Not the *date*!" Shaking his head, still staring at her exquisite face. "How did you . . . when did you—?"

"When did we what?" Simon chiding him, playing with him. "Decide? Pledge ourselves? Oh! I *see*! *Not* that! When did she *change?* When did she decide to *dump* you?"

The eye moved closer to the woman. "Colly! Look at us! Look at the *two* of us, the sort of people we are. You didn't really imagine that you . . . that you and Chloe . . . We don't *dump* people, Colly, because we don't take them on in the first place! We like to think we're above that sort of thing. Mind you, those headlines in the paper! All that detail! Now *that* was style, so *very* enlightening—couldn't have written it better ourselves, could we Chloe? No wonder you were ringing her all the time, Colly . . ."

He was listening to the words, looking at her, but listening to the words, feeling the acid burning into him, trying to make sense of them, rejecting them; but still with no response from her, his sensuous, exquisite lover. He saw now that her face was not entirely cast in stone, not the female equivalent of one of Ozzie's Greek gods, seeing there the trace of a mute denial. Of him? Of the words? Of what?

Waving it aside.

"God Almighty!" he cried, "You been telling him all about us! Everything! The two of you sniggering in a corner like two evil children! A joke! A whim! You're unbelievable! You're no better than *he* is!"

Not waiting for a reply, not expecting one, not seeing that the denial also contained a plea for his understanding, a recognition of her predicament, turning instead, to the man. "And *you*, you vindictive bastard, you told the *Screws*! It was *you* that ditched me!"

"Wouldn't like to say, old boy," the mocking eyebrow now arched almost to the hairline. "Did you say you were leaving? What a shame! You'll forgive us if we don't wave to you in church, won't you? Don't forget—the Saturday before Christmas, December the twentieth."

Two days later, a postcard arrived from her. It was unsigned, its sparse message identification enough.

"Sorry, Colly. Too many spots, too much baggage."

———

Another note.

—this time to, "My Dearest Charlie."

—this time in Colly's mannered writing.

Her immediate thought had been to fly to the phone, to tell him that she hadn't meant it! That this needn't be!

But on re-reading the note, she saw that it would be a waste of time; that each phrase was as dispassionate as the annotations on the plans he had once shown her of one of his creations, each word sculpted so exquisitely that its shape seemed more important than its meaning.

There was no urgency, no immediacy in the note. It pretended to be what it was not. And gradually, she saw there was only one conclusion. He had waited for her to make a mistake—and had seized the moment.

She sat for a minute or two, her mind curiously still, ready to accept alternative conclusions. When none came, she rose to her feet, knowing what she wanted to do. Not thinking about it, not having to.

She went to the pound at the side of the house and fed and watered the dogs, *his* dogs, *Howard's* dogs. She then washed her hands, combed her hair, and slipped Colly's note into her handbag. Into a patchwork leather holdall, a present from Howard, she placed a box of matches from the drawer by the cooker, a bottle of milk from the fridge, a green box file from the study and a few overnight things from upstairs. On the way out, she slipped into a workaday coat from the porch, a blue anorak, the first that came to hand. That done, she paused for a moment to check that she had everything she needed, closed and locked the door, walked quickly to the big Merc, *his* big Merc, put the holdall in the boot and drove to the beach house.

It was dark when she arrived and a light breeze was rustling the grass on the sand dunes. A loose board creaked in a sudden gust, the wind and the noise chilling her as she stood beside the car. She had never liked the place, had only put up with its fishy, tumbledown roughness for the sake of Howard and the children, all of whom had loved it . . . had loved him . . . adored him . . .

Had, because with Howard gone and the children, *their* children, living away, pursuing their own busy lives, not yet settled, not yet with children of their own to play with on the dunes and take on boat trips, the weather-beaten, smelly old place was redundant. For them, it was the cherished centre of their childhood summers; for her, after all that had happened, all that she had endured, its presence in her life revolted her. The happy memories she had shared there, despite herself, were for nothing—her lewd nakedness with Colly on her last visit as obscene as Howard using its isolation to hide his secret cancer, to plan his revenge.

Well, now, she thought grimly, now she would take *her* revenge.

She unlocked the doors of the rickety lean-to shed at the side of the house which they had used on occasion as a make-shift garage—that and to store the kayaks and the rubber dinghies and the beach games and a million other things. Everything was still as she remembered—including her own little runabout which she had left there that last time, not wishing to travel back to London on her own; wanting to be with Colly, always with Colly . . .

Luckily, the car's battery was still good. She reversed it out, and with its headlights playing into the shed, spent a minute or two stacking the paraphernalia around the walls. When she judged there was enough room, she parked the runabout by the front steps, edged the Merc, *his* Merc, into the shed, retrieved the holdall from its boot, and entered the house.

In the same precise fashion, she switched on the electricity and made a mug of instant coffee, which she poured down the sink, flushing it away with the tap. The mug with the dregs still in it, she placed on the worktop with the milk beside it.

That done, she drew the living room curtains, lit the half a dozen scented candles scattered around the tables and window sills, and removed from the box file a wad of Howard's correspondence with his cancer specialists. This, she began screwing, page by page, into loose balls, throwing them at the bamboo waste paper basket by the bookcase, not caring if some missed the target.

In the kitchen was a box of tall white candles kept for emergency lighting in case of a power failure. She lit one, dripped its wax onto the centre of a saucer and stuck the candle in it, placing it on the table next to the curtains. From her bag, she took Colly's note, crumpled it a little and laid it on the table so that half of it was under the curtains. The tall candle she detached from its bed of wax and placed it lengthwise, one end next to the saucer, the other overlapping the note.

With a raised eyebrow, she watched as the tiny flame ignited the paper and slowly spread to the curtains, waiting by the door, clutching her handbag, as the flames raced upwards . . .

The greedy fury of it, the shadow of Howard suspended within it, made her gasp and draw back. She ran down the steps to the runabout, searching her bag for her mobile, but delaying the 999 call until the flames were licking along the roof of the shed . . . until they were dancing in the dormer windows of the bedrooms . . . until they had consumed her passion for the two men she had lain there with . . . until they had cauterised her memories . . .

Until they had put an end to all of it.

Chapter 23

Breakdown

After two, perhaps three days, two, perhaps three weeks, his office manager drew up a chair and sat before him, her worried face looking up at him, saying, quietly, kindly: "Colly, you must take time off . . . go home . . . relax . . . rest. It's not good for us all to see you like this . . . sitting there . . . doing nothing . . . saying nothing. You need to see your doctor. Promise me . . . ?"

Ignoring her, asking her to please mind her own business, an hour later realising she was right. He'd reached the end of the road. He couldn't go on. So he went home, but forgot what she'd said. There was something else, something for him to do. But he couldn't remember. It didn't matter, anyhow. He'd just have another drink, and it'd be alright, it'd sort itself out.

What he really had to do was to get rid of this patch of blackness. It was like a mote in his eye, drifting around, uncontrollable, hanging over his head, as if watching him, marking him out, growing from small and dense to sprawling and gauzy, multiplying, seething like frantic insects, blocking out the light, mating on the wing, dying in the frenzy. And then, three days (three weeks?) later, something different. The blackness descending, transforming bit by bit into a huge, upturned crotch, its mouth gaping, sucking him in, its corrugated walls transmuting into jagged cliffs.

Trying to get to his community service jobs. But rocks drifting down like Space Wars, passing through him; his hands bigger than he remembered, one larger than the other, fingers thick, misshapen, face lumpy, tongue choking, feet leaden but still not reaching the ground; buses and taxis grinding, the road endless, going nowhere; going backwards when he knew he must be going forwards, forcing his mind, trying to get it to accept what he knew must be real.

Trying to get to his anti-booze sessions. Failing; swivelling in his seat on the bus, alarming the man next to him and the women behind him, staring at the people on the pavement, all of them striding forwards but disappearing backwards, even when the bus was standing still, engine revving, revving, revving, seats and windows juddering, juddering, juddering. Gnashing and mashing like truant false teeth chattering their way across a dance floor.

His head ready to explode, ready to splatter his brains, the ooze hanging from the bellstop, dripping down the neck of the man next to him, stumbling to the door, tripping into a pair of huge soft tits, bouncing off, the woman hissing, *"F'Christ's sake!"*, a mottled arm pushing him away, out into the open, into the sickening, oily stench of the exhaust, down and down to the distant, heaving pavement, joining the ugly pockmarks of ancient, spat-out gum.

The blackness suddenly glaring white.

Huge lights.

—pinned to a high, narrow shelf by huge glaring lights.

The doctor, not his doctor, prodding and poking and peering.

Saying Hmm!

Saying are you eating?

Saying are you drinking and smoking and popping and sniffing?

Never sweating or coughing or aching or pissing or shitting or shagging or weeping or wanking.

Never how's the self-hate, the self-loathing, the self-disgust?

Always how many bottles, how many fags, how many spliffs, how many pills?

Saying are you sure it's not more?

Saying Lizzie this and Sally that, when he couldn't know them. How did the doctor know them? Who *was* he?

Saying funny things these breakdowns.

Saying take these pills, finish the course, stop the booze, stop the spliffs, stop everything.

Acting normal, saying yes he would, yes he would, yes he would.

Saying plenty of walks, plenty of rest, plenty of sleep.

Yes he would.

When he must have known the sleep bit was impossible.

How didn't the doctor know that?

Sitting beside that morning's sick, the wall cold against his back, staring at the cracks, memorising them, knowing that if he didn't keep his eye on them, they would snake down the plaster and drag him away, force him to look in the cot.

Shuffling to the bread bin, head screwed round to the wall, shuffling backwards to the loo, daring the cracks to come nearer, crapping quickly, staring at the shit on the paper, frightened to pull the chain in case it woke the baby, placing the paper in the sink, carefully. So he didn't make a noise. So the cracks wouldn't see.

Watching the sun go up, go down, go up, go down, go up, go down. Like the curtains at a theatre, but sitting in the stalls on his own and nobody on the stage. Waiting for the cast to come on, all the people in his life, but nobody bothering.

The days getting shorter, not realising. Needing warmer clothing, not realising. Out to the shops, shivering and shuffling along next to the wall, carrying his bags, four of them, swapping them over, putting two down to slip the shifty kid fifty smackers for some more supplies, forgetting one of the bags, the one with the bread and the ten cans of tinned beans in it, not noticing until he got home. But the booze safe! Carrying it upstairs at night, all twelve bottles of it.

Shutting the curtains to keep the moon from stealing it, forgetting to open them.

Listening to the rain pounding on the windows, wondering who was trying to get in. Keeping the curtains tightly closed. Hiding behind the table.

Dragging himself upstairs, dreading the cold sheets, wriggling down, his clothes still on. Ignoring the cracks. Saying if you're going to get me, then come and fucking get me. Pulling at his tie, trying to tighten it, shouting, I'll fucking do it for you! Hauling at it with two hands, the blood pounding, his voice, not him, his voice, croaking, shouting How d'you like that, you stupid bastard, you stupid, blundering, brainless bastard? How d'you like that?

Trying to get to the doctor, his own doctor, remembering what the kind, faithful Mandy had said, but missing the bus, forgetting where the taxis were, turning round, feeling his way back along the wall.

Vomiting, missing the bowl, using *The Church Times* to mop it up, leaving what was left, sinking back into bed, his clothes off, his hands stinking.

Why had he taken his clothes off? Why bother? It wasn't as if he was in bed with Lizzie, trying to be one with her, saying sorry, sorry, sorry for the now wizened, shrunken baby, for being away, for not being there with her, for blaming her, trying so hard to melt into her, to get past the once joyous entry.

Curled up on his side, shaking his head, purging the memory, freezing hands between his legs, pulling the pyjama top down over his cock, trying to keep warm. No bottoms. Where were the fucking bottoms? Where were they?

Shivering, weeping, wishing he'd kept on pulling at the tie, remembering the cracks, twisting his head to watch them, daring them to move, staring at the ceiling, forcing his eyes to stare at the ceiling to stop it sinking, to stop it crushing him.

Wondering why on earth he was now buying *The Church Times*.

———

Making it to the shops and the surgery, gobbling the doctor's pills, choking on them, forgetting them, confused by the instructions, taking double later, no glasses, no cups, washing them down with whatever, listening to the defiant glugs. Whisky one day, sherry another, port another, gin another . . . Like it mattered! Like he needed to remember what he was drinking!

Cackling at the thought of it. Lighting a spliff, popping more pills, not the doctor's. Popping and sniffing. Acid? Brain ticklers? Coke? Crack? All of them in the same box, waiting their turn, snatched at random.

Floating away, drifting around great rolling fields of blue grass and orange and purple flowers, the colours bright, electric, like a cartoon, like poster paints on a child's drawing. Bemused by them. But horrified that Howard and Charlie and Chloe were now all caught in the cracks, hanging there under the ceiling, but still laughing at him, the man's flesh charred, sliding off the bone, the women using pointed fingers to pull themselves open, grotesquely, unmistakeably; chanting c'mon then, c'mon then, c'mon then, their black, ugly hairs like fat old Mrs Groom's, like the crooked legs of dead flies.

Fleeing from the sight of them, falling onto the lounge floor, another joy stick burning his lips, staring back along his body at the idiot's guide to the universe, its blank screen ready to flicker into life.

Roll up! Roll up! Tune in for your favourite reality shows ("See Barbie Bimbo marooned on rat-infested island!"), and quiz shows, ("What are the countries of the United Kingdom?"), and chat shows, ("So you caught your wife of three weeks in bed with the milkman, is that when you stopped fancying her?"), and earnest wall-paper gardeners, and sweating wall-paper chefs, and yah-yah wall-paper gurus. Prattling on and on, the audiences lapping it up, so long as it was no effort, so long as it was being handed out on a plate, so long as the bomb blasts and the pools of blood and the pieces of gristle were kept in their allotted, careful places.

Nico suddenly shimmering onto the screen. Nico! Nico on the telly! Standing up by himself! Standing in the shower with a hard on! Jumping out on bent, wasted legs, his knob waving like it used to. Dancing around with a bunch of Iraqi prisoners, war grime smearing their bruises, the Iraqis forced to enter that hour's quiz show—that, or another kicking. One of them getting the answer, shouting, "Kelly! That's the answer! Kelly!"

The weapons expert, the negotiator, the man who pulled the plug, blew the whistle, who did for himself in a wood, so they say, ended it on the edge of a wood, transformed the whole fucking, mismanaged, rotten business into a world scandal, the cordoned-off death spot flashing up on the screen, again and again and again like the retakes of a goal at Wembley, but not yet able to cheer the poor man's name himself until suddenly up popped another face, the Iraqis chanting, "Gilli, Gilli, Gilligan . . . Gilli, Gilli, Gilligan"

Gilligan, the reporter, the maverick who scooped the world. Glad, glad, glad that he'd spouted it out on the news. Even if Campbell, the Blair man, the camp-follower had raged and danced and screamed, saying it was a fucking lie, it didn't fucking fit, didn't fucking gel. Even if Gilli-Gilli's bosses at Broadcasting fucking House couldn't stand the heat, even if they dithered and shook and shat themselves.

So cheering and weeping for the sad, decent little weapons man, not for Blair or Bush or Campbell or the whitewashing Hutton and his inquiry, or the footling Tories, or the weak-kneed broadcasting bigwigs or all the faceless goons, the JICs and the MI5s and the MI6s. No tears for them, none of them—no tears for the people who had not stood up, not dared to be counted.

Pushing his way through them, looking for Nico. Wanting to say: Once I had a son, my own baby son and I loved him and I failed him and now I love you and if you can risk me failing you, if you want, you can be my second son. I would like that, I would so much like that.

But God! Oh God! Oh God! Not saying it. Not properly.

———————

Another blackout.

Dark, darker than the darkness behind his eyes.

Darker than the shapes that were crushing him.

Darker than a womb; than the journey down; than the thousand, urgent, desperate journeys back.

Darker than a mind.

Darker than a churning mixer bucket.

Where am I?

What's happening?

Where's Nico?

Where is anyone who loves me?

Why is it so dark?

Voices and movement and flashes of dazzling light, but still not seeing, his eyelids heavy, weighing like tombstones, one for Nico and Lizzie and Sally and one for Charlie and Howard and Chloe, the epitaphs scrolled elaborately, tangled, the letters escaping, flying around, fusing together.

———

Lying spread-eagled high in the air, the ceiling so white he couldn't see whether it was coming to crush him or was zooming away like in Star Wars. As if he couldn't see the bedside screens even if they happened to be spinning around him like fucking Daleks, couldn't feel small, deft hands pulling at his clothes, cool air cloaking him, pimpling the fetid skin; cool air and warm, wet hands, a careful, deadpan voice saying on your side, on your front, on your back, the hands soaping him, drying him, the lickerish pulse coming from nowhere, sweet, involuntary, a stiff finger striking him down, an unshockable voice saying We'll have none of that.

And another voice saying, No, and you'll have none of your booze or your pills or your sniffers and your spliffs. You'll have what we give you and only what we give you. And you'll sit in a chair and look out of the window and be grateful.

———

Somehow—after more pills, more gripes, more sweating, more pleading, more lectures, more psychos, more nurses, more of everything but the one thing he knew he couldn't, shouldn't have—somehow them thinking him well enough, in control enough, to live back at the cottage. Medics and cleaners and detox merchants in a disinfected, sanitized stream, rapping on the door, fussing around, pulling and pushing him, shouting out, being cheerful, doing their job. *Their* pills when they were there, *his* booze when they weren't; rooting out the booze and his own pills from their hiding places, his craving the only reality, the only part of him demanding an answer.

Saying sod the fucking doctors, sod the whole fucking lot of them. Locking the door, shouting to them to leave him alone.

Sitting in a chair the whole day, enjoying the quiet. The odd smoke, the odd glug, moving just the once to go to the loo, making a mistake, pissing on his hands, weeping at the wet patches on his trousers.

Spoiling it.

Suddenly frightened of the phone, of what might be inside it, of what might be watching him, listening to him. Beating it by playing his own quiz game, answering each third call, but only allowing himself to say one of two words.

Saying, "Yes" to was he feeling better?

Saying, "Yes" to had he been to the doctor, been out walking?

Saying, "Yes" to was he bearing up.

Saying, "Yes, yes, yes," to Angie. Was he eating, was he looking after himself, was he keeping himself busy? Knowing that she didn't believe him, that she would be on the phone to someone, telling them.

Saying:

"No." He didn't feel like going to the pub with Ozzie.

"No"—or out for a meal with the Brownloves.

"No"—or out for a spin with the Callows.

"No"—he wasn't weeping.

"No." He wasn't.

"No." He really wasn't.

Amazingly, Sally arriving with a flask of homemade soup, a plastic box of his favourite fried sausages and a loaf of bread, saying it's from the bakers, it's the one you like, pretending all was normal, that he wasn't sitting on the floor, hunched up against a wall. Ignoring the food, watching her screw up her face at the pot-filled sink, turning to pick up bottles, dropping them into a sack, neither of them talking, their minds circling. Then something clicking and him saying:

"What's that you've got on?"

"My leathers. They're new ones. You can grow a lot in a year."

Memory turning bleary eyes crafty.

"It was *you* wasn't it? *You* following me? *You* sending that letter?"

"Might have been."

"Not might. It *was*, wasn't it? Interfering, upsetting everything."

"I don't think so," her back to him, washing the dishes.

"*I* do. You should have minded your own damned business."

Turning to face him, a pan, the frying pan, in one hand, scrubbing at it with the other. "It *was* my business. My business as much as anyone's."

"I didn't ask you to interfere."

"I didn't ask you to walk out of my life. I wanted my father back."

Groaning, the cracked record playing the same tune again and again: Sally and Nico, Sally and Nico . . . Saying the same things . . . Always the same.

"And who's this cretin with a motorbike? Zooming you around everywhere?"

Putting the pan down, squeezing the dish cloth, hanging it on a tap, beginning to move away, reaching for the door, opening it, standing there, looking back at him.

"He's a friend. A good friend. But what do *you* care? You're not my father, not really. And you're not my friend, not any more. Don't forget the soup—and don't choke on it. We wouldn't want that, would we?"

Closing the door behind her.

Silly girl! Saying a year! When it couldn't have been a year! Just couldn't have been!

Could it?

<hr>

Nico ringing.

Leaving the phone till it stopped, then checking for a message. Again and again, always the same message. "It's Nico. Ring me."

Not ringing, not daring to.

Gradually, gradually building his courage. Picking up the phone, CD guitars twanging down the line, thumping his eardrum, removing his words.

A voice, the boy's voice, grating out, "Where've *you* been then?—the other side of the moon?"

Silence—followed by the same voice.

"If you're there, why don't you get round here and wash my arse? The others have no idea and the room's like a bloody cow byre."

—the two of them not daring, not knowing how to say I miss you, I love you, how are you; he realising that, not being so freaked out, so fucked up as not to recognise a man being a man hiding behind fond coarseness.

Grateful for the message, even if coded. But able only to see himself; wanting to consider all the rest of them; Nico and the rest of them, wanting it, but not ready to put the pieces back together, to venture from the spinning hub.

Wanting to say he'd be round, that it'd be like the old times. When he knew that that could never be, that they could never go back.

Ringing back, snatching up the phone while he had the courage, saying, "Nico, you don't understand. I've let you down. All of you. I'm a prick, a pathetic, useless prick."

And the casual, matter of fact voice coming back.

"So what's different? You always were."

<hr>

Chapter 24

Theatre

The third or sometimes the fourth Saturday of each November, depending how the dates fell, as a way of easing them all, once again, into the idea of Christmas, the de Mangers organised a Sink Set theatre visit to the West End.

In recent years, one or two of the women, Charlie Sinclair and Jessica Callows among them, had canvassed strongly for them all to travel in a couple of stretched limos—"grot with style." But with Charlie no longer attending such events, Jessica didn't care one way or the other—which left no opposition to the de Mangers' preferred mode of transport, a 1930's-type double-decker omnibus. It was nowhere near as warm, nor as comfortable, but it allowed them to reply: "Style with style."

Charlie's absence gave Lizzie a chance to mix Christmas charity with her resolve to win Sally her father back. If Colly couldn't find it in him to come round to the house, perhaps a trip to the theatre might be a step in the right direction.

"It'd do you good to get out," she said to him on the phone. "I take it you're not getting out. But I don't want to go on my own—too many wagging tongues."

"But . . ."

"Charlie won't be going, she's already said."

"But . . ."

"Look, I'll double check. I'll find out exactly who's going and what we're going to get up to. I'll ring you back."

So when she innocently divulged that Chloe Jones and Simon Mount would also not be going and heard the longing in her voice, her loneliness, how vulnerable she was, he allowed himself to be persuaded. It would scare him shitless, but if he could manage it, it might break the ice with the people who had been his friends.

In the ancient bus on the way to the show—he didn't remember which one and never did find out; all he knew and was thankful for, was that it wasn't a Lloyd Webber—he and Lizzie had first of all been sitting downstairs. In the excitement, he had allowed himself to be pushed into the seat first and thus found himself at the window, watching the people on the pavement. Like before.

This time, so long as he concentrated, they seemed to be behaving properly. He checked by swivelling in the narrow, wooden seat, waiting until the bus stopped in the traffic, pretending that he was turning round to talk to Ozzie but keeping one eye on the pavement people, watching them walk past, relieved to see that none were disappearing backwards.

The effort of keeping his mind in order, of not allowing it to run away with him, was making him sweat. And in any case, there was something else—

"Can you smell oil, Lizzie?"

"Oil?"

"Yes. Fumes. Do you mind if we go upstairs?"

So they made their way down the bus and climbed the swaying stairs, Lizzie raising her eyes, the others impassive, keeping to themselves the silly, jocular cat-calls that would have flowed had it been a happy couple, had one of them not gone do-lally, had he not let them down.

"I didn't know we were coming here first," he said.

"Yes," she said, the evening breeze blowing her hair, her face lifted, breathing in the cold air, allowing it to cleanse her, to blow the nightmares into a dark corner. "I rang back to tell you, don't you remember? Here to eat, then the theatre. Marvellous, isn't it?"

They were standing on one of the Festival Hall's enormous outdoor balconies, behind them the sound of a jazz band serenading the pre-show diners, beneath them the inky black, glittering Thames, the fairy lights of the far away Embankment; Big Ben and the Eye to their left, Tower Bridge and the City skyscrapers to their right, the magical city laid out before them, a black velvet cloak with twinkling diamonds.

He pulled his collar up around his neck, one hand gripping the rail, the other holding his coat closed across his chest as if to guard his memories of London—the deadly serious client meetings . . . opera and ballet at Covent Garden . . . nights at the Savoy with Lizzie . . . soaring music at the Albert Hall . . . clinking, sloshing glasses at half-forgotten parties . . . anonymous receptions . . . the age-grained pews of a medieval church . . . the Space Wars attack that had settled like a black cloud over two birthdays . . .

He swallowed and screwed up his face, shutting out the sparkling anthill, its illuminated immensity still pulsing behind his eyelids.

"Lizzie, I—"

"Hugo and Elizabeth thought it would be romantic," she said, not hearing him, not catching his torment, peering back through the glass, turning from him. "C'mon," she said, "the others are already sitting down. A quick meal and then on to the show—you'll love it. Lovely songs, lovely kids."

Like a dependent, protesting child, he followed her across the concrete, pushing into the raucous restaurant, anxious not to lose her, dreading, even then, the coming imprisonment, the seat in a sea of seats, transfixed by the swirling dancers, the shrill singers belting out their hope, crooning their love, leaving him their heartbreak. Nico and Sally and Charlie and Chloe and he and Lizzie and poor, dying, dead Howard, poor dying, dead Robert, all his failures swept up into a pile of autumn leaves, the fading, crackly deadness too big to be brushed aside by a few syrupy songs.

215

But his suffering interrupted by a sudden rumpus among the tables occupied by the Sinks—a mobile phone going off, Anna Brownlove searching for it in her pockets, then her handbag, failing to find the thing, standing up to search her pockets again, her bowl of pasta crashing to the floor.

"Anna, please be careful," said Paul, looking around, beckoning a waitress.

"Yes, think of the starving children of Africa," sniped Ozzie, his jibe bringing smiles to a number of strained faces, but not Paul's.

"A bit unnecessary, even for you, Ozzie," he snapped, his irritation transferring itself to Anna. "Haven't you found the bloody thing, yet?"

"Here it is!" she exclaimed, the phone in her hand at last. "It's stopped," she said, unnecessarily, stepping back from the table, watching the waitress clean the floor. "I'll see if there's a message."

They watched as she stood, listening. "It's the charity," she said, straining to hear, "Something about Harold. I'll have to ring back."

"About *who*?" asked Jessica.

"About Harold. Harold Wensum of Boring Hall, Hertfordshire." said Ozzie. "I wouldn't bother if I were you, Anna," he called over his shoulder. "They probably just want to check his latest trivia—you know, what happened on the Delhi flight ten years ago . . ."

But they weren't listening to him. They were watching Anna slowly turning to stone, shouting to overcome the weak signal—

"When . . . ?

"How long . . . ?

"Where . . . ?

"How many . . . ?

"What's the embassy saying . . . ?

"And the Americans . . . ?

"Just reports . . . ?

"Yes, if necessary, of course I can go. I would *want* to go . . . .

"O.K. Ring back. Soon as you can."

—switching off the phone, slipping it back into her pocket, swivelling to face Ozzie.

"You really are a small minded little shit, aren't you, Ozzie! An ignorant little twerp who hasn't the faintest idea what he's talking about! Harold Wensum doesn't have a big house in Hertfordshire, as some of you seem to think. He lives in a squalid semi near Heathrow. And when he says he paints, he does—he paints happiness for children."

"So he tells us," said Ozzie, rising. "Forgive me, Anna, but we don't need this. Like Harold, it's boring."

"Like Harold, it's the truth—unlike your vindictive allegations about him and children. Yes, you heard—the scandalous rubbish you threatened him with to keep him quiet about you and Hector Grammaticus."

"Ozzie and my brother?" asked Honey.

Swinging round to her. "Honey, darling! You really can't be that naïve! Or that ignorant!"

"Anna! For God's *sake*!" cried Paul. "You can't *say* such things, you—"

But the phone was ringing again and Anna was saying, "Yes . . . Yes . . . I understand . . . Yes . . . Absolutely . . . I'll see you at the airport," turning to them, white-faced, saying, "That was my charity again, confirming the reports about Harold. He's not a paint salesman, Ozzie! He's a hero, an aid worker who travels the world helping children. But he's into all sorts of things that need to be kept quiet. One of the gangs in Iraq, one of the rabid anti-American lot, are saying he's MI6. They've taken him hostage."

Into the silence, she added, "I'm sorry, Paul, I should have . . . I must go to him, I must go and help . . ." Making her apologies to the de Mangers, hurrying to the door, her husband following, saying, "But, Anna . . ."

The silence continuing, the stunned audience trying to come to terms with a new board game, trying to evaluate it.

Jessica Callows saying, "I can't believe it—Anna and *Harold . . .*?"

Amelia Platt-Smith saying, "Wow" and "Bloody *Hell*!" and beginning to sympathise with Honey but thinking better of it . . . others looking at Ozzie, grimacing, saying nothing . . .

Honey suddenly jumping up, snapping, "Take me home! Now!"

Lizzie staggered like the rest, aware that Colly was again speaking to her, his face up close to hers, picking up where he had left off, as if Anna's extraordinary disclosures had never taken place.

"Lizzie. Lizzie, I've been trying to tell you. I don't think I can do it. I'm not ready. I can't . . ."

Turning to him, as to a child, her mind elsewhere.

"Can't? Can't what?"

Bowing his head like before, muttering, "I can't go . . . I can't . . . I'm sorry, I'm not . . ."

Looking for the stairs, hiding his tears, his wafer-thin resolution gobbled up by the colossal city, cloistered in the back of a taxi with Lizzie, leaving what remained of the Set to their new excitement, freeing them to shake disbelieving heads:

"Christ! If it's not one, it's another . . . !"

"Harold Wensum . . . ?"

"MI6 . . . ?"

"Harold and Anna . . . ?"

"Ozzie and Hector? Honey's brother! Closet gays . . . ?"

"Unbelievable!"

"So what . . . !"

"*So what?*"

"At least Colly kept it straight!"

"I'll say!"

"Where *is* Colly, anyhow? Where's he pissed off to *this* time . . . ?"

Not knowing about him and Chloe, despite Anna Brownlove, and not understanding, not properly, about the cot death and about Nico.

And he not able to tell them, not able to seek their sympathy, because if he told them about Chloe, his real love, the one he ran at the same time as Charlie, their favourite, and about his other love, his pure, beautiful love for Nico, they would revile him.

Like they reviled poor Harold.

"It is now abundantly clear that the evidence which Tony Blair presented to Parliament in 2002 about Saddam Hussein's weapons of mass destruction was exaggerated and misleading"—BBC correspondent, John Simpson, in his book, 'Not Quite World's End.'

Chapter 25

Après Theatre

The next day, Ozzie coming to see him, standing at the door winking as if they were co-conspirators, raising his eyebrows, waiting for an invitation to step inside, clearly determined not to be refused.

The two of them sat in the kitchen having coffee, Colly feeling more secure now that he was back within his own four walls, but saying nothing of the blackness, that he was still floating in the blackness; Ozzie trying, haltingly, to deliver his message, saying one thing, meaning another.

"It's been a funny old year," he said, perturbed by the other's pallor, his hunted eyes, aware that his usual silver tongue had deserted him, was of little use in such situations, anyhow.

"And which year would that be—the first when I was handed Charlie, or the second with the men in white coats?"

"Well both, I suppose."

"You think so?"

"Well, a mite different, wouldn't you say?"

"Different for me and different for you"—thoughts jumping into his head, not caring if he inflicted hurt. "So what's your analysis? Does Heraclitus still rule?" Or does being accused of slander and homosexuality in one night not count?"

"You'd think so, wouldn't you?"

"You would if one's a hero and the other's your brother-in-law . . ."

"Hmm . . ." said Ollie, "but like most of Anna's stories, only half true."

"And which half is that?"

The empty, sloshing oceans were washing away at the stains, but were failing. Why didn't Ozzie fuck off home? Why couldn't he see he wasn't interested? Why didn't he just ask him to leave? Instead, he rose, his teeth clenched to stop the pounding, and disappeared into the tiny lounge. A quick slug and a quick sniff before returning.

Ozzie watched him sink back into his chair. Another time, he might have commented on the glassy eyes, the red nostrils, the abrasive stench of whisky. Instead, wary of the other's mood, he continued his tale, determined to justify his side of the record.

"Harold rumbled poor old Hector when we shared a flat at uni. We only had him with us because we couldn't afford the rent ourselves—he wriggled his way in before we had chance to ask anybody else. But he got round to thinking I was Hector's other half. So to stop him spreading it around, we told him we had photographs of him in a children's playground. A student prank, a simple tit for tat. You think everything's watertight and then—ping—off comes the wrapper. These things have a time of their own. *You* know that."

"What things?"

"You. Your . . . philandering. Your . . . illness."

"Oh and not you! Screwing up your own little trio! The three sad little aitches—Honey, Hector and Harold. Honey taking time off to do a bit of pimping! Pushing into my life! Into Charlie's! Pushing us together like some ghastly Jane Austen matchmaker!"

"C'mon, Colly, don't be so damned dramatic! Hector and I were close friends. But there was nothing between us, certainly not after I married Honey. And as for Harold Wensum, we didn't have any photographs, of course we didn't. But he *did* visit children's playgrounds. And we're *not* pushing into your life . . . into *this*." He gestured at the room, at Colly's state.

"Ozzie, I didn't ask for any of what you call, 'this'. That New Year's party at Charlie's, I was mooning around thinking how dreary, how bloody dreary, life was, when I find Honey setting me up for Charlie. She—"

"She felt sorry for you both."

"Oh, sure, thank her for the thought! But when things went wrong, she didn't stop to think, did she, about what else in my life might get broken?"

"But she didn't know, none of us could guess, that Howard . . ."

"I wasn't thinking of Howard."

"If Howard hadn't died . . . if you'd held your nerve, it would have sorted itself out."

"You think so? And what makes you think that—another of your bloody Greek heroes?"

"Sorry, old mate, but it's *you* acting out the Greek tragedy."

"And it's *you*, Ozzie, not facing up. Why is it that *I'm* the only one being judged around here? If *I* betrayed Lizzie, so did Honey. And if Charlie chose to believe that I betrayed *her*, not with *Angie*, like she says, for Heaven's sake,"—*with Chloe, with fickle, unnameable Chloe*—"but by not telling her about a poor, defenceless boy, the one I maimed and look after, saying nothing about him, not to Lizzie, not to anyone, well, that's *my* business, nobody else's. And if I want to grieve over it, I will. It was something Lizzie should have worked out. And so should Charlie. And so should you. It still is!"

"But why the mystery? What's the 'it' in all this?"

"It's rather like you and your suddenly unsavoury life, Ozzie. Work it out for yourself."

At that moment, all Ozzie could work out was that their friendship appeared to be foundering. The thought dejected him. He resented the puzzle and wasn't even sure whether he had succeeded with his own denial of the sweet, long ago times with Hector. After a while, he stirred and put his coat on, looking around while doing so. From the state of the house and the smell of booze and pot, he was back in la-la-land.

"Colly, if you can't tell me what's on your mind, what's torturing you, I can't help. Honey just wants me to say—"

"Ozzie, tell Honey to stop worrying. Lizzie doesn't know the part Honey played and I shan't be saying anything. I don't blame her—I just want the record straight. She should have kept out of it and I should have taken no notice. As it is, if I say there's nothing else on my mind, you'll not believe me, and if I told you, you'd not be able to help me, anyhow."

"Well, I just hope you're not still worrying about Charlie."

"Oh, yeah! And why's that?"

"Because she's trying to pick herself up." He hesitated, perhaps it wasn't the right time, even now . . . "I don't think you know, do you, that the beach house burned down?"

"The beach house!" Laughing incredulously, not, at that moment, recognising the significance. "When?"

"Ages ago. We all thought it best not to tell you . . . you know . . . because of how you were."

"So why should I be upset? What was the beach house to me?"

"Think about it," said Ozzie. "For once in your life, just think!"

But he was greeted by more disbelieving laughter and left in a huff, irritated as much by his own ineffectiveness as by the other's wilfulness, upset that Honey's meddling was so clearly perceived and, despite Colly's words, clearly not forgiven. He had failed to win his friend over and he had also failed to pass on the rest of his news—that after the beach house fire, Charlie had sold up everything, the dogs, the cars, and had gone off back to Wimbledon—to a tired old street just round the corner from where she had been brought up—and that, unbelievably, her house had been bought by, of all people, Herbie Kirby.

" . . . the more evidence comes to light that we fought the war on a false prospectus, that there were no weapons of mass destruction and that we have not diminished but may have boosted world terrorism, the less people ask me (whether he regretted his decision to resign). *My only regret was that I was not more successful in preventing the war in the first place."*—Robin Cook, the former leader of the House of Commons and former Foreign Secretary, a year after resigning from the Blair Cabinet on March 17, 2003, in protest over Britain's decision to invade Iraq without the authorization of a second U.N. resolution.

Chapter 26

Cell

Two people.
A man.
A woman.
Both haggard.

The man sitting in a police cell, leaning forward, head bowed, naked except for a vest, hands clasped in front of him, cuffs biting into his wrists, thumbnails pressing against dry lips, the lips working but soundless, short, sobbed breaths warming his fingers, the man with him, the one in the white coat, telling him to sit up, c'mon now, let's have a look at you, doing as he was told, the glistening, open bruise on his cheek seeping tiny droplets, the purple necklace tight around his throat, fastened there, indelible.

The woman sitting in an office in the same police station, her face white, no makeup, her mind taking time off from the crisis, dulled by the littered shelves, the filing cabinets, the pile of folders, the computer screen with her husband's name on it. Sitting beside their flabby lawyer. Mr Stirling. Sam. Sam Stirling. A name, she thought idly, more fit for film credits than a shiny brass plate:

A film of our time

"While They Were Dying"
Acted, written and directed by Columbus Wolfson
Screenplay by Sam Stirling
Special Appearance by Warren Nichols
Supporting Cast: The Sink Set.

Fancy thinking such rubbish! At this time! But it fitted. All of it.

The two of them waited in silence, Lizzie trying to get back to reality, the lawyer rehearsing what he might say in court, both of them now watching a large square man across the desk scroll up and down the computer screen, flicking impassively through the case file before addressing them, his voice sonorous, deliberate.

He was reminding them of the terms of Colly's sentence for annihilating the baby Fiat while under the influence. "As you know, the sentence required him to (a) attend rehab classes for alcoholics and addicts and (b)—"

"We know all this," Lizzie interrupted. "What we're here for—"

The inspector sighed. "—and (b) complete the required number of hours of community service. Even allowing for all the time he has spent in the hospitals and the private nursing homes, he has failed on both counts. And we're still looking into other possible contraventions in relation to drugs. But the primary reason for him being in custody is tonight's charge of assaulting a police officer.

"Now," he said, changing his tone, trying to sound sympathetic, "you want him released on bail, and I can understand that. But I have to tell you, Mrs Wolfson, that in the police surgeon's opinion, he still poses a threat to his own life and—"

"Like the threat he faced while in custody?" she snapped.

"An inquiry is still proceeding into that incident and—"

This time, it was Mr Stirling interrupting. "And what are the early findings? My client has a right to know."

Another sigh. "When Mr and Mrs de Manger called for assistance, the officers found Mr Wolfson in a demented state, throwing rocks at his car. One of these hit, and seriously injured, one of the officers. He was brought in, searched and the usual precautions were taken. Unfortunately, Mr Wolfson was being—" he rummaged for an acceptable word—"*difficult* and the desk sergeant failed to notice that his underpants were in fact short pyjamas and that he was wearing them back to front—i.e. the tie cord was hidden away at the back. It was this cord that Mr Wolfson used to try to . . . harm himself."

"To hang himself?" It was the woman again.

"Yes."

"While he was left on his own?"

"Yes."

"And the bruise on his cheek?"

"Sustained in the earlier struggle to quell him."

"And you think we couldn't do a better job?"

"With respect, despite what has happened, that is not quite the point. Mr Wolfson has been contravening his sentence. He is still drinking and taking drugs and is quite clearly a potential suicide. He is now facing a serious additional charge. He will be kept here tonight for his own safety and will be put before the magistrates tomorrow. My guess is that he will be sent to a secure psychiatric ward for a full examination before a second court appearance."

Lizzie Wolfson felt herself slipping from her skin, an icy reptile sliding through the dew, leaving her past life behind, rejecting, for the moment, the inspector's picture of a suffering future, wondering what she was doing in the police station in the first place, why she was bothering, pondering whether the inspector's skin was his uniform, whether, when his wife peeled it from him in their bedroom, he stopped doing things by rote.

"It is not justified to jump to the conclusion that something exists just because it is unaccounted for"—Hans Blix, chief U.N. weapons inspector, June 2003, on the Western failure to prove the existence of WMD in Iraq.

Chapter 27

Flowers

A lifetime later, when he was back home, when the walls had stopped cracking and the ceiling had stopped crushing and the phone and the war reports no longer terrified—during that uncertain, nervous time when it seemed he might at last recover, when he was at last managing to wash away the worst of the sights and sounds and smells of the wards and the cells—he received a surprise visit from Lizzie. She was dressed in sensible, clubby shoes, grey tailored slacks, a navy blue donkey jacket and a faded, electric blue, silk scarf that he recognised.

He smiled ruefully and she tossed her head, challenging him, forbidding him to ask why she had chosen, for this visit, to wear a fragment from their honeymoon, his gift to her at that time.

From where she was standing at the car, he looked halfway decent: jeans, a light grey sweater over a white polo neck, no socks, no shoes.

"My, my," she called, busy yanking stuff from the boot, "you certainly look better than when I last saw you." She didn't tell him he still looked awful, that she was still afraid for him.

"And when was that?" he asked, stepping out gingerly, taking a newspaper and a bunch of chrysanthemums from her, leaving her to carry in two bags of food, toilet rolls, disinfectant . . . .

"You don't remember?"

"I remember seeing you . . . hearing you. And Sally. Sally coming to see me. But no, I can't remember. Not properly."

She could see, understand, that getting things in the right order, even trivial things, was important to him, would ease his way through the blur, even if he couldn't remember them himself, but was told them. And she was only too grateful that they had found a starting point, a way of easing their conversation into something meaningful . . .

"The first time was at the hospital—when you collapsed the first time. They asked if you had a wife and you said yes and they sent for me. Sally came, too. To make sure I was OK!" She shrugged, wondering whether he remembered that he had walked out on her; that their marriage had come to an end . . .

To calm herself, she began arranging her flowers in a vase, spacing out the yellow, bronze and purple. "I brought these to cheer the place up. Thought you could do with a boost."

"You didn't come a second time, then?"

"Well, I saw you at the police station," she said, dodging the question. "Do you remember?"

"Not really."

"And I came to the ward once after that."

"But not again?"

"No. Not again. You . . . you weren't yourself. It was too upsetting."

"For you?"

"For you."

He nodded and looked around, trying to think of something else to say to prolong the revelation that she still cared. Instead, blurting:

"Ozzie used to come."

"Ozzie? Are you sure?"

"Yes. Why not Ozzie?"

"Yes, why not? He's never said anything. Neither has Honey."

"No. Well they wouldn't."

"Why not?"

He shrugged, alarmed, not telling her why not. Not telling her any of it. Not sure any longer whether any of it was true. Or which part of it. *But visited by Ozzie. Always Ozzie. Shouting at me, telling me to stop making so much bloody noise, to shut up. Saying he didn't care a monkey's about the ceiling and the cracks on the wall, that I'd got it wrong, that he wasn't bloody Hector, that he hadn't come to bugger me, that he loved me like he loved Hector, but still reaching for me like I had reached for Nico, his hands reaching for me . . .*

Saying instead, "I didn't know you were coming—I'm out of milk," rapping the table with his knuckles, upset with himself, not wishing her to see him still inadequate, deluded, still not trusting his re-emerging ability to sort things out.

"That's alright," she said. "I've brought some. You put the kettle on and we'll have coffee."

Like the flowers, her voice was bright, but careful and arranged. It was a time for careful talking, a time when whole days stood still, limp washing on a grey, windless day, the gloom kissing damp rooftops, dulling the tiles, wreathing the high trees, the wet, spent leaves spiralling down, the garden birds stifled, waiting like her—like both of them, she supposed—for the pall to lift, for the road ahead to clear.

They settled in their chairs like courteous strangers, poised and attentive.

"You don't remember me cursing you?" she asked, a little smile softening the sadness. "Cursing you, saying I could never forgive you?"

Saying, if that's wrong, if it's un-Christian, then that's what you've done to me—you've lost me my faith. Not in God, in you, perhaps even in God.

He shook his bowed head and she continued to speak slowly and quietly, without heat, into a silent void. "I cannot believe how we have allowed this, all of this, to fester; how we've wasted our lives, when there was so much promise, so much love, so much to live for. I cannot understand what I've done that was so wrong, how you felt driven away, how you felt you had the right to leave us, to sleep around, to ignore us."

"I didn't," he said, still not looking at her. "It just happened."

"And what part of it 'just happened?'" Drawing it out of him, acting out the thin, calculating psychiatrist at the hospital and the neutral, careful counsellors at his clinics. "Sleeping around? Or letting Sally think she didn't exist?"

A heavy stirring, a slow scrutiny of her before the head bowed again. "Both. It's terrible, I know, but both."

"And what about Nico? Did it just *happen* with him? Pouring your life into *him*?"

"Nico was different."

"Nico was a stranger who came into our lives. If I can learn to live with the idea of Nico, if I can forgive myself for Robert's death, you can learn to accept that your son died peacefully, that it was unknowable, unpreventable, a tragedy waiting to happen, that Nico is *in addition* to him, not *in place* of him, that Sally needs you. The two of you, you and Sally, you're dying on the inside. If you're ever going to save her, if you're ever going to redeem yourself, you must start again; you must forgive—be thankful for—her part in this. No more self, no more bitter questioning."

He glanced at her again and grimaced. "She told you?"

"Yes."

"The soup was good . . . she was being so brave."

"Then give her a chance. Start visiting us, start talking to her, accepting what she is, what she has become while you've been looking the other way."

Lizzie's visit—their conversation, his recognition of his guilt, his brief spark of perspective, was followed by a euphoria that boiled like cumulous clouds into a pure blue sky, each of them a kingdom of past happiness—his ever-upward career, his first major commissions, his decision to go it alone, his burgeoning construction business, his beautiful wife, his glossy marriage, his glittering prizes . . .

He found that if he unrolled the kingdoms carefully, the sunlit lands within them spread to the horizon, and there was no need, no need at all, to venture down the dark corridors that led off from each of them.

So he travelled eagerly to each new bend in the road and happily splashed his way through each sylvan pool, realising that he was deluding himself, of course he was, but reluctant to leave his re-found oasis. Better than anyone, he knew that the dark corridors had to be faced, that the doors within them had to be opened.

But not now.

Not yet.

Later, perhaps.

But not now . . .

So Lizzie's appeal for a new beginning was left hanging in the air—the visits to the family home were never made, the phone was left unused, perfectly, uncomfortably aware that resentful inquiries would be made, that Lizzie would ring Angie, anxious to know whether he was the same with her, with Nico. Learning that, Yes, he was!

But he not hearing Angie's concern and sympathy, nor Lizzie's apology for troubling her. So also not hearing Angie's reply:

"It's no trouble, Mrs Wolfson. I wish I could tell you differently. Other people ring, too, and I have to say the same to them. He doesn't want me around, doesn't want anybody around. I ring him and ring him, trying to encourage him, involve him. I can hear that he's stronger, that he's better in himself. But he won't let go of it. None of it."

After a three-month search, the Iraq Survey Group told Congress that it had found "dozens of WMD-related programme activities and significant amounts of material that Iraq concealed during the UN inspections that began in late 2002 . . . (but) we have not yet found stocks of weapons"—The Daily Mail, October 2003.

Chapter 28

Wedding I

As it does, life continued for the casualties, each day melting into the next with a gentle resignation, a childlike surprise that each new sunrise included them. For some, it was an awakening, a numbing realisation; for others, a continuing unawareness, a feeling that if they took care not to peer too closely into themselves, they could get by; they could accept the sensation of being carried along.

In the first moments, the first few months of her sudden life on her own, Lizzie Wolfson had concluded bitterly that the Set's anger and disgust over Colly's behaviour was not so much to do with how he had let *her* down, but with the fact that the *other woman was his friend's wife;* that in their view, he had crossed the line. As a result, she noticed that there were few, if any, attempts made to bring them together; to dust them down, to say, C'mon now, you two, these things happen. Face up!

Later still, after the drinking and the drugs and the violence and his detention had all become common knowledge, the faces had become more closed than ever, the brief inquiries more polite and meaningless. The reason, she supposed, was a mixture of shock and embarrassment—quite clearly, with the sole exception of Ozzie Leverington (why Ozzie? Why the guilt?), none of them wished to remember that once upon a time, the wreck that was now languishing in a psychiatric prison had been one of them.

But there was more! Because the message that came over to her, that flitted among the headshakes and the shrugs, was that, somehow, she was to blame! That had she been stronger, had she been a better wife, had she given him what he wanted, it would never have happened. He would never have fallen into Charlie's bed, never hidden Nico away, never gone off the rails . . .

The message remained forever unspoken, and she had no idea whether it was intended or not. But it lived there in its dark lair at the back of her mind and multiplied. And however much she denied it, tried to laugh it away, banish it from her thoughts, she came to accept that the wagging tongues might not be entirely wrong. Colly's world had collapsed. And since he had always said that *she* was his world, that it was through her that he saw everything, that without her involvement nothing mattered, it was logical to suppose that a wrong corner had been taken, and not just by him . . .

The realisation humbled her and gave her the strength to survey the wreckage. As a first measure, to prove to herself that she wasn't entirely a failure, that she still had a grip on at least part of her life, she decided to give up drinking. It was a dreadful bore, worse even than the empty ache of her sexless non-marriage, but it gave her something to curse Colly for, something specific, of the moment, not the deadweight of years gone by, and not his self-imposed depression, his long-term breakdown.

So she sat and suffered and missed him, finding herself thinking, perversely, of Paul Brownlove, wondering what was on his mind, how he was coping, the house empty, his wife skedaddling half way across the globe after someone so strange and colourless.

Sally had thought the story about Harold was cool. Romantic and dashing, she had said, her imagined hero sliding in and out of the shadows, answering her mother's snort, her, "For God's sake, we're not talking Graham Greene," with a resentful, "No, not Greene—Dickens! Charles Darnay . . . Sydney Carton. At least Sydney did the right thing in the end," not comparing her father by name, not having to.

She could see that her daughter was coping by pretending to turn her back, and could sense the girl's prayers that, somehow, Colly would return from the dead, and that they would be a family again. Where Nico fitted in to Sally's mind, she had no idea. Having exposed her father's secret life with the boy, she had never asked to meet him and seemed to be concentrating instead on Leroy, growing up in a hurry with him, schooling him, determined to change him, saying, "If Dad doesn't like Leroy now, I'll have to buy him some glasses."

Joking.

Deadly serious.

As regards Nico, the non-brother, the non-son, she knew from Angie that he was also in a hurry, getting on with his new life, his love for someone called Kate, their all-consuming plans, his restored friendships—the boy shrugging like Sally, telling Angie to have faith,

So all of them, in their different ways, hiding their anxiety, waiting for the man at the centre of it all to inch his way back, the non-son aware that Colly was still appalled by the world and its doings; but unaware that a silver envelope embossed with the words, "A Wedding," had been thrown into the glowing coals, the man revolted by it, declining to open it, getting the years wrong, forgetting the passage of time, labelling it another of Simon Mount's cruel taunts.

After the 2001 attack on the World Trade Centre and after the official ending of the Iraq War—the "War To End Terrorism"—bombings continued to make headlines in newspapers around the world. Among them:

March 2004: 10 bombs exploded in four commuter trains in Madrid, killing 191 and injuring 1,824.

July 2005: suicide bombers in London set off three devices on three Underground trains, and a fourth bomb destroyed a London bus. Fifty-two commuters were killed, 700 injured.

Chapter 29

Menagerie

Even now, when my mind slips, I see the cot death, the wicked guilt and the long, grinding fight with Lizzie.

I see the cement mixer still turning its load: the mangled boy, the dead baby and the two puffballs, Bush and Blair. The four of them sticking up like stuffed dolls, their heads lolling, the spinning, grating roar drowning their cries, all four bound together by manic co-incidence, sharing the same point in time; the boy and the baby born in the same month and on the same date as that chosen by the warmongers to launch their desert picnic. The coincidence unbelievable, predestined.

I see the plumes of flames and smoke hijacking the innocent birthday wishes, the one boy long dead, crying for peace, for the two of us to put an end to our bitterness; the other crippled, a boy soldier pleading for love, for a better deal, hoping for candles, receiving missiles; the senders isolated, derided, their delusions unproved.

I see a fifth head: Howard's. Howard's head above the other four, poking from his cockpit, his plane in a never-ending dive, screaming down, aiming for the cement mixer . . . never reaching it.

I see the desperation in Charlie's eyes and the veiled flippancy in Choe's.

I see that when the odious Simon cracked his whip, his pimping days over, and she obeyed him and stood there before me, admitting nothing, denying nothing, it seemed that my Judas was to be double-headed, their two heads on one body; my madness decreeing that it had to be the two of them, Chloe and the half-man-half-goat, sharing their sniggers, sucking the juices from me, their shared body mating with itself, her porno parody the funniest thing in Christendom . . .

And there, at the back of everything, I see the drooping shroud, the herald of the darkness that had been waiting for me; that had handed me over to the booze and the snorts and the pills; that had put me with the cons and the loonies and the white-coats; that had shoved me into the vomit bowls and the shit pans—but Anna Brownlove still involved with her own obsessions, still whizzing around trying to get Harold Wensum away from his kidnappers, her mind still not yet idle enough to start spreading its poison again, so the Set not yet knowing, at that point, about my second affair, my *real* affair, thinking that perhaps the wedding, *Choe's* wedding, was of no consequence to me, that I was too busy going crazy, so them not reminding me; or doing so and me being too flaked out, too scrambled, to take it in.

All I know is that by the time I was more or less sane again, by the time I had worked out just exactly what the burning beach house meant, just exactly what Charlie had done, must have done, Harold Wensum's headless corpse had long been forgotten by all but his secret lover. And with Anna's bitter tongue now searching for new targets, Lizzie and the rest of them soon knew all about Chloe.

So by then, I could see that not even Lizzie was sure she wanted to talk to me and I never did find out precisely what came immediately before and immediately after that day, the Saturday before Christmas, 2003.

———

While it lasted, the Sink Set was the best thing in my life, I guess in all our lives. Introducing me on that first evening, they had said, "This is Jill Maybury, her husband's a weather man"—as if I didn't have an identity of my own. But the weather bit seemed to amuse them, and in the end, I didn't mind the tag because they were all so exhilarating, so free and easy, so mannered and droll.

—So different from Barns and my life with him.

Funny! All those lovely, classy people—and the one I ended up in bed with was the snake-eyed Simon. And the one I fell for, would have given up everything for, was the one without style, the kind, thoughtful one that the others humoured and tended to avoid; treated like a harmless trespasser on their lives.

So just as I was the only person to love Herby Kirby and to hear him say he'd bought Charlie's house for *me*, that he wanted to share his life with *me*, but that he wasn't Colly Wolfson, that he was old-fashioned about marriage, that he would wait until I was single—so I also knew that however much I now regretted it, I had already broken his trust; and that with Simon Mount's loose tongue in the background, I was going to have to find some way of telling the moralistic Mr Kirby that thank you very much, but I couldn't risk breaking his heart—that I'd be staying with my faithful, tedious weather man.

—————

When you come up the hard way, like I did, and you're small and ugly and you're mixed in with a whole sea of people not so much different, the Herbert thing was never going to stick. So I became Herby. And my silly rhyme of a name never troubled me, not until I made it with the toffs. And by then, it was too late.

So I never did understand people like Colly Wolfson—or for that matter, his pal, Howard Sinclair. Both of them public school and Oxbridge, family money, background to match. Not sure about that . . . but tall, good looking. Colly quiet, debonair, Howard one of the boys, a joke-teller, a bar fly. Top notch businesses, lovely wives, homes, kids, a place on the party round, nothing in the world to worry about—not until the bust-up, not until Colly started screwing Charlie.

Jill said it was because he was still unhappy about that dead kid of his. But I didn't buy that. He did it because she was there, because she put it on a plate for him. In his shoes, I'd like to think I'd have done the same. Had it been Charlie, that is. But when it happened to me, it was Jill. And I couldn't do that to Jill.

Not because she was still married to Barns, and not, as Jill thought, because I was gelded by high-flown, working-class decency, my dick limp with morality.

But because I cared.

Because I'd never screwed a classy bird like her before.

Because I didn't know what to do, didn't know what she'd expect.

Because I wasn't ready for her to see me all small and ugly, dick included.

So to give me time, I told her that we'd have to wait until she'd divorced Barns. That it was no big deal. That we weren't kids. That the sex thing would save.

And at first she seemed OK about it. We kissed and got on with life.

But then, out of the blue, she said she couldn't do it, she couldn't leave him, he'd never manage.

I knew there had to be a catch. That we couldn't be great together one minute and not the next. Not for nothing.

But like women do, she worked herself up into a strop.

I've told you—it's because of Barns, she shouted. Just Barns.

So I had to accept it.

Pity about buying Howard's house, though. Chucking two mill at it, having to sell it, looking a fool.

—Howard in his pyre.

—Colly in his Funny House.

—And me and Jill nowhere.

That night at the Festival Hall when my then wife's mobile rang, reducing to nothing the million times it had rung before—when it rang that time and started us on the forked road to our different voids, I could see the sideways glances of the rest of the Set, see them trying not to embarrass me, see them trying to sum up Anna's agitation, to fathom this hitherto unguessed emotion, to place it amongst all the other things they knew about her, or thought they knew. And when she fled abroad, needing to be near her love, needing to try to rescue it from the horror—this one desperate act the pinnacle of her entire existence—I suppose they tapped their noses and nodded sagely.

Wensum's death wasn't the turning point in Anna's life, nor her scrawny assignations with him, nor even my marriage to her. It was the unsuspected, insidious, silent horror that I passed on to her in our youth, that wormed its way deep into her after one drunken, adolescent party when I'd already dipped into one girl and was now writhing with another, unwashed, unguarded.

It was Anna's first time. And she never took a lover until Harold Wensum—long after she learned she would never conceive. Because of me, she was barren. And she would stay that way, the magic, for her, being not merely in having children around her, something she could do, already did, with half the world's waifs and strays, but in being part of the natural, heaving, everyday point of existence, the effortless mixing of eggs and sperm in the rest of the world's beds, the rest of the world's back seats and fields and woods, the rest of the world's walls and desks and floors and couches. Every second of every year, vast vats of the fused miracle.

But not for her.

I loved her. She was my life, my soul, the sorrowing receptacle of my unthinking treachery. She saw this, and saw that I would forever try to make amends, that I would accept her bitterness and would forgive her acid ways, her mongering of gossip and rumour, her method of repleting her unfulfilment with scorn and scandal.

And she saw, too, that when Harold floated in on a cloud of children, his efforts abroad paid for by her efforts at home, that I would look away, that I would allow her this one chance of consummation beyond conscience, beyond conception, that I would ignore the humiliation of her lover's casual, callous cock.

His death, his lonely, pitiless execution, I would have wished to have been different, if only for her sake. But I could never, cannot now, pretend that I wished he was still alive, using her, prostituting her, even if I knew then, know now, that with him gone, things could never continue as before, that she would need, at last, to be rid of me.

I met Ozzie Leverington in a coffee shop across the road from our uni building in Edinburgh, buying his drink for him when he couldn't find enough money, the innocuous, innocent act an intriguing precursor, the first wheel-turn into a different existence, into the discovery of hitherto unknown, unplumbed depths.

With the student thing still new for both of us, I watched him carried aloft by the cascade of ideas, was there at his shoulder, summoned there by his call ("Hector! Where is my grandly named Hector, my Hector Grammaticus?"), thrilled to be there, laughing with him, drinking with him, watching him womanise, fascinated by his charm, he suspecting already that that side of it was not my scene, but saying nothing, revealing nothing until the day in early summer when we were bucketing along on the train, determined to spend the boiling day on a sunny beach, sitting opposite each other before an open window, feet up on the seats, sandals off, the breeze billowing our shirts, lifting the hairs on our bare legs, my straining left foot suddenly where it shouldn't have been, but leaving it there, the perverse, furtive toes exploring, he sitting there for a life-time of long seconds, allowing it, amazing me, then shuffling, knocking my foot away with a half-snort, half-laugh, the man across the aisle looking up from his newspaper, meeting Ozzie's hot stare, smiling.

We never spoke of it. And we never spoke of the other, later times, either. Those crystal times when he would sense my need to convey my love for him, not turning the corner with me, but recognising my agony, willing for me, in those rare, special moments, to refashion his own unspoken feelings, to realign and consummate them.

Years later, when Ozzie and my sister had their five children and I had my own life away from him, my permanent life with Andy, I was so miserable for him, so unhappy, when he came to see me and told me of the extraordinary scene at the Festival Hall—how Anna Brownlove had revealed her affair with, of all people, Harold Wensum, how she had outed the two of us and had laid bare our pathetic, adolescent scam.

"Harold Wensum! What, in God's name, does she see in *him*?"

"I don't know and I don't care," he said, interrupting me, annoyed that I had not yet focussed on his own predicament. "All I can think about is Honey."

I put my arm around his shoulders and gazed into a face that I still loved.

"Don't worry about Honey," I said. "I'll speak to her. She'll listen. She'll be O.K."

He nodded what I took to be his thanks and I watched as he moved to the window, glancing down to the ground far below, knowing, guessing, that it reminded him of the view from his loft of that earlier scandal, of people that he also loved; admitting I was right, but adding a new dimension, saying that it wasn't that simple, that it wasn't merely what he let happen between the two of us, that that was now mixed in with something else—that Honey couldn't forgive herself for her *own* indulgence, for interfering in other lives, for ruining the lives of four people.

"But we all do these things," I said, "we all do what we think is for the best."

"But they were dear friends! One word from your soft, sentimental sister—and one's dead, one's a screwed up widow, one loses his mind and one's left wandering in limbo land!"

"But you can only point people, show them how things might be. If they mess up, isn't that *their* business? You can't take all the blame!"

"No, but for Honey's sake, if nothing else, I can try to put things right. Not all of it. I can't undo you and me. I can't bring Howard back, and I can't make Colly love Charlie. But I can bring Colly back. I can give him back to Lizzie and Sally."

"How? How are you going to do that?"

"By visiting him. By loving him."

"Loving him?"

"Yes. Like I loved you. Like I showed you my love."

"You mean . . . ?"

"No, I don't mean that. Not that."

He sighed and when he spoke again, his voice was as gentle as it had been all those years before.

"When we're down, when there seems nothing but blackness, we all have our own particular Hells. Colly's Hell is a never ending nightmare, a place where his demons are out to punish him by doing to him what he feels he did to other people, scarring them, destroying them. His guilt is bottomless. When I visit, I think he sometimes recognises me. But mostly, I can see him watching me, trying to work out who I am, crawling into his corner when it's bad, begging me not to hurt him. 'Hurt you?' I say, 'I'm not here to hurt you! I'm Ozzie. Look at me!' But he can't. He can't bear the sight of whatever he sees."

"And you?"

"I just want to bring him back."

———

But who are you, he asked me

I'm here to help you.

But who *are* you?

You know who I am. I'm Victor. Your nurse.

My *psychiatric* nurse?

Yes.

So who's *he*?

He's your friend.

I don't know him.

You do. He's called Ozzie.

I don't want him here.

Shhhh . . . .

And I don't want your help. Your detox. Your rehab. You *know* what I want.

But we can't give you what you want—not for ever.

You could if you wanted to.

But we *don't* want to. And we don't want you to do what you've already tried to do. We want you to hang on.

Hang from a cord . . . ?

No! Wrong word! We want you to persevere. You're over the worst.

Who says?

We do.

But you're wrong.

We don't think so. Ozzie doesn't think so.

What's *he* know? What's *he* care?

He's your friend.

He doesn't care. All he wants is to . . . is to . . .

———

241

At the start, when they took him away that second time, I thought I was going to lose it, zoom off in a tide of booze and coke, tell Angie to fuck off out of my crippled life so that she couldn't see me, see what I was thinking, see me shouting out, sobbing like a kid, blabbing for a lost dream, believing that it had all been for nothing, that he'd not dared, for some fucking reason he'd not dared to give me what I wanted, to give himself what *he* wanted, the son bit, the father bit, *always the son and the father bit*. It could have been, I *know* it could have been . . .

So I thought I might lose it, let go, join him, float off to his fucking Never Never Land, not feeling it, not smelling it, not hearing it; not caring a toss if I ended up in some filthy back-street being buggered by morons, a fuck for a fix.

But Angie the mother-mother, *my* mother-mother, was in the way, baring those beautiful, defiant eyes of hers, daring me to hurt her, to hurt what we'd gone through, like some brave, vulnerable deer pleading for life, like in Colly's nightmare—me on the bridge with my pebble bomb waiting for a father, the Arab kids in a dusty, stony alley, their own bombs tied around them, waiting for Allah.

—The eyes revealing a vision that shamed me—realising suddenly that she was no longer young, that she looked older than she was; that the years of me and Colly, the effort of sustaining us, of trying and trying and trying to give us the strength and clarity to allow our yearnings to gel, to merge into a miraculous conception, had etched their way into her, that *our*, selfishness, *our* preoccupations with the past had drained her, had all but withered her.

And I knew then that I didn't want to fight her, that I owed her; that if that was what she wanted, *really* wanted, I would drag myself through every kind of shit for her.

I would help build it all up again.

"Soldiers are genuinely concerned to hear the population that sent them to Iraq and Afghanistan being dismissive or indifferent to their achievements . . ."—the head of the British Army, General Sir Richard Dannatt, addressing the International Institute for Strategic Studies, Autumn, 2007, on the effects of public apathy on Army morale (The Daily Mail).

Chapter 30

Wedding II

"Mrs Wolfson, is that you?"

"Yes, it's me," she said, mildly irritated, as always, at the woman's reversion to formality, a custom that somehow denied their shared closeness. "How are you, Angie?"

"I'm fine, Mrs Wolfson. But I can't say the same for my temper. Forgive me, I know it's been a bad time, but have you any control at all over that husband of yours? He's not answering the phone again. Either that or he's out all the time, which I can't believe. Can't you make him see what a shit he's being?"

"I wouldn't quite have put it that way, Angie." Her reply was unconsidered, sharp and edgy, feeding on her sudden resentment that this woman, anyone, should have such temerity. Colly might be all the things he was, but he was still hers, her responsibility. Not for the first time of late, the thought intrigued her.

After an awkward pause, she softened. "I'm not sure I need this, Angie. Not after four years. But I get what you mean. He's had plenty of chances."

"You tell him from me, Mrs Wolfson, that when it comes to chances, he's fast running out of them—at least in *this* house," ringing off, deciding, on the spur of the moment, not to explain, not to say, "It's about Colly not responding to Nico's wedding invitation. It's about him not coming round and embracing him and congratulating him and shaking his hand."

Ten minutes later, having decided that not telling Lizzie would hurt her more than telling her, she rang back and apologised.

They had a long, steady talk.

On the Saturday after Blair finally resigned in favour of the obdurate, astonishingly patient Gordon Brown, he was sitting staring at the dead coals of the previous night's fire, a robe wrapped round him, the cold encasing him, dulling his feelings—wondering about Blair, trying as always, to come to terms with the idea of him, with the ambitious ideologue who stood his party on its head, who wrested power from the old guard under a new label, who enticed millions of new voters to his cause, who excited them for a few, short years and left the old working class floundering; a war-monger who became an international Middle East peace negotiator with his own international faith foundation; his own international, shekel-rich consultancy; an international author who wrote a best-seller about himself and gave away the millions he earned in royalties . . . all this, and more, but still, he thought, ultimately a sad case, a confection—when Angie arrived on the doorstep, dressed to the nines.

"You're a disgrace," she snapped, pushing past him, striding into the kitchen, whirling around. "All this time and no reply, no word, no wish to share in the boy's happiness. You're disgusting! But you'll do it now! You'll get dressed and you'll come with me. Because if you don't, I shall come back from the register office and I shall probably chop your bloody head off!"

The tirade, her sudden presence, caught him off balance.

"*What*? What are you *talking* about? What's all this crap?"

"June the thirtieth—*Nico's wedding!* The boy who wants you for a father, though God knows why! He and Kate are marrying this morning. June the thirtieth, 2007! He sent you an invitation—but surprise, surprise, you never replied! Well, I'm *sick* of it! We have two hours. And we *will* be there!"

He allowed himself to be bullied upstairs into the shower and then into his clothes, her tongue silent while she concentrated on smartening him up. By the time he got into her car, she was already behind the wheel, gunning the engine. She looked him over, nodded her approval and shot out through the gates.

A minute later, held up by traffic lights, she allowed herself one last rant. "None of your gang will be there, thank God, not even poor Lizzie. Oh they were all there in their finery for dear Chloe and Simon, weren't they! Fawning over that preposterous man and his cynical little tart! Well *let* them!"

"Are you saying," turning to her, incredulous, "that *Lizzie* was at Chloe's wedding?"

"No, *of course* not," she snapped, braking hard for a taxi, cursing as she tried to get into the right lane. "Not *Lizzie*! And not *Charlie* either! But not for the reason *you* suppose. Because they were in mourning—for you and for Howard. Though God knows why for you. Forget Charlie and Chloe! You had your fun! Now *forget* them! Get them out of that bloody head of yours, once and for all!"

"But—"

"But *nothing*! We have something *far* more important to think about and you have a lot of people to meet and a lot of things to say!"

When he started to question her, his mind see-sawing, an elusive, reawakened excitement blinking on and off like a faraway lighthouse, shining on what appeared to be a new world, the beam failing to pick out any of his old obsessions, she said she meant it—there was no past any more, only the present and the future.

"Now, for goodness sake be quiet," she said, the anger leaving her, conscious of her victory in getting him into the car, in doing this one last, great, loving service for him and the boy. "Be quiet," she repeated, as though he had been about to answer her thoughts, as though he couldn't hear her laughing tautly through her words. "I can't talk *and* drive any more," she said, "—not this fast!"

The registry office was bleak on a bleak road. But none of that mattered. All around them, there was life. Cars arriving, pipping, doors popping open before the wheels had stopped turning, their occupants impatient to join the throng. People, young people, running up, kissing each other, shaking hands, saying "Hi!" to each other, and "Look at *you*!" and "*Great* to see you!" the girls squealing, the young men proud and awkward.

He and Angie standing across the road, watching it all as if at the theatre—the crowd on the stage, they in the darkened stalls, happy to see that there in the middle of it was Nico in a new suit, a beautiful girl standing beside him, holding flowers, greeting people, but never far from him, never straying, bending down, listening to him, looking up, searching the crowd, finding his face, *his* face, coming across to him, Angie standing at the side of him, holding him, giving him strength.

"I'm Kate," the girl said. "Warren's told me so much about you. He wants you to come over."

Mounting the stage, tweaking Nico's cheek, winking at him, marvelling at being forgiven, hardly able to believe he wasn't taking part in a sort of pantomime; being introduced, names flying around: Jim Dyson, Jerry Wilcox, Mary Duff, Dorothy Drummond. They all seeming to know him and expecting him to know them . . .

And two other men-boys being ushered in, being told, "It's O.K. Don't worry," shaking hands with the others, not needing to be introduced, but still nervous, shuffling, still calling Nico 'Nico' when the others called him 'Warren'. The realisation coming to him slowly . . .

Warren addressing him, firmly, clearly, so that all the group could hear: "Colly, this is David Moorhouse and Michael Dooley. You know who they are, don't you? Think about it and you'll know. They've never been able to face it, never been able to come to meet me before. But the others made them come because it's my wedding. And I'm so bloody chuffed! We *both* are, aren't we?"

Meaning *him*, not Kate. So he suddenly centre-stage, anxious young-old faces turning to him, awaiting his approval, his acceptance, sensing the magnitude of the moment, aware that on his reply hung the happiness of the day, and not only the day, but of all of their different lives, watching him grapple with the recurring thought that all this time, this terrible journey from the cement mixer, it wasn't he who had been strong, but Nico; Nico the rock, Nico around whom they had circled; that without Nico, he wouldn't now, this instant, realise that he had overcome his grief about Robert, wouldn't now, this instant, have been able to deal with the past terrible years; that he wouldn't have known about love; that he wouldn't have been a man, not a real man, not without Nico.

"Yes," he said, looking at the man-boy, searching his face, needing to memorise it, preserve the moment, "I *do* know them—I *do* know who you *all* are. It's taken me a long time, longer than you will ever know. But I got there. In the end, I got there. It's wonderful you all being here—and yes, Mr Warren Nichols, I'm absolutely delighted for you."

Pumping hands again, kissing Kate and the other girls; sitting with Angie at the back of the marriage room, feeling the pressure, the swimming dizziness

—seeing the vanished Bush, the receding Blair, the self-justifications, the yawing chasms between different cultures, the seething fundamentalism, the suicide bombs, the roadside bombs, the market bombs, the vicious, callous bullets, Blair shouting over his shoulder, "So we didn't find any WMD! So what? We got rid of Saddam, didn't we? We stopped him killing his own people, didn't we?" The blighted millions and the thousands and thousands of dead laughing uproariously, over the moon that it wasn't Saddam who had killed them but the West and the Bin Ladens, yelling, shouting, screaming that in the end it wasn't about Saddam or terrorism or politics or fears about Western security! It was about them, about the people! The butchers, the bakers, the candlestick makers! It was about innocent millions trying to live their lives, caught up in the conniving and the carnage, the West's and Saddam's, them and a dead baby in a cot—the dead and the wounded reaching up, urging him to listen to the tiny voice that was saying, had always been saying: "I love you. There is nothing to forgive. There is nothing that she, or you, could have done."

Knowing this now, but after the counselling and the shrinks, knowing also that the depression, the neurosis, the psychosis, the drugs and the drunkenness and the sex—the whole dreadful, paranoiac, obsessive crack-up—did not date merely back to the cot death; nor to the cement mixer; nor to his deluded affairs, nor even to his fixation with the war-mongers—fixated, like him; in deep, like him; fallible, like him; trying to do their best, like him. They were all part of it, but they weren't the start of it, weren't the start of the crawling worm in his brain that took him down and down and fed on his failures.

The start, he saw now, was the crucifying guilt that was teased out of him by patient men in white coats—the guilt of what he had done to his father; the guilt of what had happened that one time behind his closed bedroom door; that one, shattering time hidden in his mind, suppressed for thirty years, multiplied by him not knowing, NEVER knowing, whether the father had told the mother of his knowledge; he not telling the mother of the father's revealing, grieving letter, and knowing nothing of their divorce until he had shown the mother the death notice from the new wife; she, the mother, refusing, even then, to divulge the reasons for the marriage break-up; so he still not able to tell the mother that the father had known all about it. And thus not really knowing, NEVER really knowing precisely why she had ended it all; why she had saved her pills and ended it.

But at last, at last, at last opening the box, urged on by the shrinks and now by Nico's miracle, his new wife, his hopeful, joyous friends—able to see that the box contained nothing but the unjustified guilt of a boy; that the seeds of it all were not of his making; that what happened when he was thirteen, unwanted, unsought, was not his fault, had left him unsullied, that his father would have continued to forgive him, that had he seen this before, then Robert and Nico and Charlie and Howard and Chloe might not have got into his head; that Bush and Blair might never have invaded him, might not have ridden in with the others.

So seeing the need, now, to push them away forever, to put them in context, to overcome the panic and the vomit, to go with Angie from the marriage room to the reception, to exult in his sanity, to meet and talk, properly and decently with Warren's friends, he with *his* devils, they with theirs; his life, their lives . . .

"And now," said Angie, looking at her watch, "say your goodbyes and go outside." Saying it firmly but gently and kindly, the lovely eyes sweeping his face, the black hollows of her cheeks dancing again with tiny green flames, her words, he sensed, masking something equally new, equally momentous.

Aware that she was watching him push through the doors, but unaware that she was fighting not to weep, not to douse the dancing flames; that she was whispering her own goodbyes to the two of them, the man and the boy.

Both of them conjoined, but stepping out into their different worlds.

Both of them now leaving her.

In the car park, he found a young woman. Her nose ring had gone and she was dressed in a smart plum-coloured sweater, newly pressed jeans and shiny, pointed leather boots. Beside her, stood a tall, good-looking man in a navy blue roll neck, a pair of cords and brown shoes.

"Hello, Dad. This is Leroy and this is his car. We're all going off to have tea with Mum. You come and sit with me in the back."

And it was then, that second, that trembling instant, that he finally realised that the world was still built on love and forgiveness, that injustice and sadness and suffering were there, too, and that while it was right to recognise this and to speak out, it was wrong to suppose that hope and redemption had disappeared; that they were still there; that they would always be there; that it was only he who had not been able to see this.

Tomorrow, he would go up to the City. He would find the little church and he would sit in the same pew and he would pray.

He would square the circle.

Epilogue

During the creation of this book, the Arab Spring has swept through great swathes of Islam, governments have fallen, Osama Bin Laden has been sought out and killed, and Colonel Gadafi is also no more.

New flashpoints have boiled to the surface, the West seems not to have learned the lessons of the last one-hundred years, the crucial Palestinian issue still remains, and the path to a new beginning, a better way, is still uncertain.

After the 2003 war in Iraq, the task continues to put matters right. No weapons of mass destruction have ever been found; the search has long been abandoned.

Controversy continues to sweep the world about whether the war should ever have been fought; or if fought, on what grounds?

"The immorality of the United States and Great Britain's decision to invade Iraq in 2003 . . . has destabilised and polarised the world to a greater extent than any other conflict in history . . . Instead of recognising that the world we lived in . . . necessitated sophisticated leadership . . . the then-leaders of the US and UK fabricated the grounds to behave like playground bullies . . . They have driven us to the edge of a precipice where we now stand—with the spectre of Syria and Iran before us."—Archbishop Tutu of South Africa, 2012.

Tony Blair denies lying about the WMD intelligence; he says he would still have found an argument for invading Iraq to remove Saddam Hussein.

The British public has learned to respect and admire British forces serving their country in unpopular foreign wars—and to honour their dead.

The End

SPS
September, 2012.